"You Know BC and AD
Here is BS!"

"You Know BC and AD Here is BS!"

(Before Satan)

Written by
Elisa Guajardo Carothers

Library of Congress Control Number: 2016920498
ISBN: Hardcover 978-1-5245-6811-5
Softcover 978-1-5245-6810-8
eBook 978-1-5245-6809-2

This is a work of fiction. Names, characters, places and incidents either are the product of the author's imagination or are used fictitiously, and any resemblance to any actual persons, living or dead, events, or locales is entirely coincidental.

Any people depicted in stock imagery provided by Thinkstock are models, and such images are being used for illustrative purposes only.

Print information available on the last page.

Rev. date: 12/30/2016

To order additional copies of this book, contact:
Xlibris
1-888-795-4274
www.Xlibris.com
Orders@Xlibris.com
754331

Dedications

<u>Firstly I wish to thank God and his angels for helping me complete this book!</u>

This book is dedicated to certain people in my family and among my friends who helped fashion the personalities of some of the characters:

To my younger brother Nick, Inspiration for Raphael, and Little Me-el.

To Gregg: inspiration for little Raguel! (Watch out for the KING!)

To Sr. Kate Ottorox thanks for being my Gabriel.

To Fr. Tom Helfrich, my equivalent of Uriel!

For Joyce Sauber, a good friend.

For my parents: Juan and Diamante Guajardo, and my other siblings; Linda, John, Lorenzo, Lucinda, and Alma do not worry none of you fell!

For the land of Israel, God's chosen people.

For my spouse, Jim; thank you for showing me how we each have a little bit of God and Lucifer in each of us!

Also, a special thank you To Mr. John Gochennour, a computer maven!

Preface

Note to readers: This is a work of Christian Fantasy Fiction; however, the author wishes to declare three certain things she holds as truth; in her beliefs.

One: The truth of the One Triune God.

Two: The Devil is Real.

Three: No matter how good looking and powerful you are if you fail to keep your eyes on God; you will fall.

Keeping those three things in mind, it is the author's hope that this book will appeal to both believers, and non believers. This is a book for everyone; Jew, Gentile, and for anyone who values a good read! If you are a person of Faith reading the book, please be mindful that the author ıs by no means ever attempting to devalue God or the Heavenly host. The author has one main purpose for people who read this work; that they laugh and realize there is no such thing as a functional family! Only God is perfect! And; even He had one messed up kid, and NO it is not Jesus! ENJOY!

One other note: God is referred to by many ancient Hebrew names in this book; please simply remember it is the same Triune God. Yiddish and other Hebrew terms are simply included to remind the readers of the Jewish roots of Christianity. Asterisks are beside some terms that may be unfamiliar to the audience, definitions can be found at the bottom of the pages.

Chapter 1

Yahweh sat pensively on his golden throne, Yeshua and the Ruach vibrated calmly in his bosom. He had just created eight realms of Heaven, for a total of nine; this included the one he currently occupied. God's level was ethereal. A still sea of glass gave the triune deity a view of the newly composed levels. The floor on Yahweh's realm gleamed in white marble swirled with translucent rainbow hues. Majestic gates of pearl encompassed it, while the sky transmitted God's own natural radiant light, reminiscent of aurora borealis.

Peering into his reflective pool of shalom, Yahweh nodded to himself in approval as he surveyed each level; with inquisitive blue eyes enveloped in silver wire spectacles. Realm eight the next one down, the creator had equipped with a grand alabaster structure, it had etched glass doors and star shaped windows.

"Ahhh yes I shall call you Opus Angelorum! You will be a place of learning for my future children!" He mused.

Yahweh was preparing to make angels, beings of pure light, love, and grace. Elohim wanted his children to be properly educated. The school contained a massive library teeming with informative books about languages, mathematics and Pagan Mythology. There were also picture books displaying animals of every sort, along with each one's name. Upon leaving the library angels would find themselves in a dignified classroom filled with glossy beryl desktops and chairs.

"Once I create my angels, I shall need to appoint a rabbi to teach them!' He thought aloud.

An onyx ceiling coated the classroom's domed top. Glittering diamonds glazed the obsidian background, representing stars and constellations on Yahweh's first realm. The first level of Heaven acted as God's personal observatory, in a single breath God had permeated it with countless amounts of sparkling stars and whimsical galaxies.

Level two Yahweh had covered in ice and snow. Temperature is nonexistent in Heaven so no one would ever feel uncomfortable. The sleek formations of ice and individual patterned snowflakes brought God amusement.

Realm three featured a grandiose garden called, Eden. The lush paradise overflowed with trees, plants, and flowers; four rivers flowed tranquilly through the terrain, one of milk, one of oil, one of wine, and one of honey. The four met right at the garden's heart, where a tall pomegranate tree stood; the tree of life. The tree was stationed in front of an ambrosial lake where the four rivers came together.

Level four was a fulgent courtly sight, everything shined in fine cut diamonds, quartz, and zircon. The realm even had a throne similar to Yahweh's; with one exception, it was argent quartz, bedecked with every precious gem stone.

"Don't worry," God considered.

"Someone exquisite will be seated on you soon! Oh just thinking about it makes me feel *ver clempt!" Yahweh fanned his hand over his heart.

God's holy city Jerusalem found its home on level six. A towering temple of gold, adorned with twelve signature stones on each of its doors was the crowning glory here!

"**Oy! Here my sweet ones may meditate and pray!" He schmoozed.

Realm seven resembled a lofty opera house; a circular opalescent stage glowed at the center holding instruments of every kind. Red velvet chairs trimmed in gold filled the auditorium.

"My praise and worship concert room!" God quipped, delighted.

Yahweh rose from his chair.

"Okay Yeshua, Ruach, I do believe we are ready to create our first angel!'

"Yes!" The two inward entities hummed.

"He will be like a companion to us! Every other angel after him shall bow before his unparalleled beauty!

---

* Ver clempt: to be choked up.

** Oy: woe!

All our wisdom shall be embedded in his mind; he will have dominion over all realms, minus ours!"

Yahweh took a deep breath and released it. A nine foot cloud hovered over the sea of glass. God began withdrawing the best components from each level of Heaven to assist in the evolution of this angel. The first realm provided dazzle from each star. The second level added a pepper of detailed snowflakes. The Garden of Eden provided a touch of pomegranate juice from the tree of life. God obtained sparkle from every vitric jewel on the fourth realm. Yahweh then began to mingle white flames from realm five.

The fifth level of Heaven was a military training arena with diamond floors, and copious amounts of artillery; there was also a blacksmith shop which held a burning stove, this is where God took the fire from.

"Flames to forge metals will give him great strength!" Yahweh proclaimed.

The holy city Jerusalem provided Yahweh with fragrant frankincense from the temple. The seventh level Yahweh used to incorporate the sound of each musical instrument; this angel's voice would be sweet nectar to the ears! The eighth realm permitted God to infuse every trifle of knowledge from each book in Opus Angelorum, no future creature would ever match this angel's intelligence!

"As for my level, we shall give you life!" Yahweh affirmed.

God clapped his hands, with a clash of thunder and lightning, an imperial seraph manifested. Yahweh's heart jumped to his throat upon reviewing the spectacular angel. He had come out flawless. The angel's face and figure were androgynous, he had no sexual organs. White plumage and furry tufts veiled his nicely toned body. The creature's face was hypnotizing, finely chiseled with azure blue eyes, without pupils. The seraph's skin was ivory; he had twelve lofty white wings, which he wrapped himself in. The angel bowed low with reverence to his creator, his long golden hair hung well past his waist to his tail feathers.

"Your glorious mane of hair shimmers as much as the precious metal gold itself!" Yahweh gushed.

"*Kadosh! Kadosh! Kadosh!" The resplendent creature chanted in a most mesmerizing voice. Yahweh stepped forward caressing the angel's right cheek.

"Ahhh! You can speak my native language of Hebrew! Yes I am holy, holy holy! So glad to see you digested level eight so well! You are absolutely stunning! Oy! I'm ver clempt! I must garb you in the finest of armor!"

Yahweh snapped his fingers, in an instant the gorgeous angel found himself polished as a signet of perfection. God's ideal angel was now shielded in white gold vestures capped with every ornate gem; carnelian, topaz, jasper, chrysolite, beryl, onyx, sapphire, carbuncle and emerald. The seraph illuminated Yahweh's realm like a star gone super nova.

---

* Kadosh: Holy.

The debonair angel bowed again.

"Oy! Enough of that!" Yahweh teased.

"Now to name you! Hmmmmm what title befits such a ravishing angel?" He wondered. Yeshua whispered a suggestion into his father's ear.

"What about Lucifer? It means light bearer."

God hopped up and down with glee at the notion, causing Lucifer to skip back startled.

"Yes! Lucifer will be your name! Do you like it most lovely one?" Yahweh asked.

Lucifer kissed God's right hand, causing the deity to blush.

"It suits me well! Thank you most high!"

Yahweh now absolutely captivated by Lucifer's looks and charm, could scarcely wait to create more angels.

"I am going to make you some siblings! Other angels! You will still be the most beautiful by far! First..."

Elohim paused, to wave his right palm, four giant lion like beasts appeared, each having four sets of wings and bright copper hooves rather than paws.

"These are cherubim Lucifer, from them will come your first four siblings! Each beast will give birth to an exceptional angel! You and the four angels that come forth from these creatures will be known throughout all nine realms as my top archangels! You will act as their captain and general!"

Lucifer gazed at the beasts in shock, as they hunkered down; groaned, and began to lay eggs!

The eggs where large by human standards, each measured eight feet long, and eight feet wide. The superb marble objects caught Lucifer's interest. One cherub produced an azure blue egg, matching Lucifer's eyes. The elliptical orb was studded with diamonds and sapphire stones. The other three were equally captivating. One egg was emerald green, capped with rubies; another was hazy pink with yellow highlights, topped with crystals. The final egg was a sleek silver hue, lined with gold at its upper area.

Lucifer took Yahweh's hand. God spoke.

"You must be eager to see who comes out!" He commented.

Lucifer nodded, his eyes transfixed on the august blue egg, he really wanted that one to open first.

"May we see who comes out of the sapphire egg first father?" He timidly questioned.

"Too late" Yahweh responded.

"The green one is beginning to hatch! Look to your left my love!"

Lucifer turned towards the glistening jade egg, unlike a hen's it did not crack. The eggs laid by the cherubim split smoothly in halves, much like a human child's plastic

Easter egg would, when they wished to extract candy from inside. Yahweh's idea was for the angels to use their eggs as private sleeping quarters; he had reserved a huge amount of acreage west of Eden to serve specifically as an egg patch. Each egg was insulated with soft satin walls and elegant laced cushions of colored silk.

The emerald egg now with its upper half completely off, revealed another enchanting seraph. The new angel unfurled three sets of cherry blossom pink wings. The creature had tanned Semitic skin and stood about eight feet tall, amiable green eyes glanced up at both Lucifer and God. The angel shyly smiled, pushing back a mane full of chocolate brown curls, sweeping down past his hips. Yahweh had made a point of making sure every angel would be sexless, although some could come out looking more masculine or feminine; however no specific gender was to be given to any creature. The current angel appeared masculine, yet his face might easily pass as female, he was lovely.

"He is ravishing!" Lucifer stated.

God nodded in approval explaining:

"Behold your first brother!" Yahweh evaluated the angel, lowering his spectacles half way down his curved nose.

"I shall name you Raphael! I can see you will prove to be a remedy with those emotional eyes you have!"

"God's medicine!" Lucifer replied in excitement.

"Very good Lucifer! You know what his name means! That will be a big help to you when you begin assigning each angel his duties!" Yahweh exhorted.

Raphael, who was a bit fluffy around his mid section, enclosed his navel less tummy with his two middle wings, blushing as he did.

Lucifer chuckled; he saw no imperfections in him at all!

"Abba I believe Raphael feels somewhat self conscience! I don't understand why!"

Yahweh focused in on the angel, clapping his hands; with a flutter of golden light God robed Raphael in a long wispy gown, and then crowned him with a wreath of white and pink dew kissed roses. Raphael now feeling less insecure and more pleased with his appearance spoke for the first time; to Lucifer's bewilderment he had a very deep voice.

"Thank you Yahweh most high! Kadosh, kadosh, kadosh!"

Raphael expressed while bowing. Yahweh beamed a smile to the lambent new seraph, as Yeshua and the Ruach hummed happily inside him. God; now took Lucifer's hand, steering him over to the silver and hazy pink eggs, they were beginning to unveil treasures of their own.

The Pinkish yellow egg shot forth a brilliant dark African female looking angel; with locks of ebony curls mingled with red and blonde low lights. The creature flew upwards on six wings of yellow, she too was a seraph. The angel's kind silver eyes starred down at Yahweh and the morning star.

"Kadosh, kadosh, kadosh, most high! I am Gabriel!" She sang while bowing.

Lucifer thought her to be a masterpiece, black with delicate features. The light bearer nearly fell over backwards when she suddenly took on an Anglo masculine form, with blonde hair and blue eyes. Yahweh patted Lucifer's shoulder ready to explain.

"Gabriel means God is my strength, hence she will be unique among all other angels. The feminine form will be useful for teaching, if you should decide to use her as a rabbi. The masculine form..."

Yahweh and Lucifer gazed upwards; Gabriel and Raphael were playfully soaring in circles, getting acquainted.

"The masculine form," God continued:

"Will be strong and valuable to realm five, when you begin training angels as soldiers, I do hope you approve!"

Lucifer embraced Yahweh.

"Yes of course I approve! A sister and brother all in one angel! Father; look behind you!" Lucifer related.

"The silver egg is hatching!"

Yahweh and Lucifer grinned in anticipation as the silver gold trimmed egg revealed another wonderful creature. This seraph also had six wings, except his were composed of blue fire. His skin resembled quartz crystal, while his hair had the appearance of rivers or cascading waters. His eyes were gold.

"I am Uriel, also known as fire of God!"

The angel bowed low. Lucifer looked towards his Father,

"Beloved," He said quietly;

"His demeanor is frightfully stern!"

Yahweh gave Lucifer a pat on the back.

"Worry not most beautiful one, they will all be under your authority, doing exactly as their told! Even him!"

Yahweh pointed towards the glitzy blue egg that had first gained Lucifer's interest, it was now sliding open!

Lucifer waited anxiously to see who might birth out of the luxurious egg. The upper part of the object slowly lifted up; unlike the first three hatchlings, Lucifer was quick to glean; whoever was emerging from this egg was not as strong or graceful as his other siblings. Lucifer and Yahweh stood enthralled as they viewed two chubby little hands push off the egg's diamond top, with extra effort. A three foot angel awkwardly made his way out, tears welled up in Lucifer's eyes, the creature was absolutely adorable! He fell in love with him on the spot!

The mini seraph had a soft olive complexion and large curious opal blue eyes; his hair was a dark brown with hints of red in the light, full of curls. A pair of clover green wings came out at his shoulder blades. The child stumbled out of his egg waddling up to Lucifer and Yahweh on pudgy feet.

"Abba?" The newest addition asked batting his eyes up to God.

Yahweh smiled as he gazed down towards the tot. The first three archangels were still stretching their wings, practicing flight maneuvers in the sky. Lucifer alone knelt down beside the cute creature.

"Yes" The light bearer replied,

"That is our Abba! Our daddy! I am your big brother, I am Lucifer!"

The littlest angel cooed like a dove, jumping into the Captain's muscular arms, purring like a content kitten. Yahweh felt a tug in his heart as he witnessed such sweet brotherly love.

"Something tells me those two will never be separated!" God contemplated.

"Lucifer," Yahweh began,

"Would you like to name him?"

Lucifer's eyes went back to Elohim.

"What Abba? You really mean it?" He questioned.

The morning star walked towards his creator gently; as if the miniature seraph he was holding was made of glass.

"Is he not the most darling thing you have ever seen?" Lucifer gushed.

"I would be honored to name him Abba, I shall call him El; because El means lord, and you are my lord. I will honor you by giving this child a name similar to yours! I feel you made him just for me! You are first in my heart Abba, yet I sense this child has captured the remainder of it!"

Yahweh smiled, touching Lucifer's cheek, while mussing the new angel's mass of perfect curls.

"El does mean God or lord beloved one, I am flattered, but; that little matzo ball, cute as he is, will never come close to being anything like me! Add something more to the name." God suggested.

A puzzled look veiled Lucifer's face as the child squealed, pinching his older brother's cheeks.

"Very well," Lucifer concluded.

"Since I still feel you made him just for me, I shall call him Me-el!"

Yahweh's face lit up in amusement.

"Clever!" He surmised.

"Very well! Me- el it will be! Anything for my most beautiful Lucifer!"

Lucifer, Yahweh and Me-el all cast their eyes upwards, Raphael, Gabriel, and Uriel flew down in a seemly fashion, bowing as they landed.

"Well then," Elohim began,

"I would like you three to follow your Captain and general, lord Lucifer, well four including the little one!" God stopped to acknowledge Me-el. The three grown arch's reviewed the small angel as their captain held him.

"Oh he is sooooo CUTE!" Gabriel expressed, with outstretched arms.

"May I please hold him?"

Lucifer brought Me-el tightly to his chest; the tot's eyes were engrossed in his big brother's gemmed breast plate. Me-el seemed partial to the sapphires.

"Oh Puddy!" He cried.

Yahweh taking note of Lucifer's reaction intervened.

"I believe Lucifer wants full control of our littlest angel, however I do want him to give all of you a tour of my eight realms of Heaven, after you have seen all of the other levels, I trust Lucifer will appoint each of you where he deems you best fit to serve. Oh! In all the excitement I forgot to tell you something very important Lucifer!"

Lucifer glanced towards God ready to hear what he had to say.

"My most lovely one, I created a realm specifically for you alone! Level four, you even have your own palace and throne room! I do hope it meets with your approval!"

Lucifer smiled as Me-el hiked onto his wide shoulders.

"I am sure whatever you produced for me is outstanding!" The morning star affirmed.

Yahweh looked to his other three children with pride.

"Wonderful! So off you all go! Oh I'm getting all ver clempt at looking at all of you! OY! I still have more of you lovely creatures to make too! You all have fun exploring Heaven! Please remember to listen to Lucifer and to do exactly as he tells you! Lucifer may I suggest you take them to Opus Angelorum first. The library there with all its material may give you a good indication of what each of your siblings is most interested and gifted at! I trust you son, I know you will guide them all in the right direction!

Lucifer knelt in reverence.

"On my honor Abba."

"Very well! I need to resume my work, you four, minus Lucifer, were hatched from the great beasts you now see standing around my sea of glass, they are called cherubim, Their kind will be a class of angel's all to themselves! I plan to place them on realm four, a garden I named Eden. These four will be my egg layers, they will also require milking; yet they are not female per say, I plan to make several herds of them! Also, I still have five other types of angels in mind to create! Oh listen to me schmoozing on!!! *AY-YAY-YAY I really must get to work! Anyhooo.... While your all off traveling, please do not be caught off guard by some new entity, it's just me making more brethren for you five!"

---

* Ay-yay-yay: Yiddish exclamation.

God clapped his hands sending the four cherubim down to level four.

"Have a good time fellowshipping with one another!" Yahweh rang.

Lucifer and his siblings genuflected to honor their father, and then soared away.

Chapter 2

Yahweh advanced back to his Aurelian throne, Yeshua and the Ruach reverberating within him. God stretched his arms and began waving his hands, allowing his creative energy to flow.

"Now," He exclaimed,

"I shall complete my first triad of angelic beings, Hearken four winds of the North, South, East, and West!"

Yahweh rotated his right arm in a circular motion, as the collective gusts gathered to do his bidding. Elohim hoarded the four winds in his arms, then blew his breath into them.

"I now add light from my Ruach into you!" He commanded.

"Come forth my league of Seraphim! All of you shall each have six wings! Two to fly, two to cover your faces and two to veil your feet; the significance of this is to properly praise me!"

In a flash, an uncountable array of resplendent creatures saturated the ninth level, they all sang in unearthly voices, as they chanted to God in magnificent harmony.

"You will all be my personal angels of worship on this realm, later you will all become acquainted with your glorious captain, his name is Lucifer, only he aside from me may call you to do duties on other realms of Heaven!"

The copious amount of lovely beings bowed in solidarity to their father; none dared to question his motives.

"Oh yes" Yahweh halted to clap his hands, dismissing the seraphim to go hover above him to continue their unending hymns.

"I now send a throng of cherubim west of Eden!"

Upon professing this, Eden appeared in the sea of glass. Yahweh sighed in satisfaction as he beheld flocks of the majestic beasts take to pasture west of the utopian garden.

"Now," He declared, rubbing his long silver beard in deep thought.

"To finish off this triad I will create Thrones!"

God whirled one solitary finger in the air allowing his four winds to return to him again, blowing his Ruach into the cyclone he had formed, clusters of feathery wheels came forth; each had eyes of fire and mouths to give God praise.

"Kadosh, kadosh, kadosh," They rang.

"Hmmmmm" Yahweh scrutinized the last group of creatures.

"I know how I will use all of you, yet; I would like to see if Lucifer and I happen to think along the same lines, I'll wait a bit, I know he is currently getting familiar with the archangels, but I shall call upon him shortly, I want to see what he thinks of you Thrones!" God theorized.

Lucifer held Me-el by the hand as he led his other three siblings through the monumental library in Opus Angelorum.

"These are books." The morning star said.

"Please feel free to rummage through them, absorb everything that specifically calls to you, as you can all see the books are categorized by subject in each row."

Lucifer scooped up Me-el, watching as the becoming Raphael strolled directly towards the section on holistic herbs, plants and natural remedies.

"I am not surprised," Lucifer silently observed.

"His name defines him to a tee! I foresee him as our healer, what say you Me-el?"

The little angel purred into his brother's ear, still too young to completely comprehend what Lucifer was talking about.

Uriel brought in his fiery wings, it was a precaution for the reading material; he did not want any to burn. The seraph floated over to the aisle on space, gamma rays, and stars.

"Yahweh might like him on realm one!" Lucifer thought to himself.

Since God had given the captain more knowledge than his siblings; he was very cognitive of what each realm of Heaven consisted of.

"Placing them is proving to be quite simple." The light bearer conceived.

Gabriel truly astounded Lucifer; she unlike the other two who were drawn to distinct areas, teleported busily from row to row; her eyes scanning all kinds of different books at light speed!

"I think I know who the rabbi in Opus Angelorum will be!" Lucifer whispered to Me-el.

The child pinched his brother's nose, laughing like a wind chime.

"I wuv Lufi!" Me-el yelped.

Lucifer held Me-el out at arm's length as a mother would a baby, bringing him to his chest; the captain began rocking him, while humming a lullaby. The tyke began to drift into sleep.

"I love you too Me-el." Lucifer said as he decorated the little angel's face with kisses.

The captain turned, someone was breathing down his neck, he pivoted to face a sating seraph, one God had just recently made. The flaxen haired creature bowed, bringing in his top two wings to demonstrate respect to Lucifer.

"This must be the one father spoke of..." The angel contemplated.

"Yahweh said he would be the most beautiful angel I would ever see, he most definitely fits the description!"

The seraph arose as Lucifer gave him permission to do so.

"Hello, I take it Abba just made you, nice to meet you, what may I assist you with?" The morning star asked.

"Greetings lord Lucifer, I am Jeremiel, Yahweh has sent me to inform you, that he would like you and the little one to come meet with him on realm nine at your convenience, he has something he would like to discuss with you."

Lucifer nodded.

"Thank you Jeremiel, tell Abba I shall come up as soon as I can, I need only excuse myself from my three siblings."

"Of course your lordship," Jeremiel expressed as he bowed once more before ascending up through an open hexagon window on the library's ceiling which was outlined with mystic topaz gems.

Me- el awoke, he scooted back up onto Lucifer's shoulders. The child began braiding the lambent seraph's blonde locks.

"Puddy air! Lufi got puddy air!"

Lucifer put his hands to his mouth, making a sound similar to a morning dove. The utterance caught the attention of Raphael, Gabriel, and Uriel. The three archangels quickly came over to their captain and bowed.

"I'm sorry my brethren, Abba has summoned me, please continue to study at your leisure, I do believe I have a good idea of where I shall be placing each of you in Heaven! Upon my return we will travel through the other levels"

The three seraphs bowed yet again.

"Yes lord Lucifer." The trio replied.

Lucifer landed on realm nine, kneeling low before God, the seraph brought in his twelve majestic pinions. Me-el hopped off Lucifer's shoulders, mimicking him as best he could. Yahweh beamed as he approached the two.

"So glad you got the message from Jeremiel, now enough of all these formalities, how about we converse in a more relaxing setting?"

God scratched the side of his jaw, with two flickers of his eye lashes, a fine antique red velvet chair made of cherry wood manifested; accompanied by a less dignified royal purple one, and a velvet green ottoman. The furniture was propped up nicely in one of realm nine's secluded corners. A grey marble table with lion claw feet stood at the center, holding an exquisite china tea set; containing hot peppermint tea. A large golden tray was on the table, overflowing with savory blueberry and chocolate chip scones.

"Oh yes, I believe the little one might prefer ice tea with lemon and sugar." God opined.

Yahweh waved his hand causing another yet smaller marble table to erect itself right next to the footstool provided for Me-el. A tall quartz glass of cool tea harboring lemon halves and sugar cubes appeared on top of it.

"There now," Yahweh stated.

"Shall we go have tea together?"

Lucifer and Me-el both followed Yahweh to the private corner. God stationed himself on the red chair; Lucifer took his place on the laced trimmed purple one. Me-el ignored the velvet toad stool God had provided for him, and hopped unto Lucifer's lap instead. The child instantly commenced stuffing scones into his mouth. The youth resembled a vacuum set at full power, sucking in as much rubbish as possible. Lucifer shook his head, blushing.

"Forgive him Abba, I have yet to teach him proper table manners, I shall put etiquette it on my to do list."

Yahweh currently in his paternal form shrugged it off lovingly, as he passed Lucifer a lotus flower shaped cup brimming with hot tea.

"No worries Lucifer!" God related.

"Me-el now please pay close attention to what I am about to tell you," Yahweh added.

Me-el looked up fearfully upon hearing God's stern tone of voice. The child's little face was covered with clotted cream and chocolate from the pastries. Lucifer now slightly embarrassed by his sibling's lack of propriety, wiped him clean with a pink satin napkin.

"Yes Abba." The little angel stammered between mouthfuls of lavish treats.

Yahweh orated:

"Before eating it is proper to give thanks and praise!"

Me-el's large wide eyes darted up at Lucifer, the light bearer nodded in agreement with his father.

"Indeed little brother!" Lucifer affirmed.

"Abba gave us life, all we have is thanks to him; if not for Yahweh we would not have such pleasantries, so shall we pray?"

The child's robin blue egg shell eyes filled up with tears.

"Forgive me father!" He said jumping off Lucifer's lap, and to God's amazement; falling flat on his chubby self. Me-el was now prostrate chanting:

"Kadosh, kadosh, kadosh! Yahweh is kadosh!"

Yahweh put his tea cup aside, shifting his gaze to Lucifer.

"For not educating him on manners he certainly knows how to give proper praise!"

Lucifer shot Yahweh a dashing smile as he himself bowed his head.

"Blessed be you Abba who brings forth life" The sun of morning added.

Elohim elated with both his children exhorted:

"Very good! We may commence our tea and *nosh; and, get down to business!"

Lucifer crossed his left leg over his right one, directing his attention towards Yahweh. The seraph took simple sips from his tea, the perfect example of a gentleman. Me-el fumbled onto the ottoman, his feet tangling in his lavender alb; with some effort the portly angel gathered himself atop it, and proceeded to scarf down scones once more.

Yahweh started to address Lucifer about the matter he had been mulling through his mind earlier.

"I wanted to chat with you beloved about a group of angels I just made, I call them Thrones; yet, I must confess I am a bit curious about why I titled them as such, wait till you see what they look like!"

Yahweh arose, taking a shofar which was leaning against his chair, he blew into it full gusto. Me-el hopped in panic from his cushy pedestal; a blueberry scone dropping from his open mouth. The youth had never heard a ram's horn before. He ran over to Lucifer, attaching himself around his older brother's left leg, like a sloth on a tree branch. Lucifer set aside his tea, and then affectionately placed an arm around the startled child. The captain looked up as a grand wheel of feathers revolved in midair, glaring down towards them with eyes of amber. Lucifer lifted a contemplative eyebrow as Me-el hid from the immense flying wheel behind his older brother's boot.

---

* Nosh: snack, or to snack.

"Angelic creatures that resemble wheels," The captain stipulated.

Me-el was currently fixated on his reflection which shimmered on Lucifer's boot; he was like a house cat peering at itself on a glass ball hanging off a Christmas tree.

"I look funny!" The tot laughed.

"My face keeps changing from long to short!"

Yahweh to interested on what Lucifer's opinion would be gave the babbling tyke no heed.

"Yes," God confirmed.

"They praise well as you can see, and have great power, yet I did not give them any appendages, I suppose they shall merely chant for eternity.....Unless can you think of anything else they might be suitable to do most fair one?"

Yahweh presented the question to Lucifer with pseudo worry as he dismissed the Throne from their midst. The creature joined a good sized flock of its own kind which hovered momentarily over the sea of glass. Lucifer patted Yahweh's knee as the deity seated himself.

"Abba why not use them alongside the cherubim?" Lucifer asked.

Yahweh gazed at Lucifer with avid interest.

"Go on." God expressed.

"Well I have surmised" Lucifer continued.

"That realm five has a blacksmith shop, am I correct?"

"Indeed!" God verified, secretly aware of what his son of morning was getting ready to say to him. Yahweh's goal was to see if he and Lucifer thought along the same wave lengths. The triune God was testing him.

"Well" Lucifer went on.

"What if once you make more angels...? Oh perhaps some to adequately attend realm five, strong muscular types, what if I assign the black smiths to pound out argent chariots of gold and silver? I know your cherubim would be more than powerful enough to pull such contraptions; the thrones could act as wheels! Think of it Abba, coupled together these two ranks of creatures could easily coast you or angels too tired to fly between realms or even through space!"

Yahweh reclined in his chair, his face glowing in approval.

"I knew you would not disappoint me Lucifer!" Yahweh confirmed sipping his tea.

"That is precisely what we shall do! Now, before I dismiss you and the mini munch mouth..." Yahweh paused to give Me-el a friendly wink as the child stuffed scones into invisible pockets on his robe.

"Tell me how are you're other siblings adjusting? Do you have any ideas as to what levels you might appoint them to?"

Lucifer put down his tea cup after taking a quick swag; Me-el went over to grab his own glass of cold tea to drink.

"I do Abba" He replied.

"I envision Raphael in Eden, he seems captivated by herbs. Uriel would do well on realm one, he is fascinated with the cosmos, Gabriel is exceptional! I do believe I shall appoint her as rabbi on realm eight! She is terrific at absorbing huge amounts of knowledge! As for Me-el….." Lucifer glanced down, his tubby young sibling was ineloquently dipping a scone in his tall glass of tea, garnishing the lemon slices and sugar cubes with flaky remnants.

"Well let's just say I will personally educate him a bit myself, at least until you have completed creating the remaining angels, and the school can be filled."

"Splendid!" God confirmed.

"Well now that we have that puzzle configured you are both free to go back and join your siblings, I will get to work on my next triad of angels!"

Lucifer rose taking Me-el in his arms while bowing gracefully.

"Thank you most high, I shall always be at your disposal, summon for me whenever you wish."

God's eyes shined in love, reflecting Lucifer's light right back at him. The deity watched as the glorious seraph and his mini companion vanished from his sight.

"My sweet Lucifer," He swooned.

"You will ever be the apple of my eyes!"

Chapter 3

Lucifer reentered the library in Opus Angelorum, Me-el stood ever at his faulds; armor which covered the light bearer's soft white tail feathers. All three arch angels were now talking around a yellow marble table, lidded with opals and rubies. Uriel was the first to rise, upon seeing their captain come in. Raphael and Gabriel followed; all three kneeled, showing respect to the master general.

"At ease," Lucifer asserted.

Me-el struggled to his feet, he too had been kneeling, the child wanted to act exactly like the other more dignified angels.

"Its okay little brother, I know you are still learning," Lucifer noted.

"Why don't you go over to that section of the library labeled picture books?" The captain suggested, pointing towards the aisle. Me-el pitter pattered in excitement to the numerous gold paged books. Lucifer cast his magnetic eyes back to his siblings.

"Alright, so I was just with Abba, he asked about you three, from what I can see, you have been conversing among yourselves, have you gathered sufficient data from here, or; would you prefer to stay a bit longer?" He politely asked.

The haughty primed Uriel was the first to make his opinion known.

"We were actually discussing how eager we all are to visit the remaining levels my lord."

"Yes," Raphael agreed.

"I know I've got everything I need catalogued in my mind!"

Gabriel bobbed her head in approval.

"I as well captain, we would love you to escort us through the rest of Heaven, perhaps even tell us what our primary jobs will be?" she nervously hinted.

Lucifer gleamed like a prism with a ray of sunlight passing through it as he smiled. The seraph's presence filled the library in bouncy rainbow apparitions.

"I would be delighted to!" He disclosed.

"Me-el?" The captain beckoned his little brother away from a book about jungle animals.

The child upon hearing Lucifer's voice ran over to him straight away, gliding up onto his shoulders.

"Good! All set!" The captain cheerfully remarked.

"Let us go view the other great realms our father has gifted us with!"

Lucifer led his siblings out of the school. The five descended from level eight, ready to explore.

As his first five archangels whizzed throughout Heaven, Yahweh stood deliberating at his throne. The hypnotic voices of the seraphim assisted in soothing the gears turning in his mind.

"Yes, time to make more angels; this next triad will include some burly ones to help my Lucifer with his black smith shop on level five."

Yeshua and the Ruach buzzed in his bosom in approval. Yahweh began forming rhythmic gestures with his arms and hands, like a wondrous symphonic conductor. The four chief winds encircled him, as he blew life breath along with the Ruach's light into them. A burst of argent energy and sound rang through the ninth level, as a dashing company of armored angels came forth.

"You all shall be known as my Dominions!" Yahweh proclaimed.

God's desire was for the dominions to be born military figures, created primarily to assist Lucifer in realm five; some as black smiths, others as soldiers. Every newly formed creature shimmered in silver armor; each had handsome masculine faces and athletic bodies. The dominions stood approximately seven to eight feet tall, with one pair of wings, resembling those of an eagle. Yahweh smiled as the massive army bowed towards him chanting praise.

"Kadosh, kadosh kadosh!"

"My children," God began.

"I am going to teleport all of you to realm five, once you get there, I will supernaturally down load each of you with your names and responsibilities. I want to make something very clear! This is vital; you are all to be under my beloved Lucifer's instruction! You will know him when you see him! Lucifer's beauty is unlike any other angel's you shall ever see! His beauty radiates my own light!"

The dominions bowed again, before Yahweh relocated them to their level.

"Now!" God quipped, shoving his spectacles higher up his Semitic curved nose.

"To get to work on round two!"

Yahweh blew into his shofar, causing rainbows and lightning to bring about the next assembly of angels.

"Come forth ye Virtues!" He commanded.

The celestial group of creatures manifested, these beings displayed more feminine qualities, yet were not female. The virtues sparkled like crystal with wings made of light; fluorescent beams shot out of their shoulder blades, fluttering at humming bird speed.

"My dear dainty virtues, your voices will be enchanting; some of you will remain here, adding more harmony to my seraphim choir,"

God gestured for the first four rows of shiny angels to soar up over his throne. The entities obediently did as they were instructed.

"Now, I want some of you to go milk cherubim in Eden," Yahweh decided.

The translucent beings looked among themselves in disarray. God upon noticing their confused faces spoke:

"Oh no worries, I shall translocate you all there! Upon arrival you will know exactly what to do! The cherubim..." Yahweh lifted a finger to his temple, to mentally connect with the lion like beasts.

"Yes, the cherubim will know who you all are, and what you are required to do for them! I just told them, also; your names will come to you soon. Pay close attention to what I'm about to say next; although I have assigned you to particular work, your captain and my right hand, the light bearer; Lucifer, he has permission to call for any of you for other tasks if need be!"

The virtues eyes all tuned in to Yahweh's as he continued to speak.

"You cannot miss him! He is the most becoming seraph in all of Heaven! His armor is overlaid with every precious gem; he also has a fluffy little companion that follows him like a shadow!"

The fulgent scores of virtues bowed in unison as Yahweh clapped his hands, sending the remainder of the group to Eden. God paused to rub his long silver beard.

"Hmmmmm... why not make some more soldier types to keep post over all nine realms? Yes!" He answered himself.

"I am sure more military angels would please Lucifer tremendously! Also..., they may assist the dominions on level five!"

Raising his arms Yahweh called up clusters of thunder and bolts of light; also some armor from realm five, in a spontaneous combustion of glittery smoke, an aristocratic brigade of beings came about.

"My Powers!" Yahweh smiled, as the troupe of finely sculpted armed angels bowed low singing:

"Kadosh, kadosh, kadosh!"

The powers consisted of various skin tones, black, tan, Anglo, brown, and Asian.

"How lovely you all are!" Yahweh expressed, knowing Lucifer would also approve.

"Now hear me my children, I am going to send all of you to level five,"

The powers eagerly listened as Yahweh dictated, unlike the dominions these angels had wings of several colors, from hues of blue jay, cardinal, and finch yellow; they were a lambent clique, each quite masculine.

"Upon your arrival," Yahweh continued.

"You will meet angels somewhat similar to yourselves, in terms of height and garb, they are my dominions, one distinct feature they all share is their wings."

God held out his right arm, a majestic bald eagle appeared from out of nowhere and perched itself on the deity in a statuesque manner.

"Behold this regal animal, I call it an eagle, view its pinions..."

The eagle spread his wings as if it could read God's mind, or knew what he was saying.

"Every dominion on realm five has plumage like this fine bird."

Yahweh released the eagle; the animal ascended upwards and vanished.

"Listen to the dominions, by now they all should be attending to basic duties on level five, help them in any way possible, yet; know this, your master general is lord Lucifer, both you and the dominions are under his direct orders! I shall now send you to realm five; your names should have come to you all by now."

A polished Greco-Roman looking angel with black wavy hair and dark purple eyes stepped forward, genuflecting on his right knee; his wings matched the tint of his pupil-less peepers.

"Kadosh, kadosh, kadosh Abba! I am Beleth; may I dare ask my most holy father a question?" The dazzling angel asked.

God taken aback by the creature's poise and refined character, nodded.

"Speak child, I permit you too."

"If it pleases my holy father, I shall personally see that my fellow comrades befit themselves with proper labor."

A slow smile lifted on Yahweh's face.

"I like your *chutzpah Beleth! By all means do so! In fact I recommend you enquire for a certain dominion named Azazel. A strapping well formed ruddy angel, with long red hair and armor made of moonstone! He will make sure you all get situated upon arrival!"

Beleth bowed low once more before Yahweh transferred them all to realm five.

Yahweh walked back up to his throne feeling joyous.

"Oh what glorious children I have made! Yet none in their entire luster will ever compare to my beloved Lucifer!"

Yahweh sat down to collect his thoughts. The seraphim and virtues above him strummed on golden harps, singing.

"Hmmm...." God pondered.

"I have a stupendous idea! Oh yes! This will show Lucifer how much I love him!"

God now to wound up to sit; gaited merrily over to his corner tea area. The deity had domed the corner in glass; every breed of butterfly fluttered inside of it; Elohim thought the little sprites added atmosphere with

---

* Chutzpah: Courage.

their multi colored wings. Yahweh stretched, he was now calmer, and he seated himself on his red antique chair.

"*Oy vey!" Yahweh noticed his tea pot was empty.

Yahweh clapped his hands, summoning a virtue named Bariel.

"My lord" She said as she bowed.

"Yes my dear," God spoke.

"Would you please fly down to realm three, fetch me some senna leaves and cinnamon for a fresh pot of tea, and; if you should come across Lucifer, please send him this way."

"Yes most high!" She guaranteed leaving a trail of glitter as she left.

God watched the virtue fly off, then brought about a savory assortment of confections; scones, figs stuffed with nuts, caramelized dates, and even some chocolate cherubim milk.

"Need to be ready for Me-el! He loves to fress! I can't wait to tell Lucifer that he will be creating the final triad of angels!" He proclaimed.

---

* Oy vey: woe is me! / Fress: To eat like an animal.

Chapter 4

Lucifer and his four siblings were now hiking through Eden. Me-el skipped ahead of them all, the child was chasing tiny pixies, translucent little entities which danced on clarion wings.

"I gonna get you!" Me-el threatened as he pounced after the terrified sprite like a fat kitten.

Raphael took in a deep breath.

"Ahhh..... Yes this is the realm where I belong!" He silently thought as he took in the verdant surroundings.

The many delicious fragrances' of jasmine, mint, and roses perfumed the air, along with several other pleasing aromas were wooing Raphael, like scents from a stew pot to a famished human. Lucifer smiled as he took note of his brother's reaction.

"I knew Raphael would love Eden!" The captain evaluated.

Lucifer was anxious to tell his brother that he wanted him to manage the garden.

"Raphael," Lucifer said as he took a step towards his sibling.

"He can be Cinnamon! His coat matches the color of the herb!" Raphael observed.

Me-el now glad he could address the two creatures properly ran up to Lucifer and leeched himself around his right boot. Raphael bowed low to his captain.

"Thank you so much lord Lucifer!"

"Think nothing of it Rapha! I know you will do well here."

Raphael nudged back a tad as Lucifer went to stroke his cheek, it felt to intimate to the arch. Lucifer gave him a wink instead, not wanting to put him under pressure in front of the others. The morning star made his opinion vocal:

"Behold Yahweh's sweetest and most lovely remedy! My beguiling brother Raphael!"

Gabriel and Uriel saluted Raphael. Lucifer shifted his gaze to them.

"I have not forgotten you two!" The captain commented; as Cinnamon and Sugar galloped past him escaping Me-el's unwanted affection. The child frowned, the unicorns ran much faster than what he could keep up with.

"Gabriel, after we see the next realm, I assure you, you will feel quite at home! I also would be happy if you accepted the position of rabbi at Opus Angelorum."

Gabriel's eyes lit up.

"Of course I accept my lord!"

"Good" Lucifer smiled.

"Uriel I observed how reading about the stars brought wonder to your continence, I think the first realm will suit you nicely, in fact; I know it will!"

Uriel's flint face hinted the slightest form of a smile. Gabriel and he now both exchanged glances of anticipation. Me-el jumped up and down like an obese rabbit which had accidentally been fed huge amounts of caffeine.

"Oh Lufi! What bout me? What I gonna do?"

Raphael bit his lower lip.

"Please God don't allow Lucifer to let him rampage Eden!" He prayed.

Lucifer eloquently lifted Me-el into his arms, his face full of love.

"You my sweetest stuffed fig, you will go everywhere I go! The first thing we are going to do is practice your speech and correct pronunciation of words! Gabriel cannot be a rabbi to just you." Lucifer said tickle ling Me-el's scone filled tummy as the tot giggled in glee.

"Well" The captain speculated regaining his formal tone of voice.

"Shall we go see the next two realms?"

Gabriel and Uriel nodded. Raphael waved at the four as he began promenading through a vineyard, sampling juicy red grapes.

"If it is well with you captain, I will stay here on my level, I would like to make myself familiar with the grounds and its creatures."

Raphael expressed his notion while kneeling to the light bearer, his sunset pink wings curling inward as he did so.

Lucifer's eyes were now glued to Raphael's alluring soft characteristics, he particularly favored the archangel's long dark brown hair; it flowed over his torso to his knees. Me-el's paunchy hands smacked Lucifer's cheeks in impatience.

"Lufi! Look at ME!!!" The jealous babe demanded.

Lucifer snapped back to his senses and responded to Raphael.

"Of course dear brother, but on one condition, I expect you to have this entire garden memorized next chance we meet! Every herb, tree, and flower! I will escort our siblings to the final two realms, perhaps even once Abba finishes creating the remaining angels we might all get together?"

Raphael nodded. The archangel paused to look down to his waist. He was surprised to see a fully equipped gardening belt around it; with every tool needed to prune and trim the vegetation and plants. Raphael also had a magenta suede strap down past his collar bone;

it crossed his chest to a sheath on his back; which held a phosphorescent caduceus; Yahweh's symbol for medicine. God had bestowed them upon Raphael upon hearing Lucifer's declaration.

"I do hope my archangel of healing likes his new accessories!" Yahweh mused, looking into his sea of glass from realm nine.

"My captain," Raphael stammered.

"Is all this from Abba?"

Lucifer halted his steps, turning to Raphael again, Me-el who was becoming antsy, began blowing raspberries on the morning star's neck.

"I would assume so fairest of gardeners! We shall be seeing each other soon!"

Me-el waved at Raphael from atop Lucifer's shoulders as the four of them now descended to level two.

Bariel returned to Yahweh's throne room, God was now back at his tea corner. The virtue had brought up a crimson velvet pouch from Eden, filled with senna and mint leaves. Yahweh smiled as the relucent angel bowed then placed a few in his pot of hot water.

"Here you go Abba, it so happens that Lucifer's lieutenant the archangel Raphael has just been given full charge of Eden, so it was Raphael himself that put this mixture together for you!"

Bariel stopped, pulling another primrose pouch from the golden sash around her waist.

"The lieutenant also sent up some fresh figs and walnuts, he told me I had just missed Lucifer, apparently he is placing Gabriel in realm two, and Uriel is to manage level one. I told Raphael about you wanting audience with Lucifer, he promised to send our captain a messenger dove with the request, so he and Me-el should be here shortly."

Bariel placed the lid on the tea pot, and the treats from Eden on the gold tray of heaping pastries.

"Thank you Bariel! I did see Raphael's promotion, and I approve of everything Lucifer is doing so far! I knew he would make a great captain! My ears delight at your words! I must confide; when Raphael hatched I myself knew he would be Eden's guardian! He does not know it, but his job, aside from Lucifer's; is the most important! You see the creatures in Eden; they were made before I even thought about making angels! Eden is the very heart of all Heaven! I am so glad Lucifer and I seem to think so much alike! Thank you again Bariel, I will simply enjoy a cup of tea myself, and perhaps nosh on a few figs until my morning star and Me-el come round! You are dismissed child!"

The virtue kneeled as she ascended upwards to rejoin the choir above God's throne. Yahweh served himself a cup of tea, ecstatic at the report he had just received. Yeshua and the Ruach hummed euphorically within him. They were just as pleased.

Me-el trudged through the twinkling snow on realm two like a plump baby penguin that was just learning how to walk. Gabriel flitted about gaily, admire ring each individual snowflake. Uriel was the only one who appeared bored. He sulked beneath a shimmering ice formation with his wings of fire at a dim fizzle.

Lucifer snuck up on Me-el, pulling playfully at one of the child's tail feathers. Me-el jumped causing him to plop face first in the snow.

"Instant snow angel!" Gabriel jeered.

Lucifer picked up Me-el laughing.

"Sorry little brother your squeezable bottom was simply too hard to resist!"

The captain kissed Me-el on the fore head; the child giggled hopping onto his older brother's shoulders. Uriel rolled his gold eyes in impatience, an icicle landed on his head.

"Snow is bloody awful!" He silently fumed; the irritated arch finally spoke up:

"It would appear Gabriel does in fact fancy this level my lord, shall we be off to see where I shall be functioning?"

Lucifer's eyes gunned to Uriel's left shoulder, a messenger dove had just landed on the pompous angel.

"Yes, of course brother, but we have a visitor, look to your left, perhaps that dove was sent for one of us, you had better read the scroll attached to its foot, be gentle!" the captain recommended.

Uriel begrudged, carefully took the off white pink beaked dove into his hands, and gingerly detached the scroll. He opened it and began reading it over.

"My captain," He began, as the dove soared away.

"It is sent from Yahweh, according to this note Abba wants to speak with you, it also reads:

"No RUSH, please feel free to finish your current work before returning, love Abba."

Lucifer looked up, Uriel's face clearly displayed annoyance.

"Well sounds like I better get you to realm one, speedily brother!"

Uriel's visage brightened.

"Me-el and I must not keep Abba waiting too long, Gabriel feel free to make yourself at home here!"

Gabriel flitted down as gently as a snowflake; she bowed low to the captain.

"Thank you my lord Lucifer, I assure you by your next visit, I will have made myself a stunning palace of ice!" she replied.

Lucifer gave her a wink.

"Okay Uriel, let's get you to level one!"

Chapter 5

Lucifer and Me-el were now ascending to realm nine, Uriel waved from his star filled level, sparkling as bright as one of the stars himself.

"Now Me-el," Lucifer lectured over his shoulder as they glided up.

The morning star had been teaching the child better diction since their last visit with God.

"Remember when we get to Abba's throne room, you must pray before partaking of any food, also whenever I bow to father you should do the same. I hope I can count on you to do as you are told."

Me-el held locks of Lucifer's hair like reins on a horse.

"I promise Lufi!" The tyke affirmed.

"That's a good angel!" Lucifer said smiling.

Yahweh was standing by his sea of glass when the two softly landed.

"My most lovely one!" God gasped placing his right hand over his heart.

Lucifer genuflected, Me-el attempted to, but tripped on his robe, from the marble floor the little blunder mumbled:

"Kadosh, kadosh, kadosh!"

Yahweh chortled, Lucifer helped Me-el to his feet.

"Well thank you both for your praise!" The creator beamed.

Yahweh flicked his wrist, shortening Me-el's robe by a few inches. Me-el began skipping around his brother.

"Look! I move more better now Lufi!"

The light bearer gave his younger sibling a nod of reassurance.

"I see! What do you say to Abba? I do believe it was him who helped you out just now!"

Me-el marched up to God, giving him his best bow.

"Thank you Abba! You are so good!" He chimed, while batting his thick dark lashes.

"Oh you are quite welcome little one! Now why don't the three of us go over to our tea corner, I need to discuss some matters with your brother."

Yahweh led the all too eager Me-el and dashing Lucifer to their private pocket on realm nine. God sat down first, followed by Lucifer; this time Me-el fumbled up onto his ottoman and clasped his puffy palms together in prayer position.

"The sooner we pray, the sooner I get to eat!" He ruminated.

God taking Me-el's subtle hint asked:

"Lucifer would you please lead us in prayer?"

The seraph lowered his head, and reverently said the blessing:

"Blessed are you God most high who gives life"

"Amen!" Yahweh exclaimed.

"You see Me-el...." The triune deity explained:

"Amen means truly, it is my native language of Hebrew, I am sure once school starts your rabbi will teach it to you! It is proper to end every blessing as such!" He stated.

Me-el smiled.

"I will make sure to remember that Abba!"

"Well," Yahweh resumed,

"Help your selves'! Me-el I had some chocolate cherubim milk made just for you! Now no cherubim gives chocolate, but I had the virtues on realm three add cocoa from Eden's cocoa trees, let me know if you like it!"

Me-el's ever widening blue eye's fell upon the tall foamy glass of brown beverage, it looked yummy.

"Okay!" He said, putting his porcine hands around the quartz mug.

"Oh and don't worry about it going empty," God pointed out;

"It will automatically refill each time you finish a serving!"

Me-el formed an okay signal to God with his pudgy right hand, as he slurped down the savory liquid with his left.

Lucifer shook his head as Yahweh passed him a cup of senna-mint tea.

"You spoil him father!" He jested.

"Well, just a bit! But he is your favorite, so the little chub tub has a special place in my heart too!" God acknowledged, pouring himself a cup of tea as well.

"Now I want to tell you something beloved."

Yahweh spoke as he blew steam off his tea.

"I have finished creating the first two triads of angels, did you notice any of my recent work as you and your siblings explored the realms?"

Lucifer set his tea cup on an end table which stood between the two Victorian chairs he and God occupied.

"Yes Lord! They would be impossible to miss! The virtues sparkle like diamonds, and although no one except Me-el and me seemed to be interested by realm five, because of its heavy military components, all agreed that the dominions and powers were magnificent! I must say Abba; they are everything I hoped they would be! A dominion named Nergel was already hammering away on shields and swords when we visited the level! Thank you so much Abba! They will prove to be a spectacular battalion!" Lucifer gushed.

"So glad to hear you approve *bubeleh!" Yahweh sighed.

"Now I still need a final triad, however; to show my love for you, I would like for you yourself to make them!"

Lucifer took on a blutterbunged look.

"Excuse me **Avi? Forgive me for asking, but I am by no means you! How in all of Heaven could a seraph like me possibly create other angels?"

Yahweh lifted his right hand, revealing a gilded diadem with one mother pearl at its center.

"This crown is for you! All you need do is place it on that gorgeous head of yours, then using your own thoughts you will have the ability to make angels, or anything else for that matter; within reason of course! You need only think of something or some angel into existence, and it will be!"

Yahweh rose, placing the glossy band of gold around Lucifer's head.

"There now." God smiled.

"Try it out if you wish!" He urged.

---

* Bubeleh: my darling.

** Avi: Hebrew for my Father.

Yahweh glanced at Me-el, he was pretending not to ease drop while stuffing his mouth with scones, walnuts, and candied dates.

"He could be your test subject!" God suggested.

Lucifer gazed over towards his *grob younger sibling imagining him in a suit of armor just like his. The morning star caressed the diadem over his brow, a buzz of adrenaline shot through his veins.

Me-el had gone belly up on his velvet green stool, exhausted from so much chomping and chugging. The child's wings were extended in a frazzled pose. The pudgy little creature purred contently as he fell into slumber, dreaming of noshing on more gourmet morsels.

"Like me!" Lucifer whispered.

The captain depictured Me-el quietly in his mind's eye. The little angel suddenly awakened, he was stuffed into armor that matched Lucifer's. The tot resembled a fine fat hen trapped in a tight gleaming can, capped with multi colored gems. Elohim and Lucifer both burst out into laughter as the child rolled about helplessly like a turtle on its back. Me-el toppled off his ottoman like a meatball falling from a stack of spaghetti. He landed on the floor with a loud clang!

"Well," Abba snickered, wiping away tears of amusement from his eyes;

"I would say it works!"

---

* Grob: Fat.

Lucifer sat on his throne on realm four. The level was the light bearer's private quarters; God had enveloped the realm in crystal and every sort of reflective stone. Diamonds, white sapphire zircon and fine cut glass. Lucifer's palace was constructed entirely of glass itself; even the furniture mirrored the mighty seraph's beauty. The morning star situated himself upon his chair, cushioned with red velvet and glazed with rubies. Yahweh had actually given Lucifer his new awesome power of creating things with his mind upon making him, yet the deity did not share this information with his favorite son, he preferred viewing how Lucifer would use the diadem he had bequeathed him with.

"Let's see how he handles himself with his new ability." Yahweh said to Yeshua and the Ruach, as they watched the prince of Heaven from the sea of glass.

In truth the diadem was simply an accessory to aid Lucifer in not feeling over whelmed by his recent new power.

Me-el slid gleefully on the glass floors, much like a new born kitten on ice. He bounced off Lucifer's boot as he thudded against his brother's throne. Lucifer picked up the child, now clothed in a willowy robe. He placed Me-el on his lap.

"Well little brother you get to see me make angels!" Lucifer smiled.

Me-el clapped his hands.

"Make more little ones like me!" The tyke insisted.

"Sorry Me-el, I do believe only Abba can hatch little angels! But do not worry; the cherubim are laying eggs as we speak! I am sure you will soon have friends to play and go to school with!" He affirmed.

Me-el laid his head against Lucifer's breast plate, the captain removed it, so the child's noggin could rest against his downy white plumage.

"Alright," Lucifer uttered, bringing his right hand to his diadem.

"I want some princely looking angels, garbed in white choir robes with wings to match! Hair as gold as my own, I will call them Principalities. These angels will help me on realm seven, where I shall conduct great concerts and symphonies for Abba!'

Me-el sat up straight on Lucifer's lap, his eyes wide as saucers; a brilliant cluster of Arian angels came forth.

"Are they not incredible?" Lucifer remarked a bit baffled at his own power.

The exquisite principalities all gazed towards Lucifer for further instruction.

"Hello my brethren! I am your captain, lord Lucifer. However, I am by no means your father! I shall now send you all to level nine to give praise to Yahweh! After you have paid your respects to Abba, I will count on him to send you all to realm seven. I have given each of you knowledge of music and every kind of musical instrument on that level. Upon your arrival all of you should know precisely what to do!"

The principalities saluted Lucifer; as he used his crown to teleport them to God's throne room.

"Wow! Lufi!!!" Me-el shouted.

"They came out so pretty! But; not as pretty as you!" The child admitted.

Lucifer smiled.

"Yes Me-el, making angels is somewhat entertaining! Let's create some more!" Lucifer paused to rub his chin.

"I wonder.... Perhaps I should make my own Archangels... you, me and our three siblings only make for five...I do not think Abba would mind... Yes! It is decided! I will make more archangels!"

Lucifer brought his hand to his golden band once more.

"I call about a squad of mighty archangels! Each angel will know his name, be a well formed soldier and each should have a single pair of wings which vary in color! Every archangel will have long hair from dark to light! Come forth!"

Me-el bounced on Lucifer's lap in amusement as a luminous concourse of tall handsome archangels appeared.

"My archangels, I am Lucifer, your captain. I am going to send all of you to our father, Yahweh. Please give him proper praise; it will be him who will place all of you where he sees fit!"

The archangels all saluted, before vanishing.

Me-el hopped up onto his brother's shoulders, he had grown a foot, and two more pairs of wings. Lucifer looked up towards him.

"Wow! In all the excitement of creating angels, I failed to notice your new wings Me-el! Why you are even a bit taller! Some day you will be a ravishing archangel yourself!"

Me-el cooed in joy as he hugged Lucifer's neck.

"Well," Lucifer analyzed,

"I find it a bit lonesome here, with just me and you, what about I make some angels specifically for this level? They can attend to this realm, working around the palace!"

"Sounds good!" Me-el expressed.

"Okay then! Come forth Messengers, clothed in simple robes of silver, with nicely trimmed blonde hair and wings of gold!"

Lucifer declared, rubbing the diadem. A blast of light erupted, hordes of lovely angels sprang out in all directions. This group would be the very first ones to have short hair in Heaven. Me-el's eyes took in their becoming gold wings, as the messengers speckled the level like fireworks.

"Greetings my messengers, I am Lucifer your captain, you were all just now created to personally serve me and my younger sibling Me-el,"

Me-el grinned at the mention of his name; every messenger's eyes shot to him for an instant.

"You will all be working on this realm, but first all of you must go give glory to God our father on level nine, I shall get you all there promptly!"

The well polished bunch saluted as Lucifer momentarily relocated them.

"Don't worry Me-el," The morning star related.

"They will be back soon!"

Lucifer leaned back on his throne, content with the triad he had finished.

"I do hope Abba is pleased with the angels I made." He prayed.

Chapter 6

God stood at his throne overcome with pleasure as he faced the final triad of angels concocted by Lucifer. The principalities, archangels, and messengers all bowed towards him ceremoniously chanting:

"Kadosh, kadosh, kadosh Abba!"

"What a wonderful job Lucifer has done!" Yahweh marveled.

God waved his right hand, transferring the principalities to realm seven. Yahweh knew where Lucifer wanted each rank, he had been watching from his sea of glass. God now waved his left arm, the archangels were sent to realm six.

"Fine guardians for Jerusalem!" He evaluated.

The deity now reviewed the clean cut messengers, God smiled, stating:

"All of you best serve my beloved Lucifer well!"

The mass of angels bowed in agreement as Yahweh flicked his right wrist, leading them back to the light bearer's level. God sat on his throne, his lips curving upwards in a smile.

"I wonder how the lieutenants are doing" He pondered out loud,

No sooner had Yahweh made the statement than a virtue appeared kneeling at his left.

"Kadosh Abba!" She praised.

"Raphael has asked me to inform you of two new eggs which are preparing to hatch in Eden, in case you wanted to come down and witness the event first hand."

God rose from his throne.

"I would be delighted to! Tell Raphael I will be there as soon as possible! I think I will collect Lucifer and Me-el along the way! I'm sure they would also appreciate meeting two new hatchlings!"

The virtue knelt once more, she smiled and descended.

Yahweh quickly appeared on Lucifer's realm. An amiable yellow eyed messenger with the name "Rofocal" stitched in gold on his robe met God with a graceful bow, as the deity suddenly manifested on the glitzy level.

"Salutations most high! To what do we meager flocks of messengers owe the honor of your presence?"

Yahweh's face turned rose pink as myriads of Lucifer's charming angels paused to genuflect and worship him.

"Well, I would like to see Lucifer and Me-el!"

"I'll go gather them both for you!" Rofocal assured, heading towards the gleaming palace.

Little Me-el had basically moved in to his older brother's abode, he found the mirrored rooms to be confusing. Each time Me-el thought he was talking to Lucifer; his brother would sneak up behind him and pinch his hide.

"Gothca again!" The morning star quipped.

A scowl crossed Me-el's face.

"No fair Lufi! You always gotta trick me!"

Lucifer tenderly picked up Me-el, rubbing noses with him.

"Look!" Me-el shouted, pointing a stout finger towards the incoming Rofocal.

"Messenger in the house!"

Lucifer's sky blue eyes swiveled to Rofocal. The nervous angel knelt, feeling color rush to his pale cheeks. He had never entered the captain's palace unannounced before; he was not quite sure what Lucifer's reaction would be.

"Hello there!" Lucifer spoke between chuckles; Me-el was tickling his ears.

Lucifer bent down to read the name on the angel's garb.

"Rofocal, please rise, may I help you?" He politely asked.

The messenger stood, he looked to be no more than twenty, as did all the others on Lucifer's level. He shyly began to speak:

"My lordship, Yahweh himself is on our, I mean, your realm, he desires to speak with you both!"

Lucifer grinned, giving Rofocal a new reason to blush.

"Thank you! What a great surprise! Me-el let us go see what Abba has to tell us, Oh and Rofocal, thank you for being so punctual in your duties!" Lucifer winked, whilst he exited the palace with Me-el on his shoulders.

Rofocal's heart throbbed furiously in his chest.

"Oh what I would not give to be the child mounted on his bonny shoulders!" The star struck angel fawned.

Lucifer knelt before Yahweh, as Me-el jumped off his back, to do the same.

"Abba!" Lucifer's eyes glinted in joy.

"How wonderful for you to personally come down to my level!"

Yahweh gave Lucifer a tight embrace, and mussed Me-el's head of curls.

"Well," God confided;

"I have some great news! I have just been made aware that two eggs are preparing to hatch north of Eden! I thought you and Me-el might like to escort me down, to see who we welcome next!"

Me-el who was currently wearing a lavender robe leapt at the notion.

"Oh yes! I mean may we Lufi?" He pleaded.

Lucifer's ocean blue eyes twinkled; he welcomed any reason to bask in Raphael's sumptuous beauty.

"Abba that sounds like a brilliant idea! Yes Me-el we may, what are we still standing here for? Let's go!"

Raphael was pruning a rose bush with golden shears, singing sweetly as he did. In his opinion every plant, flower, or other herbage was praising Yahweh in its own personal way. The archangel's favorite examples of this were the trees. The limbs and branches of each arbor unceasingly reached upwards; as if they were continually paying homage to their creator.

"It is as if they never stop saying thank you!" Raphael thought.

The gardening angel turned his pensive emerald eyes towards the rose colored sky; it was dotted with stars from Uriel's level. Uriel had begun catering out the glittery stones, after he had been given charge of level one. All of Heaven was enjoying glimpses of them now.

Raphael put his shears back into his gardening belt; he glanced up as three streaks of light caught his attention.

"Oh good!" He exclaimed.

"Belah got Abba the message! I see our captain and his loyal inflated side kick have joined him!" The jolly angel opined.

Raphael bowed gracefully; his translucent robe fell gently over his well structured body. He unfurled his six sunset pink wings and welcomed God.

"Greetings Abba most holy, and to my great captain lord Lucifer!"

Raphael elevated himself, taking notice of Me-el's cute face. He had his lips in a pout.

"It is a pleasure to see you too Me-el!" Raphael added.

Raphael handed the child a handful of sugar coated walnuts, from a red velvet pouch on his belt. The gardener always enjoyed having a snack on hand. Me-el smiled and greedily nabbed the whole bundle from Raphael's waist. The small angel immediately dumped the complete contents of candied nuts into his mouth. Me-el chomped, swallowed, smiled and burped. Raphael looked at him aghast.

"So...." Raphael began; now sorry he would need to procure another pouch full of nuts for himself to nosh on later.

"Would you three like to go see the eggs that are getting ready to hatch from the cherubim?"

"Indeed!" Yahweh proclaimed.

"Please take us north!"

Raphael nodded as he took to flight. Lucifer and Me-el flew directly behind him, whilst Yahweh simply floated.

"Eden agrees with you brother, you are as lovely as any flower in the garden." Lucifer remarked, attempting to compliment Raphael.

Me-el who was still getting acquainted to his two new pair of wings struggled to keep up with his two older siblings. He wanted to hear what they were talking about, but he could not.

"Thank you captain," Raphael called back.

"However I am certain father would say that and more about your beauty."

Yahweh, who could hear every word, sniggered at Raphael's response. God advanced towards the morning star and his clumsy tag along.

"Raphael is correct Lucifer! Nothing nor no one will ever match your beauty!" He verified.

Lucifer, who was feeling a bit slighted by Raphael, began to perk up again.

"By the way," God continued as they prepared to land.

"I see Me-el has some nice new wings! He appears taller too!"

Me-el now aware he was being admired used every ounce of effort in his tubby body to make certain he landed just as eloquently as Lucifer. Abba smiled at the child's determination.

"Someday you will be a ravishing soldier!" God whispered to himself.

The four landed north of Eden, numerous relucent virtues were busy milking rows of hefty cherubim. The maiden type angels squeezed milk from the beasts into silver buckets lined with garnets. Belah and Gabriel were facing two of the creatures, which were lounging like oversized house cats; behind two new marble eggs. One was tangerine orange, sprinkled with specks of gold. The other egg was teal, dusted with silver spots.

"Hello!" Raphael bellowed.

Gabriel and Belah did a one hundred and eighty degree turn as they heard the manager of Eden's voice; upon viewing Lucifer and God in his company, the two bowed. The glittery milk maidens of light halted their work to do the same. The fifty foot Cherubim fell to their four furry knees, chanting:

"Kadosh, kadosh, kadosh!"

Yahweh stepped towards the beasts smiling, Lucifer, Me-el and Raphael followed close behind him.

"So;" God began.

"Are they ready to hatch?"

Gabriel arose along with the other kneeling angels.

"Yes most high, so glad to see lord Lucifer and Me-el with you! Raphael also invited Uriel and me. Alas, Uriel did not seem as enthused about the hatchlings. He did however send some special regards!"

Gabriel gazed upwards, Yahweh smiled once more, Uriel had sent them a shower of shooting stars for the event.

"How lovely and considerate of him!" God grinned.

Me-el grabbed Yahweh by the sleeve of his white robe, he tugged in anticipation.

"Abba look!" He shouted.

"The teal egg is opening!"

All eyes now fell upon the hatching egg. A four foot angel with blonde curls and wings of aqua climbed out. He was dressed in a blue tunic and had grey eyes. Lucifer inspected the lanky child.

"He is cute," He murmured into Raphael's ear.

"But my Me-el is still more adorable!"

Raphael gave his captain a nod. The new angel was also much thinner than Me-el; Raphael was impressed when the newly hatched child immediately went over to Yahweh and bowed.

"Kadosh Abba, I am Samael." He said in perfect diction.

"My you are a bright little bubeleh!" Yahweh expressed.

"Gabriel I do believe you are going to have more than just Me-el to teach in your future class now!"

Me-el's large indigo eyes stared darts at the lithe angel. Samael ran over to Gabriel, he hid behind one of her lower wings.

"Well hello!" She chimed, throwing her arms around him.

"Abba?" She asked.

"Speak child." Yahweh responded.

"Since Lucifer has Me-el on his level, would it be alright if little Samael stayed with me?" Samael gazed longingly at God, hoping he might agree.

God shook his head in disapproval.

"No Gabriel I am afraid not, Samael must stay in his egg, in the patch west of Eden that is where all hatched angels must reside. Me-el and you, along with your siblings are the only exceptions, solely because you are the five head archangels! Why Lucifer does not even have an egg, he has a palace. You and your brethren that do have them are at an advantage! You four are not required to sleep in your eggs simply because of your high ranking. However, they are at your disposal whenever you feel the need to snuggle into them!"

Yahweh finished speaking and Samael's egg vanished, headed directly to the egg patch. Samael's face took on a dismal look upon hearing the father's decision. Me-el eyed him over.

"I'm better than he is!" The tot thought, bemused that he outranked the new angel.

"Don't worry Samael" Raphael said going over to the new hatchling, and kneeling to his height.

"Look the orange egg is hatching! You will not be the only small angel resting in the egg patch west of Eden!"

Me-el's eyes lit up like fire flies as an angel just as chubby and inept as him, toppled out of the egg. He was an eye catching raven haired four foot child, with tangerine wings which matched his egg. The youth was clothed in a white robe; he stumbled over to Yahweh bowing forward.

"Ahhh hi, I am Raguel, oh yeah.... Praise you most High! Knosh! Ahhh I mean Kadosh! Kadosh, kadosh."

Yahweh chuckled at the child's less than elegant entrance.

"Hello there Raguel." God smiled patting the angel's head of jet black curls.

"I would like you to meet your two future class mates, Me-el and Samael, come now you two do not be timid, come and say hello!" Yahweh beckoned.

Samael shyly came out from behind Gabriel's wing and offered Raguel a smile. Me-el stood up straight and took a pace forward. Raguel's eyes fell on Me-el who was standing next to the most beautiful angel in the garden.

"I gotta be friends with him!" Raguel thought.

Raguel trudged up towards Me-el and Lucifer, his eyes transfixed on the captain's bejeweled armor and twelve white wings. Raguel extended a pudgy palm to Me-el. Me-el's hand which was equally as puffy met his in a handshake. Raguel's eyes smiled.

Samael frowned, he lowered his head and went back to regain solace behind Gabriel's wing.

"So much for making friends..." He moped.

"Let's you and me be besties!" Raguel said to Me-el.

Me-el's little chest fluffed up ever so slightly, he had been chosen over the other angel.

"You bet! Wanna go explore Eden! There are some awesome vineyards full of yummy grapes that should be eaten!" Me-el suggested.

Raphael's eyebrows went up in alarm; he had enough scavengers to worry about with the pixies! He did not need two semi bovine angels tearing through his terrain along with the tedious sprites. He immediately came up with another idea:

"I think it would be better if all three of you, were to accompany Gabriel to level eight, she could start you out on some elementary studies!"

Samael appeared excited, Me-el and Raguel did not. Yahweh impressed by Raphael's thinking, nodded in agreement.

"Yes Raphael that is a great idea! Gabriel what say you?"

Gabriel seemed as excited as Samael.

"Abba I would be delighted to begin teaching!"

God glanced over at Lucifer.

"My beloved one I also think some messengers from your realm might benefit from some schooling....In fact..." God now regarded some of the virtues in front of him with deep interest.

"You three virtues, Israfil, Anael, and Zephra, I want you to attend Opus Angelorum as well. Gabriel I will send you some more angels too! Every angel who I esteem worthy of schooling, I shall send your way! I guarantee your class will consist of at least twenty students!"

Gabriel bowed.

"That sounds wonderful Abba, for now I shall take these six, come along all of you, let us go prepare for our first session!" She happily exhorted.

Raphael released a huge breath of relief, as he watched "Roly" and "Poly"; or Me-el and Raguel; take off clumsily behind Samael and the three virtues. Lucifer elbowed the gardener.

"I would love to see those vine yards Me-el was telling Samael about, would you give me a tour?"

Raphael nervously adjusted his wreath of roses; he did not want to anger God by responding to Lucifer's subtle advances.

"Maybe some other time brother, I need to check on the four rivers right now."

Raphael bowed low to God and Lucifer.

"I politely excuse myself from my lords; I should get back to attending to my duties."

Abba nodded in confirmation, giving Raphael leave to be dismissed. Yahweh flung his arm around Lucifer.

"Come now beloved, how about we go back to your level and select a few messengers to send Gabriel's way?"

Lucifer smiled as he took God's arm and ascended a realm, as they went up Lucifer could not help but wonder if perhaps his beauty did not affect Raphael.

"No... Abba made me the most fair...Although he did get a crown of flowers on his head... Why did Raphael get a flower wreath before I got my diadem? No... I am being silly; I know Abba loves me most... Still Raphael is very lovely...I hope to get his interest, perhaps he is just overwhelmed with all his new responsibilities..." Lucifer concluded silently.

The captain decided to shrug the whole thing off and began concentrating on Yahweh and how jovial the new hatchlings had made him. The light bearer already had at least six messengers in mind to enlist in Opus Angelorum.

Chapter 7

"Well," Gabriel excogitated.

"Since we only have six students right now, I thought it best if we have our first class here in the library of Opus Angelorum!" She cited.

Me-el and Raguel sat side by side on the adalusite floor mounted on cushions of silver. Samael scooted away from the duo on his gold one, the two buddies kept pinching his wing tips on purpose. The three virtues from Eden sat behind the three children on golden chairs, capped with rose colored pillows, they lit up the room.

Gabriel was about to begin orating, when six spruce messengers entered the area in perfect line, with their names all stitched in golden lettering on their robes.

"Oh how wonderful!" Gabriel exclaimed.

"You six handsome angels must be from lord Lucifer's level; you all must have found much favor with Yahweh's eye! Please find a stool or chair from the surrounding tables, and be seated with our lovely virtues."

The messengers; Semjaza, Meririm, Beryth, Sariel, Asaph and Jericho diligently did as they were told. Gabriel noticed how Jericho stood out amongst the other five due to a streak of gold passing through his neatly trimmed hair; she clapped her hands and smiled.

"Great! Well welcome to Opus Angelorum, I thought we could start by learning more about Abba's native language of Hebrew, so..."

Gabriel teleported to an aisle of books titled: "Languages"

She instantly returned carrying twelve thick text books in her arms.

"Samael?"

Gabriel knelt down to the lonesome looking youth.

"Would you please pass every angel here a text book?"

Samael's sad face brightened, the child to Gabriel's amazement took all twelve books in his arms with ease and began doing as he was told.

"He is strong for being so small." She thought.

Gabriel watched benumbed by how easily the young angel handed out each text with great poise. Me-el and Raguel faced each other despondently.

"This does not look like a fun book to read! Look! It even opens backwards!" Raguel complained.

"Yeah!" Me-el agreed.

"What's with all the funny symbols?"

Gabriel chuckled as everyone opened their texts.

"Well Raguel and Me-el that is precisely why God invented this school for! All of you are about to learn! Trust me, before long you will all know exactly what all those symbols mean and why the books open as they do."

Raguel raised his hand.

"Yes dear?" Gabriel acknowledged.

"What if I decide I do not want to learn how to read?"

Me-el giggled at his friend's comment.

Lucifer ambled through level five as Gabriel taught her first class, his soldiers which consisted mostly of powers and dominions were already sparring. The captain wandered over to Azazel and Nergal who were hammering away at three sets of glossy armor. Lucifer wanted each of his lieutenants' to have their own special coat of arms. Nergel had just completed a gold one; Lucifer intended that one for Raphael. Azazel took the armor and placed it on a brass rack to cool. Nergel a tanned dark haired power began reheating his hammer and chisel in the oven made of stones; his tools required to gleam a bright yellowish orange so they could smelt metals with more ease. The two blacksmiths halted their work upon viewing their captain enter the smoke filled shop. Azazel and Nergel both bowed and saluted.

"Hello Nergal, hello Azazel, I see you have finished a suit, will the other two take much longer to complete?"

Nergel picked up his hammer and chisel as Azazel cleared the anvil of gold dust with a breath.

"Not at all Captain!" He affirmed.

"Azazel please pass me the silver and chrome, why I can pound two out at once I can!"

Lucifer smirked at Nergel's heavy English accent, it had flair.

"Great!" The morning star chimed.

"You will not need to worry about making one for Me-el, he already has a suit, in fact it's an exact replica of mine!"

The ruddy Azazel gave the captain a wink as he spoke:

"He be a little Lucifer that laddie!" Azazel said with an Irish drawl.

Lucifer nodded with a smile. Azazel took two more burnished suits to the cooling rack. One was of silver, the other shined of chrome. The angel situated them right next to the gold one. Lucifer tapped his diadem, the names of his three siblings and lieutenants were now engraved on each one's breast plate.

"Nice touch my lord!" Nergel surmised taking off his barbute helmet.

"Thank you;" Lucifer smiled.

"I cannot wait to deliver them!"

"Well you spared no expense!" Nergel laughed.

Lucifer was busy in the black smith shop while Me-el and Raguel were busy being immensely bored in the library of their new school. Gabriel was lecturing the group on the vowel marks which were placed between certain Hebrew letters.

"She's making me dizzy!" Raguel moaned.

Gabriel had developed a habit of pacing in circles while pontificating to the class; she found it helped her thinking. Me-el thumped his head with his book; he then used his right hand to mimic his rabbi's ongoing mouth. Raguel found this most amusing and began tittering in delight. Me-el taking notice of how his friend appreciated his comical antics decided to start imitating Gabriel's voice, in a most unflattering way.

"And ye shall learn every very a bull! (Variable) And memorize the whole Hebrew alphabet!" Me-el ranted, trying to copy his rabbi.

Raguel was now rolling around on the library floor, like a fat tamale that had been released from its corn husk wrapping. Samael tried hard to ignore the two mini Bulgarians and concentrate on what his teacher was actually saying. The annoyed youth finally rose. Gabriel who stood at eight feet was none the wiser of the fumbling rascals. The rabbi was entirely focused on her exhortation of the Hebrew tongue. It was not until she saw Samael stand that she stopped speaking; the angel's aqua wings caught her avid attention, she adored the color.

"Yes Samael do you have something to ask me?"

Samael's eyes shifted to his mischievous class mates. Gabriel's face took on a look of dismay as she witnessed Me-el; Lucifer's chosen: making absurd faces and trying to match her voice.

"And please note all you students, if ye are here, it is because you have found favor in Yahweh's eye!" Me-el bantered.

He held up one chubby little finger, to make himself appear as serious as possible. Raguel was now splitting his sides and crying from so much laughing.

"I need to get an authoritarian for this school!" Gabriel inwardly deliberated.

"Okay!" She yelled.

Me-el halted his comedy routine and cast his eyes over to his rabbi. The corpulent child smiled at her while batting his long lashes innocently. Raguel propped himself back onto his cushion and regained his composure. Samael sat down shaking his head.

"Enough learning for now, you may all return to your proper levels, when you hear the shofar sound from this realm, please be aware that a new class is ready to begin!"

Me-el and Raguel rose and bowed to Gabriel; they scampered out the building before anyone else. The remaining angels filed out, Samael glanced back at his rabbi.

"I enjoyed class." He said with a smile before leaving.

"Thank you;" Gabriel sighed.

The arch began mulling over an idea about finding a disciplinarian, she did not want to be the one to personally scold Lucifer's favorite. Gabriel knew she needed an angel who was not the least bit concerned about expressing how he felt or who he expressed it to. She began pacing in a circle again, when a light bulb went off in her brain.

"That's it! Uriel! It did not bother him in the least to speak his mind to Lucifer when he was bored out of his own mind on level two! He can also be quite scary to little ones, His stone carved face and fiery wings would make him the perfect principal! Oh thank Yahweh! I know Uriel has no problem being blunt!"

Gabriel now feeling some relief, descended to realm one to visit her reclusive brother, hoping he would agree to assist her.

Uriel was counting stars when Gabriel arrived. The arch's wings fizzled as he lost track of where he had stopped counting.

"Bloody well forget this!" He snarled.

Gabriel approached him with caution; she had not intended to interrupt his work.

"Sorry if my arrival caused you to stray from your duties brother, I know you do not care for unannounced visitors, but I came to propose something to you."

Uriel's gold eyes flickered with curiosity, Gabriel had captured his interest.

"Blimey, I got time to talk with my smashing sister, why don't you come into my palace, I just fashioned it!"

Gabriel sighed in relief as Uriel escorted her into his home. Uriel's palace was simple but lovely. The dwelling hung fifty light years above the Milky Way galaxy it was an argent sight composed of green moldavite; a sparkly debris left by meteorites. The star keeper was not much for décor. A grand round onyx table was at the center circled with five chairs.

"May I offer you a spot of tea love?" He asked, pulling out a chair made of moon stone for Gabriel to sit on.

"I actually prefer coffee" She confessed.

Uriel nodded.

"Than coffee it shall be!" Uriel waved his hand over the silver tea set, and then placed it on the table, which was sprinkled with star dust.

"You have a nice palace," Gabriel said lifting the copper lined tea cup to her lips, she smelled hazelnut.

"Well it is a work in progress; I still need to put in my star pool..."

Gabriel looked up.

"What is a star pool?"

Uriel's face looked excited for once, as he explained.

"Well you see the opening on the ceiling?"

Gabriel gazed upwards; a star shaped portal above them gave a splendid view of the stars and galaxies.

"Yes."

"Well I am going to put a huge water font made of marble in soon, this will reflect everything you see up there! I have not got around to it yet, been too busy counting, it seems Yahweh just keeps the stars coming! But I do so enjoy my work! Listen to me jabbing on! It was you who came down to chat with me, tell me Gabriel what can I do for you?"

Gabriel set down her coffee.

"Brother teaching is proving to be a tad more challenging than I thought! Me-el is quite the class clown and he already has Raguel joining forces with him! He was mimicking me in class! I am at my wits end! I love to teach, yet I fear admonishing Lucifer's portly pet! I need help! Please for the love of Yahweh, would you consider being my principal? I can send them all down here! You would not need to move a feather! Please say yes! I have seen how those two little sausages look at you! They find you terrifying!"

A sneaky smile formed on Uriel's flint face, his gold eyes twinkled.

"I would be delighted to do so! You may send any future trouble makers my way! I could use the extra help!"

Gabriel stood up to hug her brother. Uriel put out his wings of fire and accepted her embrace.

"Thank you so much!" She cried.

"Think nothing of it!" Uriel said, already planning punishments in his mind for more than one *chaya.

* Chaya: Unruly child.

Chapter 8

Me-el and Raguel decided to surprise Raphael in Eden after class was dismissed. The two children schlepped through bushy bunches of pittosporum, they were following the lieutenant's deep singing voice. Raphael sang while he picked walnuts from some nearby trees. The two unicorns; Cinnamon and Sugar; guarded the enchanting gardener while nibbling on walnuts that missed landing in Raphael's bamboo basket.

Raphael paused to stretch, he noticed the two little intruders as they struggled to remain unseen in the hedges. The seraph simpered, he could easily see the tips of Me-el and Raguel's wings, as well as their curly heads of auburn and black curls. Raphael decided to play along with the children.

"Hmmmmm...." He fussed.

"Is it me, or do you two..." The angel faced his two unicorns.

"Do you two feel like we are being watched?"

The unicorns snorted as Raphael stroked their silvery manes. Me-el and Raguel giggled impishly in the foliage.

"Oh I suppose I am being silly!" Raphael related.

"God is watching us! There we have our answer! Well now that we have figured everything out we should get back to work!"

Me-el and Raguel no longer able to contain themselves, stormed out of the bushes attempting to tackle the eight foot arch. Raphael held on to his basket as the two miscreants took hold of his legs.

"Hey Rapha!" Me-el yelped.

"Me and Raguel got you good! I bet ya never saw us coming!"

Raphael's green opal eyes twinkled in amusement.

"You two had me ambushed!" He sighed, setting down the basket full of sweet nuts.

"I don't suppose you two might like an after school snack?" He bid.

The rather rotund pair of paunchy angels licked their ruby lips at the sight of the walnuts. Raphael waved his left hand over the vessel of crunchy treats, powdering them with honey dust and sugar. Me-el and Raguel's eyes bulged out of their sockets as they witnessed the walnuts become more magically delicious.

"Go on," Raphael enjoined, as he pulled up a white sapphire stone to sit on.

The seraph watched discombobulated at the way the duo inhaled the goodies so fast.

"Hmmm...I wonder if Uriel is missing any black holes on his level." He contemplated.

The two friends now stuffed with nuts, went over to Raphael, they jumped up onto his lap. Raphael made a silent grunt as the two little bowling balls began inspecting his gardening belt. Raguel withdrew Raphael's gold shears.

"Oooohhh! Do you use these to trim your hair?" He asked; toying with the mini scissors.

Raphael quickly snatched the tool away from the imprudent youth's chubby palm.

"No! Those are for my flowers! Now why don't you both go east of here, Cinnamon and Sugar can lead you. I have a wonderful garden of desserts there! I am sure you will both like it! There is a giant sponge cake field, volcanoes that explode puddings of every flavor...I really like the chocolate myself... and there's."

Raphael laughed to himself; the two chunky angels were already flying eagerly behind the galloping unicorns.

"Well I guess they liked the sound of it!" He chuckled.

Raphael raised himself from his resting place; a flash of light had caught his eye. The arch bowed low, Lucifer had just arrived.

"My captain!" Raphael responded.

"Hello Raphael," Lucifer answered.

"If my lord is looking for Me-el, he just went east of here with Raguel. I used my creativity and made a garden composed entirely of sweets, you are welcome to try it out yourself if you like."

Lucifer took Raphael by his right hand.

"I actually came looking for you fair brother."

Raphael's eyes became sad in worry.

"Have I done something to upset you or Abba lord?"

Lucifer shook his head.

"No! I came because I brought you a gift!"

Lucifer gave Raphael a kind smile as he unfurled his lowest set of wings, revealing the golden suit of arms. The suit was encrusted with emeralds, green diamonds and maw-sit-sit gems, Lucifer knew green was Raphael's favorite color, the stones also would bring out his brother's radiant eyes even more. Raphael's name shined on the breast plate in silver lettering.

Raphael nearly wept as he beheld the gleaming coat of arms.

"Lucifer are you serious? Surely a humble gardener such as myself is not worthy of wearing such exquisite armor?"

Raphael humbly bent down to better admire the vesture. Lucifer prodded his shoulder.

"I also brought you this to go with it."

The morning star knelt down; he passed Raphael a gold barbute helmet studded with opals.

"You are the only one I gave an open faced helmet to," He emphasized.

"I did not want a visor clouding your lovely visage and alluring eyes."

Raphael rose, placing the armor on the stone he had been sitting on prior to Lucifer's arrival. The helmet was equally as stunning as the suit, but Raphael did not want to cover up his hair.

"So..." Raphael revolved out loud.

"Do you have any more special armor to pass out?"

Lucifer nodded, glad to see Raphael was impressed with his gift.

"Yes, I have a silver one for Gabriel. I thought she could wear it when she assumes her masculine form. I got a chrome one for Uriel, it is trimmed with sapphires. I thought you all deserved nice armor since you are my top three lieutenants!"

Raphael patted Lucifer on the back affectionately.

"My captain is most gracious! I will wear it whenever you need me to, however I should be honest with you; I prefer my billowy robe and garland of roses whilst I attend to my duties here!"

A slight frown grazed Lucifer's face.

"None the less my captain I adore the coat of arms, you were very kind to present me with such an elaborate gift, as I stated earlier, I am really not worthy! You out did yourself! Thank you so much!"

Lucifer's mood chippered. Raphael now took his brother's hand.

"How would you like to join me by the lake at Eden's center? It is where God's four rivers of milk, wine, honey, and oil meet. The four make for a tasty elixir! We could sit and chat a bit."

Lucifer smiled.

"I would really like that!"

Me –el and Raguel sat perched on a cocoa tree in the dessert garden, they resembled two overstuffed Thanks giving turkeys. The two friends rubbed their ballooned bellies in satisfaction. The branch they were sitting on practically touched the ground under all the extra poundage.

"I never knew pudding came in so many incredible flavors!" Raguel belched out.

"I just love the chocolate in these cocoa trees! They are wonderful!" Me-el added with a hiccup.

"We should come here after each session of class ends!" Raguel said dreamily.

"Sounds good to me!" Me-el agreed.

"We need to fill up with sweets after putting up with Rabbi Gabriel's super sour speeches!"

The two angels began laughing and lost their balance. Me-el and Raguel rolled off the tree's branch, landing face first into a mound of brown sugar.

"Mmmmm!" Me-el swooned.

"Did you land with your mouth open too Raguel? This stuff is scrumptious, whatever it is!"

Me-el brought up his candy coated face to check on his friend. Raguel was already sucking on the sweet substance like a fat fly on a sugar cube!

Gabriel soared to her icy level, for some reason her ears were burning.

"Hmmmmm some angel must be talking about me." She thought.

The rabbi was relieved Uriel had agreed to be her principal.

"Things just got a lot better for me!" She sang.

Gabriel was happier still because Lucifer had just presented her with some magnificent silver armor. The seraph landed gracefully on her realm, captivated by how each snowflake left a distinctive pattern imprinted on her coat of arms.

"Wow, Lucifer must have had that built in just for me! Now my armor will be decorated with all kinds of different snow flake patterns!" She observed.

"Snow ball?" Gabriel called.

The lieutenant was currently in her Anglo male form, since she was dawning her armor; shifting back into her feminine form she began scanning her level for Snow ball; her pet baby seal. Yahweh had given her the furry white companion in compensation for not allowing Samael to cohabitate with her. The seraph walked over to her palace to put away her coat of arms, she then trekked out into the snow to find Snow ball. Gabriel caught sight of him; he was sleeping on an ice foundation just a few feet away.

"Oh good I found you!"

The baby seal gazed up at her with sleepy eyes. Gabriel scooped him up and kissed him.

"At least I don't need to worry about you mimicking me like Me-el! Oh you are so cute!"

The arch went back into her icy abode, cuddling the animal in her arms, upon entering she placed Snowball on her ice couch, the seraph then advanced to her flugid snow flake shaped table.

"Now to get my notes together for my next class! Hmmm what to do next...Oh yes! We can continue going over the Hebrew alphabet!" She decided.

The rabbi placed a crystal quill behind her right ear.

"Okay Snow ball, pray for me, I am off to Opus Angelorum, I hope Me-el and Raguel have done their prescribed studies!"

Snow ball looked up at her with heavy eyelids, making a gentle bark as Gabriel left the palace, and ascended upwards.

The dozen students droned into the courtly library, Remiel's shofar blast had sounded, signaling a new class. Me-el and Raguel reluctantly shuffled in last. Samael eagerly skipped in ahead of them.

"What's he so happy about?" Me-el sneered.

"Who knows?" Raguel whispered.

The three little angels took their usual places on the floor pillows. Samael sat upright, holding his Hebrew book. Me-el removed his from the new red silk back sack Lucifer had gifted him with. Raguel's face displayed a mask of worry.

"I know," Me-el huffed.

"It's not the funnest stuff!" He said, as he went through the alphabet at the very last minute.

"Ahhh Me-el, I think I left my book in Eden next to the cocoa tree we fell out of!" Raguel nervously confessed.

Me-el scooted his cushion closer to his friend.

"It's okay just share with me, besides we will probably go down to Eden after class any ways."

Raguel feeling more relived, now also began reviewing the Hebrew letters for the first time out of his buddy's text.

Gabriel ambled in bringing down her finch yellow wings; now that she knew she had Uriel as back up the rabbi felt more confidant.

"Hello every one, we will be going over the Hebrew alphabet once more. I recall giving each of you two letters to study; I hope everyone is prepared to recite!" She screed out, while holding a quartz ruler in her right hand.

The messengers, virtues, and Samael nodded in agreement. Me-el closed his eyes and began repeating his two letters in his mind; he was hoping to have them memorized by the time he was called on. Raguel hid his face with his sherbet orange wings. Gabriel began with the virtues and messengers, much to the two friends' fortune; when Samael stood to say his letters that is when the pair began to panic, they realized they were next. Samael spoke, divulging his assignment perfectly.

"Tav, which means Yahweh's law, will go forth. Resh, which means corner stone."

Gabriel gave the youth a look of approval.

"So far everyone is doing excellent!" She disclosed.

"Me-el your turn."

Me-el heaved himself up; he was still bloated from all the noshing he and Raguel had done earlier in the dessert garden. He rose, and then straightened out his blue alb. Me-el took a breath and recited:

"Shin, meaning.....Ahhh.....Ummm...Oh yeah! Shin means messy!"

Gabriel's face sunk at the definition, Shin actually stood for Shiloh, which translated to Messiah! Me-el continued while chafing inwardly.

"Peh, meaning.... Ahhh ...Ummm Oh yeah it means wonderful cashews!"

The rabbi sighed in disgust, Peh actually meant wonderful counselor. None the less Me-el plopped himself back down on his pillow, glad it was all over with. The entire assembly, aside from Raguel and himself; burst out laughing. Gabriel bit her lower lip in annoyance.

"Quiet Please!" She snapped, slapping her ruler against her left palm.

The students quickly hushed up. Me-el now also hid his own face with his top two pair of emerald wings.

"Me-el! You have shown complete disregard for Yahweh's chosen language! The assignment was by no means overwhelming! The correct definitions for your two letters are very important!" She scolded without mercy.

Me-el whimpered behind his pinions, he had never heard Gabriel sound so mean towards him before, it hurt.

"If you put such little effort into your studies you will never grow up to be as wise and noble as your older brother and hero Lucifer! Is that what you want?"

Me-el felt tears rush down his cheeks; she had hit him where it really hurt. Raguel put a comforting arm around his weeping friend. Gabriel gave him a feisty once over as well.

"What of you Raguel? I see you have no book with you! I shant not even bother to ask you to recite!"

Raguel cringed.

"In fact," Gabriel continued now enjoying her teaching authority.

"I think I shall send you to level one!"

Raguel's eyes dimmed, as did Me-el.

"You see class," The rabbi went on.

"We now have a disciplinarian for angels who fail to do their assignments or enjoy mocking their rabbi!"

Me-el gulped, he knew who she was talking about.

"My brother Uriel is now the principal of this establishment, and is all too happy to be receiving angels that will not take my orders! So you see Raguel this is where you shall be going, and who you will be spending the rest of class with!"

A tangible silence came over the library. Raguel's eyes grew wide in fear. The archangel Remiel came in; Gabriel had sent him a telepathic message to come and collect Raguel for realm one. Raguel attempted to swallow the large lump in his throat as the seven foot shofar blaster took him by the hand. Remiel ended up dragging the reluctant Raguel out of the library. Gabriel now less flustered, glanced down in Me-el's direction.

The child was enveloped in all six of his wings now. He was completely hidden.

"Class dismissed!" The rabbi broadcasted.

"Our next session will require each of you to have the entire Hebrew alphabet memorized!"

The angels headed out of the building, Samael was the last to leave. Me-el stumbled to his feet, trying to follow the group out, with his wings still covering him; it was proving to be difficult. Me-el had the likeness of a walking feather duster. Gabriel placed her hand on the youth's head, causing Me-el to bump into a wall.

"Me-el," Gabriel knelt down to the child's level.

"Please let me see that cute little face of yours?" Her tone was gentle again.

Me-el hesitantly lifted his upper two wings, he was sniffling.

"I am so sorry rabbi! Am I ever gonna see Raguel again? He left his book in Eden, and it was all my fault! I am the one who took him there! Would you at least let me go get it for him?"

Gabriel gave the concerned little angel a pleasant smile.

"Of course you will see Raguel again! I'm sure a bit of discipline will not hurt him in the least! As for his book, I am sure Raphael has teleported it to his egg by now, Eden is his territory. Now listen to what I am about to tell you Me-el." She advised.

Me-el looked at her with remorse.

"I only yelled at you because I know you have the greatest potential!" Gabriel's eyes shined with sincerity.

"Really?" Me-el asked, as his lips trembled.

"Really!" Gabriel validated.

"You are one of Yahweh's top five archangels, you heard him say so yourself! You are also my brother! And...you are Lucifer's favorite. As a future lieutenant, you must strive to not only know every form of military technique, but you should also be very knowledgeable! I know Yahweh and Lucifer have great plans for you, now; why don't you dry up those tears. I suspect our captain will soon be outside waiting to receive you. Do not worry; I will not exchange any of what happened during class to your older brother. However I would like you to promise me that by the next class you will have your home work memorized!"

Me-el smiled as he extended his six wings.

"I promise rabbi! And if I should run across Raguel before our next class, maybe we can study together!"

"That sounds great!" Gabriel winked; she rose back to her stance.

"Now go, and please give Lucifer my regards!"

Gabriel watched as Me-el left the school with a bounce in his step.

"There is something very unique about him! Whether I want to admit it or not!" She silently confided.

Lucifer stood outside Opus Angelorum waiting for Me-el; his arms were out stretched to receive him. The child flew into his brother's safe warm embrace.

"So how was class?" Lucifer asked.

"Well Rabbi Gabriel say's I have the greatest potential!" Me-el laid forward, steering clear of disclosing anything else.

"I must agree with her!" Lucifer said as he took to flight with Me-el on his shoulders.

"Abba has requested us to meet with him at his throne room for tea; so I hope you were not planning to meet with your friend Raguel in Eden."

Me-el painted a fake smile on his face.

"Nah...we decided to take a break from Eden for awhile, we both are gonna try to focus more on our studies! We wanna be as wise as you Lufi!"

"Well I am pleased to hear you both are taking school so seriously, I know Abba will be glad to see you with me!"

Me-el released a big breath of relief upon hearing Lucifer's response.

Chapter 9

Lucifer landed with all the skill of a ballet dancer and as silent as a cat on Yahweh's ninth realm. Me-el clumsily slugged off his brother's shoulders and landed with a loud bump. Yahweh's face radiated with admiration from his golden throne, as the two siblings kneeled before him. God rose from his seat ready to speak.

The chanting seraphim, thrones and virtues above him stilled their continuous praise to give heed to Yahweh. The deity lifted his golden shofar to his lips; blowing into it with the combined force of Yeshua and the Ruach. The ram's horn resonated throughout all nine realms of Heaven. Yahweh wanted every angel to hear his decree.

"I hereby command angels of every rank to pay homage to my most precious gem, Lucifer. You will all bow to him, just as you do to me! Lucifer is the most glorious jewel in all nine realms. He makes the finest diamonds look dull and yellow! My magnificent light bearer holds no equal in captivating my heart! I hereby officially announce Lucifer as my divinely assigned regent and right hand!"

God finished, a mystical phenomenon occurred. The sea of glass shot out a three dimensional image, or hologram. Lucifer stumbled back, while Me-el's eyes got wide in amazement. The two brothers saw angels in every level stop whatever they were doing to do exactly as Yahweh had indicated. Every angel was bowing to Lucifer. The morning star teared up as he witnessed the gargantuan cherubim pay their respects. Me-el, who was standing to the right of his brother, also knelt towards him. Lucifer was blown away. To top everything off, Yahweh was also giving him a slight bow.

"I do not deserve all this..." The captain thought.

Yahweh apparated in front of Lucifer, he gave Me-el the okay to rise. The little angel quickly erected himself. Elohim took Lucifer's right hand and placed a band of gold on his right ring finger. The bauble held a solitary red diamond at its center. Yahweh felt Yeshua and the Ruach throb violently within his chest; they were three in one, yet only Yahweh was visible. The triune God was utterly smitten with Lucifer.

"My lord," Lucifer began.

"I am not worthy of all of this."

Yahweh kissed the shocked seraph on his right cheek.

"This and more!" God exclaimed.

"To you alone I have gifted the ring of omnipresence, it will allow your eyes to see as I do, it may take awhile for you to get the hang of it, but when you do, you will find it comes in most useful! I have no doubt I can trust you with this ability."

Lucifer blushed as he examined the ring.

"On my honor father! I would never go against your will; I am truly at a loss for words!"

Yahweh smiled while stroking the seraph's long blonde tresses.

"I know my child, just remember with great power comes tremendous responsibility"

God turned to Me-el; the child's eyes were drawn to the domed tea corner.

"I do not suppose you and your sibling would both care to join me for tea?"

Me-el bowed.

"I would be most delighted too Abba." He accurately phrased.

The three made their way over to the private corner. Me-el's face went aglow upon viewing the heaping mount of pastries which awaited his drooling mouth. Yahweh and Lucifer took their usual spots; Me-el brought in his wings and gently sat on his velvet foot stool.

"Well," God remarked.

"Someone is more refined."

Me-el smiled, he knew God was talking about him; he took a pink silk napkin and placed it over his lap.

"Indeed!" Lucifer added, crossing his right leg over his left.

"I believe Opus Angelorum is molding him into an even finer future lieutenant, or; perhaps my future co-captain!"

Me-el tried to ignore the words "Opus Angelorum", as he reached for a confection which was new to the golden tray.

"Ahhh!" Yahweh exclaimed as he passed Lucifer a cup of chamomile and rose bud tea.

"I see you found my favorites! Those are called Sufganiyot, the lesser archangel Jeremiel just brought up a batch from Jerusalem, or realm six; please try one! Tell me what you think."

Me-el gunned his eyes towards Lucifer, remembering his manners; he hurriedly put his hands together and insinuated:

"Big brother shall we pray first?"

Yahweh put down his tea cup, the youth's demeanor impressed him immensely. Lucifer bowed his head and said a blessing of thanks. The captain was also taken aback by Me-el's charming gesture.

"I am proud of my Me-el Abba! He is beginning to mature in wisdom!" The morning star stated.

Me-el now feeling more at ease, grabbed one of the new crunchy coated balls, and shoved it into his pie hole. The Sufganiyot melted in his mouth. The dessert was basically a deep fried donut.

"These are wonderful!" He blurted.

Crumbs began erupting as Me-el spoke with his yapper full. The little angel snagged four more.

"Is there any chocolate cherubim milk?" He asked, wiping his face with the sleeve of his robe.

God chuckled.

"Why of course there is! Look past the tray, your glass is full and running over!"

Me-el inched the foaming milk his way with his upper right wing, his hands were still busy gathering Sufganiyot. Lucifer sipped his tea daintily.

"Well," The light bearer gathered.

"He still has one small weakness I suppose!"

Yahweh raised his tea cup to Lucifer and winked.

"You alone I created perfectly beloved!" He commented.

"Me-el might get close to being like you some day, but he will never replace you!"

Yahweh leaned in towards Lucifer and gave him a fatherly kiss on the fore head.

Me-el to busy eating failed to overhear the comment. Lucifer gave Yahweh a smile then pitched:

"I enjoy our time together Abba, but I should go do some training on level five."

"Of course." God concluded.

"I hope to see you both again soon!"

"You will!" Lucifer assured.

Lucifer signaled Me-el who was still *fressing.

"Me-el say thank you to Abba, we should get going now."

The little angel made a small frown as he finished off another glass of chocolate cherubim milk.

"Okay I'm coming."

The child began stuffing his feathery paired appendages with treats from the gold tray.

"It looks like you will be sitting on my shoulders on the way home with that load!" The captain exclaimed

* Fressing: To eat like an animal.

Chapter 10

Lucifer placed a sleeping, pastry filled Me-el on his glass couch which was topped with soft white cushions. The tot had completed devouring his hidden stash of goodies from Yahweh's throne room on the flight down to level four. He had then dozed off. Lucifer kissed his little brother's head, and then covered him up with a blue satin blanket, salted with mini gold cherubim. The morning star pivoted, someone was at the door way of his living room, he could see a shadow.

"Hello, do come in." The captain posed.

"My lord,"

Lucifer did a full turn and was now face to face with Azazel from realm five. The dominion was genuflecting.

"Oh hello Azazel, please come in, be *schtum, Me-el is napping, he tends to drift off after eating a lot of sugar."

Azazel rose slowly and spoke quietly.

"Well I just wanted ta be congratalatin ya!" He saluted with a wink, in his Irish drawl.

---

* Schtum: silent.

"God's right hand! That be somethin to be right proud of! Will ya be comin ta spar with us soon? Beleth's been asking fer ya, as have many others! Meself included! Yer lieutenant Gabriel be with us too! She be in her soldier form! Oh and Nergel just pounded you an the laddie..." He winked at the purring Me-el.

"Well, he just hammered out a new sword for each of ya!"

Lucifer smiled.

"Of course I am coming my friend; Abba just gave me a fantastic new gift."

The light bearer said as he showcased his ring to the goggling dominion.

"Oh that be a right nice gem!" Azazel crooned.

"Yes, Abba calls it the ring of omnipresence; if Me-el should awaken while I am gone I can look for him with it!"

"That be right useful me lord!" Azazel added.

"Okay friend let us be off; I shall come for Me-el once he has gotten enough rest." Lucifer affirmed silently as he left his palace with Azazel.

Me-el lethargically opened his azure blue eyes. He sat up on the couch and caught sight of his many distended reflections staring back at him from the mirrored walls. Rabbi Gabriel had left the child with some encouraging words after school; but his young mind still kept replaying the words which had caused him the most pain.

"If you put such little effort into your studies you will never grow up to be as wise and noble as your older brother and hero Lucifer!"

Me-el began to moan like a dove that had just lost its lifelong mate. No angels outside Lucifer's clear palace heard him; they were way to busy cackling on about how the star of morning had just been promoted. On realm five, Lucifer was preoccupied having fun scuffling with Beleth, Azazel and Gabriel. The light bearer had lost himself in merry making and forgotten to look into his ring, in order to check on his younger brother. He did not know he was now awake.

"Rabbi is right! I will never be like Lufi! I look like *schmaltz!" The child cried taking hold of one of his love handles.

"Even if I studied and got perfect grades, I would still always be nothing but a pork bun! I'll never be **kosher!"

Me-el began to sob into his satin blanket. The gentle little wails reached Raphael's ears, he was feeding his unicorns some oats and grapes; the seraph was standing almost directly beneath the spot where the child was on realm four.

"Is that little Me-el?" He wondered.

The soft hearted healer ascended upwards. He swooped into Lucifer's palace and wandered over to where he heard the crying come from. Raphael felt a tug

---

* Schmaltz: dripping lard.

** *Kosher: appropriate.

at his heart, as he beheld the adorable child weeping. The seraph approached him.

"Me-el whatever is the matter? If it is about Raguel do not worry; I found his book and returned it to his egg. Uriel also promised he would be returning your friend back to classes upon your rabbi's request."

Me-el looked up at the gardener with trembling lips, and shook his head. Raphael now sat next to the youth, and put him on his lap.

"Come now little brother; tell me what is making you so sad?"

Me-el wiped away some glittery tears with his sleeve.

"Oh Raphael, look at me! I'm never gonna be like Lufi! The only thing I am good at is eating!"

Raphael held his brother close, it saddened him to see such a lovely child so against himself.

"You are right Me-el; there can never be another Lucifer! Just as there never will be another you! You are as unique as one of Gabriel's snowflakes! No angel in Heaven can ever be exactly alike! You are special because Yahweh made you! Why look at yourself, you have six beautiful emerald wings, which by the way happens to be my favorite color!"

Raphael batted his eye lashes.

"You also rank as a seraph, the highest set of angels in all nine realms! Not only that, Abba hatched you as one of his future archangels!"

Me-el sniffled, and peered down at his tummy.

"Yeah but ... I wish I was taller and more graceful like Lufi." He moped.

Raphael bounced the child on his knee and touched his fore head to his own.

"Oh Me-el! You were blessed by hatching in a small body! Why take me for example...I came out of my egg this big! So did Gabriel and Uriel, we all did! Much was required of us so soon...We had no fun frolicking, or playing with friends, Yahweh gave you a tremendous gift by allowing you to come out as a child! However, I know Yahweh also has big plans in store for you! I do not imagine you will stay the size you are for very long!"

Me-el's eyes stopped watering. He placed his pudgy palms on Raphael's chest. His face was brighter.

"Really Rapha? When do you think I will start growing?" He begged.

Raphael made a pensive face.

"Hmmm....I'm not quite sure... but wait! I think perhaps right now!"

Raphael jolted up, bringing in his top two wings, he hoisted Me-el up onto his back.

"Behold yourself in the many mirrors Me-el! You are now even taller than Lucifer!"

Me-el laughed as he viewed himself on Raphael's shoulders. Raphael undid the strap which held his caduceus and removed his gardening belt; dropping them both onto the translucent cushioned couch. The seraph spun Me-el around in circles. The little angel chortled gaily as they both teleported down to Eden.

The two were now at Eden's heart, the lake which held the continence of the four rivers of milk, wine, oil, and honey. The towering pomegranate tree, known as the tree of life, shaded the placid pool, from the south edge. Me-el took in his surroundings in wonderment. The youth had not once been to this particular part of Eden before. Rows of shiny trees filled the area. Some gleamed with silver pears and sugar glazed plums; others were veiled in radiant flowers, nuts or ripe olives.

Raphael put Me-el down on the soft blue violet grass, sprinkled with white butter cup flowers and fritillaries. Me-el inhaled deeply, the lake smelled delicious.

"Wow Rapha! I don't ever remember seeing this part of Eden!"

"Lucifer has." Raphael admitted.

"I thought it only fitting to bring you here too, your brother and I sat and spoke here, we shared some of the pool's sweet nectar. I wonder would you like to do the same."

Me-el clapped his hands in approval.

"You bet I would!" He declared.

Raphael smiled; he knelt down carefully to pick two daffodils which were growing near the lake's edge. The seraph then removed the stems. He said a silent prayer to thank the flowers for their sacrifice and service. Raphael then hardened the foliage with his angelic power; which he mainly used in Eden. The daffodils could now be used as drinking cups for him and his younger sibling. The gardener passed one to Me-el.

The child watched astounded, as Raphael gathered two immense glowing stones, one in each arm. One was amethyst; the other was a glossy yellow citrine. The archangel situated the two large gems right next to the ambrosial scented lake.

"These will be our seats." Raphael stated as he helped Me-el onto the purple amethyst rock.

The seraph then took the two homemade drinking cups from the little angel. Raphael dipped the pair of stiff flowers into the pool, making certain he procured more milk and honey for Me-el, and more wine for him. Raphael took his place on the citrine stone and handed Me-el his cup.

"I propose a toast!" He chimed, as he held up his drinking receptacle.

"To Me-el! The one and only!"

Me-el giggled then tipped his cup to drink. Raphael did likewise.

"Yum!" The youth hummed.

"That is almost as good as chocolate cherubim milk!" He said.

Raphael's eyes glinted in joy. He was glad to see the child in good spirits again. Me-el noisily slurped down every last drop. The elder angel suddenly became despondent. Raphael frantically touched his waist; the seraph had just realized he was not wearing his gardening belt and caduceus holder. He had left them at Lucifer's palace. Raphael immediately became embarrassed, he glanced down at his torso, without his leather band of tools; he displayed the tiniest spare tire. The seraph brought in his middle set of wings, as he outstretched the upper two. Me-el examined his brother's anxious green eyes.

"What's wrong Rapha?"

Raphael arose, layers of his silken robe wisped eloquently against him.

"Me-el I should get you back to Lucifer's; I forgot my belt and scepter, come we better get going right now!"

Me-el hopped off the glistening gem, he looked up and his face brightened. The child bowed low. Raphael froze and did a one hundred and eighty degree turn, he also fell to his knees. Lucifer was directly in front of him.

Lucifer stood statuesque against a tall quince tree.

"Forget your equipment Raphael?" The morning star uttered.

Lucifer's dark blue eyes drilled into Raphael. The healer rose to his feet slowly.

"Hail captain, forgive my irresponsible behavior, I heard your little one crying, and decided to go check on him. I did not see you anywhere near the vicinity, so I brought him down with me. Unfortunately I left my gardening vestures behind." He stuttered.

Me-el ran up to Lucifer and wrapped himself around his right leg.

"Where were you Lufi?"

Lucifer took Raphael's belt which was currently hanging around his own neck, and flung it towards his brother.

"Oh yes.... I brought your scepter down too."

Lucifer released the caduceus from his lower left wing.

Raphael seemed *firmisht.

"It is alright Raphael, I saw you two together. I am the one, who should have glanced into my ring sooner, but I was in the middle of a joust with Gabriel, she is proving to be a good fighter."

Lucifer went silent as Raphael began refastening his belt and caduceus strap. The morning star felt somewhat

* Firmisht: Disturbed.

annoyed that Raphael was not yet sporting his own coat of arms.

"You know we could also spar some time, I have yet to see you in your armor." He hinted.

Raphael blushed.

"Yes well I appreciate the offer my lord, but I find it more comforting to perform my duties in Eden without wearing armor; it's easier to get around ..."

Lucifer cut him off.

"I mean you could come up to realm five, wear it there and take a break from your gardening job, besides I bet you look absolutely ravishing in your gold suit!"

Raphael felt his face go red again. A slight frown formed on Lucifer's pink kunzite lips. Me-el hobbled into the light bearer's bottom left wing to hitch a ride up.

"I am not a big fan of jousting great lord, yet as I said when you presented me with the armor, I will wear it if you ever really need me to."

Lucifer's eyes studied Raphael's well sculptured body.

"Well I just hope you put it to use! You are also considered a soldier whether it becomes you or not!"

Raphael winced as his captain bolted out of Eden.

"I better wear my armor soon..." He thought.

"He sounded a tad upset with me."

Raphael shrugged and began meandering over to the tree of life. He yawned then curled up beneath it to take a nap.

Small magenta petals showered the snoozing angel as he brought in his six pink pinions. Raphael's two unicorns stationed themselves next to their sleeping master, they decided to join him. The lieutenant drifted off into dream land. Raphael now found himself in a reverie. He was in God's throne room, yet someone other than Yahweh was seated on it. The figure's face was obscured in light. On the right side of the throne, there stood a magnificent archangel. He was utterly hypnotic and vested in armor. The seraph had lush long wavy auburn hair. The unfamiliar angel nearly matched Lucifer in beauty, yet his eyes which gleamed like blue opals, appeared very forlorn. A singular tear drop fell from his face.

Raphael awoke, feeling somewhat troubled.

"I have had that same odd vision since the day I was hatched!" He contemplated.

"I wonder who those two stunning enigmas are. I have not once seen either of them in any of the nine realms...of course I am here most of the time....Oh well it is just a dream."

Raphael lifted himself up, coaxing Cinnamon and Sugar to do the same.

"Oh well. I should go gather some potatoes to send up to Jerusalem, Jeremiel could be down here any moment! I would not want to delay him or the others on realm six the joy of making latkes! Yes, Abba does love those potato pancakes... I enjoy them myself!"

The two unicorns followed Raphael as he went east of Eden where he farmed.

Chapter 11

On realm four, Me-el was in his own special room which Lucifer had furnished specifically for him. The tot was lying belly down on his cloud shaped bed, made of spun colored pink, yellow, and blue cotton. A mobile of gold and silver angels dressed like knights hung above him. Me-el's top two wings were arched up, his palms balancing his head. The child was reading through his Hebrew alphabet, making sure he had each letter along with its proper meaning carved correctly into his brain.

Me-el's room was the only region in Lucifer's palace that was not bound in mirrors. The child's walls were overlaid with blue decorative paper, dotted with pictures of silver swords and helmets. Me-el's bed hovered suspended six feet from his royal purple carpeted floor. Archangels from level six had been the small angel's interior decorators. Me-el's suit of arms hung over in a corner on a hook of gold.

Lucifer walked in to check on his younger brother.

"Still studying hard?" He quizzed.

The light bearer petted Me-el's two sets of sprawled out wings.

"Yeah I think I finally got em all memorized. I hope Raguel has been studying just as hard. I have not seen him since our last class."

Lucifer ruffled Me-el's curls.

"I hope he is going through his lessons too!" He agreed.

"By the way Me-el, while you were down in Eden with Raphael, I was on level five, I got a chance to chat with Gabriel, she said you all have a new principal now. Uriel; she further told me that your chum Raguel was his very first customer!"

Me-el closed his book and sat up.

"What else did you two talk about?" He nervously prodded.

"Oh not much, I am just glad she did not mention having any qualms with you. I think Raguel is blessed that you have taken him under your wing, hopefully he picks up your good study habits!"

Lucifer smiled as he left the child's room.

"Thank you Abba!" Me-el prayed.

The youth flopped back down on his bed in relief.

"Oh Me-el." Lucifer called.

"What is it?" Me-el flew off his cloud and into the room his older brother occupied. He bowed upon entering.

"I am thinking about putting together a concert for Abba on realm seven soon. I would like you to go there and...." The archangel Remiel's shofar blast cut the morning star's sentence short.

"Sorry Lufi! That is the signal for school! I gotta go!"

Me-el bowed as he scampered off to his room to retrieve his books and back sack.

"We can talk about it later!" He said as he passed by his older sibling.

Me-el screeched to a stop with his bare feet on the glass floor.

"You are gonna come pick me up after I am done with class right?"

Lucifer embraced his brother.

"Of course! With my new ring, I will be able to see you coming out of school! I promise to remember to peek in on you! I do not want to miss you again!"

The captain kissed Me-el on his right cheek.

Me-el returned the gesture than soared out of the palace. He did not want to be tardy, and incur Gabriel's wrath.

Gabriel floated into the library; Me-el was already telling Raguel how happy he was to have him back. Samael sat quietly on his cushion keeping to himself. The messengers and virtues were also seated and leafing through their Hebrew texts. The rabbi was about to begin class when a rush of wind and flapping wings caught her off guard. Gabriel turned to face eight more angels.

"Oh wonderful! Yahweh has sent me more students! Class we are officially up to twenty, that means we may all now relocate to our actual classroom!"

The seated angels rose to follow the new ones and Gabriel to the location. The freshly arrived angels consisted of two lustrous seraphim with adolescent visages; if human one might have guessed them to be about sixteen years of age. The seraphs were named Jehudiel and Razziel. Razziel had to be the tallest out of the entire group. He lumbered at nine feet with rainbow wings. Gabriel smiled as she waved three of Lucifer's archangels from the holy city in. The archangels were Haniel, Hamiel, and Cervill; their names were imprinted on their breast plates. The trio saluted the rabbi as they ventured across the library to the class room.

"How handsome they all are!" Gabriel appraised.

The final three could be compared to human High school jocks, they were two dominions, Hasmel and Yahriel and one power; Camael. These hulking angels were from Lucifer's military training arena on realm five; they also wore their titles on their coat of arms.

"Good that some of the new pupils have name tags already!" Gabriel thought.

"You three might help keep my smallest angels in line!" She secretly surmised.

Me-el and Raguel ran into the class room first, the virtue Zephra and Samael were politely holding the twin glass doors etched with angelic symbols open. The room itself had a dignified appearance. A high domed ceiling of obsidian glazed in moving diamonds; which represented Uriel's first realm of stars and galaxies loomed above them. The desks were all crafted of vitreous yellow beryl. The head of the class room held Gabriel's desk, it was long and gold with a clarion quartz chair, capped with a silver cushion for her to be seated on.

Gabriel went over to her new desk, and began prepping her notes for her first official session. Raguel went and took a desk right next to a six tipped star shaped window. Precious gems surrounded it. Me-el released a groan; he had wanted the window seat. The youth sighed.

"At least Raguel got it and not Samael!" He brooded.

"Hey Me-el come check this out! You can see thrones from realm nine through here!" Raguel excitedly revealed.

Me-el scooted his desk closer to Raguel's; he had observed that only he, his friend, and Samael were stationed up front. He did not care to be so close to his rival.

"Hey Raguel..." Me-el whispered as the remaining students and eight new ones continued entering.

"How did it go down there?" Me-el's voice spoke at a hush as he covered his mouth with his left hand, and pointed downwards with his chubby right one. The child's agate blue eyes looked deathly serious. He had been too scared to bring up the matter in the library, but now he had the luxury of distraction from the new students. Raguel cased the room like a timid hen on the watch for a hungry fox, which had missed more than two meals.

"Well." He whispered back, sensing it safe to speak since their rabbi was indisposed handing out books to all the new students. She was also giving each one a rundown of what they had missed, so they could catch up.

"Okay I'll dish... Uriel is the king of mean!" Raguel conveyed.

Me-el's eyes widened like a hoot owl's as his friend continued to divulge his terrible ordeal, and everything he had gone through. Raguel resumed giving Me-el the low down.

"He made me count all the stars on his level! And just when I would get finished counting...."

Me-el's eyes began to nictate in horror.

"God would make more! And he would make me start from the beginning!"

Me-el gasped, and brought both palms to his gaping mouth.

"That is not the worst part!" Raguel assured.

Me-el gulped, not sure how things could get even worse than that.

"Me-el, I got really hungry when I was counting! It takes a lot to do that you know!"

Me-el nodded, he completely understood.

"Well I asked him if I could have a snack, and do you know what he told me to eat?"

Raguel's eyes went into slits upon reaching the climax of his loathsome anecdote.

"What??" Me-el yelped, not sure if he wanted to listen to the ghastly response.

"Well, that *meshuggina Uriel fed me air!"

Me-el's jaw dropped.

"He told me to take in extra deep breaths and swallow! He is a total drill sergeant! He claimed that his level was filled with nutrients from stars! The angel is meshuggina I tell you! No wonder he is so mean if that is all he ever eats!"

Me-el shook his head in disbelief.

"I thought you looked thinner!" He avowed.

"I know! Look at me, I'm wasting away!" Raguel claimed, as he grabbed one of his jelly rolls.

"Everything you just told me is sheer travesty!" Me-el added.

Jericho the messenger referred to as gold streak, laughed out loud. He could not help but over hear the

---

* Meshuggina: Crazy.

intriguing dialogue between the two little angels. Raguel and Me-el gazed over their shoulders to the chuckling angel.

He found Raguel's tale of woe to be rather amusing.

"You think my painful experience is funny gold geek???"

Raguel challenged, as he shook a pudgy fist.

"Sorry kid," Jericho snickered, now wiping tears of laughter from his hazel eyes.

"It's just.... Well you don't look any different from when I last saw you! Seems like you have plenty of reserve on ya!"

Raguel's face now red with anger, turned to Me-el. Me-el patted Raguel's wing.

"It is okay, I can tell you need nourishment! After class we can go down to Eden and..."

Gabriel interjected; she was ready to start class.

"Every angel please give me your attention!" She ordered.

The assembly silenced.

"As you all may have noticed we now have a complete class, with eight new angels, so since we have fresh faces, I think I will break you all up into pairs. You will all get to know each other a little better this way!"

Raguel and Me-el clutched hands beneath their desks, hoping they would be paired together.

"However, I am well aware that some of you tend to stick rather close."

The rabbi hinted as she lowered her glance to her two famous klutzes.

"So..." She went on.

"I will assign you each your own partner, rather than have you select your own. Once together you and your team mate can go over the Hebrew alphabet together. You will both recite to one another than also grade each other."

Raguel and Me-el exchanged frightened looks.

"The grading scale is as follows... A: A is for angel, it is the highest score one can achieve for perfect memorization."

Gabriel picked up her quartz ruler and began lightly thumping it in her palm, much like a Catholic school nun. She began pacing about the room.

"B," She narrated.

"B is for beacon; a beacon is a ray of hope, so if you get a B the hope is that you will later obtain an A! Lastly is C, C stands for catastrophic. If you receive a C you have obviously put little or no effort into your homework! Now, I do not expect our eight new students to have anything memorized yet, so; they may assist in my grading process by using the Hebrew text book. When those of you who have memorized your alphabet have finished and are ready to recite, you must do so with your book closed." She concluded.

Me-el frowned, he really wanted Raguel as his partner, but, he knew his rabbi. Gabriel would never allow it; he could see it in her eyes.

"Alright, first pair." She allocated.

"Me-el and Samael!"

Me-el slumped in his desk as Raguel did the same.

"Whoever you get," Me-el said.

"At least you don't get stuck with the *kolboynick Samael!"

Raguel nodded, he did not care to be stuck with the teacher's pet, he felt sorry for his friend.

"Next pair... Raguel and Jericho!"

Raguel's orange wings stood on edge, his feathers ruffling, like a rooster ready to fight.

"NO! I refuse to work with that **bupkes!" He hollered.

Gabriel glared at Raguel and snapped her ruler over his cream filled fingers.

"OUCH!!! Owie!! I get punished for speaking the truth!?" The child wailed.

---

* Kolboynick: A knows it all

** Bupkes: goat droppings.

Me-el covered his eyes; he did not want to see the hideous events unfolding. It was more than he could bear.

"You dare use such Yiddish terms in my class??? That is entirely uncalled for Raguel!" The seething rabbi stormed.

"I did not mean to say it out loud!" Raguel squawked.

"Sounds like some angel is going to level one again!" Jericho jeered.

"Give the drill sergeant my best regards!"

The archangel Remiel entered the classroom, once more upon Gabriel's mental request. Raguel wrapped his chubby feet around the legs of his desk, hoping Remiel would not be able to remove him from it. The trick did not work. Me-el watched with one eye from behind a right wing feather.

"Travesty!" He whispered, terrified for his friend.

The archangel picked up Raguel by the nape of his fatty neck, and dragged him out of the class room kicking and screaming, his wings flapping in tumult.

"This is not fair! I will waste away to nothing! Help!!! Someone help!!! I know my rights!!!!"

Remiel lifted the screaming tot to his face.

"Yes, you have the right to remain silent!" He sneered.

Gabriel closed the twin doors shut after the unnerving departure.

"Very well, enough spectacles for today! Class will proceed as if nothing just happened!"

Everyone was deathly quiet, especially Me-el as the rabbi resumed naming pairs. Me-el not wanting to be Remiel's next delivery to Uriel hesitantly moved his desk up to Samael's.

"So…Guess we better get to work." The child suggested.

Chapter 12

Lucifer was sitting on his throne stewing in his thoughts. He had been looking into his ring of omnipresence.

"Well it appears Uriel has his first regular client!" The morning star giggled.

He was checking in on all eight realms. Lucifer had no need of looking at realm nine, that was solely Yahweh's territory, and he respected that. The light bearer could not have been more pleased with all the levels, except for one; Eden. Lucifer resented Raphael a bit because the healer had still not worn his armor even once.

"I had his fashioned so perfectly too..." He contemplated.

"I thought he would have least tried it on by now."

Lucifer simply could not grasp Raphael's mindset. Uriel wore his, Gabriel also was attentive in exhibiting hers when she was not teaching; while Me-el even dawned his any time he took him to level five to practice his military skills. The son of morning's eyes focused on the circular red diamond. He could see Raphael, he was gathering olives, and using his two middle wings as a basket to hold them.

"He is so beautiful...yet, I am captain! I must not let his pretty face dissuade me from taking action! I must make it clear to Raphael that I will not put up with such insubordinate behavior! After all I also speak for God! I shall call for a summons! "He decided.

Lucifer gaited out of his palace, every messenger bowed like a strand of dominoes as he passed.

"Since Gabriel is busy at Opus Angelorum, I shall go see Uriel." He determined, as he descended to realm one in a tizzy.

Uriel handed the moping tub of goo Raguel, a black silk cloth. Raguel stared up at him with timid eyes.

"So you got in trouble yet again? Well that suits me to a tee! I do believe all my stars are in need of a good polish! If I may say the exercise might do you a bit of good young chap!" Uriel commented as he surveyed the little angel's pot belly.

"Jolly good, I would like you to start on Ursa Major! Go quick now, lest I think of something a bit more sinister!" The lieutenant snarled.

Raguel flew off, occasionally looking over his right wing, to make sure the bitter archangel was not at his tail feathers, trying to yank them out.

"Cherri-O!!" Uriel waved.

The principal released a laugh.

"Well," He theorized, setting his flaming blue wings at full power.

The arch knew they created more intimidation this way, for his repeat offender.

"I do need to maintain an apropos reputation of King of Mean!"

Uriel loomed over to the Big Dipper and began scrutinizing the young angel with icy gold eyes.

"You missed a spot!" He hissed.

Raguel began wiping harder and faster. A comet went past Uriel's left, causing his attention to stray from his occupant.

"Blimey, it's Lucifer!" He chimed.

The morning star emitted rays of light when he flew at high speeds, Uriel had easily mistaken him for a comet. The chrome armored star keeper bowed low and saluted.

"Hail my good captain, tis a pleasure to have you on my realm. How may I be of service to thee?"

Lucifer stood balanced on a meteorite.

"Hello Uriel, I came to inform you about a summons I would like to have. I was wondering if we could hold it here on your realm. If you have no problem with this request I would also like to have it as soon as possible. Can you do this for me?"

Lucifer took a quick gander at the fumbling Raguel; he had just tripped over a small star while polishing a bigger one.

"Of course my lord! It would be my pleasure! I shall begin prepping for it immediately!"

Lucifer nodded then gave his brother a half smile.

"I do hope this will not interfere with your disciplinarian duties?" The captain bantered.

Uriel gave him a wink.

"That little crumpet will be kept working until Remiel sounds the shofar for the next class, or; until Gabriel requests him. In fact; he may still be tending to my stars when you have your summons here!"

Lucifer held back more laughter as he ascended to Eden. He wanted to give Raphael one more chance to try on his armor, before he officially held his meeting.

"I really do not want to criticize him in front of our other siblings..." He repined.

The power Beleth's purple eyes twinkled in approval, Azazel had made a request of him; He wanted Beleth to go search for Lucifer, there was some new drills Azazel wanted to go through with the captain on level five; Beleth had eagerly accepted to go. The power cherished any chance to bask upon Elohim's most brilliant angel. Beleth began to scout levels, as his heart pounded unceasingly beneath his armor.

"I do not see him anywhere" He fretted.

"Wait! I have not gone by Eden yet!

Beleth suddenly recollected how Azazel had spoken of how their captain seemed to be particularly watchful of realm three, especially as of late. The power glided down towards Eden's atmosphere and its compelling guardian; the archangel Raphael.

"Hail lieutenant!" Beleth called as he saluted.

Raphael looked over towards his visitor, returning the salute. The gardener was dumping freshly picked olives into a large wicker container. The archangel Jeremiel was going to pick them up any moment now, to transfer them to Jerusalem, so they could be pressed into oil.

"Hello Beleth." Raphael cheerfully responded.

"Come have a seat, and rest your wings a bit." The lieutenant cited.

Raphael dragged over two stones for him and the handsome power. Beleth raised his palm in cordial objection.

"No that will not be necessary lieutenant, I cannot stay long, I only came by to ask if you have seen our lord Lucifer recently."

Raphael adjusted his wreath of roses and pushed back some curls which framed his face.

"I cannot say I have." He replied.

The gardener took a juicy olive from his basket and tossed it in his mouth. Beleth released a sigh of despair, he seemed dismayed. Raphael rose from his seat; a smile now crossed his lips.

"It is okay Beleth; every angel is hypnotized by our captain's beauty. I presume I am a smidgen off in that respect. I am boarded by so much loveliness here, that Lucifer's good looks fail to overwhelm me as much. I really am fonder of all the flowers here!" He confessed.

Raphael nabbed a yellow rose from his head adornment and handed it to Beleth.

"Yellow roses represent friendship."

The lieutenant explained as a shy Beleth accepted the token of kindness.

"He is not Lucifer..." Beleth privately analyzed.

"Yet Raphael also displays the work of Abba's fine artistry!"

Raphael patted Beleth on the shoulder.

"Well if you would pardon me, I need to resume my work now. My berry fields need picking. I am sure you will encounter Lucifer fairly soon, he is impossible to miss!"

Beleth held the yellow rose to his chest as he beheld Raphael promenade through a thicket of trees.

"He is as pretty as this flower..." Beleth murmured.

"Why thank you!" Lucifer answered.

The captain had just landed right in front of a befuddled Beleth.

"My lord!"

Beleth crashed to his knees in shock. Lucifer examined the rose in his hand. The kneeling power discarded it; it fell next to Lucifer's left *saboton. Lucifer clenched his jaw; he knew what had just transpired between Beleth and his fair brother. The morning star decided right then and there that no further talks with Raphael were required.

"Never once has he given me a rose!" Lucifer languished.

"I trust you still find me more becoming than my lieutenant?" The light bearer cynically bid.

"By all means!" Beleth avowed upon rising to his feet.

"I was sent to find you,"

"I know." Lucifer interjected.

"Azazel wants me on realm five to go through some drills and he sent you to find me."

Beleth swallowed anxiously.

"Yes my lord I assume we can expect you momentarily?"

Lucifer now reviewed the serendipitous power with calculating eyes.

"Yes of course, yet when Me-el is dismissed from school I shall need to leave."

---

* Sabaton: Armor that covers the foot.

"By all means!" Beleth bowed.

The power took to flight after paying homage. Lucifer stomped on his forgotten yellow rose in a tantrum.

"Raphael you give tokens to every angel minus your captain!" He mulled over.

Raphael, who was avidly picking mulberries, glanced up from his work. A flower had just been hurt; he could feel it in his heart. He also sensed Lucifer was in the garden.

"When he is in Eden the birds stop singing..." He thought to himself.

"I assume he ran into Beleth by now."

Raphael resumed his berry picking when the archangel Jeremiel arrived to pick up his load of olives for Jerusalem.

"Hail lieutenant, I am here for the olives."

Raphael glanced up.

"Ah yes... I had a power from level five distract me a bit ago, but I did get them all gathered for you, come with me!"

Raphael flew over to the olive trees with Jeremiel. He passed him two heaping baskets crammed with green olives.

"Thank you Raphael, I am sure you will be seeing me again soon."

Jeremiel saluted then soared off. Raphael was about to head back to his berry bushes, when he heard a shofar blast.

"That is not Remiel, that shofar was Gabriel's that means we are being summoned."

Raphael released all six wings as he descended down. The ram's horn was sounding from realm one.

Lucifer's summons was preparing to start. Me-el although not very thrilled about going to Uriel's level voluntarily, still was more than happy to accompany his older brother to an adult archangel meeting. The youth was interested about what his older siblings would be discussing. He also expected refreshments would be served; this was his main reason for tagging along.

"Maybe I'll see Raguel polishing stars..." He conceived.

"I might be able to help him escape if I do..." He further thought.

Uriel had just put the finishing touches on his grandiose palace, after Lucifer had requested the summons take place at his abode; he decided to spruce it up a tad more. The lieutenant wanted to make certain everything met his captain's full approval. Uriel knew this also meant catering well to his lord's pet bottomless pit; Me-el.

"To bad I still have not gotten around to putting in my star pools..." He evaluated.

"Oh well, I cannot rightly worry about that at the moment, I see the captain and his little matzo ball are on their way up, I better make sure I have real food to feed him!"

Uriel said in a begrudged tone as he pandered on what treats to serve with tea.

The first realm was glorious, as the keeper of the stars Uriel found himself responsible for the entire abyss of space. Elohim was still far from creating the planets of the solar system; nevertheless the first level was nothing short of brilliant. The cosmic realm glowed with scores of glittering galaxies and innumerable stars; much to Raguel's dismay!

Uriel's palace gleamed in radiance; he had added fire opals around the outside to make it more fetching. The lieutenant sighed in relief as a virtue named Comfort apparated in his home.

"I brought up a basket of black licorice and Jasmine tea, three bottles of chocolate cherubim milk, and a pouch of scones and cakes." She communicated.

Uriel set his silver tea set on the table.

"What about coffee for Gabriel?"

Comfort smiled and extracted another smaller pouch from her golden sash around her waist.

"Fresh hazel nut coffee straight from Eden's farms!"

Uriel gave her a look of consent.

"Well done Comfort, you may be dismissed, I see all my siblings are at my door, I need to let them all in. Thank you!"

Comfort vanished from Uriel's midst, as he went to open the door; he made sure to put out his flaming blue wings.

"No need to scare off Lucifer's little dough roll during our gathering." He surmised.

Uriel opened his door to let the archangels in.

"Good day to all of you! Please be seated at my table!"

Uriel bowed as Lucifer walked in first.

Lucifer sat at the table's head, Me-el sat right next to him. Raphael stationed himself left of Me-el and gave him a smile.

"Hello little one."

"Hi Rapha!" Me-el cooed back.

Gabriel and Uriel took the remaining seats.

"Well first I would like to extend my thanks to Uriel for permitting us to have this summons in his palace."

Uriel nodded.

"Tis an honor lord!"

Lucifer continued.

"I called this summons for a couple reasons; I also wished to congratulate Uriel on his recent promotion as principal to Opus Angelorum, Gabriel you chose quite well."

Gabriel blushed, and for once Uriel's stone face melted into a tiny smile. Me-el cringed, he did not find the news worth extolling; he was to worried about what his chum Raguel might be suffering through at the moment.

"What if Uriel made him eat so much air, that he popped like a balloon?" He speculated in fear.

The child reached for some nosh from Uriel's copper tray. Uriel had not noticed, but Comfort had also dropped in cheese cubes and sugar coated fruits. Me-el knew he could always count on food to calm his nerves at moments such as this.

"Well," Lucifer continued

"I called you all here for one other reason as well."

Gabriel lifted her hand.

'Yes?" Lucifer asked.

"My captain are we going to discuss the concert you proposed we do for Abba when we were jousting on realm five the other day?"

Lucifer raised his right eye brow in demonstration of his subtle annoyance.

"Gabriel who is leading this meeting? I was under the impression that as captain I was, yet perhaps you are? Did Abba promote you without my knowledge?"

Gabriel lowered her head in shame.

"No my lord, by all means you are in charge, please forgive my imprudent behavior."

Me-el began scarfing down cheese, fruit and cakes all at once. The little angel now had the likeness of a chipmunk with overstuffed cheeks, preparing for a long winter hibernation. He was thoroughly entertained by his rabbi getting corrected for once, rather than him. Me-el had also just aced his Hebrew alphabet recitation at the last class which only added to his confidence; so far he was finding the summons to be very much to his liking.

Raphael grieved by his sister's embarrassment withdrew a red rose from his head garland and gently nudged it her way, with a friendly wink. Lucifer's face became distorted in an outraged sneer.

"That's it!" He fumed.

Every angel's eyes except Me-el's gunned towards the captain. Me-el was oblivious to any one's reaction as he slowly commenced inching the tray of edibles over his way with his top right wing.

"Raphael, you are the other reason why I called this summons!"

Raphael's face dimmed. He had not been expecting this; apparently he had angered his captain.

"Me lord? But what have I done?" He stammered.

Lucifer rolled his eyes and grunted.

"Is it not obvious? Every angel here is fully suited in their armor with the exception of you!"

Raphael hung his head in humiliation. He did not dare contest his captain, he was correct.

"Forgive me lord." He sadly let out.

"I will forgive you when you begin doing as you are told! Why just look at yourself in comparison to the rest of this company..."

Raphael's eyes were fogged in ignominy. Lucifer was not finished scolding him yet, he picked up where he left off.

"I know Abba crowned you with that wreath, but for goodness sake must you make a spectacle of yourself and wear it every day?? I mean really... brother I can honestly say ...you look more like a cake and nothing like a soldier!"

Uriel and Gabriel timorously sipped from their cups as the captain went on.

"Raphael, what sort of example are you to less mature angels when you gallivant in Eden all the day like some....." Lucifer hesitated before he spat out his final blow.

"Like some oversized culinary pastry!"

Raphael's visage went red, he felt mortified. Me-el now at full attention since he heard the word cake put in his own two bits.

"Lufi where is the cake? I heard you say cake? All the ones on the tray are tiny!"

Uriel all to glad that the semi elephantine youth had changed the subject, waved his right hand over towards Me-el's direction. A decadent chocolate cake lidded with cherries and whipped cream manifested in front of the tubby tot. Me-el instantaneously started eating it by the handfuls. The less than proper child's eating habits went ignored; even though every angel around the table rapidly became drizzled with chocolate drops.

Uriel telepathically sent silk napkins about the sitting area to carefully dab each of the angel's faces.

Raphael attempted to plead his case one last time.

"My lord has every reason to be upset with me, once more I beg you to please pardon me."

Lucifer gazed into the healer's miserable eyes.

"Even when distressed he looks becoming...." The captain reflected.

"Very well Raphael, you may resume speaking." He acknowledged.

Raphael swallowed then began.

"I love the beautiful armor you gifted me with, I just have yet to wear it because.... Well quite honestly it is much easier to tend to my gardening duties dressed as I am."

Raphael bit his lower lip; he was ready for another rebuttal. He halted his explanation, Lucifer's eyes drilled into his with antagonism. Raphael felt a shiver of fear run down his spine and into all six of his pink pinions. Gabriel now wanting to defend her petrified sibling spoke out much against her better judgment.

"If my lord would reconsider, I am certain Raphael would be glad to fly down to his realm right this moment and properly attire himself just for you."

Uriel who was now in absolute shock began pouring himself another cup of tea. He could not conceive how his two siblings were daring to upstage Lucifer with their various opinions. He knew his place; he was not going to say one single word! The archangel nipped away yearning to be in any realm but his own.

Lucifer arose his eyes were now blazing with indignation. The captain pounded his right fist on the table causing Uriel's decorative star dust which veiled it, to levitate in mid air. The tea set began to shake, whilst Me-el landed face first into his cake. The toddler munched on completely unaffected by the commotion.

"I will not be bombarded by your persistent unwanted words Gabriel!" Lucifer roared.

Gabriel who now felt like crawling under the table, nodded. She was shamed.

"My many pardons to my most lovely captain!" She begged.

Lucifer sat back down, he was a bit calmer now.

"Well now that we have discussed that matter, I shall in fact be conducting a concert soon for Abba, as some angel previously mentioned..."

Gabriel drank her coffee and kept silent; she knew who he was talking about.

"I expect you all to be in attendance and wearing your armor. I would also like Raphael to begin nesting late hatching cherubim eggs."

Raphael's jade eyes regarded Lucifer. The captain had a coy look on his face; it was almost as if he wanted Raphael to challenge his request. The gardener knew better than to fall for his bait.

"Yes my lord." He responded.

"I did not think you would mind brother after all you do seem to enjoy flitting around unarmed... so I thought you could put your two bottom wings to a better use! Why in a way it's an elevation of sorts! You could now be considered Eden's head Cherubim!"

Raphael managed out a smile.

"My lord is too kind." He said.

Lucifer went on,

"So any new eggs which are released from creatures and do not open immediately, you shall nest in your lower wings. You may do this while you are gardening, it's actually rather convenient!"

Raphael spoke not a word, yet nodded.

"I would also like to take a moment to remind each of you lieutenants, that with my new ring of omnipresence I am at leisure to evaluate any of you at any moment, so... I would greatly appreciate every angel's cooperation in future matters."

Lucifer heightened himself after his speech. The three lieutenants rose along with him to formally bow. Me-el who was now entirely bloated, resembled a dumpling wrapped in tin foil; he was also wearing his armor. The child heaved himself up to do the same. Lucifer hoisted him up onto his sturdy shoulders.

"This concludes the summit; I will have one of my messengers bring news to each of you when I orchestrate my first concerto for Abba."

Me-el exploded with a loud burp as they departed from their view in a glare of light. Uriel inspected his siblings with accusatory eyes.

"I am glad I kept my opinions to myself!" He brooded.

Chapter 13

Yahweh sat back smiling at Lucifer, the morning star was discussing how his first summons had gone. God was a trifle confused when Lucifer disclosed his displeasure with Raphael's head piece.

"Bubeleh I am glad you are beginning to be a good leader…" God expressed.

"However I do not understand your anger with Raphael, I am sure he would have eventually worn his armor. Do you think you may have been a bit harsh?"

Lucifer began sipping his lemon ginger tea. The captain started grappling over how to answer.

"Perhaps you misunderstood me Avi, I was not really angry, I just wanted to make sure he followed orders."

Lucifer contrived while pulling on his gold *gorget. The light bearer did not want Abba against him in any way; he needed a path out of this maze he had weaved. He thought out his next words carefully.

"I suppose I was a tad annoyed…yet I know there is no lingering hurt feelings, you see Abba I actually gave Raphael a promotion! He is now chief cherubim!"

---

* Gorget: Mesh metal on a coat of arms which protects the neck.

Lucifer failed to reveal how this act of pseudo up grade was actually an attempt to debase Raphael's self worth.

God's face brightened.

"Well now, that is wonderful! Forgive me for questioning your tactics! I assume our gardener will be helping nest eggs then?"

Lucifer grinned; happy to witness Abba saw it as a good thing.

"Yes Abba!"

Yahweh rose his cup to salute the captain.

"I am pleased with you beloved, but please do remember, since I have entrusted you with the ring of omnipresence I seldom reconnaissance over my sea of glass. I am putting a great deal of trust into you!"

Lucifer patted Yahweh's knee in assurance.

"I know Avi; I will do my best to make you proud."

Me-el was seated on his ottoman with a silver plate of strawberry bon bons balanced on his lap. He beamed up at Yahweh and his older brother in adoration. The little angel once more indulged himself in sugar crusted bliss.

"Well," Yahweh sighed, removing his spectacles to give them a polish with his sleeve.

"I should let you two get about your business! I have no further doubt I made the perfect angel when I created you sweet Lucifer!"

Lucifer's cheeks went red as Yahweh kissed his right hand.

"Oh and Me-el please feel free to take those bon bons with you!" God related.

"Don't need to Abba." Me-el blurted.

"I already finished em all!"

Yahweh and Lucifer both let out a guffaw. Me-el was now looking like a cream filled bon bon himself. One enclosed in shiny wrapper.

After tea with Yahweh ended, Lucifer and Me-el flew down to the seventh level of Heaven. The morning star set aside his jeweled armor and garbed himself in a flowing white choir robe, lined with gold. Me-el also tediously undid his own coat of arms and pulled a robe over his stout body. The child's pudgy feet kept tripping over the hem. A multitude of dazzling angels stood in a grand mystic quartz coliseum. It was Yahweh's worship realm. The choir of level seven consisted of seraphim, virtues and principalities. The lower part of the majestic stage held a bronze pedestal for Lucifer to perch himself on. The morning star wanted to have a rehearsal with the ensemble before actually putting on his official concerto.

The light bearer went over to his pedestal to commence conducting the assembly. Lucifer lifted his gold baton, the captain then with the elegance of the finest symphony maestro; started motioning his white gloved hands. Me-el sat obediently at his brother's feet. He began to *duven like a faithful Orthodox Jew would at the western wall. The dulcet angelic voices and divine instruments came together in agreeable harmony.

Lucifer's head swayed softly as he allowed the brilliant praise music to enchant all his senses. The choir reached a climax; this is when Lucifer interwove his own voice. On realm nine, from his throne room Yahweh listened as Yeshua and the Ruach vibrated in his chest. The deity reclined on his aurous chair and closed his eyes. Yahweh simply soaked in the melodic chants of the recital. Yahweh's heart skipped a beat upon hearing Lucifer's signature vocal cords. He resonated above all the others.

"Oh how I love him!" God mused.

"No one nor nothing will ever out shine you my glorious Lucifer!"

Lucifer's choir practice permeated through all nine levels. On realm two Gabriel could not help but hum along. The seraph who was seated at her snow flake styled table going over notes for her next class, abruptly halted as an idea entered her mind. Gabriel morphed into her masculine form and girded herself with her armor, she fastened her bracers; then using a silver ribbon, she tied back her blonde hair with her upper two wings.

"I think peeking in on his rehearsal in my coat of arms might put our captain into a more cheerful mood." She theorized.

---

* Duven: How the Jewish people rock back and forth in prayer.

Gabriel's eyes glanced back at her table of ice. The quartz vase at its center held the rose Raphael had given her at the summons. The flower was now encased in ice itself, for preservation. It shined exquisitely. The seraph recalled Raphael's saddened face after receiving correction from Lucifer; she walked over to the vase and gently ran a finger over the token the gardener had presented her with. Snow ball barked affectionately at her feet.

"Yes my pet," She said as she rubbed the furry white seal.

"I think I will visit Eden. Raphael is the tenderest hearted angel out of all of us, I wonder if this music is cheering him as well?"

Snow ball barked again as if he comprehended everything she was saying. Gabriel gave the animal one last pat on the head, and then ascended up to level three.

Raphael upon being admonished by his captain; now had his long sinuous curls tied back in a pony tail. It streamed well past his tail feathers and was knotted with a gold ribbon. The lieutenant also no longer wore his wreath of roses. Raphael did not want any more conflicts with his general. The seraph was enjoying Lucifer's run through of the concert. Raphael had become inspired to manufacture garlands of flowers to place around the necks of his two unicorns.

These adornments not only contained roses, but poppies, hyacinths, and jasmine, garnished with sprigs of baby's breath. Raphael smiled as he fastened the wreaths about the two venerable creatures.

"There you go!" He chimed.

"Lucifer should not mind you two wearing them."

The unicorns nuzzled Raphael in approval; the seraph gave them each a kiss on the snout. Gabriel, who had just arrived, coughed to get her brother's attention.

"Well hello sister! Although you look a tad more like a brother at the moment, either form suits you nicely!"

Gabriel smiled at Raphael's constant courtesy; she removed her helmet.

"I am glad to see you in better spirits brother, after the summons... well I thought..." Her words trailed off as Raphael dismissed the whole matter with a wave of his hand. He straightened out his gown and tightened his belt.

"Oh that is water under a bridge! Besides, I had it coming, why look at me!

I'm still *shlubbing...I fail to wear my armor even after I got the third degree! The only reason I have yet to put it on is because I know he is way too preoccupied making beautiful music at the moment! So...I don't believe he is gazing into that ring of his! However, I did remove my gaudy wreath. By the way Gabriel how do you like my new hair style? Does it become me?"

---

* Shlubbing: To be sloppy.

The gardener asked with a mischievous uplifted eyebrow and demy smile.

Gabriel chuckled and gave him a hug.

"Raphael you can never look bad!"

Gabriel plucked a ripe fig from a nearby tree to nibble on.

"I thought you, Uriel and I might fly up to realm seven. I know I felt simply awful after putting my foot in my mouth at Lucifer's meeting. He is God's right hand. Anyhow... I came up with the notion of the three of us arriving at his rehearsal fully armed; I thought it would liven him up a bit. You know allow us all to get back in his good graces?" She proposed as she finished up her fig.

Raphael moved his head to the side, his eyes were inquisitive.

"Or... I could just send Me-el baskets full of chocolate and desserts." He fostered while dismissing Cinnamon and Sugar.

Gabriel's brow lowered in concern.

"I was joshing you sister!" Raphael winked.

A breath of relief escaped Gabriel's lips. In a flutter of his six wings, Raphael went from a willowy robed holistic doctor, to an argent gold soldier. However, he was not wearing his helmet.

"Helmet Rapha??" Gabriel enjoined.

Raphael grinned roguishly.

"Hey I got rid of the wreath and put my hair back! Besides we are not gonna train on realm five, if or when I ever go to duel on that level; I will make sure to wear my helmet! But for now, let's just go pay our captain a visit." He concluded.

Gabriel shook her head. Raphael definitely walked to the beat of his own drum. She signaled a messenger dove over, and placed a tiny parchment around its leg.

"Take that to Uriel dear."

The bird cooed in sanction, as it flew off with the note.

"Very well Rapha, but if that is your final decision, perhaps we should take a goody basket to Me-el. if you make that little marshmallow happy, Lucifer might be a bit more lenient towards you!" She advised.

"I'm on it! I'll go east of here to my garden of sweets and gather a big care package for my favorite little angel!"

Uriel had just acquired the invitation Gabriel had sent him via messenger dove. He was always fully suited in his chrome armor.

"By Jove that sounds like a jolly good plan!" He quipped.

He ascended up to Eden without further delay. The star keeper landed right next to Gabriel. He tapped her on her upper right wing.

"Wow!" He expressed.

"The bloke cleans up rather nicely in his coat of arms! No wonder Lucifer was so adamant about him wearing it!"

"Yes he looks very handsome!" Gabriel agreed.

"Why the bloody stars is he carrying a huge basket of food?"

"Insurance!" Raphael explained.

"I assume that would be to suck up to our captain by gaining points with his pet baby cow?" Uriel remarked, unafraid to speak his mind.

Gabriel and Raphael gaped at him appalled at how he referred to Me-el.

"Oh come on, I was jesting!" He insisted.

The three admirable archangels took to the air, they emanated light, poise and grace; as they ascended upward, angels of lower rank all gazed up. They were infatuated by the triad of Yahweh's chosen throne room lieutenants.

On level seven, Lucifer's choir chanted in symphonic unity, they displayed beauty and royal presence. Gabriel, Raphael and Uriel sat spell bound in fine red velvet chairs trimmed with gold. Lucifer had yet to realize that his siblings were watching from the luxurious auditorium. The three archangels looked on in astoundment as they faced the bedazzling coliseum of singing angels. There was no doubt in any lieutenant's mind why Yahweh favored Lucifer so much.

The chief seraph not only had perfect beauty and military savvy, he also proved to be a magnificent praise and worship leader, the best. No angel in all nine realms had all the wisdom, skill, and brilliance Lucifer over flowed with. He truly was Yahweh's master piece! The lieutenants continued observing as the master general extended his twelve white pinions as delicately as a rose opening it's petals in the morning; his arms and hands eloquently gesturing the ensemble.

Little Me-el was still rocking rhythmically beside him. The morning star's beguiling blue eyes remained closed as he waved his gold baton, causing the singers to decrescendo and slur. Lucifer gracefully moved his head along with the melody, his lissome blonde locks waving back and forth. He outstretched his two arms wide and opened his eyes crying:

"Now for the finale! Sing to Abba with all your strength! I want a full crescendo aldante!!!"

Me-el jolted to his feet upon the declaration, he could not wait to see how his big brother would conclude the spectacular event. Lucifer flicked his baton up with his right hand, A great throng of heavenly beings brought forth an overwhelming chant of:

"Halleluiah!"

Behindthequartzcoliseumanetherealpyrotechnics display erupted. Shooting stars and rainbows pervaded the celestial back drop. Little Me-el bounced gleefully and banged his tambourine. Up above a deluge of thrones with glowing eyes encircled the pleochroic ceiling. The horde was reminiscent of a grand opera house chandelier, except this one rotated in circles and had feathers!

Gabriel, Raphael, and Uriel all rose clapping vigorously. Lucifer was receiving the universe's very first standing ovation. The captain turned; bewildered to see he had an audience. Lucifer shyly removed his white gloves and put down his baton. He took a slight stage bow. The morning star then stepped aside to allow the choir to receive its due recognition. Raphael put two fingers to his mouth and whistled. Gabriel and Uriel shouted:

"Brava! Brava!"

Lucifer smiled as he dismissed the singers and herd of thrones from the auditorium. He scooped up Me-el, and then went over to his siblings. He floated towards them with swan like motion. Lucifer seemed happy.

"Wow! You all look so dignified in your suits of armor!" He rang.

The three lieutenants knelt to pay homage to their captain.

"Lucifer that was brilliant!" Gabriel commented.

Raphael and Uriel nodded in concurrence.

"If that was simply a run through it's hard to imagine how the actual concert could be any better!"

Uriel sighted with shining eyes.

"Oh yes!" Raphael reminded himself.

"I got you something; I brought a gift for Me-el too."

The golden suited archangel unfurled his bottom two wings. The left pinion held a stunning bouquet of white dew kissed roses. The right one contained Me-el's basket of sublime treats. Me-el's eyes grew the size of Frisbees; he swooped down off Lucifer's back, and dove into the boatload of nuts, fruit and chocolate. Raphael reached down for the roses and handed them to Lucifer, he chivalrously kissed the captain's right palm.

"Bravo my lord!" Raphael related as he presented the flowers.

Lucifer's eyes met Raphael's.

"Why I am speechless brother."

The light bearer uttered. He now fought back emotion. Here was the one thing he had always coveted from Raphael, but it was more than just one; the gardener had just bestowed him with a whole dozen! Lucifer genuinely felt guilt for trying to belittle his charming sibling at his summons.

"I do not deserve these," He admitted, beneath his breath.

Me-el looked up; sugar covered his tiny ruby lips, from the powdered walnuts and cashews.

"Those are really pretty roses Lufi!" He gushed.

Raphael smiled at Lucifer with his eyes.

"You most certainly do deserve them my captain, though I must say they pale against your beauty."

As Lucifer inspected the bouquet his face took on a look of discernment. He felt compelled to do something nice for Raphael's sake; to make up for how critical he had been; yet, he did not want to come off as obvious. He would need to include his other two lieutenants as well.

"Captain?"

Gabriel remarked, becoming astute of Lucifer's dissociation.

"I just got a great idea!" The captain expressed.

"The concert we do for Abba will be more personal than this lavish rehearsal! Besides, I'm sure he heard it just as all of you did. How about the five of us perform privately for our father?"

All three archangels traded gloppened faces. Me-el clapped his hands; his mouth was full of chocolate covered berries. Lucifer went on discussing his notion.

"Allow me to explain, we could sing as a quartet, Me-el could play an instrument, or dance with his tambourine, Raphael I adore your strong baritone vocals; Gabriel you are what I would refer to as a mezzo soprano, your voice is high and saccharine! Uriel your unique sound is like serene waters running over stones; add my own, and we would impress Abba beyond measure! What say you all?"

Raphael spoke first.

"I say I am in!"

Gabriel and Uriel both seconded the motion.

"Count us in too!" They replied.

Lucifer brought his four siblings in towards him with his twelve wings, for a bear hug. Me-el caught off guard by the sudden embrace, chucked out a pecan stuffed fig from his throat. He watched in regret as it spewed under a chair.

"My poor goodie!" He wailed.

Yahweh who was watching from his throne, at his sea of glass, beamed with fatherly pride. His children had formed a warm circle of love; it caused his heart to pump faster.

"My dear archangels!" He smiled.

"Your fondness for one another touches my spirit like oil running down my beard! You all anoint me with shalom!"

Chapter 14

On realm one Uriel was naming stars, Raguel currently polished Ursa Minor. The star keeper halted his task; a still sound began beckoning him by name. Uriel flew over to Raguel; the portly ham hock of an angel began wiping faster.

"You best keep working! I need to attend to something! If you should stop for any reason, I will know! My stars talk to me! They will tell me if you even try to convalesce or; fly off! Understood?"

Raguel bobbed his head up and down at the fiery principal.

"Yes sir!" He yelped.

Uriel gave him a tiny:

"BOO!"

The seraph then went over to the area of space where he heard the voice coming from.

"Here I am." Uriel revealed, as an orb of light not from his realm danced around him in playful formations.

"Hello my child, do you not know who I am?"

Uriel's eyes scintillated. It was Yahweh, yet in a different form.

"Abba?" He questioned.

"Yes, this is me as the Ruach." The triune God exposed.

Uriel could not be certain but he thought he could make out the silhouette of a dove fluttering from within the silver sphere. The luminous ball began pulsating. Uriel bowed to pay homage to his creator.

Every angel was conscious that Yahweh was known for having three distinct personages; yet up until now, God had only displayed his fatherly figure. Uriel felt honored to be viewing the Ruach; who knew, he could even be the first!

"Yes lord, speak for your servant is listening!" He said in excitement.

"First," The Ruach disclosed.

"I want you to know, If by any chance Lucifer is looking into his ring right now, he will see me as Yahweh, you are the first to see me in this form!"

"Blimey! I was right!" Uriel appraised.

"Yes, your thoughts are accurate. You must promise me to not tell anyone else of me coming to you in this way; your siblings will also see my other images soon, understood?"

"Of course most high!" Uriel pledged.

"Good, now follow me."

The Ruach flickered towards Uriel's palace then into the Milky Way, there at the center of the spiraled galaxy stood an opaque structure glowing brightly.

"Come!" The Holy Spirit hearkened as he locomoted over to the vibrant building, bound in spectacular gems of every sort. Uriel entered through a tall round door, he gazed around dumbfounded. The seraph found himself entrapped by limitless ticking items. Some were small; others large, each one had a peculiar face.

"Bloody stars and comets! They have arms and hands on their faces!" Uriel blurt out.

The abnormal objects also had no eyes, yet some displayed long ghastly swinging tongues of bronze or copper.

"Can't say I know what Yahweh was thinking when he created these oddities!" Uriel thought.

He shook his head, observing these curious specimens made his mind boggle. Like a cat pawing at a pendulum, Uriel swatted at one, it gonged in response. The seraph stumbled back in timorous fashion. The Ruach chortled causing the orb he was in to change colors. He spoke:

"I want to invent something called time Uriel, these are clocks, do not worry they are quite harmless."

Uriel blushed.

"Now no angel or creature in all nine realms will be physically affected by my new creation. All angels shall never age past twenty five years..."

Uriel looked a muddle of questions.

"Beg pardon lord... But what are years?" He asked.

"Allow me to finish." The Ruach put forward.

Uriel nodded.

The Holy Spirit turned the confused angel's attention to a massive font of water which reflected the stars.

"It's my star pool!" He merrily took in; Uriel had yet to place any in his own palace.

Uriel peered into it; he noticed two new additions to his realm! A big beryl star that shot flares of flame; and a much smaller round rock that lit up just like his own skin.

"These two will assist you with studying time, the yellow one, I call the sun, and the lesser is called the moon. This pool of water will allow you to calculate time by the cycle and alignment of these two bodies, along with all your stars. You will configure months, days, years, and so much more!"

"Abba I just want to take a moment to thank you," Uriel bowed.

"I've wanted to put some star pools in my palace, but have yet to do so! But may I also ask how will I do all you are telling me to?"

The orb now clearly showed a dove inside, its eyes fixed on Uriel's.

"Firstly, you are most welcome, and when you return to your palace, you will find two star pools as you call them, I put them there for you too. As to how you will ascertain everything, I shall personally bestow you with all the wisdom you need to do this!" The Ruach answered.

The dove inside the sphere of light began flapping its wings, a gush of the creatures breath whammed right into the archangel. Uriel gradually felt a surge of knowledge whip through him. The Holy Spirit manifested heaps of scrolls atop a quartz desk equipped with ink jars and quills.

"By Jove I understand everything now most high!" Uriel yelped.

"Wonderful!" The Ruach related.

"When you have your first drafts completed, come alone to realm nine so we may converse, I am confident time will bring more order to Heaven!"

Uriel bowed again.

"Yes my lord! I will do as you say!"

The Ruach affectionately jostled Uriel's fire blue wings.

"Oh, you might want to put those out when you begin scribing!" He suggested as he fizzled out of the angel's sight.

Uriel dimmed his wings to a birthday cake candle level, and then walked over to the desk.

"Well time to get to work!" He stated.

Outside Raguel fainted at the sight of two new things to polish.

"Why me!" He cried as he fell over back words.

Taking to his desk, Uriel began writing as inspiration stormed through his mind. The concept of days, weeks, months, years, hours, minutes and seconds cyclone in his brain. The seraph's refined hands began scribbling at an unfathomable speed. Uriel occasionally glanced up at the vast array of chiming clocks; he now could make out numbers on each of their faces.

"Yes!" Uriel leapt from his cushioned crystal chair.

He raised his quill, and re dipped it in ink.

"Twenty four hours in a day, seven days in a week, twelve months in a year! Jolly good!"

The ecstatic angel finished a stack of scrolls within minutes. The first certified drafts of calendars were now completed. He had made two separate copies, one strictly coincided with the phases of the moon; where upon every three years par the cycle of nineteen years the third, sixth, eighth, eleventh, fourteenth, seventeenth, and nineteenth years would have an extra day; or be months of leap year. Uriel also added an entire month every three years in correspondence to the lunar routine.

Uriel's second calendar was simpler; it consisted of twelve months, with only one out of the twelve being a leap year.

"I shall allow Yahweh to choose which one he sees fit to use in Heaven." He decided.

The archangel had just finished both Hebrew and Common time calendars. Both drafts shared twelve months; however the course of each differed due to the celestial orbits of the sun and moon. Uriel sealed up his work, and then recalled he still had a small angel to pick on.

"Better check up on Raguel!" He smirked.

Chapter 15

Yahweh sat at his tea corner, he had sent for Lucifer; knowing Me-el to be always at his side, Yahweh had made certain to place an order for a full tray of assorted goods. One of God's lesser archangels Seraphanel had just delivered some new lip smacking morsels from Jerusalem. He bowed low to Yahweh as he brought in his blue wings.

"I was promenading about the temple court, acquainting myself with the several vendors, many are virtues from Eden." Seraphanels' left hazel green eye twinkled; he was partial to the dainty feminine looking angels.

"The lovely creatures assured me that Me-el would love these delicacies!"

Rising from his bow, Seraphanel lifted a lacey pink cloth from a silver spun basket he was carrying. The dusty blonde Hispanic angel disclosed:

"We have Baklava, Turkish delight, and coconut macaroons dipped in chocolate!"

Yahweh smiled as the suave Seraphanel carefully stacked the treats on a tray which laid on an end table close to Me-el's velvet footstool.

"OY!" God whooped.

"They all look good, but I do not know if it will be enough to keep Me-el satisfied!"

Seraphanel let out a small snicker as he poured Me-el's gallon sized quartz mug full of chocolate cherubim milk; at least he knew Yahweh had made this receptacle automatically refillable.

"I hope it is enough most high! Please give the captain and the little one my highest regards, fare well Abba."

Seraphanel genuflected then disappeared back to realm six. Yahweh was still preoccupied about Me-el's ravenous appetite.

"I need to make sure his hunger is subdued." Yahweh pondered.

God snapped his fingers, some succulent dates covered in rum sauce and ripe cherries coated with dark cocoa appeared alongside the other edibles.

"Better!" God chimed.

His face lit up as he perceived Lucifer and Me-el arrive and kneel before him. Yahweh held his right hand over his heart, as he fawned over his most fetching angel.

"Be still my beating heart! Welcome bubeleh!" Elohim bellowed.

"Lucifer, fairest of angels you overwhelm me with love! I'm getting ver clempt! You make me turn my eyes away! Come my most beautiful one, you too Me-el! Both of you come and join me!"

Lucifer rose, in a balletic stride he went over to his royal purple chair and sat down. Me-el not nearly as stylish, hobbled up unto his green ottoman. The child's eyes automatically shot to the scrumptious loads of desserts. God stationed himself last; he wanted to convey his bountiful love towards Lucifer by doing so.

"I am a servant." Yeshua whispered into Abba's ear.

The advice had compelled Yahweh to do as he did. Once God was seated, Me-el clasped his hands together, bowed his head and began to screed a prayer.

"Abba we praise and thank you for giving us life and for loving us!"

Lucifer and Yahweh were both daunted by the young angel's recitation. They smiled at him and together finished with:

"Amen."

"Very good!" Lucifer expressed, flashing a grin of admiration to his little brother.

Yahweh passed Lucifer a cup of rosemary tea, his eyes smiling under his silver wired spectacles.

"He has a great example to follow, with you as an older sibling bubeleh!" Yahweh divulged.

Lucifer's lengthy gold lashes fluttered, he lowered his head.

"Abba you are the best example to all of us!" He shyly said.

God put down his tea cup, and tenderly lifted the seraph's bowed head with two fingers.

"Enough of that Lucifer." Yahweh cheerfully jeered.

"Let me gaze upon your lustrous eyes!"

Lucifer blushed, as he faced his father.

"Well I called you here to make you aware of a few matters. I do not know if you have been looking into your ring as of late, but in case you have not; I wanted to tell you about some new assignments I have given to Uriel."

Before Lucifer could respond, the three were taken aback, a messenger; by the name of Rofocal, spontaneously emerged, he began refilling Lucifer's tea cup, yet failed to give Yahweh's cup a warm up. Rofocal immediately realized the flaw in his actions when he witnessed the shocked glances shared between Yahweh and his captain. Lucifer did not appear amused in the slightest. God lowered his glasses and commenced surveying the tense fidgety messenger from Lucifer's private realm. He was stupefied by his inappropriate behavior.

"What compelled you to come up here and begin tending to me? Do you not know that Yahweh is above all of us? Rofocal your actions are reprehensible!" Lucifer challenged.

"When any angel comes to the throne room, they must always pay tribute to Yahweh first! Rofocal you trod on dangerous grounds by committing such unneeded discord!"

Rofocal fell prostrate on the floor in front of Yahweh's chair.

"Forgive me most high! You are worthy of all praise! My captain is correct to scold me! I got caught up in trying to please him, please have mercy on this imprudent fool of an angel!"

Yahweh touched by the messenger's sincere contrition, lowered his hand and patted him on the head.

"Of course I forgive you my child, I can easily comprehend your fixation to find favor in Lucifer's eyes, now please rise, and I just got an idea!"

God clapped his hands, causing Rofocal to jolt up. A medium sized gold harp was now at his feet.

"Take it." Yahweh recommended.

"We could use some extra music while we enjoy tea."

Yahweh snapped his fingers; a bronze stool appeared a few feet behind Me-el's ottoman.

"Can you play?" Yahweh posed.

Rofocal bowed.

"Yes I can, it would be an honor to play for all of you!" He replied.

"Good!" God expressed.

"See, no harm done Lucifer, it turned out to be for a good reason that one of your messengers showed up!"

Rofocal flew over to the stool and positioned himself. The angel commenced strumming notes of melodic serenity. Lucifer was impressed. He would have never presumed Rofocal a musician.

"Indeed Abba!" The morning star confessed.

"Rofocal is proving to be full of hidden talent!"

The messenger shyly smiled at the captain's compliment, happy he was no longer upset with him.

Yahweh shifted his attention to Me-el, the tyke had baklava and Turkish delight in one cream filled hand, and chocolate cherubim milk in the other, this was not all; Me-el had apparently developed a unique technique with his upper pair of feathered appendages. The tot skillfully used each plume on the top two wings; much like a human would use their fingers. Each of his feathers held either a cocoa dusted cherry, or a rum coated date; God's eyes widened beneath his spectacles in disbelief.

"He's a regular food *maven!" Yahweh esteemed.

"How are you Me-el?" He asked.

The gifted eater was in his armor, however unlike his older brother, he did not wear it as well. On the high ranking Lucifer it served to embellish his ravishing

* Maven: To be an expert.

presence; whereas on Me-el, it gave the child the likeness of a plump sausage ready to burst from its skin! The youth sat opened legged, as tiny tufts of white fur and plumage shot out from under his arms, waist, and neck. Me-el's ability to nosh was by no means diminished. The little angel easily continued to shove pastries in his mouth and chug down chocolate milk at warp speed.

Me-el released a small belch, and then daintily wiped his cupie doll lips with a blue satin napkin. He looked up at Yahweh and responded.

"I am marvelous Abba! Thank you for all the wonderful things to eat!"

The tot patted his gem stone covered belly, Lucifer and Yahweh fought back laughter as one third of the precious rocks ejected off the suit of arms, due to Me-el's over consumption. A sapphire clanged on Lucifer's boot, while an emerald plopped into Yahweh's tea cup. God removed the stone and wiped it clean on his robe. He positioned it on the end table between him and Lucifer. The morning star's cheeks turned pink as he sipped his tea. He did not know what to say, he felt a tad embarrassed. Me-el seemed unaffected in the least.

"Oh sorry about that, it happens a lot when I eat with my armor on," He emphasized as he reached for more baklava.

"Rofocal," Me-el pointed back to the harpist with his right upper wing.

"He always replaces the gems for me on level four."

Rofocal nodded in the child's direction.

"Sure do!" He verified.

Lucifer cleared his throat; Abba turned his gaze back to him.

"So Avi, you were telling me about some new work you assigned to Uriel."

Yahweh still floored by Me-el's strange table manners, regained his composure to finish speaking.

"Ah yes, well beloved, I have given Uriel the task of handling time! Although no angel in Heaven will ever be subjected by its effects; such as aging. I feel the concept of time will bring more balance; also, with time will come days."

Lucifer listened with avid interest. God went on.

"I suspect Uriel has come up with a seven day week by now! But here is the best part of the whole plan!"

Yahweh now pushed the end table back allowing him to lean into Lucifer. God took the morning star's hand in his.

"One special day I will have set apart just to bask in your glorious beauty! A day of repose, a Shabbat! Oh and Me-el is welcome to join us as well." Yahweh added.

Lucifer's eyes glimmered.

"I cannot wait Avi, it sounds wonderful! Spending time at your side brings me immeasurable joy! I have been so busy training on realm five and practicing music on level seven, that I barely ever look into my ring, not that I do not value it! Your notion of a day of rest is pleasing to my ears!" The light bearer exclaimed.

Yahweh lips formed a smile, he was glad to see his favorite angel so bemused. The ease dropping Me-el now fully overloaded with sweets slid off his velvet green stool; mesmerized at spending more of this thing called "Time" with Abba. The little shiny pudgy ball was now belly up on the marble floor. Me-el gradually fell into a whimsical daydream. Images of dancing, walking, talking, culinary delights seduced his mind with a catchy rhyme; Pastries of all sorts now waltzed as they serenaded:

"Eat us for a whole day soon! Eat all of us till you balloon!"

Me-el's large blue eyes closed as he hummed along with the scrumptious vision.

"It will be worth the pain of ballooning!" He thought.

Me el attempted to grasp a pirouetting chocolate chip scone with his right hand. Lucifer and Yahweh both turned to examine the perplexing gesture of the young angel, since there was actually no moon walking baked good busting a move above him; it would appear anomalous to any onlooker.

"*Nu?" Yahweh wondered.

"Whatever is he grabbing at?" Lucifer said, answering Yahweh's nu.

---

* Nu: huh

Me-el perpetually pandered until he caught hold of a monarch butterfly; with eyes still closed and the dream still going on in his brain, the child thrust it in his mouth. He purred away while licking his lips.

"Oy!" Yahweh yelped.

"Poor Seth!"

God knew each of his creatures by name, no matter how insignificant.

"Well, in his defense Avi, you did name them butterflies!"

Yahweh put a hand to his fore head and chuckled at Lucifer's reasoning.

"You got me there bubeleh!"

Chapter 16

Uriel rose from his bow to face Yahweh. The archangel had just flown into the throne room prepared to show God his first calendar drafts. The flint faced lieutenant struggled to maintain his immovable features when he tried to fathom who Abba portrayed. He was not in his paternal form, nor was he the Ruach.

"Is this Yeshua I am beholding?" Uriel pondered, he was certain it must be.

Yahweh was in a young masculine body; his skin was unlike any angel's. He also had a nicely cut beard. Yeshua's eyes were a soft hazel brown; his hair was shoulder length and dark. He wore a white robe and was approximately six foot tall. Uriel found him even more attractive than Lucifer. Yeshua smiled as he walked up to Uriel. The seraph handed him two scrolls sealed with red wax stamps. The God man carefully opened the parchments. Uriel's flaming wings gave off tiny spats of sparks as he nervously watched Yeshua survey the two drafts. After what seemed like hours to Uriel, Yeshua spoke up.

"Wonderful work! Very concise! Well done!"

Yeshua beamed at the anxious angel. He gave Uriel a wink as he rolled up the papyrus.

"I am very pleased with both calendars! I especially like how you put together the Hebrew one!"

Uriel released a sigh of relief.

"Thank you Abba, of course we can go by whichever one you like best here in Heaven."

The archangel could not take his eyes off Yeshua; he knew he was viewing God's third form. He could feel it in his crystal veins. Nevertheless, the angel remained reserved, he was all too aware of how Yahweh did not appreciate rumors spreading about what his other two personages might look like.

"I shant be Heaven's first *YENTA!" Uriel quietly evaluated.

The angel lowered his gaze as Yeshua approached him to shake his hand. Uriel a master of disguising his emotions gave Yeshua another low bow of respect, without moving one facial muscle.

"I am so glad they have found favor with you most high!" Uriel proclaimed.

Yeshua now reopened the common time calendar and gave it another once over.

"I adore how you named the days of the week on this one; I think we will use this one in Heaven for awhile." He commented.

---

* Yenta: A gossip, or busybody.

"The first day you obviously titled after my new *spodumene star, Sunday...clever...Then, what genius, you named the second day after the moon! May I ask how you got Twosday?" Yeshua inquired.

Uriel's fiery wings sputtered out to a fizzle.

"Well my lord, I am a bit leary to say...it was not one of my most candid moments. You see I had just come up with Sunday and Moonday, and, I was floundering about what to name the next one, I thought to myself, well... you bloody well got two titled! And..."

Yeshua smiled as Uriel's gold eyes shifted from side to side, in paranoia.

"Well the outcome of Twosday was as it sounds, I figured I had named two already, so the third day of the week became Twosday!" Uriel mumbled.

"I really like it!" Yeshua claimed.

"I think you are quite clever!"

Uriel's wings sprang up to full vibrant blue flames again.

Uriel was clearly relieved, his face even lit up a tad. Yeshua simpered at Uriel's unmerited worry, he was true God and true man; thus Yeshua knew beforehand what each day of the week would be called; yet, the love he had for his angelic children was so great, he permitted them to use their free will when performing various duties. With false curiosity, Yeshua resumed quizzing the star keeper.

---

* Spodumene: A gemstone known for its yellow color.

"Tell me, how did you get the names for the remaining days?"

Uriel now excited by Yeshua's obvious interest became eager to divulge more.

"Well lord, Windsday came about rather comically as well, you see while I was writing a slight breeze from Gabriel's second realm came through one of my window's I left ajar, well that breeze jolly well knocked over my ink jar! It fell and mussed some of my parchments....This well it angered me a trifle, which led to Thorsday, yet I digress, did you catch how I named Windsday after the bothersome breeze?"

Yeshua nodded and smiled.

"I rather guessed that! Please do go on with your story!" He insisted.

Uriel coughed then continued.

"Jolly good! Well as I was saying it led to Thorsday because the ink spilling caused me to pound my desk in dire frustration, I may have yelled a bit as well...I am sure Raguel could attest... I tend to scare the small bloke rather easily! Anyhow I was rather loud I suppose. My yells of torments reached Gabriel; she apparated right in front of me, apparently she assumed I had beckoned for her with my...oh how did that stitch of a sibling of mine put it? Oh yes with my thunderous voice! After observing her true concern over the whole silly matter, I got a bit of a chortle out of the whole bloody mess! I then decided to take advantage of her scholarly mind since she was already on my realm and all."

Yeshua stepped closer to Uriel. The fact that the days of the week came through a team effort pleased him immensely.

"Please don't stop!" Yeshua implored.

"Well Gabriel and I shared a hardy laugh after I told her how the fourth day of the week got its name from her unwanted wind. I got the notion of asking her if she might enjoy assisting me in naming the days that remained. She thought it brilliant! Gabriel came up with Thorsday because once more she said my hollering had reminded her of thunder, apparently my dear sibling is a sage with Pagan Mythology. She told me about a book she had read about a false God by the name of Thor who could produce thunder and lightning with a magical gold hammer. Gabriel fancied the name Thor for the fifth day, thus we got Thorsday!"

Yeshua brought up two silver stools for them to sit on.

"How studious she is!" Yeshua remarked.

"Please do go on!"

"Well Thor, I must admit, I was a bit fearful of running past you, after all you alone are God, and there is, nor ever will be another, yet Gabriel gathered you would see and appreciate the humor of it, seeing as how she would have not thought of the character unless I myself had not gotten a tad perturbed and thundered as I did."

Uriel paused to check if Yeshua was still in accordance with the decisions he and his sibling had made. The lieutenant knew they could run a risk of offending their father by using a pagan name, as far as Uriel could see; Yeshua seemed charmed by the complete discourse thus far. The archangel breathed a sigh of relief as he noticed Yeshua quietly chuckling.

"Why did you stop?" Yeshua asked with all the eagerness of a child.

A very miniscule smile crossed Uriel's lips.

"Yes well I continued to consult with Gabriel and she came up with some smashing ideas for the last two days, she really is a genius if I do say so myself. Gabriel decided to use your native language of Hebrew as a source next! Being a rabbi, she said she would not mind one day of rest from her teaching functions! Blimey I cannot say I blame her there! I'm sure my lord has been made familiar with the hooligans she handles?"

Yeshua's eyes blinked.

"I actually think all the students in Opus Angelorum are all very sweet." He challenged.

Uriel let out a fake titter.

"Oh quite so! I was just joshing...getting back to what I was saying Gabriel thought Shabbat would be perfect, since it literally means rest! I must confess lord; I too look forward to it...although as your humble lieutenant I am well aware of the fact that Shabbat was conceived of, entirely by you and for you."

Yeshua nodded in approval.

"Correct, I want a day to simply rest my eyes on Lucifer and his beauty, but please you were saying?"

"Oh I was just identifying with the notion of rest my lord, Although I do believe my little maverick Raguel will value it more since I keep him so detained polishing your stars! I even got the little blighter waxing up the moon now!"

Yeshua sniggered at Uriel's comment about Heaven's notorious repeat offender; The S.P Raguel, S.P stood for star polisher, a nick name Raguel had earned from his fellow class mates. A picture of him was posted on all nine realms of him, snoozing on a star, courtesy of Jericho. The messenger proved to be quite the artist. It read:

"Do your homework or do Uriel's!"

Yeshua handed Uriel his copy.

"Jolly good likeness wouldn't you say?" Uriel bid.

Yeshua smiled and waved his hand.

"So tell me how you both got the name for the final day." Yeshua said.

"Well we used Hebrew to name the day Shabbat, as I prelude to earlier, then Gabriel decided to use it again to come up with Sederday."

Yeshua's eyebrows rose.

"We both thought Seder felt right, especially once Gabriel reminded me that above all, you are a God of order! Why the very conception of time brings so much more clarity to our nine realms, Gabriel's reasoning was to have rest; or Shabbat, one must also have Seder or order. I do think it all turned out rather splendidly!"

Uriel jumped an inch or so off his stool, his flaming wings popping off sparks as Yeshua transformed back into Yahweh again.

"BOO!" God bantered.

He could not resist taunting the archangel a bit, as he knew Uriel adored teasing his chaya Raguel. Yahweh felt he owed it to the a.k.a S.P to give his principal a startle, he had succeeded. The stoic seraph's face went paler than usual.

"What's wrong Uriel; you can dish it out but can't take it in?"

Uriel's gold eyes fogged in awkwardness.

"You should see yourself Uriel! Come now I was only teasing, I am actually well pleased with you and all the drafts you brought up! I just thought you might want to feel Raguel's sense of fear! I know I got a good kick out of it!" Abba laughed.

Uriel arose from his stool and bowed to his creator. He had been more than a bit put off by Yahweh's strange sense of humor, yet; he was not about to let on about it.

"Thank you most high! You are quite the jokester when you want to be." Uriel stated most cautiously.

"Now then," Yahweh began.

"You my fine English angel have had the honor of observing me in all my three forms, your siblings will also see them in time...get it?"

Uriel lifted an eyebrow.

"Beg pardon lord, but did I get what?"

Yahweh now rolled his own blue eyes, Uriel was too serious.

"It's a pun on words my child! We were just discussing time and I said..."

Uriel cocked his head to the side like a dog who could not figure out a human's command.

"Oh never you mind! Just know that in time, meaning, when I wish to reveal my other forms to your siblings I will, as we discussed before when I came to you as the Ruach even if Lucifer had happened to peek in on our meeting, he would have only seen me as you now do; as the father. Uriel I need you to solemnly swear that you will not speak of my other two solid persons to any other angel! Can you promise me this?"

Uriel still a bit unnerved by Yahweh's scare fell prostrate on the marble floor. In a muffled voice he uttered:

"I assure you most high! My lips are sealed!"

"Good!" God cheerfully replied.

"Now rise, for today is Sunday! The first day of our first official week in Heaven! I thank you once more for all your dedicated effort in this project! By the way, glad you were willing to glean some of Gabriel's ideas and intermingle them with your own; this tells me you are a fine archangel! Rather than horde all the credit to yourself, you were humble enough to hearken to one of your siblings! Keep up the good work, my great star keeper!"

Yahweh kindly helped the worshiping seraph to his feet. The lieutenant gave his father a stately smile; bowed again then turned to exit the throne room and descend back to his realm.

Yahweh strolled over to his throne and waved down one of his singing seraphim.

"Ezekiel would you please come here a moment?"

An enchanting masculine angel with a big smile flew down and knelt before God.

"Yes most holy one."

"Would you please go to all the realms and distribute these."

Yahweh handed the gleaming angel a pile of small calendars. The deity had mentally concocted them after looking over Uriel's copies.

"You won't need to take any to level one; Uriel has all the information already."

"Yes most high I will do as you say." Ezekiel answered.

"Oh by the way, tell Gabriel she need not begin classes for the students until Twosday, The angels might require some adjusting to the various changes." Yahweh speculated.

"As you say most High!"

Ezekiel soared off in a dartle of shimmer.

"Shavuot tou!" God hollered, meaning; have a good week!

Lucifer's eyes reviewed the eight realms, with his ring of omnipresence. He was currently on level five with Me-el.

"I wonder when we will get our calendars from Uriel?" He said aloud.

Me-el waddled over to his older brother with curiosity. The child resembled a shiny stout tea kettle in his tight fitting armor.

"What is a calendar?" He questioned.

"Oh something to help us keep track of time, remember Abba talked to us about it at our last tea?"

Me-el's face became absorbed in thought.

"Oh yeah when we talked about Shabbat!"

"That is correct, a calendar is a piece of papyrus that displays days, weeks and months, it will be useful for you, because you will know what day school starts on!"

Me-el scowled.

"Don't worry," Lucifer offered.

"Right now we are going to practice your swords man ship!"

The captain handed Me-el an agate blue sword, as soon as Me-el took it in his chubby hands, the weapon's weight caused him to fall to his knees; just then Ezekiel arrived and passed Lucifer a new calendar.

"Thank you!" Lucifer said as the seraph bowed before descending to the next realm.

"Hey Me-el there is a note attached to this calendar from Abba, it says that even though the first week has officially begun, you will not start school until Twosday! Isn't that nice! Usually you would all be starting today which is Sunday, according to this. Me-el???"

Me-el sat on the clear diamond floor, holding the sword had not been his expertise; yet what concerned him more now was that Raguel's terrible sentence of doom had just been prolonged by God giving them an extended leave of absence from Opus Angelorum. The small angel's eyes looked gloomy.

"Poor Raguel! That means he has two more days of travesty!" He cried.

Lucifer knelt down to comfort the concerned tot.

"Oh come now Me-el, Raguel will be fine until Twosday, you'll see!"

Me-el shook his head in disbelief.

"We do not really live in time Lufi! I know it's Sunday but what about tomorrow?"

Me-el's lower lip was now trembling. Lucifer regarded his brother's troubled countenance.

"What about tomorrow? It's just two days! You shall see Raguel very soon! Whatever is the matter?" The captain persisted.

Me-el fell into a daze, as the realm went a buzz with activity. Lucifer's training area overflowed with angels practicing dueling drills. Among them was Gabriel, she was jousting with Azazel with a Falchion sword. The lieutenant lifted her shield, a signal to her partner that she needed a break. Azazel sheathed his own weapon and gave the silver armed archangel a salute. He wondered over to spar with Beleth.

"Thank ya fer thee duel fair Gabriel!" He called back.

Gabriel removed her helmet, revealing her blonde curls.

"You are most welcome Azazel!"

She was in her Anglo male form; the archangel had seen Me-el's looks of dread and decided to make sure everything was okay. Gabriel gaited over to the pair, she genuflected to Lucifer.

"Why look!" Lucifer exclaimed.

"Here is your rabbi now! Why don't you ask her about your time concerns? If anyone knows how time works in Heaven it's her! Then you can be worry free about your friend!"

Lucifer turned the reluctant youth towards Gabriel who was now standing.

"Hopefully she can calm his mind." The captain thought.

Gabriel smiled.

"Oh hi there Me-el, what can I do for you?"

Me-el elbowed Lucifer to hand over the calendar. The captain passed it to the child; he held it up to Gabriel as he stood on his tip toes.

"Well rabbi, Abba started up time..." He began from behind the paper.

Gabriel snatched the calendar to get a better gander of it.

"Oh so I see! It came out great! You know I aided Uriel in naming a few days of the week!" She giggled.

Me-el bit his lower lip in impatience; he really did not care to hear his rabbi glorify herself.

"Yeah...that's real nice...What I wanna know is, Lufi said that Abba said that us your wonderful students did not need to start school until Twosday..."

Gabriel interjected before Me-el could finish what he was going to say.

"Oh well Abba has blessed you by far! As I recall he told Uriel and me that one day is like a thousand years to him! So I will not be seeing any of you wonderful students for two thousand years! Well I'm going to go see if I can spar a bit more! See ya!!"

Gabriel flew off to start a fun brawl with one of her student's, the power Camael.

"Oh Camael shall we duel?" She called.

Lucifer picked up Me-el, and attempted to shake him back to reality. The child was shivering in horror; he resembled a chicken that had just seen it's mate get its head hacked off.

"He's toast!" Me-el sputtered.

Lucifer patted his younger brother lightly on the cheek.

"Me-el! She was joking, come now why don't we see how much progress you made with your sword?"

Me-el's eyes now glossed over, nodded with a spaced out look to him.

"Poor Raguel! What if he is not in class on Twosday because Uriel does not feed him! Lufi he could be evaporated by then!!!"

Me-el wailed so loud, that the entirety of the fifth realm halted, thinking Yahweh or Remiel had blown a shofar.

Lucifer put his brother down and addressed what had just happened.

"It was just me!" He masked.

"I was teaching Me-el a new battle cry!" He jested.

The troupe of armored angels shrugged it off and returned to their drills.

"Now, now, if we do some training it will make time go much faster, I promise! You know I never break a promise right?"

Me-el nodded and sniffled. Lucifer picked up the little angel's sword again, hoping he would take it up.

"Well I guess I will take your advice Lufi." Me-el said as he extended a portly hand to gather the shiny weapon.

"That is my Me-el! Now I'll let you get acquainted with your new sword, and I shall go have a word with Gabriel about her sense of humor, I'll be right back!"

Lucifer kissed Me-el on top of the head and soared off.

Me-el now had both hands on the sword's handle. He could barely lift it. The child curled up in a ball in effort to do so; he was reminiscent of a fat constipated kitten covered in tin foil, as he hunched down with all his strength. He barely got the weapon three inches off the reflective floor. Dumah and Molech could not help but notice the youth's struggle. They were two of Lucifer's frequent patrollers on level five. The two dominions had been clashing scimitar blades.

"Hey little Lucifer, try bending your knees more." Dumah suggested, as he blocked a swipe from Molech.

"Kay!" Me-el mumbled.

The child did as requested, only to fall flat on the floor. Me-el could not bend his pudgy knees in his armor.

"Help!" He sobbed.

Dumah raised a hand to Molech.

"Better go find the captain." He advised.

Molech halted the match, as Dumah assisted Me-el back to a standing position.

"New sword to heavy?" Dumah asked, wiping some tears from Me-el's face with a satin handkerchief from beneath his right bracer.

"I'm a lousy soldier Dumah! I will never be like Lufi!"

Dumah placed the glossy roly poly tot on his knee.

"I am sure your older brother would say otherwise!" The suave angel assured.

Lucifer swooped in, he appeared very concerned.

"Thank you Dumah, I got him," The captain tapped the angel's left red wing, smiling.

"No problem general." Dumah smiled back.

"I'll go finish my duel with Molech!"

Lucifer came down to Me-el's height.

"Hey I told Gabriel to be a bit more sensitive, she sends her apologies." Lucifer disclosed.

Me-el's lower lip hung down in a pout.

"That's nice.... But Lufi it's not why I'm firmisht!" He moaned.

Lucifer's right eye brow jolted up.

"Firmisht, that's Yiddish for disturbed, you really are quite smart!" The morning star grinned.

"Then tell me bubeleh what is wrong?"

Me-el frowned.

"It's me! Look at me! I cannot even pick up a sword! I'm *garnisht! I will never be anything like you!"

Teardrops commenced raining down Me-el's visage again. Lucifer gathered the weeping youth in his muscular arms and nuzzled him.

"Well, then that would be my fault!" Lucifer claimed.

"Nu?" Me-el gazed up at his older brother with mystified eyes.

---

* Garnisht: To be beyond help.

"Me-el, I have been to focused on making you fight and act just like me, I even made your armor identical to mine....I have been selfish. You are special, you are the only you there will ever be! You should have armor that suits you! Trust me, if you allow me to, I will make things better! Give me a chance to fix everything?"

Lucifer now formed his own luscious pink lips into a big silly pout. Me-el giggled at the captain's funny face.

"Okay Lufi, but how ya gonna do it?"

"Well," Lucifer opined as he set Me-el down to evaluate him.

"First you need some armor you can really move in! I think I'll have Nergel make you a suit hammered out of blue opal to match your eyes!"

Using his magical diadem Lucifer removed Me-el's tight fitting coat of arms and replaced it with a comfortable silk robe. Me-el's face seemed less blue now.

"You give me a few minutes and Nergel will get it right out for you!"

Me-el clapped his hands in delight as Lucifer headed towards the blacksmith shop. He could hardly wait; it was also nice to be able to breathe a tad better again.

The corpulent child squealed in glee, his new coat of arms was perfect! Lucifer gave Nergel, the smiling Blacksmith a two thumbs up.

"Thank you Nergel! It fits him spot on!"

"Not a problem good captain, call on me anytime, I hope the tyke enjoys it!"

Lucifer dismissed him, and then surveyed Me-el with joy. His little brother looked happy; Me-el's new armor was thin and flexible. Nergel had also smelted it out to be very light, almost like a second skin. The child whizzed about easily, he felt like he was wearing nothing more than his robe. Me-el soared high into the air on all six of his emerald wings, his opal blue armor emitted blue streaks of light as he whirled in loop de loops. The whole fleet of sparring angels on realm five, Gabriel included, stopped to marvel at the rampant sapphire laser ball cruising above them. Me-el truly shimmered in the lucid aquamarine suit.

"He is so fast now!" Gabriel admitted stunned by how agile her chunky student had suddenly become.

"Captain that new armor seems to have made all the difference!" She assured.

Lucifer smiled.

"Indeed, I bet he can handle any type of weaponry now too."

The morning star gazed up at his preferred brother with pride; Lucifer flung a cruciform sword Me-el's way. Gabriel winced, a sword of that caliber was usually only handled by realm five's finest fighters. Lucifer took note of Gabriel's unease.

"Worry not Gabriel, just watch!" Lucifer recommended.

Many other bystanders now gazed up to see what would happen. Dumah and Molech even dropped their scimitar blades in anticipation.

Me-el snatched the sword with all the skill of an expert base ball catcher. He grabbed it right by its helm. Every angel clapped, each one bowled over by Me-el's expertise. The child began performing well advanced swordsmanship in mid air.

"WOW!" Lucifer proclaimed.

"He must have been really studying me each time I sparred some one!"

Gabriel nodded, she was equally impressed.

"His military techniques are identical to yours my captain!" She observed.

"Me-el, come down!" Lucifer hollered.

Me-el trickled down as graceful as a petal frolicking through the air; he landed in an aesthetic manner, bowing right in front of his older brother. He looked up.

"Did you see me Lufi? I can be a good soldier!" The excited youth chided.

Lucifer gleamed at Me-el with joy. He picked him up; and smothered him with kisses.

"Yes! I saw you! So did every other angel here! My sweet Me-el, I knew you had it in you!"

"Aye!" Azazel commented.

"With lord Lucifer as your trainer and brother, ye be out brawling the whole lot of us soon!"

"I'll get you right now!" Me-el snickered.

Azazel lifted his shield as Me-el flew out of Lucifer's arms and went at him in full charge.

"Mercy!" The ruddy power pleaded, Me-el was proving to be stronger than even him!

Gabriel gave Lucifer a pat on the back.

"Well done captain, I must admit I had my doubts... but I should have never questioned your tactics! You have a fine prodigy in Me-el, forgive me again for hurting his feelings earlier, I really did not mean to." She bowed then marched away.

Lucifer called over to Me-el who now had Azazel at his knees, in a blocked position. The captain let out a small laugh, it was funny to witness a big power overwhelmed by such a small angel.

"Me-el, come here." He beckoned.

Azazel rose excogitating how the lad had gotten so good so fast.

"He really is a little Lucifer!" He sighed, as he caught his breath.

"Lufi thank you so much! I love you!" Me-el shouted.

The child sheathed his sword, and then wrapped his arms around Lucifer's right boot. The light bearer heaved him up.

"My Me-el, I am so proud of you! I better watch out!"

"Why? Is Uriel up here?" Me-el asked with panicked eyes.

"Uriel is not here. I said I better watch out, because at the rate you are going at, you might be better at dueling than me some day! You might take over my job!" Lucifer teased.

The captain hugged his brother tightly to his heart. The onlookers all applauded shouting:

"Hail Me-el! Hail lord Lucifer! The best fighters Yahweh ever created!"

Me-el cooed in amusement, even Gabriel was praising him, which really felt good.

"Lufi." The youth exclaimed.

"I want to play soldiers with you now! Can we?"

Lucifer's lips curved upwards as he reviewed the tiny patroller, he had helped mold.

"You bet!" He crooned, as he placed Me-el back on the transparent floor.

The morning star waved his gilded gauntlet to dismiss the crowd of angels.

"Go joust among your selves, I am going to spend some quality time with my newest soldier!"

The mass of glowing creatures bowed in unison as they hurried back to their sparring. Lucifer turned and bowed to Me-el in a gentleman's way. Me-el returned the gesture.

"On guard!" The son of morning expressed as he withdrew his broad sword.

Me-el procured a serious look and held out his cruciform. The two brothers began innocently scuffling. Lucifer could not help chuckling as he witnessed Me-el match his every move and attack accurately. The child's jousting ability was utterly astounding. Lucifer lost himself in thought.

"Someday." He pondered silently as he continued to duel.

"Someday Me-el you will be my co-captain! You shall supersede Gabriel, Uriel, and Raphael! You will be the greatest archangel, well; except for me of course..."

Lucifer resumed clashing swords; his mind began to imagine Me-el as a full grown seraph.

"What a spectacular specimen you will be little brother!" He inwardly deliberated.

"With my training and your God given beauty, I can easily envision you standing next to me to the south of Abba's Aurelian throne! Yes we shall make a most handsome pair!"

Lucifer now panting put up his shield, to let Me-el know he had enough and needed a break.

"That was great Me-el!" He said as he inhaled.

Lucifer shot a debonair smile at Me-el as he sheathed his sword.

"Well, why don't you head to Eden, I was looking through my ring earlier, I think Raphael is nesting his first egg!"

Me-el's eyes widened in expectation, he put his weapon away.

"Really?" He yelped.

"Yes a new angel! Oh and please remind him that I decided to do our quartet concert for Abba this upcoming Sederday; would you please do that for me?"

Me-el bowed to Lucifer before rocketing up.

"You Bet Lufi! I'll see ya later!"

"Oh Me-el." Lucifer spouted.

"Meet me back at my palace when you get through, Raphael has a sun dial on his realm, tell him to send you back my way around the third hour, he will know what that means! I love you!"

Me-el advanced upwards and blew Lucifer a kiss.

"I love you too! I will do everything you told me to I promise!" Me-el verified as he descended to Eden.

Chapter 17

Raphael hummed melodically to himself whilst tending to a trellis of pistachios; every so often the archangel would sample one.

"Mmmmm...These would make an excellent pudding!" He repined.

The lovely gardener was working as he nested an egg in his lower two wings. Raphael had ingeniously brought together his bottom pair of pinions like a feathery basinet. The five foot magenta elliptical orb rested comfortably inside; as the lambent archangel went about his tasking, the egg incubated itself securely like a human babe in its mother's arms. Every so often it would vibrate. Raphael made his way over to a doum tree, heavy with ripe ginger bread fruit. The seraph instinctively knew that by the egg's peculiar movement, it would soon be hatching.

"Hmmm I wonder who you will be." The nurturing angel mused, as he plucked an orange red ginger bread citrus.

Raphael's jade eyes scanned the foliage, a mild breeze blew through, allowing his cherry blossom trees to cascade dainty pink petals. The archangel took in a deep breath and absorbed the delicious scents of jasmine. Raphael was about to bite into his freshly picked gingerbread fruit when a loud "Kirthump!" caught him unawares, Raphael threw the whole fruit into his mouth, chewed, swallowed and traversed over to the pittosporum hedge were two familiar emerald wings were sticking out.

"Hello Me-el." The seraph said.

The lieutenant was further taken aback when the child stepped out into full view. Me-el looked nearly as radiant as one of Uriel's stars in his new flugid blue armor.

"Sorry about my landing." Me-el offered.

"I was trying to surprise you." He quietly confessed.

"Well" Raphael expressed.

"You have! You look as dashing as ever! Is that a new coat of arms?"

Me-el blushed as he politely saluted Raphael.

"Sure is! Isn't it the best?" He chimed.

"Lufi had it tailor made just for me! I can fight a lot better in it! Anyways, he's kinda busy right now, so he asked me to come down here and keep you company. He said you were nesting a new egg!" Me-el now carefully inched his way over to Raphael, he did not see any egg; he was curious as to where the seraph was hiding it.

"Where is it Rapha?" Me-el prodded.

"Don't tell me you left it alone somewhere so you could prance around snacking!" Me-el screamed.

Raphael's peaceful green eyes went into incensed slits as Me-el carried on.

"Lufi told me how sometimes you just meander around collecting honey dust and noshing on Eden's vegetation! Oh the travesty!" The alarmed child let out.

Raphael narrowed his brow in subtle annoyance.

"So...That is what Lucifer says about me. Well for your information, I am nesting the egg at this precise moment!" He contested.

"You just cannot see it." He snapped with a sneaky grin.

The admirable Raphael shook his long, dark pony tail loose. Me-el watched in wonder as the archangel's silken mane of curls flowed about, actually releasing miniscule drops of golden honey.

"So where is it?" Me-el hammered while stomping one foot. The youth was taking his mission from Lucifer very seriously, this amused Raphael.

"Oh calm down little Lucifer, come look behind my back and down at my bottom two wings." The seraph recommended.

Me-el casually pattered around the lustrous archangel, like a nosey cat. He peered into the cradle of pink plumage.

"Wow! Are you keeping it nice and cozy like that?" Me-el questioned.

Raphael smirked, he was tempted to say:

"No it's actually freezing!" However he knew better than to antagonize his captain's favorite sibling.

"Yes." Raphael admitted, as the egg began vibrating once more. This time there was extra kick to it.

"Me-el I do believe our new angel is getting ready to make itself known!" The lieutenant declared.

Me-el glanced up at Raphael with excitement.

"Neat! What sort of angel do you think it will be?" He asked.

Raphael shrugged whilst gathering his long locks back into a pony tail.

"I am not really sure, but we better head west of here to the egg patch, remember the one Yahweh sent every angel's egg to?"

Me-el appeared disappointed; he tugged at Raphael's silken robe.

"Yeah, I remember but can't we go east, to the dessert garden instead? You could let it hatch on your sponge cake field!"

Me-el smiled innocently as he batted his eyelashes.

"I'm just trying to look out for the angel Rapha," Me-el stammered.

"You know sponge cake is so nice and bouncy, and if the angel comes out small, I would not want it to bump it's head on another egg or anything."

Raphael's emerald eyes smiled at Me-el's clever reasoning, he knew Me-el really just wanted to be in the vicinity of large quantities of sweets to nosh on when the egg hatched. The enthusiastic child's eyes widened larger than a hoot owl's as he awaited Raphael's reply.

"Oh very well, but we are only doing it for the safety of the angel." He insisted.

"I shall take you up on the offer so the new angel comes out very safe, come let us fly over to the sponge cake field!" He proclaimed.

Me-el took to flight first, rapidly flapping all six of his wings; he knew his way to the dessert garden with both eyes closed.

Raphael glided rhythmically beside him, using only his first two pairs of pinions.

Upon arriving east of Eden, Raphael caught up with Me-el who was already seated on the fluffy arena of sugar, munching on cocoa fruit. The archangel roved over to the field, and tenderly unfurled his lower pair of wings. An august magenta egg rolled out onto the bouncy sponge cake field. It had grown two feet taller and wider.

"No wonder it was moving so much." Raphael theorized.

"Not only is it ready to crack open, it's gotten bigger!" He exclaimed.

Me-el now too enthralled over the egg to resume licking chocolate from his cocoa fruit, joined Raphael in scrutinizing the dark pink object. Raphael looked down at Me-el and wiped some *schmutz off his cocoa covered face.

"You wanna look your best for the new angel don't you?" He smiled.

Me-el nodded as Raphael removed some cocoa residue from his upper lip.

"Hey Rapha look it's sliding open!" He shouted.

Both Raphael and Me-el turned to face the egg. In a burst of rainbows and light a six foot male androgynous angel came forth. Raphael and Me-el stood staring spell bound. He was magnificent. Blonde tresses fell well past his shoulders, his white satin robe barely veiled his athletic body; Raphael took note of how the name, "Rahab" was stitched in gold lettering upon it.

"Hmmmmm that is usually only seen on Lucifer's messenger angels..." Raphael stipulated,

The newly hatched angel displayed fetching bronze wings and dazzling grey eyes that shined like steel.

"I am Rahab." He announced in a tenor voice; with slight sarcasm.

---

* Schmutz: something you wipe off your face.

Raphael and Me-el were equally impressed by the hatchling's conduct. He was obviously endowed with Yahweh's wisdom. Me-el tottered over to the new angel; he extended his hand to properly greet him.

Raphael saluted Rahab, it was a common courtesy for a newly hatched angel to return his nester's gesture out of respect and thanks; it had been a condition Yahweh had put into place after Lucifer had given Raphael the task of Chief Cherubim. In other words it was a standard protocol.

Rahab cocked his head to the left, like a confused puppy, as Raphael held his salute. With a flutter of his golden lashes, the angel vanished faster than a snowflake on a hot stove in July. Me-el's jaw dropped, he was confuted. Rahab had also failed to shake his hand too!

"What? He did not return your salute! He just left! There is no excuse for that Rapha he came out really smart! He even knew his name! I don't get it! He did not show you any respect!" Me-el said with a flushed face.

Raphael now stretching out his tired bottom wings did not seem overly concerned about the angel's behavior. The seraph knelt down to tear a chunk of sponge cake off the field. Raphael tore the piece of cake in halves and offered some to Me-el.

"No worries Me-el, a thank you is not necessarily a requirement for my job just a sort of polite suggestion; Rahab would only need to be concerned if he failed to not give praise to God! I know he came out way too smart to not do that!"

Raphael bit into his sweet bread while mentally relocating Rahab's egg to the egg patch, west of Eden. After he swallowed he continued speaking.

"Yes, thanks and praise to Abba is what really matters in Heaven, I'm just a humble gardener after all."

Me-el sat next to Raphael Indian style as he too began noshing on his treat. The child tried to evaluate Raphael's hidden feelings.

"If I was him, I know I would feel bad, I mean I feel like bupkes after he ignored shaking my hand!" Me-el sweat out in his mind.

"I am sure that lovely angel is presenting himself to Yahweh as we speak! As you pointed out, he came out very intelligent! He probably just wanted to get to his creator and not be bothered by our insignificant technical formalities." Raphael added in his usual cheerful way.

"I guess Rapha, but just so you know, and please do not tell Lufi I said this..." Me-el looked around to make certain no other creature who could talk was nearby.

"Next to Lufi, you are my second favorite brother! If you would have nested me, well I not only would have saluted, I would have hugged you too!"

Raphael's green eyes twinkled. Me-el had touched his heart.

"Thank you my little pomegranate! I am rather found of you myself! Now," The seraph lifted up a single finger.

"I got something on my belt that makes this sponge cake taste even better than what it already does! Are you interested?"

Me-el nodded with hungry eyes.

"You bet!" He assured.

Raphael smiled taking a small crystal flask from a velvet purple pouch on his belt; the receptacle's contents consisted of a bright red liquid. Me-el watched as the archangel twisted a cork off the vessel, and poured a few dabs of the substance on each of their portions. Me-el sniffed it, than shoved it in his mouth.

"Mmmmm! That's wonderful!" He mumbled as he spewed out tiny remnants of cake.

"What is that?"

Raphael tucked the clarion beaker back into his belt pouch.

"Juice from strawberries." He related.

"I found it goes along excellently with sponge cake, or as Yahweh calls it, Angel food cake!"

Me-el spit out the food in his mouth, his eyes quivering in disgust.

"Angel food cake! You mean we are eating other angels! Rapha how could you let me be a cannibal!" Me-el shouted.

Raphael began laughing so hard he choked.

"Me-el it's not really made out of angels, Abba calls it that because it is light and fluffy!"

Me-el's face took on a look of relief.

"I knew that, I just wanted to see you laugh!" He bid.

Raphael cleared his throat, than finished up his piece. Me-el got closer to his sibling and remembered what else he was supposed to remind him about. He poked Raphael on his top right wing.

"Yes, what is it? You want more cake?" He kindly asked.

Me-el thought about saying yes, yet resisted and got down to brass tact's.

"Ummm no, it's Lufi, he wanted me to remind you that the special archangel quartet concert for Abba will be this Sederday. I think he's going to have me play an instrument or something."

Me-el stated as he mulled over what he might be doing at the performance.

"Well," Raphael expressed as he grabbed some more sponge cake.

"That sounds great! I can hardly wait, I really enjoy singing."

Me-el thumped his fore head with his free hand.

"What's wrong?" Raphael quizzed.

"I am supposed to leave at the third hour! Is your sundial anywhere around here?"

Raphael closed his eyes and zoned in to the north of Eden where the sun dial was located. Using his angelic vision, he reopened them after catching a glimpse of the time.

"You have fifteen minutes before the third hour, I am sure you will make it back to Lucifer in fifteen seconds! Especially now that you have that nice new armor!" Raphael winked.

Me-el saluted then bowed towards Raphael, before taking to flight.

"Thank you for everything Rapha! I can't wait for you to hatch another egg!" Me-el disclosed as he ascended.

Raphael waved goodbye to the child as he left his view. The enticing archangel stretched out all six of his wings and flopped backwards onto the squishy sponge cake.

"I know I am in no hurry to hatch another one!" He whispered to himself. The seraph shut his eyes to nap. As the lambent angel drifted to sleep, a cluster of multi colored dragon flies encircled him; their whizzing wings lulled him to his slumber. Raphael dozed off only to find himself in his same monotonous dream yet again.

"He is no more….." The baffling angel spoke.

In his reverie Raphael turned to see the enigmatic exquisite archangel, he stood next to Abba's throne and wept a single tear. This time he looked Raphael right in the eyes.

"I have lost him...."

Raphael could not take his gaze off the dashing seraph, he was truly alluring; like no other angel in Heaven he had ever seen.

"Who?" Raphael asked, hoping to solve the mystery of his repeating vision.

"I loved him, I really loved him!"

The spell binding angel of Raphael's dream began fading from his sight. Raphael witnessed another glorious entity seat itself on the throne, once more it was not Yahweh. Raphael squint his eyes attempting to make out who or what it might be; yet it proved useless, the figure was enveloped in light.

"Who are you two? Why do I fail to recognize you both? How can I help you if I do not know who either of you are?"

The throne room went pitch black, a streak of lightning jolted from the south side of God's throne all the way down past Uriel's first realm. Moans erupted from all around. Raphael awoke.

"That is bizarre! I never had such a realistic dream! I wonder who that angel is. Does he even exist?"

Raphael rose and decided to go check on his egg patch.

"Maybe he has yet to hatch." He contrived.

"Yet who could be the stranger on Father's throne?" He thought.

"Every angel knows only God himself may sit there... Yet I cannot say who was sitting on it!"

Raphael shook his head mystified at his own whirling theories.

"It was just a dream!" He told himself.

Chapter 18

Me-el landed just outside Lucifer's glimmering palace, copious amounts of messengers parted like the red sea as the small distended future archangel hobbled to the doorway.

"Greetings Me-el!" Rofocal smiled, giving the toddler a slight bow as he flew by.

Me-el saluted the cordial messenger, he was ready to rush inside and give Lucifer a big hug; until something unusual drew his attention away.

Rahab the angel he had just witnessed come out of his egg not too long ago in Eden, was bowing before Lucifer's throne. Me-el could not believe it.

"He should be with Abba! Unless... maybe he already went to praise God...yeah I bet that must be it." The child decided.

Me-el entered levitating so he would not make any sound; he carefully hid his semi bovine body as best he could behind a tall crystal pillar.

"Maybe Yahweh sent him down to Lufi." Me-el determined.

The child was interested to see how his older brother would handle the new angel, or what duties he might give him. Me-el simply loved to snoop. Lucifer sat majestically on his vitreous throne, a look of mystified bewilderment coated his finely sculptured face; his blue eyes practically sparked fire.

"Lufi does not look to happy!" Me-el appraised in secret.

Lucifer heightened, extended all twelve of his wings and thundered:

"Why have you insulted my beloved father by coming to bow before me first? Art thou so dim, that you do not know that every newly hatched angel must go pay homage to Yahweh first!?"

Me-el quivered behind his hiding spot; glad he was not the object of Lucifer's bad mood.

"So I was right!" The child evaluated.

"I hope he's ready for a scolding!"

Me-el was not at all surprised by Rahab's lack of priorities; after all the hatchling had also neglected to salute Raphael or even give him a thank you. Rahab now feeling uncomfortable rose timidly to his feet. He began fidgeting his hands.

"Forgive me lord Lucifer, for some reason I felt led to come praise you first." He stuttered nervously.

Lucifer's eyes flickered in aggravation; he then noticed something he had not taken into account before.

The angel's name was branded on his garment, much like those of his messengers.

"Could he be a messenger?" The son of morning deliberated.

Lucifer dismissed the notion.

"No, Yahweh would not bother to hatch any messengers...He is way above me, the very concept is preposterous!" Lucifer thought.

The captain now took a step towards the bustling angel; a look of indignation swept over the light bearer's visage.

"Rahab you have acted foolishly! Yet I am by no means Yahweh, so I cannot punish you! Go now to realm nine; present yourself to Abba our most high father pay homage to him! For he alone deserves all the glory! After that perhaps I will receive you back here, if and only if you find favor and forgiveness in my father's eyes! Understood?"

The morning star concluded his admonishment on a softer note; he brought in all his pinions and reseated himself. Rahab nodded, bowed then darted out of the palace.

Me-el hesitantly came out from hiding, Lucifer's countenance transformed into pure joy as he noticed his little brother coming his way.

"Me-el!" The seraph bellowed cheerfully.

"So glad you are back!" Lucifer realized Me-el seemed a bit shaken.

"Don't worry bubeleh, Rahab will be fine, I just need to be sure every angel has their heads on right! We all must give all laud and honor to Yahweh above anything or anyone else!"

From his glitzy throne, Lucifer patted his lap, hinting for Me-el to come hop up on it. Me-el jumped onto his older brothers knees and threw his arms around him. Lucifer bounced the tyke up and down, causing Me-el to laugh; the child's voice rang through the palace like a strand of silver bells in the wind.

"So," Lucifer began.

"I have met Rahab, how is Raphael? Did you remind him about the concert like I asked you too?"

"Yup!" Me-el asserted, pleased he had done his job correctly.

"Good!" The morning star quipped.

Me-el rubbed his chin with his tubby sausage link fingers, portraying the picture of someone in deep thought.

"What is it bubeleh?" Lucifer asked.

"Well," Me-el disclosed.

"If you four are gonna do most of the singing at Abba's concert, what exactly are you gonna have me do?" The preoccupied child presented.

Lucifer ran his fingers through Me-el's auburn curls and speculated.

"Well I was thinking you might play your tambourine, or perhaps fly above us as we sing; you could do some nice air dance formations now that you have your new armor. Which one sounds good to you?"

Me-el jumped off his brother's lap, his arms crossed and eyes serious.

"I would personally love to show Abba how much better I fly now with the new coat of arms you had made for me! I bet I will really surprise him!" He sang.

Lucifer snapped his fingers.

"I agree with you! Abba will most certainly be delighted at all your progress! I think I shall have Rofocal place some nice silk ribbons on golden poles, so you can hold them in your hands when you do your flying maneuvers! You shall soar among the ninth realm as brilliantly as one of Uriel's comets!"

Me-el embraced his older brother's left leg.

"I can't wait Lufi! You always have the best ideas!"

Lucifer patted Me-el's head.

"We will have a wonderful time!" The captain assured.

Whilst Lucifer and Me-el were going over the details of the upcoming archangel quartet; Rahab lay prostrate on Elohim's marble floor in front of his throne.

Yahweh was well informed of how this angel had unusually given praise to Lucifer before paying homage to him. The creator's refined hands stroked his silver beard in perplexment. He was absolutely *fertummect.

"What," God silently contemplated.

"What would cause any fresh angel to act so meshuggina?"

As Yahweh continued rolling the situation around his triune mind, he could see the creature was very penitent. Rahab whimpered for mercy as he lay face down on the ground.

"OY! Enough child! Rise I forgive you, I can see you are sorry."

Rahab up cast himself, keeping his gaze down; it was then that God became aware of the title engraved in thread on the angel's alb.

"Oy vey! You are a messenger!" The flabbergasted deity expressed.

"Pardon me most high?" Rahab said, his grey eyes flashing in panic.

Yahweh frowned as the poor creature's lower lip began trembling. God approached the angel and gave him a hug. Rahab calmed in the father's bosom, his nerves no longer marbled.

---

* Fertummect: Confused.

"Listen my child." Yahweh exhorted as he placed his hands on Rahab's shoulders and looked him straight in the eye.

"I see you are a messenger! The gold embedded name tag on your stole makes that quite clear!

Your breed of angels were originally formed by Lucifer himself! You are the very first of your kind to hatch directly from one of my own cherubim! Thus you're dashing appearance; you are a bit fancier than any messenger created by Lucifer himself, for example; you are the first of your flock to have long hair!"

Rahab blinked, he did not fully understand.

"Rahab as a messenger you are required to serve Lucifer on realm four! That is your top job! The fact that Lucifer was originally responsible for creating your rank of angels; just might be the key as to why you felt compelled to go worship before him first!"

Rahab retained a blank look on his face, as God resumed to explain.

"You see bubeleh, since you are a messenger that means your primary function is to serve on Lucifer's realm. Yet you were hatched from a cherubim egg; well, I feel this may have clouded your judgment. You poor dear!"

Yahweh caressed one of the messenger's bronze wing's making Rahab purr.

"No more worries!" Yahweh smiled.

"By your actions I can see you now got your priorities in order! You have paid me proper praise and have received my full forgiveness!"

Yahweh dug his right hand into an invisible pocket on his robe, pulling out a small scroll, stamped with a flat red wax mark.

"Now take this with you and go back to level four to serve your captain. Everything we just discussed is catalogued in the contents of this parchment. I'm sure when Lucifer reads it, he shall put you straight to work without further delay. There are no hard feelings to preoccupy yourself about!" Abba grinned.

Rahab bowed low to God then took the sealed scroll.

"Thank you Yahweh, all praise and glory be to you alone forever more!"

The messenger rang as he obeyed and descended downward.

"Simple mistake!" Yahweh concluded.

Rahab landed in the outer quart yard of Lucifer's realm. He began analyzing his surroundings, myriads of messengers encompassed him. All the angels on the fourth level wore robes quite similar to his. Rahab was unique in more than one aspect. Aside from his lavish locks, he was also taller by at least a foot and his wings were bronze, rather than gold. Every one of Lucifer's cookie cut messengers were beautiful, yet they all had the same short cropped army style hair. They fluttered to and fro performing various tasks; they were all quite synchronized in their performance; almost robotic.

"Do they even see me? They all look so animatronic!" Rahab conceived.

Just as the very thought passed through Rahab's mind, a smiling messenger with the name Rofocal printed on his alb, bounced gleefully towards him and waved.

"Hello I am Rofocal, as you might see!" The friendly angel pointed at his name.

"I saw you fly in, are you a power visiting from realm six? If you are I bet one of us made your robe! It's an obvious guess since your name is spelled out on it! Am I right?" Rofocal snickered.

Rahab shook his head.

"No friend, I have just come from level nine, our most high father told me I was one of you! A messenger; Abba said my job was to serve lord Lucifer here with the rest of you."

Rofocal skipped back a few paces upon hearing Rahab's declaration.

"You must be a hatched messenger! It would explain your regal appearance! In case you have not noticed, we all kinda look alike around here, except for our eye color. Oh; and Jericho, he has a gold streak that runs down the right side of his head."

Rofocal took in Rahab with interest; he was tall and quite attractive. Rofocal felt a bit intimidated by having an angel of his own rank look so much more appealing than any of them on the forth realm. It was a tad unsettling.

"I guess my yellow eyes are all that help me stand out." Rofocal sighed.

"But enough about that come follow me! I will escort you to the captain, he and Me-el are both in the palace. Now just so you know, Me-el is Lucifer's prize gem! He's a little angel in bright blue armor, with lovely emerald wings, a future archangel and seraph. Perhaps you may have seen him."

Rofocal mentioned as he looked over his shoulder towards Rahab who was behind him. Rahab's wings cringed as he flew, he had seen Me-el, Rofocal had just described the same small angel whose hand he had refused to shake earlier.

"How could I have been so foolish?" Rahab silently admonished himself.

As both messengers arrived at the door way of the palace, Rahab began longing he could simply evaporate. Rofocal turned to look at him, taking notice of his fellow angel's apprehension.

"Everything okay Rahab?" He asked.

"Rofocal I am ashamed to admit I did meet that child! Upon my hatching, he tried to greet me and I ignored him! There was also a ravishing seraph crowned with roses who saluted me; I failed to properly return his gesture! I do not fully know why I acted the way I did... How could I have made so many idiotic mistakes! What if little Me-el has informed lord Lucifer of all I neglected to do? He most certainly will not like an angel like me on his realm!"

Rahab bowed his head low with strife and guilt.

"I do not deserve to serve him!" He wailed.

Rofocal put a hand on Rahab's shoulder to comfort him.

"Come now, in all fairness you are the first of our kind to hatch from one of God's own cherubim, and; if Yahweh has forgiven you, I am sure Lucifer will do likewise! Besides, that other archangel you saw; the pretty one that nested you, that would be Raphael.

He is known for being the seraph with the sweetest disposition in all of Heaven! Raphael never holds on to a grudge, as for Me-el, well, I am certain Lucifer will help clear things up in that department! Our captain is actually quite soft hearted. Sometimes he can yell or scream, yet no sooner than he does; He becomes vehemently apologetic. Now enough of your worry! Lucifer and Me-el are right through this door way. I will hold your hand if it helps."

Rahab nodded, he swallowed the lump in his throat and took Rofocal's palm. Together they entered the glass dwelling.

Lucifer's nimble fingers danced across the keys of his mystic topaz grand piano. Me-el sat next to him on the nicely crafted crystal bench, topped with a red velvet cushion.

"I have just composed a new hymn for Abba." Lucifer said as Me-el cozied up closer to him. The morning star began singing in his hypnotic voice.

(Sounds like: "Yahweh I know you are near.")

"*Yahweh I hold you so dear.... I'll be always at your side.....*"

Lucifer's golden vocals resounded throughout the realm. God himself shed tears of joy as he watched from his sea of glass. The ethereal lyrics were enchanting his ears. Lucifer picked up on the next stanza:

"*Oh I love you soooo.......... You are my love everlasting........*

Rofocal and Rahab stood enraptured as they walked into Lucifer's piano room. Rofocal gave Rahab a jab with his elbow and interjected;

"His voice is by far the most tantalizing! Tell me if any other angel has ever sounded lovelier?" The messenger related.

Rahab nodded in complete agreement.

"Yes" He asserted.

Rahab felt his heart pump faster as he spoke.

Me-el's keen eyes shifted over to the pair.

"Messenger and Rahab in the music room!" He taunted.

Me-el held out a chubby finger towards the two. Lucifer yielded his melody, and rose from his bench. Rofocal and Rahab fell to their knees in reverence.

"Rofocal I see you have come with Rahab. Rahab I have witnessed how you went and paid proper praise to our father. I saw it all in my ring. Abba has forgiven you, so I do as well. Now tell me what can I do for you both?"

Rahab was confused, if Lucifer had seen everything, why did he not already know why he was in his palace.

"I thought you would know my lord." He timidly answered.

The light bearer raised an eyebrow.

"My ring of omnipresence allows me to view all I want to, however I cannot hear anything that is spoken or thought by any angel, nor by God, in fact I usually do not even bother to look into realm nine, yet I did so this once to make certain you were doing as you were instructed to. So; tell me what is it I may do for the two of you?"

Lucifer seemed in good humor, but Me-el glared at Rahab with accusing eyes. Rofocal urged the frightened Rahab to speak. The new messenger rose hesitantly and took a few steps forward; trying to ignore the little angel's disgruntled face.

"My captain, Yahweh sent me back here and....He told me to give you this." Rahab nervously withdrew the scroll God had given him from behind his left ear. Me-el's eyes lit up with fascination; as Lucifer slowly unrolled the papyrus and read it through.

"Well!" Lucifer exclaimed.

"You are a messenger! I had a slight inkling you might be...but I was not completely sure." The captain looked Rahab up and down.

"So you are the first of your rank to come from one of Abba's cherubim! I must say this would explain why you are so easy on the eyes. Our father spared no expense when he formed you! For a low ranking angel you are quite becoming!"

Me-el joined his older brother in scrutinizing Rahab.

"He's okay looking..." Me-el put in.

"But he could have way better manners!" He spurted out sarcastically.

Rahab lowered his head again as Rofocal fought back a chuckle.

"Me-el whatever are you referring to?" Lucifer asked.

Me-el crossed his arms and stood up straight, he was all too ready to hash this matter out.

"Well Lufi, it might interest you to know that when this pretty angel hatched; he completely ignored Raphael! He did not salute or even say thank you! And... This is really the most disturbing part, get ready..."

Me-el began thumping his left foot in anger.

"He did not want to shake my hand! Me your most wonderful little brother!"

The tyke finished his heavy nagging with a pout.

"It is all true lord Lucifer!" Rahab said as he collapsed onto the relucent floor groveling.

"I am so sorry little one! And if your lordship desires I will fly down to Eden straight away to beg Raphael to forgive me as well!"

Lucifer lips made a slight pucker.

"Please get up Rahab. Me-el..." Lucifer turned to face his riled up younger sibling.

"Come now Me-el please be a bit more compassionate to our new friend. After all, Yahweh has forgiven him; should we both not strive to act just as our father does?"

Me-el gazed up at Lucifer; sorry he had made a spectacle of himself.

"You are right Lufi, I forgive you Rahab." The child professed.

Me-el extended his right hand to the new messenger, this time Rahab kissed it.

"Good!" Lucifer uttered.

"Rise now Rahab, since you are such a stately creature, I shall make you my own personal palace butler!"

Rahab stood shocked by the captain's words; Rofocal sneered at his companion.

"I knew the lord would favor him because of his beauty!" Rofocal ruminated.

Rofocal had always envisioned himself as Lucifer's own go to guy. Lucifer's brilliant eyes scintillate, as he beheld Rofocal's negative reaction.

"Rofocal," The mighty seraph spoke.

"I will make you Rahab's supervisor! After all no one knows my home better than you! You shall both be in charge of all my personal indoor needs! I do hope that sits well with you?"

Rofocal could have leapt in jubilation, but he simply bowed.

"I accept, and I would be most honored to my lord! You can rest assured I will train Rahab well! Why, by this time tomorrow he shall have every nook and cranny of your palace memorized! He will be able to sift through everything blindfolded if you so desire!"

Rahab coward at Rofocal's proposition; Lucifer noticed.

"Oh that will not be necessary my friend! I trust you will be a good manager! Why don't you begin by giving him a tour of the place, afterwards, report back to me if there are any questions or concerns." Lucifer emphasized.

Both messengers bowed then exited the piano room. Lucifer felt a tug at his lower right wing. It was his little brother.

"Yes Me-el?"

The small angel looked up at his sibling with both arms crossed once more.

"You should have made him wear a blind fold!" He grunted still feeling a bit jilted.

Lucifer chortled and scooped him up in his arms.

"Well, maybe you can take him through the grounds that way once he gets to know the place a bit better!" The light bearer laughed as he rubbed noses with his brother.

"I will remember that!" Me-el affirmed.

The child still felt Rahab should have been required to apologize to Raphael, but he was not about to tell Lucifer how to do his job, he was just a kid.

Whilst that thought was going through Me-el's mind; down on the third level Raphael was taking inventory of the new eggs in his patch. Rahab's being one of them; as Raphael walked by the magenta egg, a strange nausea spread throughout all his senses. The archangel passed it off as indigestion from noshing on so many rum coated figs. He resumed reviewing the latest additions. Fortunately, Raphael had only nested one so far.

"Maybe that's why going by his egg made my *kishka hurt!" He speculated.

---

* Kishka: Belly.

Chapter 19

Twosday was now in full swing, Gabriel stood in front of her class eager to begin teaching. Her eyes swiveled to the three desks in the front row, an angel was missing.

"Oh dear!" She cerebrated.

"I forgot to tell Uriel to release Raguel from his detention!"

Me-el was in straits! He sunk low into his chair imagining the worst.

"Travesty!" He whimpered.

Me-el was certain Uriel had made Raguel eat so much air that he had now popped him like a balloon! The vexed child buried his head inside his folded arms on his desk top. Samael wanted to comfort him, but resisted.

"Poor Raguel!" He moaned.

Gabriel was feeling guilty over Me-el's concern; so she gestured to the seraphim Razziel. He was a large angel who enjoyed sitting way in the back. The athletic student took note of his rabbi's signal and lumbered over to her desk.

"Oy vey! I bet she's gonna get on me about my bad writing again!" Razziel gloomed.

On his last assignment Gabriel had left several comments on his paper about having neater pen men ship. Razziel did not comprehend what the big deal was since all his grades were very good. He approached Gabriel's desk.

"S'up Rabbi?"

Gabriel pretended not to take in Razziel's improper use of grammar, she was much to agonized by Me-el almost having a *plotz in front of her.

"Razziel would you please fly down to realm one and tell Uriel he may dismiss Raguel so that he can come join us for class?"

Razziel gave her a salute.

"Sure no prob, I'm on it!"

"He would be one of my honor roll students if he learned how to accurately communicate!" Gabriel grumbled under her breath as the jock soared out of the room.

"Okay everyone." The rabbi commenced.

"Please take out your Hebrew texts, today we will be reviewing."

---

* Plotz: Stroke.

Me-el raised his hand. Gabriel surveyed the child with apprehensive eyes; she already knew what his question was going to be.

"Yes Me-el."

Me-el cast a sad puppy dog face her way.

"Is Raguel ever coming back rabbi?" He implored.

Jericho sniggered from behind.

"Poor chubby!" He jeered.

Gabriel shot the messenger a stern look of disapproval, he silenced himself. Me-el let out a tiny whimper.

"Calm down Me-el your friend will be joining us shortly, I just had Razziel go down to level one to bring him back up!" She smiled.

Me-el sat up straight now. He felt more focused and alert. Raguel was okay! That morning when he had heard Remiel sound the shofar, he had packed a pouch full of sugar powdered walnuts and figs in his book sack; he knew his malnourished comrade would be ever so famished!

"He probably lost another two whole pounds!" Me-el fretted.

Me-el took out his Hebrew book and began going over his notes; his mood had gone from extremely worried to calm.

Uriel was filling ink jars when Razziel knocked on his palace door, for once the star keeper had it closed.

"Come in." He mumbled.

The principal was concentrating on not spilling any liquid on his table or scattered papers.

"Ahhh, hail lieutenant, I'm Razz, a student from Opus Angelorum."

Uriel topped off the jar he had just filled, a rush of excitement entered him. Gabriel had sent him another star polisher! The archangel turned to see a huge *shlub of a seraphim.

"He's bloody bigger than me! Well that's quite alright, I shall simply have him polish the sun! Or; he could also wind all those ghastly tall grandfather clocks!" Uriel reasoned as he sized him up.

"What pray tell; landed a lug like you here?" Uriel pried.

Razziel put up his hands in a defense position.

"No way I come in shalom! I was just sent to pick up the S.P Raguel, the little fat angel. I guess rabbi wants him back in class." The hulking youth stammered.

Uriel could not help but sneer, it delighted him immensely that he could intimidate such a large angel.

"Jolly good! Wait here and I shall fetch the little pop n fresh muffin for you straight away!"

---

* Shlub: Sloppy.

Razziel bowed, his silver hair wisped over his lavender eyes; as Uriel went past him.

"He is kinda a lot a bit scary!" Razziel thought to himself.

Uriel floated out into the vastness of his realm.

"Now where is that little ham?" He wondered.

The archangel scanned the numerous stars; his eyes landed on a sputtering meteorite. Uriel wobbled his head; Raguel was face down on top of it snoring!

"Hey you! Get up!" Uriel shouted.

"Your rabbi wants you back in class! I suppose my stars do look a trifle brighter. It shall simply have to do! After all I assume you will be coming down again, now away with you before I decide to personally prolong your stay! One of your fellow miscreants came to collect you! He's waiting for you at my palace!"

Raguel sat up with ample sized eyes, he hurriedly soared over to Uriel and handed him the silk varnishing cloth he had been using.

"Yes sir!" He chimed while saluting.

"That's lieutenant to you! Now go find that bloke who came to get you, before I make a decision to detain you both!" Uriel bellowed.

Razziel who could hear every syllable Uriel roared out, came flying out speedily and took Raguel by the hand.

"I got him lieutenant! You have a nice day!"

Uriel could not resist putting in another two cents.

"Yes! Off with the pair of you gits! Remember to mind your rabbi! If you fail to I am always ready for you!" He snarled.

The two angels flew off like a couple of life flight helicopters at maximum speed. Uriel began convulsing in laughter at how fast they left.

"I really do rather enjoy my job!" He simpered.

"If only poor Raguel and the others knew....stars, moon, and sun never actually require polishing!"

Uriel continued chuckling as he wiped tears of amusement from his golden eyes.

"Well back to my office work." He gathered, as he transferred back over to his palace.

Razziel glanced over at Raguel with startled eyes.

"Oy! Ya weren't kiddin! That Uriel really is a drill sergeant! I don't think I would have lasted a minute with him! He's like totally not nice! Raguel you got major chutzpa for putting up with him as long as you did! Just so ya know if Jericho ever gives you a hard time again, you can count on me to have your back! I like totally respect you now!" Razziel offered.

Raguel's eyes twinkled, he had earned a reputation. He found himself feeling more confident.

"Thanks! I can't wait to be back in school!" He confirmed.

Razziel gave Raguel a puzzled look as they landed on realm eight.

"He's gotta be nasty if school sounds good!" The imperial seraph conjured.

"Rabbi is a real stickler! Especially if she cannot read your writing!" Razziel thought.

Razziel found himself completely confounded when he witnessed Raguel skip merrily into Opus Angelorum; like it was Thorsday.

"I better work on my calligraphy! Rabbi Gabriel might be in one of her moods one day and have me sent down to Uriel for failure to improve my writing skills!" He deliberated as he followed the younger angel in.

Me-el's face shined as he saw Raguel stroll into class and take his usual spot left of him. Samael let out a tiny smirk.

"Glad I never get in trouble!" He contemplated.

Gabriel who was currently behind her desk pivoted to address the assembly.

"Good to have you back with us all Raguel! Oh Razziel..."

The rabbi paused as the tall seraph stride in.

"Thank you for retrieving him, by the way meet with me after today's class, your penmanship is deplorable! You also need to improve the way you speak!"

Razziel grimaced and gave his rabbi a bow as he returned to his seat way at the back of the class room.

Me-el fist bumped Raguel.

"You prevail!" Me-el said in a hushed tone.

"I sure did!" Raguel sighed, a bit taken aback to see his book on Hebrew already on his desk.

"Gabriel had a virtue from Eden bring your book up for you." Me-el communicated.

"She is actually being sorta nice today! We just gotta review!" He added.

Raguel opened his text. Gabriel seemed satisfied that the prodigal was reading for once rather than gabbing.

"Alright everyone, as I stated earlier, today will be a study period of sorts, however, I will assign homework before the shofar sounds at the third hour."

A wave of groans emanated from the rows of students. Me-el began helping Raguel get acquainted with the Hebrew alphabet, while Samael started going over the several different vowels incorporated into the language.

"Well," Gabriel analyzed.

"It would seem my youngest angels are diligently making good use of their extra time!"

Razziel rolled his eyes and commenced practicing spelling his Hebrew letters out at a more intelligible rate.

"Hopefully if I work on my spelling technique now, she won't...I mean she will not keep me to long after class!" The sulking seraph repined.

"Looks like chicken scratches!" Some angel expressed.

Razziel gave Camael a provoked stare.

"You mind your own business! At least my name does not sound like one of the weirdest looking animals in our library picture books!" Razziel bantered back.

"Everything okay back here?"

The two students nodded in unison, their rabbi had teleported to the end of the rows without their knowledge.

"We are totally...I mean we are doing just fine Rabbi!" Razziel smiled.

Gabriel tapped her ruler on his desk.

"Your letters look like chicken scratches Razziel, please resume scribing until your lettering is comprehensible!"

Camael giggled as visible steam came out of Razziel's ivory ears.

"Oh how would either of them know what chicken scratches look like? Yahweh has not even created one yet! They only exist in our freaking picture books!" Razziel fumed inwardly.

Lucifer was scoping out level eight with his ring of omnipresence.

"My Me-el! What a fine young angel you are turning out to be, I can see he is helping out that chaya Raguel catch up on all the home work he missed."

The morning star's gaze now curiously scanned over the ninth realm, this was most uncommon for Lucifer; yet lately he had been looking in on the Throne room more than usual. When he had first gotten his ring, he had made a firm decision to never invade Yahweh's privacy.

"I suppose a little peek now and then won't bother him." Lucifer presumed.

God always aware of when his son of morning was secretly spying on him blew him a kiss from his sea of glass. Lucifer's eyes flickered.

"Whoops Hello Abba, I love you!" He said aware his father could hear him.

Lucifer watched as Yahweh winked and blew him yet another kiss.

"I really should keep to my own eight realms..." Lucifer confessed.

Rofocal and Rahab's rustling wings and robes made the captain look away from his ring. The two messengers were kneeling low before him.

"At ease, you may both rise; what is it I can do for you?" Lucifer asked.

"If it would be well with my lord," Rofocal started.

"Rahab and I would like permission to go to level six, Jerusalem. We know our lord has a private concert for our most high father coming up soon, this Sederday. We were hoping to go acquire some fine linen and ribbons to begin working on your attire as well as Me-el's, for the event."

Lucifer nodded with approval.

"That is a great idea!" He affirmed.

"Please go do as you wish! Just so you both know my choir robe should be white with a pearl like sheen. I want Me-el dressed in a dark ocean blue. The ribbons should be of every color! From russet, plum and lemon! You see I am going to have the two of you twist them on two golden poles for Me-el to use when he does his dance formations for Abba! It will be like he is holding a rainbow in each hand as he flies!" The light bearer excitedly proclaimed.

Rofocal nodded as did Rahab.

"Most certainly!" Rofocal avowed.

All the while on realm eight, Gabriel's outdoor sundial was quickly approaching the three o clock time.

"Okay every angel." She articulated.

"The third hour is now falling upon us! We are approaching the end of today's session, for tomorrow, I would like all of you to identify every plant, fruit, and flower in Eden!"

Raguel looked at Me-el with hazed eyes.

"She is relentless!" He whispered.

Samael raised his hand as the rest of the class groaned.

"Yes Samael?" Gabriel acknowledged.

"Rabbi where should we write down all our findings?"

"Ahhh glad you brought that up!" Gabriel quipped.

The lovely rabbi clapped her hands; every desk was now furnished with thick gold bound note books.

"You may all catalogue your entries in these journals! My gift to each of you!"

Razziel leafed through the bulky blank book.

"Oy! More writing!" He fretted.

"I would appreciate it if all of you were on your best behavior while doing your research on Raphael's realm. Just so you all know I have given him permission to send any of you down to Uriel if you somehow manage to distract him from his duties!" Gabriel said with a cynical half smile.

Raguel snatched up both of his books, he was not about to mess up another assignment. His arms were still sore from all the stars he had polished.

"Okay." Gabriel went on.

"Off you all go, except Razziel, we have some things to go over together!"

A torrent of:

"Oys and ooooooohs, with some Ummmmmsssssssss!"

Echoed throughout the room as the angels rose from their seats in unity; tentatively heaving the new silver spiraled auric portfolios along as they were dismissed.

Before he left the class room Raguel went over to Razziel who had yet to get up off his chair.

"Whatever you do, just remember rabbi is always right! Stick with that and she will go easier on you!" The tubby tyke advised.

"Thanks little S.P!" Razziel winked.

Once outside the school, Raguel caught up to Me-el who was patiently waiting for him.

"What were you doing?" Me-el inquired, as he passed his friend the bag of goodies he had brought for him.

Raguel accepted it all too readily.

"Oh that big angel who came and got me, the one Rabbi "Wretched" kept after class; I was just giving him a few tips on how to steer clear of old drill sergeant!" He divulged while dumping the entire contents of the pouch into his mouth.

Me-el cased his surroundings.

"So, now that you brought up the mean tin can Uriel, how did it go down there? I mean what did "IT" make you do?"

Raguel chewed, swallowed then belched louder than Remiel's shofar which had just blasted.

"Me-el let's just say I will never sing "Twinkle Twinkle Little Star" ever again!" Raguel pledged, as he wiped sugar off his lips.

Me-el shook his head.

"To think that used to be your favorite song! He has scarred you for life!"

Raguel nodded in absolute confirmation.

"At least our next assignment is in Eden!" Me-el chimed.

"After all the terrible travesties you suffered, you need to re nourish yourself! Luckily Raphael just loves us!"

The two slightly elephantine youths took to flight together. Gabriel, who was overhearing the conversation on the sly; chuckled, then went back inside Opus Angelorum to retrieve her own belongings.

"Those two never fail to keep things entertaining up here!" She laughed.

Chapter 20

Lucifer sat sipping red wine at his banquet table. Rofocal and Rahab had just returned from Jerusalem on realm six. The two messengers had brought up some groceries from the several markets around the holy temple; they wanted to prepare a nice repast for the captain and his small prodigy. The morning star's eyes glint in pleasure as Me-el came sliding into the dining room on bare feet. The child was a big fan of the smooth glass floors.

"What's for dinner Lufi?" Me-el prodded as he flew up onto his chair; just right of Lucifer.

Lucifer pinched Me-el's button nose.

"I hope you were not over snacking in Eden! I saw you go down there with Raguel after school." The captain disclosed.

"Ahhh no" Me-el answered.

The child did not consider a basket full of caramelized dates and stuffed figs any type of considerable snack. It was more of an energy booster.

"I made sure Raguel got plenty of food though! Did you see him?" Me-el's eyes now displayed incredible discomfort.

"Lufi I barely recognized him! He must have shed two and a half pounds off this time around! Uriel is such a slave driver!" Me-el presented with earnest concern in his voice.

Lucifer covered his mouth with his right hand so Me-el would not see him holding back laughter.

"So when we gonna eat? I am starving!" Me-el spouted.

"Well," Lucifer related.

"I do believe Rofocal and Rahab have cooked up a surprise for us! A new recipe Raphael came up with."

Me-el's eyes brightened, if anyone knew food it was Raphael.

"I thought I saw those two in Eden! Did Rahab ever apologize to Rapha?" He asked.

Lucifer moved his wine glass in a circular motion, taking in its scent.

"He did!" The captain promised.

Me-el smiled.

"Good! Now I like him more! Plus now I don't really need to take him around the palace blind folded!" The child added.

As Me-el finished his sentence, the two messengers entered.

Rofocal and Rahab genuflected, each bowed on their right knee, whilst their wings handled a large round silver tray. Rising comely the pair placed the dish on the quartz table and unveiled it.

"Yum! It smells almost as good as Abba himself!" Me-el cried.

The child began vigorously inhaling the freshly baked pita shaped food. It was a sort of un lidded pie. The flat bread was immersed with thick crimson tomato sauce, and a heavy blend of cheeses, including; provolone cheddar and feta. Some savory mushrooms and olives from Eden also garnished it.

"Well, by the looks of Me-el's drooling mouth, I say we all better pray."

Lucifer took his younger brother's hand, and then motioned for the two messengers to come join them. Rahab and Rofocal although somewhat mystified by the captain's notion, were both immensely thrilled to assemble with Lucifer and Me-el, at the dinner table in giving thanks to God. The morning star took Rahab's hand, Rahab in turn took Rofocal's, while Rofocal completed the prayer circle by connecting palms with Me-el. Lucifer lowered his head to say the blessing.

"We thank thee Abba for bringing us food from your heavenly garden, blessed may your name be, let all who love and serve Abba agree with me now and in Hebrew say..." Lucifer opened one eye to see if the other three responded correctly.

"We say amen, amen, and amen." The trio chanted, Me-el being the loudest.

"Amen!" Lucifer repeated with a grin.

Me-el rubbed his porcine hands in anticipation.

"Gimmie!" He expressed, as he licked his salivating lips.

Lucifer smiled as he brought the tray forward. Rahab passed him a golden slicer. The captain winked at the flaxen haired angel, causing him to blush. Rofocal then gave Lucifer two clear plates adorned with rubies around their edges; he too received a wink from the son of morning. Rofocal and Rahab were now both beet red in the face.

"Me-el," Lucifer recommended, while he commenced slicing his sibling an extra large piece with all the fixings.

"What would you think if I invited these two very attractive angels to join us at our table from this day forth?"

The messengers exchanged hopeful glances; they were going to be endowed with even more privileged benefits; by Lucifer himself, if Me-el thought them both worthy. Me-el snatched his plate and bit into the oozy nosh before answering with his mouth full.

"This stuff is divine!" He swooned.

"As long as they keep cooking like this, they can sit anywhere they want to!" Me-el proclaimed as a clump of cheese made its way down his chin.

Lucifer looked up at the pair with his enticing eyes.

"Well, you heard my Me-el, both of you shall dine with us from this day onward! My table is large and we would both adore your company, so please be seated and acquire some plates for your selves as well."

Rahab and Rofocal speedily went to gather two more plates from the kitchen, they returned, bowed then seated themselves. The duo was still in disbelief that this was all actually happening to both of them.

"The pie looks quite appetizing; I know Me-el is enjoying it! Your hard work and clever hands helped make it, so please by all means join us!" The captain opinioned as he now began cutting a slice for each of them.

"Thank you most gracious lord!" Rofocal smiled.

Rahab still somewhat floored, simply nodded in agreement.

"My lord, aren't you going to eat?" Rahab finally managed to phrase.

The angel became aware that only a few meager mushrooms from the round confection had found themselves a home on Lucifer's plate.

"A simple taste will do for me." The captain pitched.

Lucifer cocked his head towards Me-el. The child was famously performing his traditional wing movement, and inching the silver tray his way with his upper right feathery appendage. Three succulent slices remained, and they had Me-el's name written all over them.

Rofocal and Rahab immediately comprehended, Lucifer was leaving his remaining pieces of pie to his younger brother. The two messengers each took only one piece for themselves and ate in slow small nibbles.

"It is very good!" Rahab affirmed.

"It is WONDERFUL!" Me-el gushed as he swallowed down a whole slice without chewing; it seemed to go down rather easy.

Lucifer threw a mushroom in his mouth.

"Not bad at all!" He verified.

The four angels were enjoying the very first pizza!

Chapter 21

Raphael was peacefully reclining under a tall cedar down in the realm of Eden. Gabriel's class had just bombarded his level with notebooks and quills; on the up side, every angel had comported themselves very well. The archangel breathed in the aromatic smell of infinite flowers and fruits.

"I adore this level." He remarked.

Cinnamon and Sugar Raphael's two unicorns came up to rest beside him. The creatures still were wearing their flowery garlands around their necks.

"Hello my friends!" The seraph kissed each animal on its muzzle.

While the gentle gardener was petting his two companions, a subtle crackle of twigs and leaves diverted his attention.

"Perhaps some angel forgot their notebook, most likely Raguel." Raphael murmured.

The seraph hiked whimsically over to where the noise originated. Raphael found himself walking towards the tree of life.

"Odd." He speculated.

"None of the angels from Opus Angelorum came anywhere near this section of Eden."

The lieutenant advanced.

"Hello, who is there?" He called as he morphed into his golden armor.

"It is I." The response came.

Raphael nearly fell over backwards as one of the obscure entities from his reoccurring dream apparated right in front of him; however this time his face was not overshadowed by light.

"This is surely the being I saw seated on Yahweh's throne!" The angel contrived.

Raphael's entire body tingled; somehow he knew he was staring into the face of God. The archangel dropped to his knees and paid homage.

"It is Yahweh in one of his other forms." He assured himself.

"Salutations most high!" Raphael saluted.

"I am honored to have you here, forgive my conflicted actions and behavior, is it safe to presume that this is you in the form of Yeshua or the Ruach?"

The solid figure which was Yeshua smiled as he assisted the dashing lieutenant to his feet.

"I am who I am, but yes; this is me your father in the form of Yeshua." He responded.

Raphael took in Yahweh's other personage in awe. He was even more beautiful than Lucifer! A light like no other in Heaven shimmered through Yeshua's hazel eyes.

Yeshua's body was unlike any angel's in Heaven; he radiated pure love and grace, yet was composed out of something altogether unequalled.

"He almost smells like the soil in Eden." Raphael surmised.

Raphael had in no way ever assumed what Yahweh's other two forms might look like. This was his first time viewing God outside his paternal figure; still every angel knew Yahweh consisted of three total separate ones.

Yeshua stood at six foot; he was broad shouldered with tanned Semitic skin. As Raphael gawked at him, Yeshua threw back his head to laugh, allowing his dark brown wavy hair to rustle through the wind. Yeshua was youthful and seemed very bemused with Raphael's reaction to meeting him.

"If he took away the beard, and added some wings..." Raphael imagined.

"He could easily be the most exquisite angel in all of Heaven!"

Yeshua took Raphael by the hand.

"Come with me my child, I want to tell you about the tree of life, there is something very distinctive about it which I need to discuss with you."

Raphael felt warm fuzzies permeate through his body as Yeshua's hand grasped his. The archangel struggled to maintain his composure as he recommenced to study Yeshua. The two tarried over to the lush pomegranate tree. The abashed angel realized how when the breeze wafted through Eden, Yeshua's hair moved with it. As an angel Raphael was fascinated by this, for example; if Lucifer plummeted through all nine levels of Heaven, not a single strand of hair would be out of place; Yeshua on the other hand differed in this aspect, aside from so many others; His hair flowed with the wind, it was lovely.

Yeshua's divine yet rare characteristics made him the fairest creature in Heaven by far! Yeshua stopped when they reached the tree. He reached up and plucked a pomegranate from it, then tossed it to Raphael.

"Feed that to your unicorns, and they will be just as immortal as you!" He smiled.

Raphael examined the unusually large fruit, up until now he had not given the produce of the tree much thought. Now that he thoroughly handled it, he could perceive that it was grander than any other pomegranate in the garden. The fruit also had a specific gloss to it. Raphael's emerald eyes met Yeshua's.

"A thousand pardons most high," The seraph began.

"Yet I am not familiar with the term you spoke just now, the word immortal, what exactly does that mean?"

Yeshua smiled again, he picked another fruit from the tree and bit into it himself. A trickle of crimson juice ran down the right side of his lips, he licked it away.

"The word is not known to you because your kind; angels, are just like Yahweh none of you will ever die." He said as he swallowed.

Raphael's eyebrows narrowed in confusion.

"You lost me again my lord, what does die mean? I have never heard that term spoken either."

Yeshua finished up his pomegranate than explained.

"Death, or to die, is something that will never exist to angels, or to Yahweh. Your unicorns and the other animals here in Eden which are few; they will someday."

Raphael pursed his lips, he still did not comprehend. Yeshua expanded on the matter.

"Raphael this tree is called the tree of life because any creature that eats from it will live forever just like you and your siblings! The fruit of this tree allows one to become immortal. To be immortal is to live for all eternity while staying young and beautiful! Just as you are!"

The pensive lieutenant put the pomegranate in a pouch attached to his belt which held his shield.

"I still do not understand what death or die means, obviously to be immortal is to live as we do here in Heaven, but what precisely is this thing called death?"

Raphael sighed as Yeshua sucked some of the leftover pomegranate juice off his fingers; this further jogged the archangel's mind. Yeshua was God, he was Abba himself, he was the original immortal Raphael knew that much; all life came from God, because he had always existed, so why was he eating from the tree? He had no need to, it also perplexed the angel that Yeshua referred to himself or his primary form of God as if he was not completely three in one! Every angel was aware he was, yet in this form Yeshua's dialogue was utterly odd.

"Death or to die," Yeshua put forth,

"Is for a creature to cease to live, to simply lose one's life force; hence vanishing into nothing and being separated from Heaven and God forever."

Raphael's eyes started to enlarge in sheer terror; if that was the case he would personally see that every bird, butterfly and pixie; however annoying they might be, would partake from the tree; along with his two unicorns. He did not want to lose any of his garden creatures to this fate of death, it sounded horrifying.

"Abba," Raphael spoke with caution.

"If I may be so bold to ask, you are, and have always been, although your figure is momentarily different, why do you eat from the tree? You obviously do not have too..." The angel cut himself off; perhaps it was unwise to pose this question to God himself. Yeshua simply smiled.

"Raphael you are correct! I am and have always been three in one! I am Yahweh; but, I am also who you now see, Yeshua; and the Ruach, I do as I please. Perhaps I just wanted to sample the fruit for myself, to make sure it tasted okay for all the animals. I'm sure you of all angels would understand that? I have caught you noshing on the clock at times, while looking into my sea of glass." Yeshua winked.

Raphael blushed; Abba had him there, guilty as charged.

"Yes most high it is important to know the fruits and vegetables are well ripened."

Yeshua caressed the tree's bark, then turned back to face Raphael.

"Raphael I am glad to see you in your armor, because I want you to guard this tree. Remember this; no angel need eat of it, only the creatures in Eden. After all, I already tasted the fruit; it seems to be just fine! Will you accept this responsibility?"

Raphael bowed low and put his hand over his heart.

"On my honor most high." He pledged.

A piercing thought suddenly rocketed through the kneeling seraph's brain.

"Pardon me once more most high, yet if I am to guard this tree, how shall I attend to my other duties, such as gardening and nesting eggs? I can only be one place at once."

Yeshua walked up to Raphael, his eyes were smiling.

"From this moment on, you, Lucifer, Gabriel and Uriel will be given the power to bilocate!"

Raphael looked up he could not believe what he was hearing. Yeshua resumed speaking.

"Since Lucifer is your captain his ability will be far more advanced, Me-el is still quite young, but when he matures he too will acquire the same gift."

Yeshua helped Raphael to his feet in an act of chivalry; he also grew two feet to match the archangel's height. The seraph seemed amazed at all the new information he was just given to digest.

"Do not worry my lovely one; everything is going to be just fine!" Yeshua assured as he leaned in to kiss Raphael on the right cheek. The angel tingled as the warmth from Yeshua's lips rushed through his senses.

"Now Raphael, you must promise me that you will tell no one of our meeting. I know Lucifer can see whatever he wishes with his ring, after all I did give it to him, yet; if he were to by chance glance into it now, he would see me as Yahweh. When the time is right, I will reveal Yeshua to him, but that is up to me alone, do you understand?"

Raphael nodded and bowed once more. Yeshua went back to his fatherly image before leaving Eden.

Raphael closed his eyes to try and get an idea of how his new-fangled ability of bilocation worked. The archangels six pink wings sprung out as his mind's eye displayed him north of Eden, monitoring milking virtues.

"Astounding!" He expressed.

"Here I am fully armed, posted at the tree of life, yet I am clearly north of here as well! Not only that, I can feel and see myself just as well in my other state! It's almost like dreaming but more vivid!" He contrived.

Raphael picked up a bucket of cherubim milk in his other self, he hummed. The seraph was rather pleased, he could wonder through Eden in his gown and wreath of roses; while still being a completely suited sentinel at the tree of life.

"Now everybody can be happy!" He sang, while carrying the pail of foamy milk to a lesser archangel who was headed for realm six; or Jerusalem. The milk was bottled in quartz containers there.

"I can be a solider as well as see to all my other tasks now!" Raphael analyzed.

As the jubilant Raphael traipsed through a tulip field, he could not help but think back to his encounter with Yeshua. A song began to form in his head. The lieutenant began singing sweetly as surrounding birds hushed their chirping to listen to his.

(Sounds like the Hymn: "The garden")

"He came to my garden alone....There was dew kissing my roses... and the words he brings were like love to me... and he walked with me and he spake with me...I felt as if I was his own..."

Each tulip in the field opened its petals a touch wider as the archangel's melody filled all of Eden.

Lucifer had not been gazing in his ring when Yahweh had visited Raphael as Yeshua. The captain was occupied monitoring principalities and messengers as they ascended and descended between realms. Although Yahweh had given the chief seraph his own God like vision, Lucifer seldom used it. The morning star stood perfectly perched on a cloud; suspended between levels five and six; every so often a lesser archangel or power would catch sight of him, stop, bow, and salute. Lucifer responded each time with a smile and nod. The light bearer's cotton white pinions fluffed up in contentment.

"Abba's concept of time really brought new order and stability to all nine realms." He gathered.

Lucifer glanced up at the sun, according to its position, the captain configured that the noon hour had arrived. He smiled to himself.

"Me-el is probably breaking for lunch in Opus Angelorum just about now." He hypothesized.

Lucifer had slipped a crystal container into the child's book sack; Rofocal had filled it with a personal size disc pie, along with a sweet peach from Eden and a bottle of chocolate cherubim milk from Jerusalem.

"I need to get him to Abba's holy temple on level six...he keeps dropping hints as to when we are going to go." Lucifer reminded himself.

The meditative captain was caught off guard when Rofocal, who he had just been thinking about; bumped smack into him. Lucifer looked over at the befogged messenger. A basket full of dates, figs, and matzha went flying from the angel's arms; Rofocal had just gone shopping. Now his goods were scattered everywhere, and he was disheveled. Rofocal appeared *fertummect; or confused.

"Lord Lucifer?" Rofocal stammered, as he attempted to pick up his spilled items.

Lucifer lifted an eyebrow.

"Whatever is the matter Rofocal? You look like you just saw a leviathan, from one of Gabriel's picture books come to life!"

The messenger shook his head in disbelief.

"No lord you look nothing like a leviathan! Your beauty is flawless as always; please do not take my unseemly conduct in that manner." He begged.

"Then what is it?" Lucifer asked.

The captain now began helping the messenger refill the dropped contents from his basket.

"Well," Rofocal put forth.

"As you might see, I was in Jerusalem; I was procuring some necessities for Me-el; when I thought

* Fertummect: To be confused.

I'd drop by the temple for a moment of prayer." Rofocal paused; his citrine eyes began darting in all directions.

"And?" Lucifer bid, as he flung some figs into the carrying container.

Rofocal looked into Lucifer's eyes and gulped, before answering.

"Well you were there!" He spouted at last.

Lucifer rose, and assisted Rofocal to his own feet. The captain handed the perplexed angel his basket.

"Why do not be absurd my friend, as you can clearly see, I am right here! I have not moved for well over five hours, Wait... were you wine sampling in Jerusalem?" The morning star joked.

Lucifer regarded Rofocal, he could tell his messenger was by no means fooling around, he was being quite serious.

"My lord, no angel in all of Heaven can ever come close to matching your extravagant beauty! I tell you, you were there! I dared not disturb you, you were playing a lyre in front of the alter you sounded very well." He verbalized.

Lucifer looked into his ring.

"Show me the inside of the holy temple on realm six." He said.

Rofocal was right! An equivalent of a human brain freeze struck the confounded captain, causing him to fall to his knees, as he caught sight of what Rofocal had just described. He was in the temple! The morning star brought a hand to his fore head; he could actually tangibly feel himself on not only level six; but on five and four also. On level five he was dueling with Dumah, on level four he was sitting on his throne.

"How can this be? Has Abba made replicas of me?" He repined.

"My captain are you alright?" A concerned Rofocal asked.

"Yes my friend, yet I can now comprehend your bewildered reaction. Every angel is avidly aware that only Yahweh may be in more than one place at a given time."

Rofocal nodded, he did not know what else to say.

"I shall go see father myself, to find out what is actually happening." Lucifer expressed as he carefully regained his footing.

"Are you sure you are okay? I could come with you if you wish, you look a bit peaky." Rofocal offered.

"No friend that will not be necessary, please continue about your work, I'm sure Yahweh will clue me in as to what is taking place."

Rofocal bowed and took back to flight. The disoriented captain ascended up to level nine, still rather mystified.

"What is happening?" Lucifer whispered to himself.

Lucifer landed in front of the gates of God's level. The morning star found himself in further shock as he saw Uriel posing as a porter amongst the pearly gates.

"That's it! I am going meshuggina!" Lucifer spluttered.

He roved over to Uriel.

"Let me guess, even though you are here, you are also still on your own level?" The light bearer questioned, now feeling completely out of his mind.

"Quite so my lord!" Uriel affirmed not seeming the least bit bothered by it.

"Abba has made me the door keeper of his realm, yet I still retain my duties as star keeper and principal on realm one!" Uriel noticed Lucifer's gloppened expression.

"Don't fret lord." The lieutenant touted as he unlocked the gates.

"Yahweh will explain everything to you properly."

Lucifer nodded, looking over his shoulder he began admiring how statuesque his brother appeared standing vigilant before the entrance with sword in hand.

"He resembles a frozen quartz figure veiled in chrome." He appraised.

Chapter 22

Lucifer entered the throne room, his jaw dropped.

"I am here too!" he blurted.

The morning star crashed to his knees before Yahweh. Lucifer saw himself levitating south of his father's throne, holding a scepter of fire. Yet this was not all; Uriel who had just let him in a moment ago, stood north of Yahweh, holding an hour glass filled with swirling silver sands. Gabriel floated to the west, balancing a sphere of water in her right hand and a sword in her left. Then; to the east, Raphael gloriously flew on all six wings. They were all chanting:

"Kadosh, kadosh, kadosh!"

A throng of shimmering seraphim echoed the praises above them.

"How can we all be here, yet still somewhere else as well?" Lucifer puzzled.

Yahweh always glad to receive Lucifer, clapped his hands, bringing the throne room back to its normal state; Lucifer blinked as he and his three siblings vanished from around the throne. The captain was still on his knees.

"Get up bubeleh! It's just you, me and the usual seraphim choir again!"

God now teleported from his golden chair, over to the morning star who was just a few feet away from the sea of glass.

"Surprise!" Yahweh yelled, as he hugged the dazed seraph so tight that the angel found it hard to breathe.

Lucifer grappled to his feet.

"You can bilocate now! Your siblings can too; of course you most likely figured that out by now! Unlike them however, you can be in all nine realms at once if you so desire! You get special treatment because you are my favorite after all!" Yahweh avowed with a grin.

Lucifer scrutinized his father with baffled eyes.

"Forgive me Avi, but I am more than a little confused, why have you decided to give us, especially me; so much power? I seldom keep up with my ring of omnipresence as it is, Abba, I fear I may disappoint you with all the new responsibilities you have given me." Lucifer dismally confessed.

"Lucifer I do not like hearing you talk that way! That is meshuggina! You could never disappoint me! Why that would be impossible for my preferred son to do! Come, let's schmooze over some tea, you look a bit ver clempt; some nice ginger lemon always helps calm the commotion in my mind! I know it will put you at ease too!"

Lucifer took Yahweh's hand as they sauntered over to their secluded domed tea corner. Elohim waited for Lucifer to be seated, and then positioned himself on his own chair. The pair cast their eyes over at Me-el's velvet green ottoman with longing eyes.

"It's not quite the same without our little food *maven!" Abba expressed.

"So he cannot bilocate?" Lucifer asked.

"Oh when he matures he will!" God added.

"Oy vey! I pity all the pastries and edibles on that day!" Yahweh chuckled.

God passed Lucifer a cup of tea. The captain let out a small laugh. He suddenly envisioned Me-el bilocating to every realm with food on it; and inflating up to the size of a behemoth.

"You got a point there!" He quipped.

Abba smiled while sipping. He set aside his tea cup, and lifted his spectacles to survey Lucifer.

"I know you feel a bit overwhelmed bubeleh, but think of all the benefits this will give all of you, I know your siblings all seem thrilled!"

Lucifer looked up from his tea abruptly.

"Avi, why did you discuss this new ability with them first, I am the captain, why was I not personally informed by you; instead I get dumb struck by the news by one of my messengers!" Lucifer's eyes drooped at the corners, in sadness.

Yahweh now pushed back the table which stood between him and the morning star; he took his hands and placed them on his own lap.

"Forgive me my bubeleh; I simply assumed that with your ring and unsurpassed wisdom, you would easily catch on before anyone else."

The seraph now put his own tea cup on the shoved back table; he knew Yahweh was being sincere.

"Avi, you are correct, you have no need to apologize, I have been so preoccupied on realm five practicing my swordsmanship....or I begin composing a song. I just need to come to terms with all the awesome supremacy you have bestowed upon me. Why I regret to say it, but I hardly ever gaze into my ring the way I used to. Maybe I am not the right kind of captain, maybe I am flawed."

Lucifer's eyes now began welling up with tears. He felt like he was disappointing God.

"Bubeleh how can you say such nonsense! When I made you I created you using only the finest ingredients of Heaven! You are by no means flawed! Lucifer you are the most perfect thing I have ever made! Now enough crying! Tears pollute your beautiful face!" Yahweh tipped.

Yahweh lifted the captain's chin with his right palm.

"You are my beloved; with you I am always well pleased!"

Yahweh asserted.

The light bearer's face went pink.

"I suppose I do actually like the whole conception of bilocation, yet how will I know what I am doing on other levels? As I stated earlier, I seldom even look into my ring." He fretted.

God gazed at his most ravishing creature a bit daunted; Lucifer honestly had no clue as to how powerful he had made him.

"My love," Yahweh questioned.

"How is Gabriel's pet seal Snowball?"

God decided to throw his son a curve ball to see if he would catch it; without thinking Lucifer responded automatically.

"Oh alright, it's munching down a pomegranate from your tree of life, apparently Raphael gave it to Gabriel so Snowball would never cease to exist or die, it will also allow for the seal to ever remain a baby."

Lucifer brought his hand to his mouth unnerved.

"How did I know all that?" He conveyed in disbelief.

Yahweh kissed Lucifer on the cheek, he had passed the test.

"My bubeleh you need no magical diadem or ring of omnipresence, they are but accessories! When I created you I made you to be my companion and equal!

You automatically know everything I do! I only gave you the crown and ring to aid you in better comprehending your own supreme authority! They also both look lovely on you!"

Lucifer could not believe what he was hearing; if he wanted, he could be just like God; it was somewhat intimidating. The captain closed his eyes and cleared his mind; he was trying to get a better grasp of all his capabilities. He decided to try and get an enhanced feel for bilocating.

In his mind's eye Lucifer could see what was happening on every realm. Abba was right.

"Bubeleh," Yahweh smiled, he was pulling an ornate talisman from his long silver beard. It was a gold medallion with the image of the moon eclipsing the sun on it. Lucifer opened his eyes and stared at the rarity, he had a weakness for receiving gifts from his father. The most dazzling feature of the medallion was that the moon actually moved over the sun, it was magical.

"I have yet another token of love for my most beloved angel." Abba presented.

God clasped the necklace around the son of morning's neck; it looked glamorous on him.

"This talisman is a bit of a booster, to go with your ring." Yahweh explained.

"Although you are beginning to see yourself on other realms, I realize you still are struggling a bit, this medallion should make things easier for you until you can adjust to your new abilities more. My hope is that someday you will be so advanced; that you will simply wear these fineries as jewelry and nothing more!"

As the medallion fell against his chest, Lucifer felt his entire body surge with force; without shutting his eyes he could now see himself on all the realms! It was remarkable.

"It really is helping!" He yelped.

On level eight he was keeping watch over some messengers Gabriel had sent to the library, to gather some new reading material; they saluted and bowed as Lucifer went past. On level seven he was preparing to run through a new hymn with his worship choir. In Jerusalem the morning star was praising in the temple; just as both he and Rofocal had earlier observed. On realm five he jousted with Beleth. In Eden he passed Raphael another egg that had come out somewhat small and required his nesting. Realms two and one were a trifle foggy, but he could see the snow on Gabriel's icy palace and her silly pet seal; he also made out Uriel patrolling about the stars.

"Wow!" Lucifer gasped.

"Abba this is incredible! I actually feel more at ease if I really think about it! I'm just glad I don't hear everyone's thoughts that would really drive me meshuggina, I don't know how you do it!" The seraph emphasized.

God smiled and kissed Lucifer's hand.

"Well, not yet you can't." Yahweh winked; the truth was that God did plan on giving Lucifer that ability later on.

An incredulous look whammed the captain's face.

"What do you mean by that Avi? Please tell me you are joking!"

Yahweh waved his hand to signal he was only jesting; he did not want Lucifer to become more alarmed than what he already was.

"Calm down Lucifer, that is something only I can do, I do want you to be aware however that your ability to bilocate supersedes that of your three lieutenants; you can easily be on all nine levels of Heaven at a time if you so desire; they may only apparate three to four places at a time, if even that many. I have chosen you alone as my primary seraph of choice, another reason for your new glittery decorum." Yahweh disclosed.

Lucifer smiled he did enjoy the variety of bling Yahweh kept presenting him with, it was a nice perk.

"Thank you for everything Abba, I shall continue practicing my bilocating, the talisman really does help, I love it!" The captain admitted.

"I knew you would!" God chimed.

"Bubeleh I have complete trust in you! Now you are dismissed, I look forward to our upcoming Shabbat together! Don't worry; I will have plenty of treats here by then for our little Me-el!"

Lucifer rose, he elegantly bowed, and kissed his father's hand. The light bearer then descended.

"I really feel like I am one with Yahweh now!" He considered.

The seraph gleefully soared down from the ninth realm; Uriel saluted Lucifer as he flew by him.

"I love this bilocation." The chrome covered porter whispered beneath his helmet.

"Now I can be Abba's door keeper, stand north of his throne, and yet still keep a close watch on my own realm; thus permitting me to tether the occasional tantrum throwers from Opus Angelorum! I am sure lord Lucifer is equally pleased!" Uriel concluded, as he relocked the gates of pearl.

Chapter 23

It was now Windsday, Remiel's shofar sounded the beginning of class. Me-el and Raguel trudged into Opus Angelorum toting their note books full of data from Eden. As usual they were the last two angels to take their seats.

"Who's that?" Raguel asked as he elbowed Me-el.

Me-el looked up, an older man in a light brown pant suit and dark blue Yakama; stood behind Gabriel's desk. Me-el's azure eyes flickered at the figure; there was something vaguely familiar about him.

"Is that Yahweh?" He wondered.

The figure turned to face him and Raguel, revealing silver spectacles and blue eyes beneath them that twinkled.

"Abba!" Me-el squealed.

Yahweh nodded with a wink to the youth. Upon Me-el's serendipitous announcement the entire student body rose, bowed and chanted:

"Kadosh, kadosh, kadosh!"

Gabriel, who had purposefully obscured herself way in the back of the class room, joined God up front after the pupils had finished praising him.

"Me-el is quite gifted!" Yahweh remarked, as he allowed his long silver beard to reappear over his jaw line.

Me-el grinned triumphantly.

"Well we can all recognize him now." Raguel proclaimed.

Gabriel smiled as she took her place right of Elohim.

"Class, we are very privileged to have Abba himself giving you a special lesson today!" She orated.

All the angels in the class room nodded, their eyes fixed on Yahweh.

"Abba," Gabriel offered.

"Please begin when ready."

The archangel gave her creator a bow as she stepped aside to give him all the space he might need.

God nudged his spectacles further up his curved nose.

"Well hello my sweet children! I am honored to be talking to all of you! Some of you might have noticed that Lucifer and my three top lieutenants, your pretty rabbi included; now have the ability to be in more than one place at a time! Raise your hand if you have witnessed what I have just spoken about."

Jericho's hand sprouted up first. Raguel and Me-el rolled their eyes.

"Ah gold streak, or Jericho!" Abba acknowledged.

"Our *kolboynick!" Raguel whispered.

Me-el brought a finger to his lips to warn his friend. He did not want Raguel getting sent down to Uriel so soon, he had just got back. Yahweh, although aware of Raguel's comment, dismissed it and carried on.

"Tell me Jericho, what have, or rather who have you seen, and where?" Elohim asked.

Jericho rose from his seat to properly address God.

"Well, just this morning before class even started, me and my fellow companions from realm four, decided to fly up here early. Rabbi always tends to arrive a few hours before class, so we thought we would spend some extra time studying our Hebrew; you know, before Remiel actually sounded his shofar."

Me-el felt nauseated, Jericho was really brown nosing.

"Mega suck up!" Raguel sighed aloud.

Gabriel shot the two chaya a cold stare. Me-el smacked his friend on the cheek in angst.

"Owie!" Raguel yelped.

"It was a pixie!" Me-el innocently conjured up.

"That is why the both of us were rolling our eyes earlier; I saw it land on Raguel's cheek, so I slapped him!" He claimed.

---

* *Kolboynick: A knows it all.

Raguel picking up on his friend's covert job bobbed his head in agreement.

"It was! If Me-el would not have hit me, I think it would have tried to bite me! Sorry rabbi, sorry Jeri joke, I mean Jericho." Raguel mumbled.

Razziel sniggered in the last row.

"Right on S.P!" He evaluated, he was not a big Jericho fan himself.

Gabriel tempted to lash her quartz ruler over both the children's knuckles, held back when she saw Yahweh chuckle. To her amazement a tiny neon pixie zoomed right on top of Yahweh's Semitic nose.

"I got it!" Abba proclaimed.

God cuffed his hand over the celestial pest.

"Come here Sarah, you have caused enough trouble here! Go fly back to Eden were your kind belongs! Shoo!"

The mini creature cruised out the window, blowing a raspberry towards Raguel and Me-el who were utterly shocked. The friends exchanged commingled glances. God had just taken their side! Both small angels gazed up at Yahweh with eyes full of silent gratitude. Yahweh winked at them, before resuming.

"So sorry about that Jericho, please my son, you were saying?"

"Yes well..." Jericho continued.

"As I said we had come to do some extra studying, when about an hour passed. We saw Rabbi Gabriel come in, since we were already here; she asked if we would not mind going to the library for her to gather some books on Mythology. While we were doing so, we saw lord Lucifer there! We were all a bit blown away, since we knew he was usually on realm five when we are in school; yet, there he was! We all took time to bow and salute to him" The messenger concluded. Jericho bowed to Abba then took his seat again.

"How did a rouge pixie get way up here? I thought those two matzo balls were making it up!" The messenger conceptualized.

"Well there you have it!" Yahweh tipped.

"I shall further explain, front row you three make sure to pay close attention!"

The three small angels now sat up straight and properly poised, with quills in hand, ready to jot down notes. Gabriel could not help but be impressed.

"Bilocation for an angel," Yahweh exhorted.

"Is similar to splitting a multi-dimensional hologram in several slices with a laser, when one of my four top archangels has a need to be in more than one realm, they now can!"

Me-el and Raguel gulped, Uriel could be watching them at this very moment if that was the case!

"Now I really better behave!" Raguel deliberated.

Yahweh went on with his lecture.

"For all of you to fully comprehend this, I will form an illustration, Me-el, will you please come stand next to me?"

Me-el rose, bowed to God, then went to stand on his left. Raguel looked over at Samael, amused that Abba had called on his friend rather than him, who happened to be Rabbi Gabriel's favorite. Samael ignored the taunting sneer; he preferred to take the upper hand, thus keeping his reputation unblemished.

"Okay Me-el." Yahweh commented.

"For us to formally demonstrate, we need everyone to see what we are discussing don't you think?"

Me-el affirmed God's question with a nod.

Yahweh waved his hand; the movement of his palm triggered a liquid screen to root up behind Gabriel's desk.

"I call this a projector," Yahweh disclosed.

Gabriel mentally locked this display in the vault of her brain.

"I shall do the same in the future when teaching; the whole class can easily see what we would be discussing." She analyzed.

"Now," Abba went on.

Me-el turned himself to completely face the wall with the placid screen. The assembly began cooing:

"Oooohhh" And,

"Ahhh!" as the rugged power Beleth appeared on the projector, sparring at a hacked up sand bag, with a falchion sword.

"So," God spieled.

"Let us suppose this angel who is clearly practicing his swordsmanship on level five; suddenly remembered he forgot his helmet. He gets frantic, because he recalls he will need it later to duel with his captain, what if he reminded himself that he had left it in his egg west of Eden; how might he retrieve his head gear if he could bilocate like one of my archangels?"

The class went silent, no angel seemed eager to communicate an answer that might be way off. Yahweh's eyes landed on Me-el, who was apparently responsible for resolving the situation Yahweh had presented. Me-el felt like a chubby fly caught on sticky orange tape. The tot searched the faces of his class mates, they were all clearly clueless. Raguel now held his tubby hands together in prayer for his friend to gain some divine knowledge from the Ruach. The child remembered Raphael telling him stories about how the Holy Spirit's job was to help angels become wiser; right now he knew Me-el could use a revelation.

"Well Me-el, you are my chosen volunteer! What say you?" God challenged.

He knew that Me-el had great potential; he just needed a gentle push, to tap into it. Me-el's indigo eyes narrowed whilst he contemplated.

"Well Abba, maybe if he thought about it hard enough, I mean really concentrated; he could make his helmet come to him with his telepathic angelic brain waves." Me-el stopped.

Gabriel stood dumbfounded, his answer was uncanny!

"Me-el actually said something intelligent!" She silently opined.

The students all began murmuring over how Me-el came up with such an informed resolve.

"That's my friend! He is a genius!" Raguel bragged as he clapped.

Yahweh patted Me-el on the head affectionately, and then kneeled down to his height.

"Precisely!" God asserted.

Yahweh knew the tot would not disappoint! After all, Lucifer was his mentor!

"You may go back to your seat bubeleh."

Me-el let out a sigh of relief as Yahweh continued with his disquisition.

"All my archangels need to do to bilocate," God indicated.

"Is think about a realm which requires some of their extra attention, the mere thought will automatically transfer them straight to that level! However their primary selves will remain on their initial realm of focus! It's like me right now; even though I am currently teaching all of you at the moment, I am still on realm nine watching myself teach all of you from my sea of glass! It's actually quite simple! Do you all understand bilocating a bit better now?" Abba quizzed.

Raguel whose mind was now a hodge podge of commotion lifted his hand.

"Yes my child?" Yahweh smiled.

"Ahhh, does that mean Uriel is still mainly focused on level one and being a principal; or does he poke around other places too? I mean; with all due respect to you most high, I think you might be over working him; I'm just looking out for him, I mean I would not want him to wear himself out or anything."

Gabriel embarrassed by Raguel's false sense of concern, thumped her hand to her fore head; while Me-el released a smirk.

"Father forgive him, he knows not what he ever says!" She quietly languished.

God merely chortled at the child's statement.

"Do not worry Raquel; I have it on good authority that Uriel has plenty of help! Especially from this level!" He claimed as he vanished from their midst in a flurry of sparkle.

Raguel moaned in defeat, he was afraid Yahweh might respond that way; and he did.

Gabriel approached her desk as Yahweh dissipated.

"Alright everyone, I do hope you all took good notes on Abba's speech, we have a whole hour before Remiel sounds the shofar; I would like each of you to write a short essay on bilocating. When the ram horn dismisses class, please leave your completed papers on my desk."

The rabbi seated herself and turned over her sand filled hour glass.

"Begin now!" She ordered.

The students all commenced scribing, Raguel groaned as he wrote.

"I get what he said; I just don't think I can articulate it well on paper!" He moped.

Gabriel glanced up.

"By the way, I will have everyone's essay graded by tomorrow, so please make sure you leave nothing half finished."

The rabbi's eyes seemed to be nailed on Raguel.

"I think she can read my mind!" The tyke worried.

Chapter 24

Raphael gently nudged the opal egg blanketed by his bottom wings. Although posted at the tree of life, the archangel's main area of focus was on nesting. The gardener was selecting olives and placing them in his middle pair of pinions. Jeremiel, a lesser archangel from level six was going to arrive later to collect the olives for pressing in Jerusalem. The egg began vibrating; Raphael popped an olive in his mouth, and looked back at his passenger.

"Well I better get these in a basket for Jeremiel; I think you might be coming out soon!"

Using his telepathic skills, Raphael called on the virtue Lucia; a fair Hispanic angel, with delicate female features; she apparated in front of the blushing lieutenant, holding a large empty basket.

"Hello lord Rapha," She smiled.

Raphael stepped forward as he dropped the olives into the silver and gold threaded receptacle. The seraph felt his cheeks go warm and pink as he studied Lucia's avocado green eyes and thick black hair.

"Thank you Lucia! I appreciate your promptness; I think the egg I am nesting is getting ready to hatch!"

The gleaming feminine virtue gave him a smile, and then positioned the basket on top of her head; she balanced it with one arm.

"You are a sweet angel Senor Rapha." She winked.

Lucia secretly had an eye for Raphael, as he did her; she loved when he beckoned for her specifically, after all he had myriads of other virtues he could choose from.

"I will make sure Jeremiel get's this Senor!" She promised.

Lucia knelt carefully so as not to spill any olives, then flew off. Raphael watched the pretty creature until she was completely out of sight.

"She is as lovely as a rose!" He conceived.

Raphael roamed over to a soft meadow of bright purple, blue, and white hyacinths; he tenderly unfurled his lower wings to allow the egg to roll gingerly out onto the brilliant flowers. The great archangel brought in all his pinions, and seated himself cross legged on the grass to observe its hatching. An incoming rush of wind caused Raphael to jump back to his feet and turn. The lieutenant bowed and saluted upon his rising; Lucifer had landed and was standing right in front of him.

"Hail captain." He rang.

The morning star's eyes searched out the egg he had personally handed over to Raphael earlier. The lieutenant moved to the side as he took note of his captain's interest. Lucifer's eyebrows went up as the elliptical orb started buzzing.

"Why is it doing that?" He asked.

Raphael went over to stand next to his eldest sibling.

"That vibration means it's getting ready to open! Would you like to watch it hatch with me?" He offered.

"Yes." The captain affirmed as he advanced towards the shiny object.

"I am curious to see who comes out of this one." Lucifer confessed.

Raphael patted a zircon stone to his right; he pulled it up for his captain to sit on.

"Have a seat my lord and make yourself at home." He broached.

The light bearer gave his brother a smile, and stationed himself on the clear, glowing rock.

"Thank you Raphael, what about you?"

Raphael plopped himself back on the ground Indian style once more.

"I'm fine right here!" He guaranteed.

Both seraphs watched in amazement as the egg spurted two superfluous feet in length and width; as it opened, a wondrous seven foot angel emerged. He was clothed entirely in light with three pairs of opaque wings which fluttered in *labradorence. His rainbow eyes radiated purity. The hatchling's hair whirled whimsically around his face, white as fallen snow on realm two.

"A seraph!" Lucifer yelped.

"Yes and quite a splendid one!" Raphael conveyed.

The creature bowed low towards both angels. Raphael saluted, this time his gesture was politely returned.

"Thank you for nesting me great prince Raphael, all praise, glory, and laud to God most high! Hello good captain Lucifer, I bid you greetings, my name is Cassiel."

Lucifer felt a pull at his heart. Why did this handsome new angel greet him last? He was aware of Yahweh's formalities of hatchling's saluting Raphael, but even still; Lucifer was the captain! Cassiel should have paid tribute to him, before thanking his sibling. At least this was how the son of morning saw it. Cassiel clearly needed no schooling, so why had he missed his opportunity to give Lucifer praise before Raphael? The irate captain hoisted himself up from his feet.

"You would do well to remember I am God's right hand and regent young Cassiel!"

Raphael surveyed his older brother, the only other time he recalled Lucifer taking this tone, was when they had the summons; and Lucifer had accused him of resembling a cake in his rose wreath. The new angel genuflected towards the towering light bearer.

---

* Labradorence: To give off all the colors of the rainbow, some diamonds do this.

"Of course my dear lord Lucifer, a thousand pardons, now if given permission, I should like to go pay homage to Yahweh."

Lucifer now went eye to eye with the sating seraph. Raphael made sure to stay close by. The captain's look seemed somewhat menacing.

"Yes go! All respects should be made to Abba first! Just never forget who his equal is! That would be me!" Lucifer chided.

The seraph bowed, and then ascended. Raphael all too happy that the whole scene had ended released all six of his wings and yawned. Lucifer gave him a look of repulsion.

"Must you act so nomadically Raphael? For goodness sake, even Me-el covers his mouth when he yawns! You sound like a moaning grizzly bear!" The fiery captain spewed before soaring away.

Raphael jiggled off the comment; he did not even know what a grizzly bear was.

"Must be an incredibly ravishing beast if he compared me to it!" Raphael said with a guffaw.

"I do think he should apologize to Cassiel for coming off so snarky," He thought.

"Then again, Lucifer does speak for God, so who am I to judge him?"

The archangel promenaded over to a weeping willow which was drizzling mini white buds. He slunk down and leaned up against its trunk, he then enveloped himself with his wings. Raphael decided to nap. Cinnamon and Sugar snuggled up next to him as he drifted into slumber.

Up above Eden, Lucifer glanced down; he was thrown for a loop to see Raphael fully armed at the tree of life, while dozing off elsewhere. He paused in mid air. The captain began deliberating how his brother seemed to contain his bilocation to the celestial garden.

"I really like the way he looks in his armor." He evaluated as he resumed ascending.

Raphael now completely asleep, found himself once more plagued by his same persistent dream. This time the archangel knew the person on the throne was Yeshua, there was no doubt about that! Yet, he still could not identify the aristocratic angel who always appeared so dismal. His beauty as before was nearly equivalent to Lucifer's; yet his lustrous mane of hair was dark and wavy, with a few curls.

"Who is he? Why does he weep?" Raphael stipulated.

The seraph awoke abruptly; his two unicorns were munching on his head wreath.

"Hey! I just made this one! Did Lucifer put you two up to this?" Raphael jeered.

He commenced filling the open gaps of his flowery crown with boisen berries and fig leaves from some nearby bushes.

"Okay, I'll get you both some oats and sugar cane, so you'll keep away from my wreath!"

The two beasts grunted in approval as Raphael stumbled to his feet.

"I just wonder why I keep having that same vision." He expressed.

The unicorns skipped gaily through Eden's lush foliage as Raphael marched over to a field of sugar cane. The seraph pulled out some verdant stalks for the bonny animals to crunch on; as the angel fed the noble creatures, a still whisper of a voice caught his attention. Someone was calling him by name. The unicorn's tentative regal heads arose as their ears twitched in all four directions of the utopian garden.

"So you both heard that as well," Raphael remarked.

"I better go see who it is."

The seraph undid a leather suede sack he carried over his back; he placed it down for Cinnamon and Sugar, oats sprinkled with nutmeg streamed out of it.

"Here are those oats I promised." Raphael smiled.

The unicorns whinnied in gratefulness. The archangel pat each creature on the nose, then took to the air; he could not distinguish from which particular area the voice was coming from. It was almost as if it moved with the wind.

Gliding high in the cerulean blue and violet tinged sky, which was shining with Yahweh's own light, Raphael peered down on the entirety of Eden. He saw himself guarding the tree of life, while shimmering pixies swarmed over various plants. The voice kept heralding; this time Raphael's ears perked straight to the source of it; almost one hundred yards from his shielded pomegranate tree, the seraph caught sight of a new gargantuan arbor; harboring luminous apples. The voice was clearly beckoning from this exclusive addition to the garden.

"When did Abba plant that? I should have noticed something so imperial." He ruminated.

Raphael gracefully landed next to the ethereal tree. Looking up, he saw a white over sized dove starring down at him with inquisitive eyes.

"You found me my son!" The bird related, as it cocked its head to the side.

Raphael rubbed his eyes in astoundment.

"Abba is that you?"

"Yes it is I." The dove replied, as it flew down a branch closer to the puzzled seraph.

"You have seen me as Yeshua, and know me as Abba, this is me in my third form, the Ruach, close your eyes Raphael, envision yourself east of my throne on realm nine, as you give praise there."

Raphael obeyed, the archangel now viewed himself chanting in mid air, with his other three siblings; however above him there danced a silver orb with a dove at its center. Raphael eyes unbolted in epiphany.

"Of course! You are indeed the Ruach; you are that very sphere of joy which is enraptured by my low vocals! You are my most high!"

Raphael bowed.

"What an honor that you're Holy Spirit tends to gravitate my way in your throne room! Please forgive me Yahweh for not recognizing you sooner! What pray tell brings you to Eden?"

The Ruach tilted his head, blinking as he answered.

"This tree, in case you have failed to notice, it is new."

Raphael's face flushed, he was a bit ashamed he had not deduced the obvious.

"Yes Abba, although I must confess, I just recognized its presence recently. I saw it from the clouds above. Did you plant it overnight? It is magnificent! Eden's finest gem by far! The apples shimmer with auroras light!"

Raphael's appetite was getting the better of him; he goggle the voluptuous fruit and stretched out his hand to pick one. The Ruach immediately perched himself on the seraphs extended palm, and began pecking at it. Raphael quickly withdrew his hand and began soothing the red abrasions the dove had left with his lips.

"No my son!" The Holy Spirit warned resting itself on the archangel's shoulder.

"You have no need to eat of this fruit. This is the tree of wisdom."

Raphael's eyes gazed up at the forbidden produce in caution while the Ruach flitted back up to one of the branches.

"Forgive me Yahweh; I suppose I let my noshing habits get the best of me." The lieutenant frowned.

"Yet if I might ask Abba, why have such a great tree in this garden, with such a grandiose title if no angel may eat from it? Or do you want the animals of Eden to become smarter?" Raphael boldly queried.

The seraph felt his cheeks go red again in shame; perhaps his sudden inquisition had angered God. The Ruach simply cooed he adored Raphael's childlike innocence and sincerity; he also had chutzpa to question him as he did!

"Sweet child you are my chief gardener and overseer of this realm, the entire garden is free to you and to the many others, yet only Lucifer shall be permitted to taste of this tree; no animals, only him."

Raphael's visage took on a fazed façade.

"Pardon me most high, but did you not make Lucifer intelligent enough? I mean he knows things that I have never even heard of; like grizzly bear!" Raphael cupped a hand over his mouth.

"I talk too much!" He chafes.

The Rauch blinked its deep black eyes and almost seemed to smile, he did not respond to Raphael's slip of the tongue; yet resumed communicating mentally with him. To any onlooker it would appear that the angel was bird watching, the Holy Spirit was only making himself known to Raphael.

"This tree," The Ruach explained.

"It will also help the rest of you to gain discipline, due to the fact that no angel or animal may eat from it, except my beloved Lucifer. It will serve as a sort of guide to assist you all in resisting future temptations."

Raphael felt a lump grow in his gut, perhaps Yahweh had picked up on how he had been gushing over Lucia earlier in the day.

"Is her charm equivalent to one of those prohibited apples?" He contemplated.

"I think I understand Abba." The angel shyly admitted.

The Ruach flapped his wings, he had not meant to make his son feel unwarranted guilt; Raphael had done nothing wrong.

"My sweet Raphael." The Ruach began.

"Love is by no means a temptation; there is nothing wrong with admiring a pretty rose like Lucia. This tree is here to give you and every other angel more insight into how to tithe."

Raphael's face fell into stupor.

"You lost me again lord, I am not aware of the term you just used, what is a tithe?" He bid.

The Ruach flew down from Raphael's shoulder and changed into Yeshua.

"Yeshua!" The stunned seraph proclaimed.

Lucia was now utterly erased from his train of thought; Yeshua had him captivated. Yeshua took Raphael's hand in his; as he pontificated.

"A tithe or tithing is another way of worshipping, and since Lucifer is now one with me, it will also be a way of giving back to your captain. This tree is composed of every angel's first fruits!"

Raphael entranced by the God man's lovely eyes, found himself tripping over his words.

"Forgive me my lord, but I am still confused. If you made this tree by your own power how have we angels put anything into it ourselves?"

Yeshua smiled warmly.

"Well, when all angels hatch an aura of light and grace emits from them as they spread out their wings, for the first time. After each hatchling leaves their egg, Yahweh removes a tenth of each creature's essence; which he as you can plainly see planted right where this very tree is located. Raphael this arbor was not cultivated by a regular apple seed, it blossomed and will continue to do so; from miniscule drops of purity taken from each angel in Heaven, minus Lucifer himself."

Raphael's wings went limp, as he took in the enormous tree.

"You mean to tell me that Gabriel, Uriel, and Me-el along with me and other egg hatched angels helped this tree become what it now is?"

Yeshua nodded in affirmation.

"Yes!" He excitedly made clear.

Raphael's eyes blinked, a thought crossed his mind.

"You appear to have another question Raphael." Yeshua posed.

"Yes the truth is I do, Yeshua Lucifer created the last triad of angels, although some from the final three ranks are now actually hatching out of eggs; The greater portion did not, most high how do the creatures Lucifer himself made give any offering to this tree?"

Yeshua raised his right eye brow, bemused by the lieutenant's keen observation.

"Very good Raphael! The answer is they need not give any of their essence! Since Yahweh himself created Lucifer, and Lucifer in turn was specifically given the task of forming the last triad, only those such as Rahab for example, which as you pointed out hatched, will tithe; or rather, did tithe to this tree. However, Lucifer's self made angels will still pay a certain tribute to Yahweh none the less..."

Raphael fought back the urge of asking Yeshua why he was referring to himself as if he were separate from his paternal form of Yahweh; it was somewhat strange; He was still the same God after all.

"Maybe he just likes talking like that." The angel thought.

Yeshua picked up where he left off, not paying mind to Raphael's disturbed glances.

"The tribute Lucifer's self made angels make, is actually more of a sacrifice. They pay by not having eggs of their own; you see eggs are actually quite a luxury to have! When I created the cherubim, I only selected four to be egg layers, as you well know,"

Raphael nodded; Yeshua was finally saying "I" rather than making himself separate from Yahweh who he was and always would be.

"My dear Raphael although you seldom sleep in your egg you cannot deny how quaint it is to have your very own private chambers. Lucifer's angels must all go to his realm when they desire to repose, and only if they have his permission! All hatched angels may enter their eggs whenever they so choose!"

Raphael rubbed his chin, he had rarely thought of it, but eggs were quite nice to have. They were insulated with plenty of room. An angel's egg would be easily comparable to a human home. Some of the oval orbs enlarged up to forty feet wider and taller after releasing an angel. Raphael's egg was the largest in the patch west of Eden. The lofty emerald col de sac sat at the very center of all the others.

"Lucifer, he has no egg, has he ever asked for one?" The seraph casually slipped in.

Yeshua gave the archangel a demy smile.

"No he never has, and why should he; your captain has a massive mirrored palace! Why I architected it myself just for him. His reflection shoots out of the prism castle to all nine levels of Heaven! I cannot ever get enough of his perfect beauty!"

Raphael tried to ignore the queer feeling in his stomach, at Yeshua's final statement; it made him want to prod his creator with one more question.

"Yeshua, what about Lucifer? Does he or rather will he ever be required to tithe?"

Raphael bit his lower lip after chucking out the words. Yeshua switched back into Yahweh and went nose to nose with the rattled angel. God seemed goaded by Raphael's probing.

"Why can't I just keep my big pie hole shut?" Raphael sweat out.

Yahweh answered with sparking blue eyes.

"NO! Never!" The deity snapped as he took a step back.

God caught hold of his anger, and calmed down. He had not meant to come off so aggressive to the sweet gardener. The seraph lowered his head, disappointed with himself. Yahweh now feeling bad for hurting the angel's feelings lifted Raphael's chin with his right hand.

"Forgive my bitterness dearest Raphael, a hungry mind is a good thing, yet, you must understand I formed

Lucifer myself; he is my signet of perfection! He is my equal and beloved! For this reason my glorious light bearer need never worry himself with tithing. His unparallel beauty is gift enough for me! I do hope you comprehend what I am saying?"

Raphael's eyes undimmed, Yahweh's voice was soft and loving again. The emotional archangel fell prostrate before Elohim, causing the apples on the tree of wisdom to tremble.

"Thy will, not mine Abba." He muffle from the ground.

Yahweh sighed, feeling he may have come off like a nasty ogre.

"Oh please get up Raphael."

The angel rose slowly an adjusted his crown of roses.

"Now I want your brother Uriel to guard this tree, please make sure to remind him, that Lucifer alone may eat of it."

Yahweh took Raphael's right hand and held it to his cheek.

"I promise to do exactly as you say." Raphael avowed.

"I know you will, I do hope Lucifer tastes some of the tree's fruit, I've noticed he is not much of an eater; perhaps you or Uriel might persuade him to partake of it?"

Raphael nodded as Yahweh kissed his hand. The love emanating from his father's eyes was food to the angel's soul.

"On my honor Abba." Raphael promised.

Yahweh's face lit up as he slanted in to plant a kiss on Raphael's cheek; He then disappeared from his vision.

No sooner had Yahweh left, then Uriel arrived. He fixated himself directly beneath the tree in full armor. Raphael rushed over to embrace his brother, careful not to get his plumage intermingled with the star keeper's wings of flame.

"Oh sorry, let me diminish them." Uriel commented.

He lifted his visor to reveal his golden eyes.

"I'm used to keeping them at full charge since I have become Gabriel's principal! But, I shant think you will dare to cause me dire problems!" Uriel's eyes shined with good cheer. Raphael laughed as they greeted one another.

Chapter 25

Gabriel sat at her snowflake shaped table sipping hazelnut coffee; it was her flavor of choice. Snowball was curled up on her lap. The archangel busied herself grading student essays on bilocation.

"Well, Me-el scored highest out of all the class, Raguel on the other wing, faired the lowest! Oh well, at least he put genuine effort into his work this time; Ahhh……. Razziel, I should not give you an A, I can barely make out what you wrote! But you really do know what you are talking about, soooo…even though I wish your penmanship was better; you will still get a good grade!" She reasoned out loud.

Gabriel suddenly turned; her pet seal slid off her lap and began barking. A gust of wind coursed through her moonlit palace of ice. The seraph always left every window in her dwelling open; since temperature ceased to exist in Heaven. On level two, both sun and moon were clearly visible, they added extra panache to Gabriel's superb clarion fortress. The burst of wind had come from a window just left of her, it was Me-el; the portly snow covered tot resembled a white powdered donut hole.

"Me-el?" Gabriel spouted.

"What are you doing here? I assumed you would be in Eden with Raguel; attacking Raphael's garden of delights!" She teased.

Upon her declaration, an epiphany came to the rabbi.

"Lucifer is with you isn't he?" Her voice quickly went from sarcastic to tender.

Gabriel knew all too well that if Me-el was not with Raguel he was always active being their captain's loyal side kick.

"Yup!" Me-el grinned as he made his way over to her table.

The child climbed up one of her ice cube stools, like a roly poly baby polar bear as he settled himself atop one.

"Lufi is waiting right outside your door, not to be one to tell you what to do rabbi, but; if I were you I would not make him, your great captain feel unwelcomed!" The tyke expressed in a conceited manner.

Gabriel now alarmed, ambled over to her crystal doorway, sure enough Lucifer stood dignified right outside. Gabriel flung open the door and bowed low.

"Hail my most beautiful lord Lucifer! Please enter my humble abode."

The morning star removed a bouquet of pink roses from beneath his upper right wing and presented them to Gabriel as she elevated from her subservient position.

"Thank you for finally letting me in," He winked.

"These are for you sister, I picked them in Eden, Me-el told me you might be grading papers today."

Gabriel took the flowers with hesitance, her mind in a tizzy.

"That grob little sprite!" She silently pondered, as she glanced back at him.

The little angel batted his heavily lashed eyes at her in total false innocence. Gabriel sighed, trying to not give heed of Me-el's apparent bribe of roses via his older brother. Lucifer walked past her and took a seat next to Me-el at her table.

"My lord is too kind, the flowers are lovely!" She smiled.

Gabriel joined the pair and formed a vase made of ice with a breath from her mouth, to place the bouquet in. The flowers obtained a sating sheen as they became overlaid with frost.

"So, aside from bringing me a nice gift, to what do I owe the honor of my great captain's presence?" Gabriel put forth, as she sat herself just right of Lucifer. Me-el released a tiny grunt, his face taking on an appearance of remorse, he spoke at last.

"Ummm excuse me rabbi but don't you know how to properly entertain company?" The child asked, as he ran his pudgy palms over his jelly belly. Lucifer's eyes gave Gabriel a questioning glare.

Gabriel forced a smile onto her visage.

"Oh of course! How silly of me, give me one second!"

The seraph clapped her hands; a steaming brass cup of hot cherubim cocoa, accompanied by a glass tray of blue berry scones capped with clotted cream; manifested before the ever hungry Me-el and his elder brother.

"Forgive me captain; I seldom get many visitors on my realm, aside from Samael..."

Me-el rolled his eyes as he heard his rival's name uttered.

"May I conjure up anything special for you my lord?" She amiably offered.

Lucifer shook his head.

"No, I'm fine, but thank you for meeting my Me-el's needs!" He cheerfully expressed.

Lucifer was completely captivated by his younger sibling's ability to chug down steaming milk so fast. He looked back over at Gabriel.

"Actually," Lucifer picked up.

"I was wondering if you had been to Eden lately."

Gabriel pushed an ebony curl away from her fore head, as Me-el snorted piggishly whilst gorging on scones.

"Does Me-el even breathe between bites?" Gabriel wondered.

She cast her eyes back over to Lucifer.

"No, not as of late my captain, yet Uriel did inform me about the new tree he now guards, it is called the tree of wisdom."

Lucifer pounced on Gabriel's statement.

"There is yet another new tree?" He yelped; now feeling infuriated at himself, for failing to keep up on what occurred on each realm; the captain was still adjusting to all his new power.

Gabriel's eyes fluttered.

"I assumed you'd know." She timidly alleged, as she took sips from her cup of coffee.

"That is just it Gabriel, I should know!" Lucifer sulked.

"Sister, the truth is I am feeling disappointed in myself, Abba has given me the gift of omnipresence; several ways to bilocate, and I.... well I am so self absorbed in level five that I fail to notice something right in front of me! I mean...I was just recently procuring those roses for you only a few minutes ago in Eden, yet I saw no new tree! What if Yahweh grows weary of my incompetence? What say you? My dear sister I truly value your opinions, after all you are the designated rabbi to all nine realms." Lucifer searched Gabriel with pleading eyes.

Gabriel set down her quartz coffee mug in utter disarray, she could not have ever fathomed Lucifer coming to her for any sort of advice or counsel; even

Me-el seemed astounded. He had stopped eating; a scone comically protruded half way out of his mouth.

"Great lord," Gabriel emphasized.

"I know you will never cause Abba displeasure! I believe all you need do is take a bit of time to allow all your added power to soak in. Why not place your primary focus on Abba alone for an entire day. Give yourself a retreat, perhaps in the holy temple on realm six? Meditate and pray, learn to manage your novel talents better. After all even though you still may not be quite accustomed to your skills, we as lieutenants still witness you monitoring each realm. I am sure if you seek out Yahweh with your concerns he will submerge you in his glory! Thus permitting you to become very proficient with all your added abilities."

Lucifer brought a hand to his fore head.

"Yes, I do suppose you are correct, maybe I shall try that on Sunday, or Moonday, I could spend some quality time in the temple in Jerusalem as you suggested." He replied.

Me-el, who had just finished three more savory scones, patted Lucifer's arm to get his attention. The seraph's eyes shifted to his younger sibling.

"What is it bubeleh?"

Me-el licked up some clotted cream from his rose bud lips beseeching;

"Can I come with you when you go Lufi?"

Gabriel interjected, before the captain could answer.

"I think you might want to allow your older brother some space Me-el." She kindly submitted.

A minor frown swept over the child's face, as crumbs trickled down his lower lip.

"Lucifer you could spend time in the holy temple while Me-el is in class tomorrow!" She cited.

Me-el's look of disdain grew as he lapped up remnants of pastry from around his face.

"Perhaps I will Gabriel, do not worry Me-el, I shall take you to Jerusalem sometime soon, oh by the way Gabriel before we leave; remember we have our Archangel quartet concert approaching for Abba on Sederday, I trust you will come up with some good choreography for us all."

Gabriel finished up her coffee nodding.

"I already have everything prepared my lord, I do believe you will be pleasantly surprised!"

Lucifer rose, Me-el hopped up onto the light bearers shoulders, he was way too bloated with pastries to use his own wings.

"Good!" Lucifer expressed as Gabriel up cast herself to see the two out cordially.

The lieutenant bowed low towards the morning star.

"Thank you again for the roses and it will please my captain to know that Me-el is displaying great progress in class!"

Me-el hugged his brother's neck merrily; glad his rabbi finally had put in a good word for him.

"I knew a little insurance with the flowers was a good idea!" The child secretly evaluated.

"Well, I'm sure you will be seeing me about, even though I still may not be entirely mindful of it!" Lucifer bantered.

"I know you'll get the knack of everything soon lord!" Gabriel assured.

"After all none of us is closer to Yahweh than you! Me-el, I shall see you in class tomorrow." She winked.

Me-el waved and blew his rabbi a kiss as he and Lucifer left the arctic lodging.

Gabriel closed the argent entrance and jaunted back to her table. Stubby little hand prints now varnished it, along with splotches of cocoa.

"Oh Me-el!" She mumbled.

"If only you could emulate Lucifer in your etiquette as well as you do in your swords men ship!"

Gabriel released a disgruntled breath as she commenced wiping down her finely chiseled ice slab, with a blue satin cloth.

"I am just glad I moved my papers away before he made this mess!" She noted.

Chapter 26

Lucifer had just seen Me-el off to Opus Angelorum; the captain was keeping good on Gabriel's recommendation; he was now soaring down to Jerusalem to meditate in the temple.

The sixth realm was ablaze with vibrant beings; mainly lesser archangels and powers; they encircled the temple's courtyard. Some of the celestial creatures were pressing olives into oil, while others stomped grapes into wine with golden boots. Numerous vendors passed out fruits and flowers from Eden. The virtue Lucia upon noticing the captain hurried up to him and genuflected.

"Greetings my lord, would our great captain like some fresh fruit? Or; perhaps some milk or matzo?" She propositioned.

Lucia was holding three baskets; one in each arm, the last was parked perfectly on her head.

"No." Lucifer related.

"I am here to pray, not shop!"

Lucia arose with a reddened face.

"Of course my lord, please forgive me, I do hope you enjoy your time at the temple!"

The virtue gave Lucifer a courtesy as she went along her way.

"So much commotion around Yahweh's sacred temple!" The morning star smirked, as he glided over to it.

Up on level eight Me-el's face gleamed with happiness, his essay on bilocation had earned him an A. The child flaunted his paper at Samael.

"Now we are even!" He whispered to his contender.

Samael un fazed by Me-el's squawking did not even bother to pay him any mind.

"Lufi will be so proud of me!" Me-el gushed.

Gabriel smiled as she resumed passing out the rest of the graded assignments.

"He most certainly will be Me-el," She concurred.

"Oh and by the way, you got that grade from your own efforts, the roses were not really necessary."

Me-el managed out a cheesy grin.

"Oh rabbi, that was all Lufi's idea! I had nothing to do with it!" The child warranted.

Gabriel spun her eyes in subtle infuriation at Me-el's obvious cover up; she set Raguel's paper face down on his desk and moved on.

"Pssst!" Me-el poked his friend with his left upper wing.

"What did you get on your report?"

Raguel stared at the paper as if it was hosting the Black Death.

"I need to flip it over to find out." He murmured.

"Well do it!" Me-el demanded.

"I think I'll wait till three o clock gets closer." Raguel divulged.

Whilst Raguel fretted over his score in school, Lucifer was now entering the temple piously. Twelve lesser archangels unsheathed swords of silver to make an arch for the captain to walk through. The son of morning cantered in, his eyes taking in the splendor of the inner temple. Two cherubim faced each other at the altar, between them blazed Yahweh's white holy fire; from behind the pair of living creatures and eternal flame, Lucifer could see Yahweh seated on his golden throne.

"Yes." The captain said as he fell to his knees in worship.

"This is where I will finally obtain all the answers to my questions! In my father's great temple!"

Lucifer fell prostrate before God's *haesh, Yahweh viewing his preferred son's reverent homage, began filtering the morning star's mind and fine tuning it to match his own.

---

* Haesh: Fire.

"You have sought me my son, now you shall be richly rewarded!" Yahweh appraised.

Lucifer's entire body became still; he now had single eyed vision and could understand all things in their totality. He nearly had the very eye of God himself.

"Thank you Abba most high!" He moaned, as tears began streaming down his face.

"I was blind, but thanks to you, now I see!"

Lucifer rose, his arms lifted in worship, he began to offer Yahweh a song of praise.

Meanwhile on realm eight, the third hour was only ten minutes from approaching. Gabriel had settled on ending the week by giving a lecture on the three different triads of angels; and, how each one functioned. The period had basically consisted of listening and taking notes. Razziel had gotten reprimanded for falling asleep, halfway through the rabbi's disquisition. Fortunately, he was not sent down to level one, thanks to the fact that he was not snoring; as the students began packing away their papers, Me-el's eyes shifted back to Raguel.

Raguel was still much too frightened to flip over his graded essay; he had his head bowed in defeat towards his friend.

"I just can't bring myself to do it!" He wailed.

"You turn it over Me-el!"

Me-el glanced up; Gabriel was at her desk putting her own papers away.

"Okay." The curious angel yelped as he flipped.

Raguel's report had earned him a big fat red C.

"Travesty!" Me-el whispered.

Raguel slumped down in his chair; his greatest fear had officially become a harsh reality.

"I'll never get an A Me-el! I bet she keeps me after school for some of her torturous tutoring, or….." Raguel's eyes fogged up in devastation.

"Oh don't say it!" Me-el shivered.

"I'm going back down under my friend! The drill sergeant is probably cackling away as we speak! Just pray I do not lose any more weight! Either way I am DOOMED!" The child's head thumped down on his desk; just as the shofar blasted. Samael and the other pupils rocketed out of their desks, hastily rushing out of Opus Angelorum. Thorsday after all was equivalent to a human child's Friday.

Gabriel rose from her seat, to see the students out the doors; occasionally she would pat one on the back and say:

"Nice job on your report."

Me-el feeling remorse for his friend, decided to attempt to sneak him out ninja style; without needing to go by their rabbi.

"Hey." Me-el spoke in a hushed voice, into his whimpering comrade's ear.

"I can get you outta here by gliding out that window next to you! Look rabbi is busy scolding Razziel for sleeping right now! Come on let's make a break for it! This way you can be scot free and in your egg by the time she starts congratulating her perfect student Samael!"

Raguel looked up; his eyes were puffy from tears. His orange wings perked up a bit. Samael did make a point of jabbing with Rabbi Gabriel for a good ten minutes after each class; and, he was still looming around her, whilst Razziel kept profusely apologizing.

"I swear I was just resting my eyelids rabbi!" Razziel implored.

"You sure you can pull it off? What if she catches us? Neither of us is very quiet when we fly." Raguel noted.

Me-el dumped his notebook into his back sack and gave his pal a wink of assurance.

"No chance she will catch us! Lufi just taught me how to fly without making any noise! Plus, I've been training extra hard on level five! I'll carry you out on my shoulders; that way you won't need to worry about her hearing your own wings flapping!"

Now; although in Me-el's opinion Raguel was wasting away; the child was truthfully only a tad smaller in poundage than Me-el himself. None the less, Raguel agreed to the proposition. In an instant Me-el hoisted Raguel onto his back; he was actually quite strong, the little angel made a bee line for the star shaped portal.

Gabriel, who had just finished saying good bye to Samael, heard not one thing; until, she got an earful of Raguel howling in pain like a dying rabbit. The elegant rabbi turned to face a ludicrous spectacle! Raguel was belly up on the floor groaning with a red face from hitting the wall, a tip of a star was imprinted on his forehead; his sherbet wings were frazzled. Me-el's full plump tuches, tail feathers and all, now plugged up the window completely. The tot's tubby legs kicked up and down as he tried to unsuccessfully dislodge himself.

"Oh my!" Gabriel gasped.

"I will need to get someone to pry you out Me-el! What in Heaven's sake prompted you two to try something so silly?"

Gabriel fought to contain her laughter as she bilocated to her realm to grab a silver bucket of ice and a cloth for Raguel's bruised brow.

"I suppose I am not really surprised." The rabbi chuckled as she reappeared in Opus Angelorum. Gabriel immediately began to administer first aid relief to Raguel.

"Thank you rabbi." The youth sobbed, as he compressed the cloth and ice to his wound.

"Well now what shall I do about this dire obstruction?" She evaluated as she jabbed Me-el's rear.

Me-el pumped his legs faster, he was still trying to wedge out by himself.

"Hmmm...I suppose I'll send for Uriel!" She expressed.

"NO!!!!" Raguel and Me-el shrieked.

Gabriel bilocated to Eden, she knew she could find Uriel at the tree of wisdom.

"Hello brother, ah could your level oneself please find a way up to Opus Angelorum?" The rabbi asked, her face looking as if it was ready to burst out in laughter.

Uriel lifted his visor.

"Bloody comets! Let me guess my favorite shmendrick is causing a ruckus again?"

"No," Gabriel revealed, now holding her gut as she began splitting her sides.

"It's Me-el! I need you to go up and help Me-el!"

Uriel now quite intrigued by what might be happening uttered:

"Go on back up; I'll be there in a jiffy!"

Gabriel now back in her class room witnessed Raguel rubbing ice around Me-el's drooping love handles.

"Come on Raguel! You gotta get me out! Or we will both be on level one! No passing GO! No nothing!" Me-el insisted.

"I think the ice is defective Me-el! I still can't get you out!" Raguel proclaimed as he tried with all his might to push Me-el through the window, which was congested with his friend's furry white butt.

"Your hands! Watch your hands! You are hurting my tail feathers!" Me-el complained.

Gabriel at last broke in.

"Raguel."

The child turned and dropped the ice he was holding.

"Hi rabbi, ummm is HE coming?" Raguel gulped.

Before Gabriel could answer, Uriel stealthy entered the building and removed his helmet. He bit his lower lip to maintain his flint face.

"No wonder she was laughing! This is downright jovial!" He conceived.

"Alright Me-el, get ready!" Uriel warned as he pranced over to the window and effortlessly yanked out the flabby youth.

Me-elglaredupathimwithglossyeyesandtrembling lips. Raguel held both hands over his own peepers; he did not want to see Me-el's awful circumstance.

"I got me three new jolly good tail feathers to serve as quills now!" Uriel said as he tucked Me-el's tuches plumage under his left arm bracer. Me-el began to grovel.

"Please forgive me Uriel! Rabbi have mercy! I just wanted to help Raguel, he was nervous about his essay grade, and thought he might be in trouble! I was just trying to help a friend!" He sniffed as he rubbed his tenderized tush.

"Thank you Uriel." Gabriel commented.

"You may return to realm one."

Upon Gabriel's words Uriel exited the school. Gabriel moved her gaze back to the fumbling duo.

"Now I am not sending either one of you down to level one, I think you have both punished yourself enough."

The two children sighed in relief; they had escaped the Heavenly dungeon.

"Raguel," Gabriel went on.

"Getting a C is no reason for panic of this caliber! Believe it or not, your report was not all that bad, you just have a problem phrasing things correctly; yet, you are so quick to jump to terrible conclusions! Am I really such a villainous teacher?"

Raguel and Me-el simultaneously shook their heads. Gabriel leaned back against her desk with her arms folded.

"Well I cannot say I am pleased with your shenanigans, I will simply have to overlook the whole matter. Tomorrow is Shabbat, Uriel and I both have much more important things to get done, so off you both go! Me-el, I plan on seeing you at our concert for Abba accompanied by our captain."

Gabriel shooed the pair out the twin doors.

"I am so glad Abba made a Shabbat!" Gabriel expressed; as she finished gathering up various materials from her desk.

Me-el and Raguel smacked right into Lucifer as they bolted out of school. The light bearer held up two hands smiling.

"Whoa slow down! I know its Thorsday and all, but I don't see your rabbi chasing either one of you."

Lucifer noticed Raguel shove something into his mouth.

"Me-el must have brought you another snack." Lucifer cited.

"Yeah!" The child answered; now chewing on his poorly marked paper and swallowing it down.

"Mmmmm...That's some good matzha!" Raguel said in a somewhat muffled voice.

The flustered tyke bowed towards the captain, he rose and saluted, gave Me-el a fist bump; then clumsily took to the air. Me-el shrugged as Lucifer picked him up.

"Guess he had to eat and fly!" The youth joked; not wanting to disclose what Raguel had actually just consumed.

Lucifer kissed Me-el on the cheek.

"Well I have already spent some time in Jerusalem, but I do recall promising to take you there! What do you say; do you feel like going right now?"

"Oh yeah! That sounds super! Let's fly Lufi! I can't wait to see the temple!" Me-el communicated eagerly.

Lucifer glowed with joy as they descended down to the holy city.

Me-el's eyes widened as he took in level six in admiration. The couple had landed right outside the temple.

"Wow!" Me-el exclaimed.

"Is that where we worship Abba on this realm?"

Lucifer nodded and took his brother's hand.

"Yes, isn't it glorious?"

Me-el bobbed his head in agreement as his gaze fell upon the refined principalities and virtues that had come to praise God with dance in front of the temple. They fluttered through the courtyards with tambourines and flutes. Seraphim from level nine chanted in droves above the building unceasingly singing in harmonious unity. The two brothers traversed the pearly floor while two gilded powers held up burnished swords to welcome the Captain and his guest.

The temple was ringing with choirs of glittering angels from every rank.

"Not as quiet as when I was here." Lucifer observed.

Me-el now awe struck by his surroundings; pitter pattered away from Lucifer and fell to his knees in respect before the alter.

"My brother knows how to accurately praise our father!" The morning star ruminated; he was impressed with Me-el's reverent behavior.

Lucifer knelt down next to his sibling; from the opening behind the two cherubim and fire, Lucifer saw Abba smile and wave at them both.

Chapter 27

Rofocal and Rahab were both setting up Lucifer's dinner table on level four, in the palace. Rofocal looked down at his watch; a gift from his captain.

"Rahab it's nearly six, by my calculations they have been in Jerusalem for almost three hours! I do hope everything is well!"

Rahab glanced over at Rofocal with concern in his eyes.

"My yes!" He expressed as he placed silver forks at all four table settings.

"Yet, we must remember, Lucifer did vow to take Me-el there; and, it is a grand realm to visit! There is so much to see! The temple, the courtyard, worshiping angels of each rank.....not to mention all the potpourri of goods brought up from Eden that the merchants pass out!"

Rofocal frowned as he lit Lucifer's menorah with the tip of his index finger.

"Well," He gloomed.

"I hope Me-el does not ruin his appetite, Lucifer gave us specific instructions to prepare Me-el's favorite dish, disc pie."

Rahab gave Rofocal a wink as he put down four shiny plates.

"No worries there friend! I know Me-el always has room for disc pie!"

The two messengers jolted to attention as an energized Me-el famously slid into the dining room screaming:

"Did I hear disc pie? Lufi hurry up and get in here! Rofocal and Rahab are setting up for our EATS!"

Lucifer entered looking listless; all twelve of his feathery appendages were loaded with packages and bundles from the holy city. The captain seemed lethargic, yet his face displayed pride and unconditional love. Rahab stride over to the mighty seraph, he bowed; then obediently began lifting the numerous items from Lucifer's heavily burdened wings.

"Thank you my friend." The morning star acknowledged.

Rofocal; pulled out Me-el's chair then went over to assist Rahab.

"Where shall we put all these things?" Rofocal asked after genuflecting.

Lucifer gave them a tired smile as he answered.

"It's all for Me-el, everything should go in his room...unless of course it's edible, all food must go in the kitchen."

The messengers bowed in unison as they lugged the heaps of boxes and bags to the little angel's private resting quarters. Lucifer went over to the table and sat at the head; his enamored little brother was at his right.

"Did you have fun in Jerusalem Me-el?" He asked with heavy eyelids.

"Sure did!" Me-el chimed.

"Worked up the hungries too! When we gonna chow down?"

Lucifer let out a meager laugh.

"As soon as Rofocal and Rahab return, we decided to all eat together, remember?"

Me-el rested his chin on the table.

"Yeah, okay, I just hope they hurry, I'm starving!" He whined.

"Music to my ears!" Rofocal shouted.

Rahab and Rofocal re entered the undimmed dining area with two round sliver trays, holding freshly baked disc pie. The pair of messengers set a tray on each side of the burning menorah; then seated themselves. Lucifer led them in prayer.

"Blessed are you Yahweh, king of the universe who brings us such bounty."

A loud "Amen." was uttered at the end of the captain's blessing. Rofocal was glad to see Me-el devour five slices of pie in almost five seconds. Rahab equally seemed to be enjoying the dish; however, this was the third time Lucifer failed to join them. He merely took a polite bite from a single slice; it was mainly to show courtesy. The captain chewed slowly, and then wiped his mouth with a silk napkin; he passed Me-el the remainder of his uneaten piece.

"Lord Lucifer, if you so desire, I can prepare something else just for you." Rofocal offered.

Lucifer shook his head while sipping his wine.

"I've never been much of an eater my friend, but, I like seeing my Me-el happy, you two are both fantastic servants! I'm simply not into food as much as my younger sibling."

Lucifer affectionately elbowed the gorging child.

"It's all good!" Me-el released between mouth full's.

"It means I get extra disc pie!"

The two messengers and Lucifer all snickered at the youth's blunt declaration.

"Indeed it does!" Rahab agreed.

Me-el finished off a complete pie all by himself, his eyes began looming over to four slices which remained on the tray left of the menorah. Rofocal taking avid note of Me-el's little pink tongue smacking his eager lips; suggested:

"Would you like these final four pieces? I do believe Rahab and I have had quite enough."

Rahab affirmed Rofocal's statement with a nod.

"Well..." Me-el spoke as drool dripped from the corner of his mouth.

"Only if Lufi is positively sure he really does not want anymore!"

Lucifer leaned back on his mystic quartz chair, giving the child a half smile and wink.

"I'm fine Me-el; you go ahead and help yourself!"

Rofocal levitated the left over disc pie in Me-el's direction; upon landing, the tot plunged into it like a famished shark.

"I think," Lucifer began.

"I should go see how my soldiers are doing on realm five."

Rofocal raised a hand.

"Yes?" Lucifer asked.

"Forgive me lord, yet you appear so very tired; since you are now more familiar with your single eyed power, why don't you repose a bit?"

Rahab asserted his associate's submission.

"Yes lord, I too must agree, I know you care little for sleep, yet even a captain should indulge in an occasional nap."

Me-el now hiccupping like a record stuck on a needle; from taking in too much disc pie, seemed excited about the notion.

"Yeah Lufi! I know you don't have an egg, but we can both nap in mine in Eden! It's big enough for both of us!" The tyke spouted.

"In fact for some reason, it's gotten a lot wider lately." He added.

Lucifer's eyes darted to his little brother.

"Hmmmmm... You know I have always wondered what it would be like to sleep in an egg, who knows I may like peasant accommodations!" The morning star laughed.

Rofocal and Rahab chortled hysterically with him.

Me-el not understanding the joke searched Lucifer's eyes for a positive response.

"Indeed!" Rofocal chided.

"Rahab also has an egg west of Eden am I not correct my friend?"

Rahab bowed his head with a blush; Rofocal had just reminded him that he too was also but a peasant.

"Tis true lord," Rahab sighed.

"My egg is by no means a palace, yet you are most welcome to rest in it if you so choose. It is magenta colored one; I am sure Raphael can lead you straight to it, he did nest me after all."

Lucifer gave the messengers a nonchalant wave with his right hand.

"Thank you for the recommendation Rahab, but I would rather share an egg with my bubeleh Me-el!"

Me-el's eyes lit up in merriment; his hiccups subdued.

"As you wish my lord." Rahab asserted.

The messengers bowed as Lucifer and Me-el teleported out of the royal residence.

Rofocal and Rahab started to clear the table.

"That was nice of you to offer your egg."

Rofocal murmured to Rahab as they stacked trays, plates, and silverware.

"Well, you were the one that brought it up; I was embarrassed that I did not think of it first, I was too worried about coming across as a commoner, since I sleep in it....Anyhow I am sure you would have done the same thing if in my place."

"You are by no means common Rahab!" Rofocal insisted.

"Dare I say I am a bit envious of you? You see I was created by lord Lucifer, so I have no egg to go sleep in. Our lord did however make us messengers on level four each a bed of thick spun clouds; even still, tell me what is it like to have your own egg to go rest in whenever you wish?"

Rahab who was now blowing out the menorah looked up and smiled.

"I will not lie, the egg is quite comfy! But as lord Lucifer said it is but a peasant life! I think you and the other angels made by lord Lucifer have a far greater advantage! You may all rest on simple clouds of cotton; but, your kind also may constantly gaze on Lucifer's perfect beauty right before you close your corneas each eve! Oh what I would not give to be you rather than me!"

Rofocal's face formed a simper as he responded.

"Yes, I do suppose you have a point! I never really thought of it in that manner my friend! It would seem we are each blessed in our own special way!"

Rahab gave his friend a nod as they took the soiled dishware into Lucifer's mirrored kitchen for cleaning.

Down west of Eden; Lucifer and Me-el had arrived at the celestial egg patch. Enormous multi-colored gem glazed objects encircled them. The captain struggled to locate where his younger brother's dwelling was stationed.

"So many!" Lucifer observed.

"Me-el when you hatched there was only yours and three others, then of course came Raguel's and Samael's.... But now why they are limitless! I also see more blue ones! How do you ever manage to find your own?"

Me-el smiled smugly as he tugged his brother's hand.

"Come on Lufi, I will show you how I get to my egg! It's easy!"

Lucifer overwhelmed by the deluge of oval homes, carefully followed Me-el as he traipsed through the tulips and white butter cup flowers which decorated the violet dew kissed grass under their feet. Me-el peered up at Lucifer and pointed his ring finger to a familiar diamond topped azure egg.

"Why I remember how cute you looked when you came struggling out of that!" The light bearer reminisced.

"How did you find your egg so fast?" He bid.

"Easy, our eggs sing out our names when we come into the patch!" Me-el articulated.

"The cherub that laid it infused its voice into its shell allowing our eggs to send out vocal vibrations to us the angels!" Me-el pontificated intelligently; as he slid the top part of his egg open.

Lucifer grinned in pride.

"Not only does my Me-el sound more mature, but his upper body strength is advancing quite nicely!" He appraised.

(If *only the captain had witnessed Me-el lift Raguel up onto his shoulders earlier that day!)*

"You are a good little angel Me-el! Promise me you will never change!?" Lucifer tipped; as he made his way into the lofty sapphire shell.

Me-el who had entered first was already curled up at the bottom of the elliptical orb on some princely purple cushions.

"I promise!" He wistfully replied.

Lucifer slunk up next to his sibling and flung an unarmored right arm over him; the captain had morphed himself into a satin gown upon entry to be more at leisure.

"I love you." Lucifer remarked, as he kissed Me-el's temple.

The great seraph shut his eyes for the very first time since he had been created.

Chapter 28

Lucifer awoke, he saw himself napping next to Me-el yet also hovering over all nine levels of Heaven. The captain was now more cognitive of his bilocating skills since he had meditated privately in God's holy temple. He was able to decipher the activities occurring on each realm without any problems what so ever, in fact he was currently doing it while sleeping!

"I finally got the hang of it!" He theorized.

A rush of adrenaline coursed through the seraph's veins as he swung past each level. Lucifer commenced doing all sorts of works whilst resting by Me-el's side. The captain's wings fluffed up in confidence as he began promenading through Heaven. Throngs of angels fell to their knees in worship upon seeing him. Seraphim echoed songs of praise to him on level nine; while cherubim came down to all four furry knees in servitude to him in Eden. Thrones in Abba's own throne room circled him invoking gusts of wind to tussle his streaming gold hair. Dominions and powers from his fifth realm all brazenly lifted swords to form an aisle for the swaggering angel to walk through. Lucifer also be held his brethren; Raphael, Gabriel, and Uriel all pay homage to him from their own respective areas.

"They are all under my supreme authority!" He evaluated; as the triad he himself had formed; the lesser archangels, principalities and messengers all fawned over him like young school girls at a rock concert.

"Are they actually groveling?" Lucifer revolved.

The son of morning focused on realm nine once more; this time he saw Yahweh himself give him a slight bow. Lucifer's cobalt blue eyes suddenly opened. Me-el's chunky little arm had bopped him on the brow; bringing the silk attired captain back into his brother's egg.

"I know now that even though I am here with Me-el, I am also still everywhere else! It is all even clearer!" Lucifer thought.

"Well," Lucifer whispered as he lifted Me-el's arm to relocate it over a stuffed velvet toy lion.

"Apparently you are my primary focal point my sweet bubeleh!"

The light bearer quietly left the dozing child; he wanted to go prowl about Eden a bit before Shabbat officially began, it was only a couple hours away.

Raphael bowed upon viewing his captain amble over his direction.

"Good eve to you my lord! I saw you a moment ago, flying above me; may I help you with anything?" Raphael asked; from his post at the tree of life.

Lucifer walked around the tree, occasionally he would eye the ripe red pomegranates, at last he spoke.

"Tell me Raphael are you ever tempted to taste these plump citrus? I recall hearing none of us were to eat from this arbor; I am not at all bothered by it, since I scarcely partake of any food....yet, I am rather surprised Yahweh chose you to guard this tree; after all you are known to have a tendency to sample bites of the garden's foliage!"

Raphael's emerald eyes narrowed; Lucifer sounded rather cynical.

"Actually captain it does not faze me at all, I know what pomegranates taste like; aside from that my primary focus is most often in my gardening form, which is currently snacking on plums and walnuts as we speak!" Raphael coyly divulged.

Lucifer stepped back; he began to take in his golden armored brother.

"Well I must say you look absolutely smashing! I prefer your soldier gear over your gardening garments! I really never cared for that wreath around your head; with all due respect Raphael it makes you look like one of those gourmet princess cakes Me-el loves to nosh on! You appear much more handsome in your barbute helmet!"

Raphael chuckled at Lucifer's comment.

"There he goes comparing me to a cake again!" The lieutenant per pended.

"So," Raphael interposed.

"Have you tasted from the tree of wisdom yet? I assume you know all about it by now; how only you alone may partake of its fruit; I am a bit baffled that you would come here first and not head there straight away, Yahweh expressed how happy it would make him if you were to eat from your token tree!"

Lucifer's eyes looked into Raphael's with appeal.

"Really? Abba is that eager for me to try it?"

"He most certainly is." Raphael verified.

"Perhaps once you eat of the wisdom tree, you will find yourself infused with even more new abilities!"

Lucifer's face became serendipitous.

"You could be right! Thank you Raphael, I suppose I just wanted to socialize with you a trifle; I'll go pay Uriel a visit next, oh, and don't forget about our quartet concert on Sederday!"

Raphael smiled; he was looking forward to the event as well.

"I will see you there my lord. Oh by the way have you and Me-el been enjoying the new recipe Gabriel and I put together? The disc pie?"

Lucifer nodded.

"Yes, Me-el cannot get enough of it!"

Lucifer glanced up; a large white dove flew right above him, it seemed to be sizing him up with inquisitive eyes.

"Raphael that dove is mesmerizing! I believe it is the most beautiful bird I have ever seen in all of Eden!"

Raphael put out his right gilded hand; inviting the beguiling creature to perch, the lieutenant knew very well it was the Ruach.

"Say hello." Raphael suggested.

Lucifer outstretched his palm to touch the bird; he was blown away when he audibly heard it speak with the voice of God.

"I am looking forward to our Shabbat together bubeleh!" It telepathically transmitted.

Lucifer went down to his knees.

"Abba most high! I gather this is one of your other two forms?"

The dove cocked its head and blinked.

"Yes my beloved, this is me as the Ruach, I do hope you take Raphael's advice and go to the wisdom tree soon!"

The Ruach now flew over to Lucifer, landing on his right shoulder.

"I will my lord." The captain avowed.

"Yet if it is well with you, I may wait until after Shabbat."

The dove rubbed its head against the morning star's cheek.

"Oh very well my most lovely one, just make sure you do not forget about it!"

The Holy Spirit emphasized as he ascended.

"I thought you were going to go upon leaving my company." Raphael pointed out.

Lucifer shook his head.

"No I think I should wait; I mean suppose you are right about the tree giving me more power? I have just now mastered my current gifts of omnipresence and bilocating; I believe it would be wiser on my part if I waited. Aside from all that we have a concert to put on soon!" Lucifer's voice quieted as he finished his sentence, he was hoping Yahweh had not overheard; he wanted the concert to be a surprise for him.

Raphael winked at him.

"As you so choose my lord." The lieutenant bowed as the Captain soared over in the direction of some vineyards.

Raphael found himself in a rut; he was bowing yet again; a few grapes fell from a large basket which was strapped on just below his chest, yet above his gardening belt.

"Well hello again my great captain." Raphael chided he felt things were becoming redundant.

"Sorry brother, I simply could not resist gazing at you for a second time! By the way in all truthfulness I think your wreath is actually very nice; I was just giving you a hard time about it earlier to mess around with your wits a bit!" Lucifer jeered.

Raphael somewhat disconcerted over his brother's odd sense of humor, began to adjust his gathering basket.

"Well my lord, as enjoyable as our little chats tend to be....I should really finish up my work, Lucia will be by soon to transport these grapes up to Jerusalem for pressing them into wine."

Raphael knelt down on one knee to demonstrate respect for Lucifer without permitting more grapes to escape from his basket. A swarm of meddling pixies were at the angel's feet ready to devour any fruit he might drop; they permeated the vineyards ever searching out scraps to nosh on.

"I understand." Lucifer replied; as ten pixies leeched onto one of his boots.

"Clingy little things aren't they?" The captain remarked as he gave a swift kick causing the puny beasts to disperse.

"They are not the only ones being clingy today!" Raphael secretly mused; hoping Lucifer would actually let him complete his duties before Shabbat arrived.

"Well I'll see you Sederday Rapha! Oh if you would not mind, how about not wearing your wreath for the concert? Come in your choir robe and sash, I would like to keep things simple."

Raphael gave his captain a nod of approval as he watched him trek out of the budding vineyard. The archangel glanced down at his basket full of grapes.

"I really would love nailing him on the head with one of you grapes!" He inwardly pondered.

"Our captain can never seem to make up his mind! One moment he abhors my wreath, then the next moment he is fine with it; now he is back to..."Please do not wear it!" Ugh!!! Oh he is so lucky he outranks me! I am so fed up with his meshuggina mood swings!" The frustrated seraph excogitated.

Me-el awoke rubbing dream dust out of his eyes. The little angel noticed that aside from his toy lion, he was now alone in his egg.

"Judah!" He nagged at his plush animal.

"Did you go and gobble up my Lufi? You are a very bad lion! I shall need to punish you!"

Me-el began spanking the fluffy jungle cat on its rear, when he saw a silk tag sticking out beneath its tail, it read:

"*Made in level six: By the Archangel Jeremiel*"

"Nu? Oh yeah I feel like a shmendrick! I forgot toys don't need to eat! Sorry I spanked you so hard Judah. Please forgive me?"

The child kissed his stuffed lion then set him on a pile of pillows, before he exited his egg. Me-el covered his mouth and yawned.

"Where did Lufi fly off to?" He wondered. The youth scanned the egg patch, it was evening the sun had set and Uriel's stars were now glittering over the realm.

"You guys all look good because my friend Raguel polished you!" Me-el mumbled to the stars.

He started casing the egg patch over again. Me-el witnessed several angels coming to their eggs; Rahab was one of them. Me-el flew over to him.

"Hey Rahab."

The messenger smiled and gave Lucifer's favorite sibling a hug; he had just commenced sliding his magenta egg open.

"Hello Me-el, why aren't you with Lucifer? Don't you know Shabbat has begun?"

Me-el frowned and thumped his hand to his forehead. Rahab was right! Rabbi Gabriel had mentioned Shabbat officially began on the eve of the sixth day.

"Oy! I gotta get to level nine! I hope Abba and Lufi don't lock me out on account of me being late! All the napping I did made me really hungry!" Me-el's big blue eyes filled with tears; the very thought of missing out on an entire day of noshing simply devastated him! Rahab gave the angel a pat on the head.

"I doubt that little one, in fact I recommend you take a gander behind you!"

Me-el turned, Lucifer fluttered down towards him with outstretched arms.

"I came to get you Me-el! Sorry I left without telling you! I did not want to wake you, ready to go see Abba?"

Me-el gleefully soared up into his older brother's embrace.

"Let's go!" He sang.

Chapter 29

Yahweh watched as the last grains of silver sand swirled down his hour glass; a gift Uriel had presented him with, Shabbat had arrived. The jubilant creator hurriedly rushed over to his domed tea corner to make sure everything was set. The antique chairs along with Me-el's ottoman where in place. The table hosted a tray overlaid with heaps of lip smacking; crumpets, scones, stuffed figs, candied dates, muffins, cupcakes, and an extra large disc pie; made especially for Me-el. God knew his children very well, he had even made the table longer and wider.

"My little grob angel will need even more sustenance for an entire Shabbat!" Abba sniggered.

Yahweh opened the lid of his tea kettle.

"Oh that smells divine!"

Raphael had sent up jasmine spice with peppermint leaves. God readied the two lotus flower shaped cups; and placed them on white china plates, lined with gold and rubies.

"Hmmm....I feel as if I have forgotten something." The deity massaged his beard pensively.

"Oy! The chocolate cherubim milk!"

Elohim snapped his fingers as soon as the revelation hit him. A round marble end table materialized next to Me-el's footstool, holding a large quartz pitcher full of the sweet foamy beverage.

"Now we are all set! Oh I have been waiting almost a whole week for this!" God proclaimed.

"Yes!" Yeshua whispered.

"So have the Ruach and myself!"

Yahweh took his seat as he noticed his preferred son and tag a long enter his realm with a bow.

God brought both hands to his chest inhaling a large breath, as a relucent Lucifer, the source of his affection came towards him with Me-el. The child schlepped beside his brother; ready to attack the sublime pastries which were tantalizing his nostrils. Lucifer gracefully kissed Yahweh's hand. God returned the gesture on Lucifer's right cheek; he acknowledged Me-el with a hug and a poke at his belly.

"How is our favorite little dough ball?" Yahweh smiled.

"Hungry!" Me-el answered.

Lucifer's eyelids flickered, he felt a tad embarrassed.

"Shabbat shalom to both of you!" Elohim bellowed.

"Come let's go over to our tea room."

The triune God and pair of angels jaunted to the glass masked corner.

"I hope the butterflies have nibbled from the tree of life!" Lucifer thought.

He was thinking back to how Me-el had accidentally chowed down on a lovely monarch named Seth.

"Come and be seated!" Yahweh lay forward.

Lucifer relaxed into his violet chair as Me-el jumped onto his velvet green toad stool. The youth's eyes immediately became absorbed on the table; it was lidded with every choice edible, even disc pie. Yahweh; taking note of Me-el's ravenous appetite suggested:

"Shall we pray?"

The dignified Lucifer captured his father's right hand, along with Me-el's pudgy palm, he orated:

"We thank you Abba for this Shabbat repast, blessed are you great father who has given us life."

Elohim's eyes smiled in doting approval.

"Amen." The three concluded.

"Now you are both quite welcome to help yourselves to the refreshments!"

Me-el looked up at God, he knew he truly was privileged to be where he was; the tyke smiled brilliantly towards Yahweh adding:

"Thank you Abba for allowing me to join you and Lufi! Gadol Adonai!"

Yahweh gave the small archangel a wink.

"You just said how great our God is in my native language of Hebrew! Your rabbi is doing a nice job on her teaching!"

Me-el impishly giggled; he was thankful God did not bring up the whole window scenario. Yahweh situated his chair to face Lucifer.

"So," The deity began.

"Tell me Lucifer, my most fair, how have you been?"

God started filling their two cups full of tea. Lucifer politely accepted his, the morning star's pink lips carefully embarked on blowing steam off the cup's surface. He then began to sip.

"I am well Abba, Me-el keeps me filled with vigor! Do you like the new armor I had crafted for him?"

God's eyes dotted towards the succulent angel.

"Ahhh yes!" Yahweh said as he reviewed the child in earnest.

"It is magnificent! Why it even matches his opal blue eyes! It also fits him much better than the previous one! I see no precious stones popping off this time!"

Lucifer held back a laugh, recalling how Me-el had to (kvetsh); or squeeze into the prior coat of arms he once wore.

Me-el to busy inspecting what savory delicacy to snack on first, was in a world all his own. The tot's imagination ran wild as he envisioned himself sailing through the Milky Way on a gargantuan disc pie. He was in the process of chewing away on six slices at the moment, one in each wing.

"Life's been good to me...." He hummed as he brought a piece to his oral cavity.

Lucifer faced Yahweh as his younger brother continued with his feeding frenzy.

'Abba," He imparted; as he put his tea cup on its plate, on an end table which stood between their two chairs.

"Yes bubeleh," Yahweh remarked his eyes stuck on Lucifer's.

"Please speak! I created Shabbat for this very reason! That we might talk, oh how your voice enchants my senses! Say whatever you wish! I am all yours today!"

Lucifer smiled, he pushed back the end table so he could move closer to Yahweh.

"I now understand everything about the two new trees in Eden, The tree of life gives immortality to creatures which are not angels; and, I have been told by you as the Ruach and my siblings as well of how the tree of wisdom pertains specifically to me. I must confess Avi, I cannot lie to you; I am a bit leary of taking from the wisdom tree. I have just gotten the knack of my single eyed vision and bilocating; I assume you want me to eat of the tree to become even more powerful. I do not know if I am ready for that, what if I partake of the wisdom tree and....well, what if instead of becoming wiser, I end up disappointing you! I would never be able to live with myself!"

"That is absolute meshuggina bubeleh!" Yahweh answered.

God was deeply saddened that such a silly thought had even crossed Lucifer's mind.

"The tree of wisdom will make you wiser and more powerful, but you have nothing to be afraid of! I created it just for you, once you do eat of the tree you and I will become more united than ever! You should make haste and partake of it as soon as you can!" God propounded.

"I will if you really want me to." Lucifer said.

"But would you at least give me a couple of days to pray about it?"

Yahweh placed his hands on Lucifer's lap and smiled.

"Of course, my love, your reaction to eating from the tree is what gives me total faith in you! My Lucifer you have never been one to dive into something without first consulting me about it; this is why I love you so much! You may eat of the tree whenever you feel led to!"

Me-el who had just finished fressing down a disc pie and was starting to chuck strawberry bon bons into his yapper could not help but put in his own two cents in after ease dropping; he decided to try and encourage Lucifer to experience the wonders of eating.

"Abba is right Lufi! I do not know how you have resisted the tree of wisdom! I mean I know I would have eaten at least half of all its apples by now! Eating is so under rated! It is actually my favorite sport if you must know. Oh and those apples!"

Me-el stopped talking; his face took on a dreamy look of unattainable desire, as he began to fantasize about the wisdom tree.

"Those gleaming voluptuous sweet melt in your mouth fruits! Mmmmm... just thinking about the forbidden shiny yummers it makes my kishka growl! Oh I need to eat; I'm getting faint from so much thinking! I better get back to my Shabbat noshing!"

Me-el picked up a plate stacked with matzha, cheese and ironically; apples!

"Thank you Abba! You must have been reading my mind! You added apples to my plate that I can eat! Lufi you really have it made! If Abba would have given me all those humongous apples they would have found a nice home in my belly by now! You know, I bet they taste way better than these!" The child hinted as he chomped on some apple wedges.

Lucifer now displaying subtle discomfiture, due to Me-el's table conduct, lifted his tea cup and began taking dainty nips, like a proper English gentle man.

"I hope he is watching my etiquette and taking mental notes!" The captain mused.

Me-el remained oblivious; he was slurping up chocolate cherubim milk like a fat overheated dog that had just run a triathlon.

"My little brother has a healthy desire to fress! You know Abba; I think he might be hitting a growth spurt." Lucifer cited.

Yahweh could not help but smile. He really enjoyed gazing at the light bearer's perfect beauty. The deity looked over at Me-el and simpered.

"You know Lucifer; I do think Me-el has grown a bit." Yahweh affirmed.

God somehow managed to grab a cut of cheese from the tray next to the small angelic garbage disposal.

"He has grown wider!" Abba contrived inwardly, thankful Me-el could not hear his thinking.

"Abba," Lucifer spoke, taking God's eyes off Me-el.

"Yes my bubeleh?"

"I was just wanting to let you know, my siblings and I have planned a special surprise for you tomorrow, I hope it's okay for us to all come up here."

Lucifer halted; perhaps springing an unexpected concert on his creator was not the best idea.

"What if Abba has plans for Sederday?" Lucifer repined.

The morning star's face took on a look of preoccupation; he felt like a putz for not thinking things out better.

Elohim now concerned over the frown dimming his beloved one's visage; gently took hold of Lucifer's chin.

"My most precious child, I would be delighted beyond measure at any surprise you have prepared for me! Do not look so sorrowful! My heart becomes grieved to see such beauty tainted by worry! Come now, give me a smile!"

Lucifer's lips curved upwards causing the light in him to shine through his eyes with a pulsating force.

"Thank you Avi! Your approval means everything to me!" He sighed.

"I do not know what I would do with myself if I ever knew I had upset you!"

God smirked at Lucifer's final statement.

"That," Yahweh chortled,

"That would be entirely impossible for a creature like you to ever do! Lucifer you have only ever brought me sweet vibrations of love!"

The seraph took his father's palm and kissed it. Me-el, who actually had been studying his brother's table manners, now began dabbing his mouth with a silk napkin.

"I agree Abba! Lucifer is better than disc pie!"

The trio laughed as Yahweh brought his own foot stool out from under his chair to rest his feet on.

"What a glorious Shabbat!" Yahweh trumpeted.

"Indeed!" Lucifer and Me-el both concur.

Chapter 30

Sederday was in full swing, the fourth realm was abuzz with messengers allocating feverishly about the archangel quartet that was soon to take place in Yahweh's throne room. Hordes of golden haired angels were zoning in around Lucifer's palace in hopes of catching a glimpse of him.

Rahab and Rofocal acted as bouncers; sneering at the multi- farrious blonde gawkers from one of Lucifer's upper windows.

"All of you need to get back to work!" Rofocal hammered; as held back a dozen creatures with a gold scepter, something the light bearer had presented him with.

"Yes!" Rahab interjected using a scepter of his own; it was similar to Rofocal's; yet his held up a great pearl, whilst Rofocal's was topped with a red diamond. Lucifer had given them to the messengers out of gratitude for their diligent service.

"LordLuciferisquippinghimselfforhisperformance! He has no time to dally on you lollygaggers!" He snarled.

Lucifer's two personal assistants now more aggressively took to warding off the masses, much like two thug security guards at a teenage rave. The crowd began dissipating after some angels were bonked on the heads a few times; courtesy of the morning star's secret service.

Rofocal and Rahab grinned at each other in sanction; the pair had slight egos since Lucifer had honored them with wands of gold. The son of morning had explained how the exalted batons were symbols of authority. Lucifer had exhorted the following declaration upon bestowing them with the halcyon sticks on Thorsday evening.

"All messengers on my level will now clearly know that you both have been given distinct priority among all others with these two scepters at your sides!"

Rofocal lifted his scepter high and yelled:

"All of you angels must go now! Rahab and I must help our most ravishing captain prepare for his ceremony!"

The proclamation caused the flock to dwindle out completely. Rofocal slammed the window shut, and nodded at Rahab in victory.

"You sure told them!" Rahab spewed; as he polished the glossy pearl on his wand with his loose hanging sleeve.

Rofocal smiled and placed his scepter up against a mirrored wall.

"I did didn't I? I must say I do feel sorry for the poor lot of urchins! The sad chaps just happen to lack the savoir-faire you and I have, it's really rather pathetic."

Rahab simpered at his friend's statement; he could not have phrased it any better.

"Shall I go tell lord Lucifer it is safe for him to enter the dressing room now?" Rahab asked as he leaned his wand next to Rofocal's.

"Yes by all means." Rofocal asserted.

As Rahab went to fetch the captain Rofocal sashayed over to Lucifer's tall zircon crusted wardrobe. The messenger flung the doors open, revealing the light bearer's long opalescent white choir robe and Me-el's small, yet wide blue one.

"Oh Lucifer will gleam brighter than the sun and all the stars in Uriel's realm!" Rofocal gushed, as he ran his hand under the soft silken material.

"I do hope Rahab and I got all the measurements correct when we obtained the cloth in Jerusalem." The messenger thought to himself.

Rahab came in with an unarmored Lucifer and an insecure Me-el who was hiding his naked jelly rolls beneath his six emerald wings.

"Is my concert attire ready?" Lucifer bid, purposely holding back his twelve pinions to showcase his finely carved form.

Rofocal's face went turnip red as he averted his eyes lest he fall to the floor faint.

"Yes my lord." He guaranteed.

The ver clempt Rofocal passed the captain his choir robe, while keeping his gaze down. Rahab merely focused his glance on the wardrobe. Me-el began to tug at the messenger's robe.

"Ah Rahab can I please get my robe too? I don't have the chutzpah my brother does, I prefer my fluff to be well covered at all times!" He released.

Rahab winked at the fretting youth, he walked over to the clarion dresser to obtain Me-el's alb. Lucifer now a bit amused by the thick tension which was sweltering in the room; slipped on his garment and exhorted:

"Every angel can look up now I am dressed!"

Two big breaths of relief issued out of Rofocal and Rahab's lungs; as Rahab handed Me-el his billowy blue robe. Me-el looked up at his big brother, his middle set of wings were still hiding his tummy.

"I hope my choir robe fits me that good." Me-el mumbled.

"I know it will my little Lucifer!" Rofocal expressed.

"Rahab and I took it out just a millimeter or so around the mid section this morning, only to be safe of course; now..." The messenger went on.

"Pull in all your wings and suck in your tum tum!"

Me-el hesitantly did as he was told, while Rofocal and Rahab struggled to pull the silken clothing over Me-el's portly body. The child began to sob.

"I am no little Lucifer! I'm nothing but a butter ball!" He cried.

The pair of messengers paused to rest; the task was proving more challenging than imagined: Lucifer who had been admiring his reflection in all the mirrors turned, he faced his younger brother. The captain's diadem glowed as he widened the fabric for Me-el, thus permitting the tunic to swiftly envelop the tyke's porcine figure.

"Why Me-el your choir robe fits you quite nicely!" Lucifer said.

"I even think it appears to be a bit big on you!" He added.

"Perhaps Rofocal and Rahab got an armhole confused with your head hole; isn't that right you two?" Lucifer questioned as he gave his fumbling butlers a steely once over.

"That is exactly what happened!" Rofocal promised.

"Tis true!" Rahab agreed, bobbing his head like a velvet hound on a car visor.

"A thousand pardons to you Me-el, why look how loose it fits! Your older brother is right!" Rofocal emphasized.

"I do believe someone is getting svelte!" He chided.

Me-el who was now content from hearing all the forced out compliments now displayed all six of his wings through the open slits in the gown. The child began strutting about the dressing room like a midget plus size model on a cat walk in Paris singing:

"If you want my feathers and you think I'm fluffy come on angels let me know!"

The toddler shook his tail feathers towards Rofocal and Rahab. The two messengers clapped and whistled as the little angel paraded his silk choir robe in satisfaction.

"Well," Lucifer uttered.

"I am the only one that get's your fluffy little self! So enough showing off, I might get jealous, come on Me-el it is time for us to go meet our siblings on realm nine."

Me-el flew up into Lucifer's arms as Rahab handed the youth his satin sack which contained his silk banners on poles and his shofar.

"I can't let you forget your equipment!" He communicated.

"Thank you both." Lucifer smiled making the friends blush.

"Both of you can get a good audio of our performance if you fly to the outermost ledge of level eight, I had Gabriel tell her older students to set up a listening area a bit south of Opus Angelorum. I also told her to tell them that two special places were to be specifically set apart for the two messengers which were carrying golden scepters!"

Lucifer's loyal servants bowed in sheer gratefulness as they took hold of their signet jeweled wands.

"My lord is so thoughtful!" Rahab stammered.

"Indeed!" Rofocal granted.

"Lord Lucifer dare I say you are as generous as God himself?"

Lucifer smiled.

"Well I am technically equal to Abba in some respect, so I shall receive your compliment my friend! Besides it was nothing, I am just looking out for my two favorite messengers!" The captain spouted as he teleported to Yahweh's level with Me-el.

"Let's fly!" Rahab stuttered in excitement.

"I do not want to miss a single note our lord sings!"

Rofocal nodded.

Raphael, Gabriel and Uriel stood ceremoniously posed in front of realm nine's pearly gates. Lucifer had arrived accompanied by his younger brother.

"You all look so smashing!" The captain commented.

"Brother Uriel will you please perform the honor of unlocking the gates?" He asked.

All three archangels lifted from bowing as Uriel saluted; then, with his celestial key ring; which hung from a velvet pouch attached to the gold sash around his sliver choir robe, did as he was told. A burst of wind and sparkle erupted as the doors mystically opened. Lucifer took Me-el by the hand and led the group in.

Yahweh sat on his throne basking in a joyous spirit. Yeshua and the Ruach watched secretly from within the father's bosom; they were also salted with enthusiasm over what the morning star and his brethren might have in store for them. God leapt from his throne and spieled:

"Oh how wondrous you all look! I simply cannot wait for my surprise! I feel ver clempt!"

The five classy garbed angels bowed before Yahweh as Lucifer spoke on their behalf.

"My beloved Abba, prepare your eyes and ears for a feast of the senses! Please feel free to be seated upon your throne as we sing a personal concerto to you." Lucifer halted to pat Me-el on the head; the child was beginning to take out his ribbon wands from his sack.

"Me-el will dazzle you with dancing formations in the air while we sing!" The captain concluded.

"Sounds splendid!" God cheered.

"Please begin whenever you are ready!" He exclaimed.

Lucifer and his three lieutenants took their places just a foot or so from the sea of glass. Yahweh smiled while he examined his glittery children. Lucifer raised a gold pitch finder to his lips and blew into it; this was in order to harmonize his siblings. Me-el rocketed up into the air above the glass sea holding streaming rainbow banners. The captain nodded and ordered:

"Starting on a low D, Raphael will start the first song, and a one and a two.... Come now, poco a poco just as we rehearsed!"

The four seraphs with Lucifer standing in the middle began bobbing up and down in the style of a barber shop quartet. Raphael's deep rich low voice melodically started as the others sang as back up:

(Sung to the tune of "Mr. Sand man.")

"Bom, *bom, bom, bom, bom, bom, bom, bom, bom, bom, bom, bom, bom...*" Lucifer, Gabriel, and Uriel sang as they rocked to the side while snapping their fingers.

Raphael's solo then commenced:

"*Father Yahweh, you made a dream, the fairest angel all Heaven has seen.... With a young sibling with green wings of clover.... With Lucifer and Me-el now your lonesome days are over!*"

Raphael's words caused Yahweh to grin; Me-el flew about him elegantly spinning his ribbons in circular patterns. Uriel now picked up on the happy arriety; as Raphael stepped back, so he could step up.

"*Yes father Yahweh we wish to please... although we may not be as lovely as he... we hope our voices can win you over... if they fail to, we come out looking like rovers...*"

God snickered at the delightful music; he now tapped his sandaled foot and began snapping his fingers in time with the acapella beat of the quartet chorus. Lucifer waved his white gloved hand; this was to signal in a new song. Yahweh watched as a spotlight from the glowing wings of silent seraphim which were hovering above Gabriel now showcased her. The archangel took Uriel's place and poured out the next song.

(Sung to the tune of "Blue Moon")

"Yahweh you were just standing alone.........You wanted someone to care for and a love all your own....."

As Gabriel chimed out her melody the others chanted:

"Oooohhh Yahweh....."

Lucifer now went center stage, standing next to Gabriel, their voices joined in an enticing sound.

"Yahweh I am here just for you....Oh I love you so dearly, to you alone will be true.......Oh Yahweh....."

Gabriel silenced herself, then stepped back as Lucifer outstretched his arms and beamed lovingly up to God as he finished:

"My Yahweh....................."

The trio behind the captain fell to their knees, each extending their right arms' out and repeating Lucifer's last line.

"Our Yahweh!"

Me-el fluttered overhead, he withdrew his shofar and ended the concert with a mighty blast from it. The little angel's cheeks obtained a blue hue as he sounded the ram's horn; his effort paid off, the trumpeting was impeccable! God hopped off his throne clapping his hands vigorously.

"Wonderful!" He proclaimed.

"I loved it! Thank you! Thank you all so much! You too Me-el!"

The exhausted tot dropped his ivory shofar back into his carrying bag, which hung over his back. He was just now feeling the weight of all his fancy flying maneuvers and trumpet blowing. Me-el lethargically made his way down on six very soar wings. The tyke's pinions suddenly gave out; causing Me-el to plummet down ward like an inflated bird who had just smacked into a closed glass window.

Me-el landed with a squishy plop belly down in front of Yahweh's feet.

"Oy! Are you okay bubeleh?" God questioned as he bended down to review the youth.

"It's nothing some chocolate cherubim milk would not fix right up Abba." Me-el hinted from the floor.

Yahweh let out a laugh as he picked up the hefty mini seraph and sat down on his throne, with Me-el on his lap.

"We will need to accommodate you with that then! But, first..." Yahweh's gaze went to Lucifer and his three siblings.

"My beloved light bearer, Raphael, Gabriel, and Uriel, come forward!"

The archangels and their captain rhythmically levitated and floated over the sea of glass. They stationed themselves softly in front of God's throne. Yahweh set Me-el down, giving him a gentle pat on the tuches.

"Me-el why don't you go over to our tea corner, I do believe some nice frothy chocolate cherubim milk is awaiting you!"

A panting Me-el licked his lips, he was very parched. The child obeyed; yet, since his wings were still stiff in pain, he waddled down to the domed tea room like an overweight infirm duck.

"Well," Yahweh began.

"I am in awe with all of you! Lucifer my love, tell me who wrote the lyrics?"

Lucifer's chest began to rise up a bit as he responded.

"I did Abba, however, Raphael came up with the music and Gabriel choreographed our dance moves."

"Well you all did wonderfully!" God divulged.

"I am overwhelmed and even more ver clempt that my four top archangels came together to display such affection for me! Brava to all of you!"

"Did you really like it?" Lucifer beseeched, wanting to be sure Yahweh was not simply being kind. God picking up on the son of morning's *fertummect mind; rose from his throne and planted a kiss on his right cheek; he then tightly embraced the others.

"Like it? I loved it! Lucifer I cannot fathom ever creating another entity more spectacular than you!"

Lucifer blushed, he was glad to see Yahweh's feelings were sincere.

"I am here to serve you Abba." He pledged.

---

* Fertummect: To be confused.

Chapter 31

The Sederday concert had been a success; angels in every realm were still going on about it, when Sunday arrived. Gabriel entered her classroom only to receive a standing ovation from her student body. The rabbi's face reddened as she made her way to her desk.

"Thank you all! Alas, your flattery will not get any of you spared from homework!"

The students all emitted moans as they took their seats.

"Today I would like all of you to go spend time on level seven, Cassiel..." She called.

"You may come in now."

The class went silent as a spellbinding seraph appeared in their midst. He glowed like the moon, and his eyes were like stars. The stunning creature displayed his crystal wings in a humble, yet exalted manner.

"Wow!" Raguel whispered.

"He looks like he could be a prince or something!"

Me-el nodded.

"I hear he helps out on level seven, Lufi told me all about him! In fact Lufi was there the day he hatched!"

Cassiel's opaque achroite eyes gazed down at the two little *yentas, he smiled warmly.

"Class," Gabriel explained, as she came out from behind her desk.

"Please meet Prince Cassiel, although he was born a seraph; Yahweh himself has saw it fit to elevate him as a prince and overseer of realm seven. Cassiel was hatched with God given knowledge; making him very exceptional. That is why he was not required to attend school like the rest of you."

"That lucky bum!" Raguel gloomed.

"Prince Cassiel will be your chaperone today; I will now allow him to explain the purpose of the outing." Gabriel said as she gave Cassiel the floor.

"Well greetings to all of you!" Cassiel exhorted, his visage was handsome and friendly.

"I know I enjoyed yesterday's concert as much as all of you! Today I will be taking you to the praise and worship center, we are all going to go over how to read music together! Realm seven is known to be the very nuts and bolts of all heavenly music! I do think all of you will be captivated by it!"

Me-el and Raguel shared disgusted glares. The Prince noticed the exchange between the duo.

---

* Yenta or Yentas: Busy bodies, or gossips.

"I know it does not sound like the most fun thing to do, but, it will greatly assist each of you! For example, does anyone in this class plan on learning to play any type of instrument?" Cassiel quizzed.

To Cassiel's astoundment every hand in the room went up, even Raguel's.

"So," Cassiel knelt down alongside Raguel's desk.

"What kind of instrument would you like to play little one?"

"I wanna play one that you don't need to learn how to read for!"

Gabriel rolled her eyes at her pupil's response.

"I suppose I should not be surprised by any of his answers anymore!" She silently grunted.

Samael let out a chuckle. Prince Cassiel rose to full height again.

"Well, believe it or not Raguel there is one musical instrument that does not require use of note reading."

Cassiel glanced back at Gabriel, the rabbi nodded, she knew straight away Cassiel was referring to the shofar; She picked up her small one which she kept in one of her desk drawers, and handed it to Cassiel. Me-el's eyes lit up.

"Yeah Raguel! You could play the ram's horn! I did it at the concert yesterday! I did not need to read anything! All you gotta do is blow into it! Yahweh really liked it! Trust me it is super easy!" Me-el promised his friend.

"Yes it would prove to be simple to an angel full of hot air like Me-el!" Gabriel deliberated unheard.

Prince Cassiel passed Gabriel's eight inch shofar to Raguel.

"Okay lad, just do as your friend said, and give it a nice hard blow! Don't hold back, you most definitely look like you got it in you!"

Raguel took the ram's horn to his puckered lips; he filled his lungs with air and blew. The little angel's face began to grow purple in color, as he passed out on his desk, no sound had come out at all, not even a sputter of one.

"Oh no!" Me-el yelped.

"Rabbi your shofar poisoned my best friend! Did you let Uriel borrow it? He probably laced it with arsenic!"

The class giggled in unison; until Gabriel shot them an icy stare with her ruler in hand.

"No Me-el! It is mine, I alone use it! Not every angel is meant for the shofar, it's all in the lips, and perhaps Raguel cannot blow it correctly because he spends too much time complaining!"

Me-el silenced and made a pout, Samael released a tiny chuckle.

"Raguel please get up!" Gabriel rebuked.

The dazed youth hobbled to his feet and reseated himself.

"I guess learning how to read a few music notes won't be so bad." He said as he regained his breath.

"Wonderful!" Cassiel proclaimed.

"That is the right attitude to have! Come let us all go together to level seven! Do not worry I will start each of you on the simplest of instruments for beginners, it is called a recorder; it is a sort of flute which comes with very easy notes to follow!"

The students all stood and followed the gleaming seraph out of the classroom. Gabriel went back to her desk.

"Well while they have music study, I can catch up on my own papers; I think I'll assign an essay on musical instruments for today, yes... no doubt Cassiel will show them each one on the realm. It can be a type of exam as well." She evaluated.

Gabriel pulled out her quill from her ink jar ready to write; when, she was taken aback by an outstanding figure. He was standing right in front of her desk. The rabbi's jaw and quill dropped as she froze in her cushioned chair. He had to be the most beautiful creature she had ever laid eyes on; he was even lovelier than Lucifer!

"Do not be afraid my child." He disclosed.

Gabriel slowly closed her gaping mouth, she felt a bit foolish; she recognized his voice!

"Abba?" She bid as she rose to bow.

"Yes, I AM, this is me in my form of Yeshua."

Gabriel genuflected; she began to wonder if Lucifer was watching them.

"No, and even if he was, he would not see me." Yeshua answered.

"I put a block on him, I do intend to appear to him in this person when I am ready, but today I want to discuss some important information with you and you alone."

Yeshua walked over to the glass twin doors etched with angelic symbols and carefully shut them tighter. He wanted to make certain no one would accidentally over hear their private conversation.

"Gabriel I loved the concert yesterday! Since Lucifer took the time to put something so nice together for me with all of you; I would like to return the favor! I want to give Lucifer a great surprise all his own!"

Gabriel smiled.

"Of course my lord, tell me what can I do to help you?"

"Well," Yeshua spoke as the angel pulled out her personal quartz chair for him to sit on.

"Please be seated most high, I am used to standing, in case you have not noticed, the students tend to keep me on my feet."

"Thank you dear." Yeshua smiled as he took the angel up on her kind gesture.

Gabriel watched as the God man turned the chair backwards and straddled it. Yeshua rested his arms and chin over the upper part of it, like a cowboy.

"What a curious way to sit!" She observed.

Yeshua began reciting his plans to her.

"I am going to create some glorious new additions to level one!"

Gabriel's eyes widened, and then blinked again.

"For Lucifer?" She enquired.

"Yes." Yeshua grinned, flashing white teeth her way.

"I have already discussed it with Uriel and Raphael, now; I've come to tell you! Here is the catch; it must all be kept under wraps from Lucifer! Remember this is my surprise for him! So…." Yeshua's face took on a brilliant sly smile as he continued.

"Please do not by any means allow Me-el to find out!"

Gabriel and Yeshua began laughing together.

"I assure you my lord I will not reveal any information you give me to any angel!" Gabriel affirmed.

She was all too familiar with Me-el's terrible talent of letting the cat out of the bag.

Yeshua tilted his head upward, his eyes gunning to the onyx ceiling sprinkled with clusters of itty bitty diamonds; which represented constellations and galaxies. The archangel followed Yeshua's gaze.

"Do you like it Abba? I use it to teach the students about astronomy...Oh how silly I can be! You were the one who made all of this! I just simply cannot get past your current form! If I dare say, you are more beautiful than..." Gabriel cut herself off.

"To say any one is more beautiful than Lucifer could bring offense, even if I am talking about him..." She analyzed.

"More beautiful than what?" Yeshua prodded as he shifted his hazel brown eyes to Ursa Major and Ursa Minor.

"More beautiful than all the stars in realm one combined!" Gabriel disclosed.

"Why thank you Gabriel, but, Lucifer, my Lucifer outshines everything! However, let us get back to why I came; you should know that within a few days; perhaps sooner, this little observatory of yours will need some reconstructing! I have decided to make nine planets! One to correspond to each level of Heaven! This is the big shebang I have planned for my Lucifer! I am going to create them all just for him!"

Yeshua now looked over at Gabriel, she seemed somewhat thrown.

"Pardon me father, I know I look confused and believe me I feel like a bit of a shmendrick for asking what I am about to ask, since I am the designated rabbi of this realm, but, what is a planet? Is it similar to the sun or moon? I suppose they are not; the sun is technically a large star; oh by the way did you notice those two particular bodies have been added?"

Gabriel nervously tipped; she was hoping Yeshua did not think her to be entirely unwise.

Yeshua's gaze went back up to the ceiling, his eyes traveled to the fire opal and the regular opal which symbolized the sun and moon.

"They are stunning!" He expressed, his eyes shining with love.

"Each one is precise in measurement and the right color! Did Azazel bring those jewels up from realm five?"

"He did!" Gabriel transmitted.

"He pounded them both in himself!"

"Well," Yeshua went on.

"As I said they are very nice, but, to answer your question about the planets; they will be entirely different. Gabriel I intend to fill each planet with brand new life! I am going to make new creatures! They will be unlike anything you have thus far seen in Heaven," Yeshua paused, before he picked up on his wording.

"Well for the most part anyways." He added.

Gabriel found her jaw dropping yet again; she reclined on Samael's empty desk.

"You mean some of the creatures that are perhaps depicted in our library will inhabit your planets?" She queried.

"Perhaps..." Yeshua hinted not ready to dish out all the details he had in mind yet.

"I will tell you this much Gabriel, my head is teeming with several ideas! I know what kind of beings will exist on eight of the planets as of now, however....The ninth one I am still trying to fully conceptualize but, I can give you one small clue about it."

Gabriel slanted forward, her silver eyes agleam in anticipation.

"The ninth planet, which will be the last one I compose, it will be almost like Eden, the life I put there will be by far the most enchanting of all the planets! Now as for structure; all my planets will be round; yet, they will vary in size, proportion, and color. What do you say? Will you assist me and your two brothers in keeping this on the low down from Lucifer and Me-el? We could really use your scholastic expertise and knowledge."

"YES!" Gabriel practically screamed out.

Yeshua arose and turned the chair back to its correct position, he then sat on it properly.

"You know Gabriel I have already begun working on the first one! This is another reason why I came to see you. I need a good name for it!"

Gabriel shook her head with stunned eyes.

"You actually find an archangel like me worthy of naming something of such significance to you like a new planet?"

Yeshua simpered.

"Why not? If any angel knows the library better than you, it's Lucifer! And, as I said before, this project is to be kept under lock and key until I am completely finished with all nine! Now, I could easily title each one myself; but, I would love to hear what such an exquisite angel like yourself might manage to come up with."

Gabriel blushed; Yeshua was both compelling and charming.

"Well, only if you are absolutely sure"

Yeshua nodded.

"I am! Now throw some ideas my way!"

"Very well my lord, can you tell me a bit about it?" She carefully ventured.

Yeshua opened his right palm, a tiny silver glass ball; much like a great masher in a human child's set of marbles sat in it.

"See this, my first planet will be the smallest of all nine, it is the one I am just finishing up on; also it will be the furthest from the sun; unlike here in Heaven, life on my planets will experience temperature."

Gabriel was beginning to understand things better.

"Then it would make sense to expect that your first planet will be very similar to my realm of snow and ice." She put forward.

"Exactly!" Yeshua said bemused.

"Gabriel how would you like to personally over see this planet? It would allow me to get straight to work on the others much faster. I have already created the life on it as well, now the life forms which inhabit it are suited to the planet's climate, in other words, they all do very well in the cold."

Gabriel now giddy with enthusiasm asked:

"Are the life forms anything like my Snowball?" The anxious archangel could not help but imagine countless furry White Sea lions running adorably about the planet.

Yeshua's eyes twinkled; he could read her excited train of thoughts.

"Actually yes; but, they are bigger! I call them yetis. I created them using the ice and snow, making sure their body temperatures would accurately adjust to their surroundings."

"So you are telling me that yetis are giant seals?" Gabriel blurted out.

"In a manner of speaking," Yeshua said as he began playing with the rabbi's quartz ruler.

"But, unlike Snowball, the yetis will have the ability to walk upright on five toed paws. Now some will look very similar to your pet seal; yet once full grown, a yeti can reach ten feet in height. They are all white and fluffy, also quite playful; they will all have the same diet of vegetables and milk. In fact Raphael has been feeding them as of late; but, I am sure he would not mind if you gave him a hand."

Gabriel was now bouncing on the tip of her toes in exhilaration.

"Oh let me be the one that takes full care of feeding them Abba?!"

She pleaded in a child like manner.

"Oh alright..." Yeshua smiled.

"I thought you might like to anyhow!" He winked.

"So before I go, what about giving me a name for the planet I am going to let you manage?" He asked.

"Oh yes! Well, it's cold and far from the sun, so it cannot be very bright; yet, it will be filled with playful Sea lion type creatures! I recall reading about a Pagan Roman god named Pluto; he was said to be dark and miserable, yet; you have furnished this tiny planet with such delightful beasts, so delightful that they will surely light up the planet's dismal atmosphere! So... Pluto would not be a really good name, hmmmmm; what about using the name Pluto yet also using a play on words? How about we call your first planet Playful?"

Yeshua set down the ruler, and jumped out of the chair.

"I love it!" He expressed.

Yeshua placed the marble he had been holding on the corner of Gabriel's desk.

(To this very day it still remains there.)

"And... if for some ridiculous unknown reason I ever were to eliminate the yetis..."

Yeshua was thinking out loud, but Gabriel's eyes took on a serious appearance of alarm, she really loved seals, the thought of such a thing deeply worried her.

"Oh sweet Gabriel do not worry! I never see that actually happening!" Yeshua jested.

"I was just going to say that IF the yetis were ever extinguished for some reason, we could use the name Pluto as a back up!"

A sigh of relief escaped Gabriel's lips. Yeshua concluded his dialogue.

"I should get going Gabriel, the third hour is approaching, your students will soon be returning from level seven. Remember, mum's the word! When I begin working on the next planet, I will stop by to see you again; after I complete the first eight, we will have a formal unveiling on realm nine. Lucifer and Me-el will then have the privilege of gazing upon them for the very first time! Oh one more thing; I want you to know this, it's another clue about the ninth planet! It will be so incredible that your captain will surely fall to his knees when he catches sight of the life I plan to put there! All the rest of Heaven will as well! Of course I still have a few kinks to work out; but the final planet will be the most wondrous of all!

Please feel free to write me a letter via messenger dove after you make your first visit to Playful. Oh and do not worry; I blocked Lucifer's vision in certain areas, without his knowing. He will not see you or your siblings when you travel to any of the planets to check on them. Well off I go! Don't forget to write! I cannot wait to hear what you think about my yetis!"

Gabriel gave Yeshua her best elegant bow as he dissolved from her classroom.

"Eeeeeeeeeeeeeee!" Gabriel squealed in a high pitched shriek.

"I get to feed and play with giant walking seals! I can't wait till the third hour comes! Hmmmmm I sound like Raguel and Me-el! Oh I cannot help it! I bet they are as cute as Snowball!"

The overly thrilled rabbi regained her composure as she realized her students could come waltzing through the closed twin doors at any given moment.

"I will assign them their homework, and then shove them off! I gotta get to realm one and visit Playful!" She stipulated.

Chapter 32

Lucifer and Me-el were frolicking in Eden; the morning star had gathered his younger brother once class had ended on realm eight.

"Me-el," Lucifer asked as they meandered through a field of multi colored fritillaries.

"Would you like to go visit with Raphael for awhile, I promised Abba I would try out the tree of wisdom."

Me-el was holding a vivid purple pixie in his hands; he was planning to take it to Raguel so they could encage it and turn it into their own personal little slave.

"You are gonna write out all our future homework assignments!" He threatened.

Me-el, sadly unaware of the pixie's short temper, howled in pain as the miniscule creature bit into one of his sausage shaped fingers.

"OUCH! You stupid ingrate!" He roared.

Lucifer's eyes widened, he did not know a pixie had just bitten his brother, he thought Me-el had been addressing him! He had never heard Me-el sound so furious.

"Forgive me little brother, you can come along if you so choose, I do not want you to be mad at me! It's just that Uriel guards the tree, and I know how he gives you the...what do you call it? Oh yes, the heebie jeebies, but again, you may come if it will settle your temperament."

Me-el shook his head.

"Oh Lufi, I am not yelling at you! I would never ever be mean to you! How could I ever call some angel as wonderful as you something so awful? I was yelling at a pixie!"

Me-el held out a swollen red finger, displaying puny bite marks.

"That rascal bit me!" He touted.

Lucifer picked up his brother, glad he had not been referring to him as an ingrate. Lucifer kissed Me-el's sore digit.

"Me-el I told you to leave the pixies alone! I know they are pretty, but they can be horrid little beasts! They like bothering angels; mainly because they were made by God before we were. Their terrible jealousy makes them do mean things sometimes!"

The child rubbed his finger; it was starting to feel better.

"You can say that again! One time one of them hitched a ride on my wing without me knowing it, way up to level four! I never would have found the stinker, but, Rahab got him for me! The pixie was making knots in his hair! Poor Rahab had to lose a couple inches off his long locks; at least it all grew back within a couple hours."

Lucifer tittered.

"Yes, pixies often knot up an angel's hair if they feel that the angel is more attractive than they are!" He revealed.

"Good thing it did not find you then Lufi!" Me-el related.

"Your hair would be meshuggina with all kinds of awful tangles!"

Lucifer gave Me-el a hardy guffaw.

"Why thank you brother, though I assume when you get older, you will make many a pixie envious yourself! Now, would you like to go visit with Raphael or come with me?"

Me-el escaped Lucifer's hold on him.

"I'll go see Raphael! Like you said, Uriel guards that tree! He is like a giant pixie to me! You go on ahead, oh and eat some apple for me!"

Lucifer smiled and waved as Me-el hopped through the field and collected flowers.

"Hey Lufi, I think I will weave some of these flowers together for Raphael and make him something to go with his head wreath!" The youth rang out.

The captain glanced back at Me-el one last time before heading for the wisdom tree.

"He will love that Me-el; I will come find you when I am finished, okay?"

"Okay Lufi!" Me-el hollered as he extended a threaded strand of fritillaries proudly over his head.

"Just what that cake Raphael needs, more frosting!" Lucifer thought as he flew onward.

Uriel lifted the visor of his helmet, he could scarcely believe it; Lucifer was coming his way.

"Eeegad! I wonder if he finally is going to try one of these blasted apples!" He conjured.

The chrome armored Lieutenant knelt and saluted his incoming captain.

"Hail lord Lucifer, Cheeri-O; have you come to sample from your tree?"

Lucifer's eyes reviewed the unusually large shiny apples, some were silver and some were gold.

"I have." He admitted curious if, or how, the gold ones differed from the silver.

"I would give both of them a go if I were you lord! Two hues may mean two types of wisdom." Uriel advised.

Lucifer lengthened his right arm and hand as Uriel moved aside to give him room. The light bearer's eyes caught sight of a unique apple; it was half silver and half gold!

"Uriel look, if I pick this one, why I will not need to eat two!"

"Blimey! You are right! Take it captain." He suggested.

Lucifer picked the double toned fruit. He sniffed it, hesitated; and then took a minute nibble.

"Awww dear me!" Lucifer crooned as he collapsed to his knees and dropped the apple; Uriel in instinct; caught it with his left hand.

"Captain?" Uriel hunched down and put his right arm around the morning star.

Lucifer held a hand to his brow. The seraph closed his eyes, as new-fangled energy jolted through him.

"I can hear every angel!" He cerebrated.

The captain put both palms to his cranium.

"Is this how my father Abba feels?" Lucifer wondered it was quite overwhelming.

Raphael's thoughts were the first Lucifer made out; as Me-el handed the gardener the connected garland of flowers.

"I shall wrap it about my waist, just to give Lucifer a tease; since he loves calling me a cake so much!"

Lucifer waved away the concerned Uriel, as he rose to his feet.

"I hear Me-el..." He evaluated.

"I miss Lufi, I wonder if Abba would let me lick one of his apples....Nah! I'll just ask Raphael to take me to the cocoa trees!"

Lucifer shot Uriel a baffled stare.

"Whatever is the matter my lord?" The vexed archangel asked.

"Oh nothing, I am fine Uriel, by the way you do not need to go and contact Abba. Will you please give me back my apple?" Lucifer communicated.

Uriel handed Lucifer the fruit and took off his helmet, his eyebrows were lifted in shock.

"Captain you just bloody well read my mind didn't you?"

"I did." The captain stated with equally startled eyes.

"My lord you have been given a great gift!" Uriel posed.

"Why, you are just like Abba now! This tree truly does live up to its name!"

Uriel shut his yapper; he began to strictly focus on space. The archangel suddenly became aware that now more than ever, he had to block his brain, especially since

Yahweh was planning a big surprise for the morning star. Lucifer tossed the bitten apple into a black satin pouch on his artillery belt.

"Well, I better go find my Me-el before cocoa trees become extinct in Eden!" The captain bantered.

Uriel placed his helmet back on and re stationed himself under the tree.

"Oh Uriel," Lucifer said as he glanced back over his shoulder.

"Yes my lord?" The lieutenant asked.

"The Milky Way is extraordinary! I can tell Raguel has proved to be a good star shiner!"

Uriel bowed as Lucifer took to flight, the archangel whispered for a nearby dove to come over in his direction. A delightful grey and pink one landed on his shoulder. Uriel kept his mind set on the Milky Way and pulled a feather from his avian friend.

"Forgive me love." He apologized.

The dove re grew its missing plumage within a second. Uriel removed an ink jar and some small scrolls from his own belt of novelties, then began scribbling two separate notes; one for Raphael and another for Gabriel. They both read:

"Guard your thoughts! Lord Lucifer has eaten from the tree of wisdom, and he can now read our minds!"

Uriel whistled causing the reluctant bird to come back. The lieutenant snatched a curling vine from the tree's trunk and broke it in separate pieces. Uriel gingerly tied the two messages to the dove's fragile pink leg.

"Off you go love! Deliver these notes, go to Raphael first, then Gabriel! Fly fast!"

The dove flew up into the sky; unfortunately Lucifer had already gotten a peek at Raphael's thinking.

Raphael and Me-el were laughing hysterically; the pair were flying in loop de loops over some exploding pudding volcanoes in the garden of desserts east of Eden.

"Yummm! A new flavor!" Me-el said while licking pistachio pudding from his lips.

"Okay little one, I do believe I see Lucifer headed our way, we had better go in for a landing."

"Oh goodie Lufi is back!" Me-el cheered, catching sight of his favorite sibling.

Raphael went into a seemly flight; Me-el flew less gracefully alongside him. The two angels appeared radiant against the mauve sky, which was specked with stars. Raphael's luxurious pink wings spread out triumphantly as he softly glided down into a riveting bow to his captain. Me-el landed with a thud, and then he bowed.

"At ease," The light bearer commanded.

Raphael swore he sensed some sarcasm in his captain's voice. The gentle gardener looked up and rose from his bended knee. Me-el was already up on Lucifer's shoulders, telling him how much he had missed him. Lucifer roved up to Raphael and tore the woven strand of fritillaries off from around the archangel's waist. Raphael gazed at his brother in stupor; Lucifer was not in a good mood at all. Me-el to happy to have his older sibling return, did not even notice what had occurred. The child was braiding Lucifer's hair, and making sure no mangy little pixies had made their way into it.

"Oh I am sorry Raphael," Lucifer smirked.

"I meant to give you a hug,"

Raphael's eyebrows narrowed in suspicion.

"It is alright my lord, I am glad to see you; Me-el really missed your presence."

"Of course he did." Lucifer snapped.

"Me-el is not one to try and purposely tease me as some angels do!"

Raphael's emerald eyes nictate. He felt inopinate.

"Can he read my mind?" The lieutenant asked himself.

"Yes I can." Lucifer sneered.

Raphael now standing at his full height bravely peered into Lucifer's eyes; they were different. The gardener felt as if he was gazing into the very eyes of God himself, yet; Lucifer's eyes had a spark all their own; a spark that made Raphael shiver to his core.

"Forgive me my lord!" Raphael beseeched as he fell to his knees.

"My most sincere apologies for allowing my silly mind to mock such a great and beautiful captain like you!"

Raphael went prostrate; his wreath of roses fell off his head and slipped forward towards Lucifer's feet.

"Oh Raphael you really do look lovely adorned in all those flowers...still...."

Lucifer picked up the wreath, and then tapped Raphael's fore head with the toe of his boot.

"Now that I ate from the tree of wisdom....Brother I can hear as Abba does"

Raphael continued lying flat, and spoke not one syllable as Lucifer went on.

"I remember the day you hatched, Abba crowned you with a wreath just like this one, it made you so happy...."

Raphael trembled as he stood up. He felt ill at ease, the archangel started to focus his mind on the milking virtues, lest Lucifer see into his thoughts again.

"My lord I am truly sorry." The gardener repeated.

"Oh I know you are, you know; perhaps what you need is to occupy yourself with making another flowery crown like this one."

Lucifer held up the wreath, since he was a foot taller than Raphael, it was just out of his brother's reach.

"I think the one my lord is holding is just fine." Raphael submitted.

Lucifer's eyes now appeared more like blue flame as he threw Raphael's wreath to the ground and crushed it without mercy under his right foot... Raphael cringed; he could feel the pain his flowers had felt. Me-el, who had been engaged working on Lucifer's hair, finally looked down.

"It is not so fine any more now is it?" Lucifer smirked.

Raphael swallowed a growing lump in his throat.

"Lufi, why did you do that to Raphael's pretty wreath?" The puzzled child put forth.

Raphael fought back tears as the captain elaborated:

"Oh Me-el! Well you see I saw a frightful pixie in one of the roses! I did not want our sweet Raphael to put the wreath back on his head after I had discovered it! His long hair would become all tangled in knots!" He bluffed.

Lucifer's fib fooled the naïve youth.

"Oh that makes sense! Lufi is right Raphael, I know pixies live here with you, but you should not trust them, they can be super mean!"

Raphael forced a smile onto his face.

"Both you and Lucifer are correct, I know your older brother is just looking out for me, I am most thankful for his concern." Raphael disclosed, hoping that he sounded convincing.

"I am always looking out for you!" Lucifer said in a scornful tone.

The captain rocketed upwards with his younger sibling.

Raphael now somewhat un nerved, skipped back a step; out of his left ear, he plainly heard the coo of a dove. The lieutenant turned to see a messenger bird sitting on one of his many flower coated trellises. Raphael approached the dove, taking the tiny parchment from its talon. The bird flew off and ascended to realm two to visit Gabriel. Raphael unrolled the scroll; it only confirmed what he already knew.

"So," The healer bemoaned.

"We now have an all knowing captain! I had better make certain to think about solid good things! Either that, or I shall be making myself a new head wreath every other hour or so."

The sulking angel began hiking over to the river of wine.

"I really need a pint!" He thought aloud.

Gabriel was pushing Samael down a big sleek hill of snow, on a wooden sled. The child laughed merrily as he swooshed down the mound. Samael used his aqua wings as sails in the wind.

"I am so glad he came down to see me today!" Gabriel smiled.

Snow ball barked at her feet, the messenger dove was mounted atop his furry head.

"Oh! Why thank you Snow ball! If it were not for you I might not have gotten my mail."

The dove flew up onto Gabriel's opened right palm; the seraph detached the note, and then sent the bird back to Eden. Gabriel slowly unfurled the papyrus and scanned it over.

"Oh my!" She yelped. The lieutenant instantly tuned her mind entirely onto her pet seal.

"Lucifer you will only see Snowball in my thoughts!" She ruminated.

Samael soared up to his rabbi with sled in hand.

"Thank you rabbi, I had fun, I had better get to my egg, I still need to go over my music essay one more time before I turn it in tomorrow."

Gabriel gave her studious pupil a kind smile.

"That sounds like a very wise idea! A good eve's rest makes for a good student! I will see you in the morning!"

Samael saluted his rabbi as he left with his sled.

Chapter 33

Lucifer sat brooding on his quartz throne; ever since the light bearer had obtained the ability of mind reading, he found himself overly obsessed about what his three lieutenants were thinking about.

"What idle things they all think about!" He crowed.

Lucifer's lips were at a full pout. A vision of Gabriel's brain displayed her pet seal Snow ball, he was licking icicles. Raphael's thoughts were continuously contained to virtues squeezing milk into shiny silver and copper buckets from cherubim.

"Sheer nonsense!" The captain huffed in discontent.

"Let's see what Uriel is pondering, it would be nice if some angel other than Me-el and my devoted servants were engrossed on my beauty!"

Lucifer closed his eyes and read Uriel's mind.

"That damn Milky Way again! He is such a fuddy duddy! The way he fantasizes over the Milky Way; why one would think it was made out of signature chocolate and caramel!" He scowled.

Lucifer slouched in his chair; his three lieutenants were boring him. Rofocal and Rahab entered the throne room.

"My lord what has you looking so bothered?" Rofocal asked.

"My three siblings! Raphael, Gabriel, and Uriel!" He snarled.

"Oh my, do not tell us that they are still thinking about their usual ridiculous fetishes? They should be envisioning your perfect countenance." Rahab added.

"You two and Me-el seem to be the only ones who truly understand me!" Lucifer boomed.

"Yes my friends, my siblings are still wasting their thoughts on those silly things! Rather than thinking about me in all my brilliance!"

"Well lord they most obviously need to get their priorities in order!" Rofocal enjoined.

"You are quite right that Rahab Me-el and I know how to fully appreciate you; that brings me to why we came in my lord; we wanted to let you know that the evening meal is ready."

"It is, and have I mentioned how handsome you are in the past hour?" Rahab interjected; hoping to score more brownie points.

The captain flashed him a grin.

"I do believe your little Me-el is rather famished! He has not stopped eye balling your unfinished apple from the tree of wisdom!" The angel tipped.

Lucifer had placed his apple on a gold pedestal covered by a glass domed lid. He had left it on the dining table upon their arrival. Me-el was currently squatted down right in front of the forbidden fruit, ruminating over what it might taste like.

"I wonder if you taste like all the other apples in Eden." Me-el said as if the fruit might answer him.

"Of course you look much tastier! Yummers! I know only Lufi can eat you....Everybody told me that... but..." He deliberated.

The tyke's cream puffed hands began to unveil the mouth watering pleochroic apple.

"I wonder if I could just give you a lick... I mean that cannot possibly count as eating you! Tell me my delicious friend, am I right?"

Me-el's eyes glinted as he stuck out his small pink tongue and aimed it towards the fruit.

"You look so tender and juicy!" He proclaimed as he fondled the apple with his chubby finger.

"Me-el!" Lucifer shouted.

The child hurriedly placed the lid back upon the high standing platter.

"Oh hey Lufi, for a minute I thought the apple was talking to me!" Me-el chuckled.

"Sure..." Lucifer smiled.

"Me-el I have news for you, licking would most definitely count! So do not do it." The captain noted as he took his seat.

Me-el put on a face of perfect innocence.

"Oh Lufi I was not really gonna do that." He asserted.

"Well your tongue would say otherwise by its actions." Lucifer winked.

"No worries! Because dinner is now here!" Rofocal and Rahab announced. The two messengers had brought in Me-el's meal of choice, disc pie. The tot clapped his hands.

"Forget the apple! Give me my disc pie!" He insisted.

"I would be delighted to do so!" Rahab said as he and Rofocal set down an extra large tray.

Rofocal had decided to simply bake one massive pie since Lucifer seldom consumed more than a bite; while he and Rahab were partial to two slices. Me-el would then be left with the remaining thirty five and a half pieces to himself.

Rahab passed around plates and filled Me-el's glass mug with chocolate cherubim milk. The messenger then took a bucket filled with ice carrying red wine which

Rofocal had just wheeled in on a cart; he popped the cork on the bottle, and then poured three tall stemmed goblets for Lucifer, his friend and himself. The four angels held hands to pray, after Rahab had served the wine.

"Blessed be Yahweh who brings forth life and loves us." Lucifer verbalized.

"Amen." They all responded.

"Now it's time to chow down!" Me-el touted as he greedily helped himself to five slices straight away.

Rofocal and Rahab took their usual helping, as Lucifer sipped on his wine.

"Is everything alright my lord?" Rofocal asked.

The captain's eyes shifted to Me-el, the child was practically swallowing down his disc pie.

"Little brother, you might try breathing between each slice." He jostled.

Me-el who was currently slurping up clots of oozing cheese, nodded at his older brother.

"Well," The morning star turned to face his messengers.

"I take it you both noticed my bitten apple, Me-el certainly did."

Rofocal and Rahab did their typical yes sir nods.

"Why did you take only one bite my lord?" Rahab bid.

Lucifer twirled the wine in his glass, as he answered.

"I plan to eat more of it tomorrow; the first taste already gave me the hassle of hearing every angel's mind. I do not wish for more bombardment; that said I still cannot get over how my three lieutenants all waste time thinking about such frivolous matters! It is so annoying! Even as I speak to both of you, I can see Gabriel's coddled pet fur ball barking idiotically at an ice berg! I mean you would expect them to at least be transfixed on my beauty for the better part of the day, every other angel aside from them is!" He badgered.

"Oh I agree!" Rahab added, as Rofocal's head went up and down in approval.

"Why I cannot bring myself to stop thinking of my lordship's unequalled appearance!" Rofocal confirmed.

"Why Yahweh himself praises you above all others! We only follow the example of our father Abba. How wasteful for your brethren to concentrate on petty things! Yes, shame on them I say!"

Lucifer, whose spirit had lifted after the affirmations of his butlers, smiled and took a mushroom off the giant disc pie he threw it into his mouth and chewed.

"I believe I will make you both managers on level five as well, Azazel and Nergel are in charge, since they are higher in rank, but I would not mind having some bonus help with my soldiers, what say you? Could you two handle a bit of a promotion? You can polish my various weapons, and wipe my armor down between drills."

The pair of rattled angels looked at Lucifer in disbelief, they both nodded as their forks fell from their limp fingers in shock.

"Good! I did not think either of you would mind! Me-el did you hear that? Our friends here will be assisting me on level five while you are off at school, isn't that kind of them?"

Me-el reclined back on his chair and patted his pot belly; the disc pie had found a new residence inside the tot's bulging *kishka.

"Yup! You two just better remember to get back on this level in time to keep baking me disc pie after school gets out." He warned between hiccups.

Rofocal and Rahab chuckled along with Lucifer as the child made his top priority well known.

* Kishka: belly or gut.

Chapter 34

Moonday morning had dawned; Yahweh towered over the new planets he had just completed; Neptune, Urius, and Saturn. Gabriel had helped in naming Neptune and Saturn, due to what God had primarily composed them of. Yahweh had formed Neptune entirely out of water; the planet was populated with hypnotic singing merbeings. The creatures swam freely, like angels they too were androgynous; they had glittering fish tails of blue, green, and silver. The merbeings praised God with their lovely whale like moans.

"Genius of Gabriel to think of naming this planet after a Roman pagan deity of water, it is suitable." Yahweh contrived.

"How melodic my angels of the oceans sound!" He expressed.

Saturn, which Gabriel had titled after a Pagan Roman god of agriculture; was a lush and highly vegetated home to Yahweh's winged horses. The animals fed off the foliage on the planet, then would race around its enchanting rings on their golden hooves.

"Oh Lucifer will adore all of you! I am sure of it!" Abba swooned.

"Who knew that my make believe deities and fairy tales of Mythology would prove so useful in the creation of the solar system?" God joked to himself.

"Ahhh... we did!" The Ruach jested in return.

"Oy! I know I really knew! It was an attempt of humor for my own sake!" Yahweh pointed out.

God hovered over to Urius.

"This one I decided to name after my Uriel! Although all nine planets are specifically for Lucifer, I thought my stern faced star keeper might appreciate a smidgen of recognition, after all the planets are located on his realm." He appraised.

Urius was covered with ice and water, yet it did have much more sun light than Playful. Yahweh had inhabited this planet with whale and dolphin like beasts which echoed their neighboring friends on Neptune. The creatures on Urius were bright neon colors; they could fly over the waters on transcendent dragon fly wings. God looked to his right, Uriel and Gabriel had just finished checking on the yetis on Playful. The two lieutenants bowed as they approached their maker.

"Hail Abba!" Uriel exclaimed.

"Your planets are absolutely smashing!"

"I agree Abba." Gabriel smiled.

"I simply adore the merbeings! They sound so similar to the seraphim that chant on your realm! Oh, and the whales and dolphins sing just as wonderfully! Not to mention my favorites; the yetis! Oh I also find the winged horses to be very regal."

Yahweh grinned at the pair of archangels.

"I am glad you both are enjoying the planets; Raphael did tell me how you all have had to block your thoughts quite carefully from Lucifer so he would not find anything out. I thank you all for that; I know it is not an easy task, I suppose I should have taken that into account before I pushed him to eat from the wisdom tree, alas, all things end up working together for the good. Come; let us go to Uriel's palace."

Yahweh ascended to the upper part of Uriel's realm, the solar system was a few light years beneath it; yet still considered to be part of his level. God paused as Uriel unlocked the silver gates which encompassed his private area of the realm.

"Oh Abba you need not concern yourself," Uriel fostered.

"Mind blocking is not so bad, although I must confess; Lucifer must think us daft to day dream all the day on pure meshuggina!"

Yahweh and Gabriel giggled at the porter's statement.

"Lucifer is probably sick of seeing Snow ball so much!" Gabriel chortled.

The three floated over to Uriel's abode; showers of stars wisped by them. Par God's request Raphael was seated at the star keeper's table awaiting them. The archangel rose and bowed upon viewing his father enter. Raphael was not wearing his head wreath; after Lucifer had stomped out his last one, he had failed to make another, he had been keeping to busy. Yahweh's eyes smiled in his direction.

"How is my favorite gardener?"

Raphael rose from his bow.

"I am well Abba! Your recent work is superb!"

Yahweh inspected the gentle seraph, something was different about him, he lowered his spectacles half way down his nose, his eyes became dimmed in puzzlement.

"Why Raphael, where is your wreath of roses? Bubeleh I thought you were rather found of it."

Raphael blushed; this was the first time the lieutenant could recall God referring to him as his darling.

"Oh it is gone for now Abba, lord Lucifer accidentally stepped on it when he came to see me the other day in Eden. I have not taken time to form myself another, yet; perhaps it is for the best; lord Lucifer does not seem to care for my wreaths."

God's face grimaced in blatant disapproval. He waved his right hand and a shiny garland of unbreakable crystal enclosed roses manifested on Raphael's head.

"All of you know this, Lucifer is my equal, not only that, but he has now eaten from the tree of wisdom. I trust him to be a good captain to all of you, not showing any partiality! For his sake I truly hope the destruction of your prior wreath was really an accident! I myself garbed you with those roses when you were hatched! Lucifer knows that! I think I should better have a chat with him soon, know this Raphael, you are to wear those flowers for me, not for him! Lucifer is my companion, but, you are my children. My authority will always supersede his! Never allow him to intimidate any of you! Even Lucifer must answer to someone! And, that someone is me!"

Gabriel, Uriel, and Raphael all exchanged stunned glances, God was not messing around. Yahweh's visage softened.

"Alright then enough of me acting all meshuggina! I am certain Lucifer is simply getting adjusted to all his new abilities, it can be tedious. I will converse with him about the matter. Now, let us get back to business." He smiled.

"Gabriel how are those yetis doing?"

Gabriel returned Abba's beam of joy.

"Fun and easy to love my father!"

"Good!" Yahweh quipped.

"Now all of you keep on guarding your thoughts, we must continue to keep this secret from Lucifer, if perchance he should eat more of his apple, I will make a point of installing a different power into him, something that will divert him from attempting to probe your brains."

The three seraphs' nodded in unison; it took a large burden off their shoulders to hear God say what he did.

"Alright, tomorrow I plan on having some more planets ready! Thank you all again for meeting with me, be assured that Lucifer's mind will not pick up on the gathering we just had."

Yahweh dissipated from their midst with those final words.

"Well," Gabriel began.

"I better be off to Opus Angelorum, Remiel should be sounding his shofar in five minutes or so."

Raphael and Uriel rose as their sibling saw herself out.

Chapter 35

Me-el sat at his desk in school, looking over his completed paper on musical instruments. Raguel was placing the finishing touches on his. Samael who was not the least bit concerned about his work, was reading a book about different types of clouds. Me-el cast his gaze over at his rival. Samael failed to be much of a talker, but Me-el knew how his rabbi's preferred student had recently made a point of visiting Gabriel on her level, Lucifer had told him.

"Teacher's pet!" Me-el grumbled under his breath, making sure Samael heard him.

Samael shifted his grey eyes over to his accuser.

"Take that back!" He shouted in defense.

Gabriel flew in and interposed after Samael's loud retort, she had been standing towards the back of the room, aiding Razziel with his less than perfect writing style.

"Why is one of my best student's yelling during class?" She demanded of Samael.

Samael found himself in a pickle; Me-el smiled like the cat that ate the canary, from beneath his desk, his friend Raguel fist bumped him, for a job well done. Samael however, knew if he were to rat on Me-el he might find himself in hot water with God's regent lord Lucifer; still, the youth dared not fabricate a lie to his rabbi. Samael stood up and faced Gabriel, she was now poised in front of her desk, with ruler in hand. Me-el and Raguel eyed him with reproach.

"Forgive me for the outburst rabbi." He mumbled.

"Samael," Gabriel began, as she thumped her ruler on her left palm.

"You have never expressed yourself like that before; I must therefore wonder...did some angel say something to antagonize you to commit such an odd behavior?"

The rabbi's eyes squinted towards Me-el and Raguel, the two quickly hid behind their Roman Mythology text books.

The rest of the class, not wanting to get involved, went on with their own studies.

"Little guys be cruising for a bruising!" Razziel deliberated to himself.

"Well," Samael whispered.

"Me-el accused me of being a teacher's pet, and it really hurt my feelings." He at last managed out.

"I see, thank you Samael, you may go on with your reading."

The child shyly returned to his seat and picked up his book.

"Me-el will you please approach my desk?" Gabriel ordered in a stern voice.

A series of: "Ummmmssss!" went up among the class.

"Uh... I am too busy reading." Me-el concocted.

"He's got chutzpah to talk back to rabbi!" Raguel chafe inwardly.

Raguel could already see the dire consequences that might soon befall his best bud.

Gabriel rose from her desk; she planted herself right in front of Me-el's. The rabbi gently tapped her quartz ruler on it.

"Well, I must say I am surprised, I did not know you and Raguel could both read upside down." She contended.

Raguel immediately flipped his book right side up as the assembly of students fought back the urge to burst out laughing.

"Oh thank Abba! I thought I was going batty!" Raguel jabbered.

Me-el put down his text and gave Gabriel his best cutie pie smile.

"I have a lot of untapped talents!" He offered, hoping his long lashes would get him out of his current dilemma.

"So I see." Gabriel remarked.

"Me-el before class goes on; I would like you to give Samael an authentic apology."

Me-el frowned.

"But I did not do anything wrong! I just told the truth!" He hammered.

Gabriel slapped her ruler on the child's desk so hard, that the whole class jumped in their chairs.

"You will say you are sorry or, you will know exactly what Raguel endured on realm one with Uriel!" She warned.

Me-el quivered at her threat, and turned to Raguel; his friend had brought a finger to his own neck and was pretending to slice his head off.

"You better do what she says!" Raguel suggested in a scared whisper.

"We do not have the pleasure of offing ourselves up here!"

Me-el swallowed his pride and rose from his desk. He walked over to Samael. Me-el now found himself feeling legitimate hurt over how he had treated his class mate, Samael's eyes were welling up with tears; although Me-el enjoyed teasing Samael, he had not wanted to become some sort of bully; Me-el now validly felt bad that he had ever said such a thing.

"Samael I am sorry, please do not cry I was being a bupkes, the truth is you are a really good angel, I guess I just got a little jealous. I hope we can put the whole thing behind us and be friends." Me-el implored.

Gabriel smiled at Me-el's unadulterated admission of guilt.

"Perhaps you will turn out to be just like lord Lucifer someday!" She thought.

Samael's eyes went dry and he shook Me-el's hand.

"It is okay Me-el, and I would really love it if we could all get along." He admitted.

Raguel let out a sigh of relief.

"Very good, I am glad you both made peace!" Gabriel said.

"Me-el you may return to your seat, so we can all resume class."

The child obeyed.

"Everyone please take out your reports on realm seven." The rabbi orated.

Raguel displayed a complete assignment for the very first time; Gabriel could not help but be impressed, she decided to call on him first.

"Raguel it is so good to see you finally take your homework so seriously! Would you please be the first to read your report out loud?"

The tyke rose and stood in front of the class, he felt good about himself.

"I would not mind a bit rabbi!" He stopped to clear his throat.

"I did my essay on the importance of the trouble cleft."

The entire class began snickering, Gabriel hushed them down.

"I believe you meant to say the treble cleft." She hinted.

"You mean there is more than one cleft? OY!"

Gabriel attempted to maintain a straight face, Raguel's regret was heartfelt, and he truly assumed he had gotten the name of the cleft right.

"Raguel my dear why don't you sit down, I am just pleased you completed your paper that is what really matters."

Raguel shrugged and went back to his seat; still mystified about how there might be more than one cleft in a sheet of music.

"Today," Gabriel went on.

"I am going to put you all in two groups; I shall split the class in half, some of you will discuss musical instruments; while others will practice sight reading." She communicated.

Me-el raised his hand.

"Yes," Gabriel acknowledged.

"Rabbi can Samael be with me and Raguel?"

Gabriel smiled once more.

"Well, I was going to make the teams myself, but, I do not see any harm in your request. Class, Me-el will be picking for one side, oh and let's have...." Gabriel scanned the students to choose another team leader.

"Jericho, you may pick for the remaining pupils."

The students broke up into two groups of ten, Gabriel observed as Me-el and Jericho selected who would be in their cluster. The rabbi sat at her desk and pulled out her own book on Mythology.

"While they study music, I will get more familiar with Abba's pagan stories; they have proven unusually useful in naming planets." She contrived.

The noon shofar sounded, it was time for the students to go to lunch. Gabriel glanced up.

"Me-el and Raguel are always the first ones to the mess hall!" She chuckled to herself.

As the students rushed out of the room, Gabriel noticed Samael was lingering by her side.

"Can I help you my dear?"

Samael's eyes were glued to the silver marble Yeshua had left on the corner of the rabbi's desk.

"I like your great masher rabbi, I did not think an angel like you would be into playing marbles. I mean you seem way to sophisticated for a kid's game."

Gabriel simpered at the child's comment; she did not want to disclose were it had actually come from, or rather, from whom.

"Well Samael, I do not play marbles, it was actually a gift from someone very special to me. I keep it there to remind me of him." She answered.

Samael's face became flushed.

"Well, whoever he is, he is one lucky angel!" He replied as he bolted for the doors; hoping his rabbi had not picked up on the crush he had on her.

Gabriel picked up the silver glass ball.

"He is more beautiful than any angel..." She mused, keeping her mind on Snow ball, so Lucifer would not hear her think such blasphemy.

Samael entered the dining area of Opus Angelorum, it was about as big as their class room, virtues from Eden were passing out lunch trays filled with matzha, cheese, fruit and an option of plain or chocolate cherubim milk. Samael was rather surprised to see that Me-el was in line; He was branded as a lunch bagger, who carried only the finest delicacies. Me-el's vivacious attitude and popularity had gotten him and Raguel to the front of the procession. Me-el caught sight of his new ally Samael and waved him over. Samael gave him a smile and ran their way eagerly.

"Hey you kolboynick, there are no cuts in this line! Get to the BACK!!"

A hungry Razziel made clear.

Samael lifted his shoulders and gave Me-el a sorry shrug, he was not about to anger a seraph that was five feet taller than him.

"Hey Razz, it's all good he is with us!" Raguel blurted out as a virtue placed four helpings of various cheeses on his tray.

Razziel's face suddenly became friendly.

"Oh little dude, I am so sorry! I did not know you were with the Star Polisher! Go on ahead of us! You just earned my total respect!"

Samael felt a shock wave go through him; he was officially part of the chosen clique of Opus Angelorum; even jocks like Razziel were accommodating him.

Me-el's tray was stacked high with food, mostly cheese and nuts, he also had more than one bottle of chocolate cherubim milk in each of his wings.

"I know; I usually don't like waiting in the school lunch line; but, Lufi's butlers are helping him out on level five, so; to be nice, I only make them make me disc pie for dinner now, help take some the pressure off them." He mentioned.

"Well you could always just pack your leftovers from dinner and bring those." Samael submitted.

Me-el and Raguel both swap confounded glances.

"Ahhh Samael what exactly are leftovers?" Me-el questioned in a very somber tone.

Samael chuckled as a virtue filled his gold plate.

"Oh nothing that important, I am just happy we are all friends!" He said.

The students returned from lunch, Gabriel separated them into the two groups which Jericho and Me-el had selected. The rabbi finished her book on Mythology up until a quarter of the third hour.

"Okay everyone, please return to your regular seats," She networked.

"For your homework, I would like all of you to review what you went over in your teams today; also, when Remiel sounds the shofar, please leave your completed papers of level seven piled neatly on my desk." She paused to take a breath.

"Oh and there will be no written reports required of any angel tomorrow, but, please do study! You never know when I might decide to spring a pop quiz on all of you!"

The students groaned. Raguel tapped Me-el on the right wing.

"Hey you wanna go to Raphael's dessert garden after school?" He asked.

The shofar blasted before Me-el could respond.

"Okay everyone, please remember to study! Turn in your reports and have a nice afternoon!" Gabriel urged.

Me-el looked over at Raguel as he put away his books.

"Yup! I'm gonna ask Samael to come with us this time, is that okay with you?"

Samael's aqua wings ruffled in stimulation; Me-el was actually going to permit him to join them on an excursion!

"Sure, he's cool now." Raguel answered as he placed his essay on the "trouble" cleft on his rabbi's desk.

Gabriel offered the child a wink as he caught up with his two friends and exited the school.

"I am so pleased to see those three getting along so well now!" She sighed as the adorable trio left.

Chapter 36

On realm five Azazel found himself under Lucifer's boot yet again.

"Check mate!" The captain uttered.

"Ya canna beat da best!" Azazel admitted as Lucifer assisted him in regaining his footing.

Rofocal and Rahab sat watching in awe, they were absolutely mystified with Lucifer's exceptional dueling skills. The two messengers were varnishing shields and swords on a jade bench. The black smith angels had been given specific instructions by Lucifer; all new weapons and armor were to be polished by the pair of angels which had come down with him from his realm. The light bearer marched over to his personal couple of fans. He gave Azazel a pat on the back.

"Rofocal, Rahab this strapping angel is Azazel, the only angel on realm five who can spar me for five hours straight! Azazel my friend, may I introduce you to my two new helpers; meet Rofocal and Rahab."

The shimmering eagle pinioned power shook hands with the ogling messengers.

"Tis a pleasure!" He said with his Irish drawl.

"Any friend of Lucifer tis a friend O mine! Glad ta meets ya both!"

Rofocal and Rahab went to correspond to his greeting; when all at once every clanging sword, mace, and dagger on the level went silent. Lucifer turned to see God himself standing in the midst of his training ground, it was a first. Every angel went prostrate; Rofocal and Rahab halted their work to do the same. Lucifer and Azazel did likewise.

"Please rise my beloved son of morning." Yahweh ordered.

Lucifer rose on cue.

"Abba, what a pleasure to see you here! What brings you?"

Yahweh's amiable blue eyes went dull.

"You Lucifer, I wish to meet with you privately in my throne room."

Before any other angel had time to rise, God vanished. Lucifer pivoted to face a now standing Azazel.

"Azazel would you please finish up going though drills with the others, Abba must not be kept waiting."

Azazel bowed to the captain.

"Of course me lord, twould be an honor!"

Lucifer gazed over at his pair of messengers.

"Rofocal, Rahab; after you are done smoothing out those weapons, you may both head back to the palace, it is thirty minutes after the fourth hour, I assume Me-el is working up an appetite in Eden as we speak, you should both get to realm four as soon as possible and prepare him a disc pie, dinner time will soon be upon us!"

Rofocal and Rahab bowed and saluted.

"Of course lord Lucifer, we shall do just as you have commanded."

Lucifer now knelt before God's throne. Yahweh drifted his way, he gestured for the seraph to rise and follow him to their tea corner.

"I came at once Abba; tell me, what can I do for you?"

Yahweh looked into Lucifer's eyes as they both sat down in the antique chairs. The morning star noticed that his father's gaze seem conflicted, the seraph now felt concern. It was clear his creator was deeply troubled. God rotated his seat to face the light bearer.

"My Lucifer I am just going to get straight to the point, why did you toy with Raphael's emotions?"

Lucifer's eyebrows jolted up; God had hit a nerve with him.

"Did you really crush his wreath of roses by accident as he said? Please think before responding, you see; the tree of wisdom might be giving you strange side effects, if you destroyed the wreath out of envy; which could be one of the appalling offshoots, well, then perhaps I have been a bit hasty in giving you so much power, and letting you eat from the source it originated from." A worried Yahweh elucidated.

Lucifer wrung his hands in anxiety. The morning star attempted to smile. He had felt envy long before he bit into the apple of wisdom. He simply did not know the accurate definition for the feeling. Eating from the tree had most definitely intensified the emotion. Thoughts began to cyclone through Lucifer's head as Yahweh sipped on a cup of tea. The son of morning struggled to keep his composure as his own voice commenced to haunt him.

"You know why you hate that wreath so much! Father gave Raphael a crown long before he gave you one! Oh yes.... You have a gold diadem now, but, you rule over all angels in Heaven! So...why did Abba give a mere gardener any kind of crown first?"

The labyrinth of opinions surged among the light bearer's slowly maddening mind. Lucifer had officially invited jealousy and envy into his brain; sadly it was over a very marginal matter. The seraph was not about to display his real feelings to Yahweh, he was much too clever. Lucifer masked his emotions with a fake sad face and dewy cow eyes.

"Oh Abba, please forgive me!" He cried as he fell to his knees; he procured his father's hands and plastered them with kisses while his eyes became loaded with crocodile tears.

"Avi, I really did foolishly step on the wreath, it was an unfortunate mishap on my part! Raphael went to bow; and, the crown, well it simply fell off his head. I suppose sometimes I forget what big steps I take, I was about to kneel down and retrieve it for him myself, when..."

Lucifer broke off in sobs. The morning star's acting routine, could have easily won him the universe's first Oscar, his ritual had convinced the Almighty himself. Now; Yahweh was, nor is by any means a fool, he had just come to love and trust Lucifer so much, that he found no valid reason to doubt the angel's sincerity.

"Come now my bubeleh, please get up, I believe you, I just needed to be sure about the whole matter."

Yahweh helped Lucifer to his chair and handed him a satin handkerchief.

"Dry up those tears beloved one."

Lucifer sniffed as he dabbed his eyes, he was pulling out all the stops to make certain his performance seemed kosher.

"Why now I feel silly for even plaguing you with the incident!" God said in a choked up voice.

"How could I allow myself to even imagine that an angel as beautiful as you would ever purposely offend his own sibling? Why your outer beauty reflects your inner beauty after all! Lucifer my sweet bubeleh I am afraid it is you who need to forgive me." Yahweh languished.

Lucifer looked at God with pouty lips and a pleading stare.

"Oh my Avi, do not say such things! You have done me no harm, I still love you!"

Yahweh's eyes brightened at Lucifer's statement, he embraced the captain tight and kissed him on the cheek.

"Oh I love you so much my Lucifer! Well, since you are here, would you like a cup of tea? It might help your feathers become unruffled." God bantered.

Yahweh felt guilty for making his most cherished of angels weep. Lucifer however, was inwardly burning like a tea kettle ready to screech out steam. He was still working hard to conceal what he was really feeling. The light bearer knew he had to leave his father's presence lest he give his true colors away; thus permitting God to see how he really felt about Raphael.

"I am sorry Abba but I should get going, little Me-el is probably on level four expecting me for dinner by now." He said to excuse himself.

"Ahhh yes little Me-el! Well it would be dangerous to keep an appetite like that waiting long!" Yahweh agreed.

"Here," God took a small purple velvet pouch and filled it with some raspberry scones and powdered chocolate truffles; he knotted it with a pink silk ribbon.

"Please take this to him! Tell him that Abba sends his love and many hugs his way!"

Lucifer took the bundle and gave Yahweh a kiss; this further lifted God's mood.

"I love you bubeleh! This meeting never happened as far as I am concerned; I have forgotten it completely, as far as the east is from the west! Go on your way and tend to our Me-el, you are an outstanding older brother and role model! He could not be in better hands than yours!"

Lucifer shined a radiant smile to his father; he bowed low to him then left his realm.

"To bad Raphael is one cake Me-el cannot eat!" Lucifer thought as he descended to realm four.

"He does look like one with that gaudy wreath around his head! If only he was not so damn attractive! I would have crushed his head rather than his adornment!" The morning star brooded.

Twosday had arrived, and it could not have come fast enough for Lucifer, he was still discontented over the conflict that his father had nearly discovered between him and Raphael.

"I need to teach Raphael a lesson, but I need to be very careful about how I go about it..." He evaluated.

Me-el had already left for school; Lucifer was suddenly hit by an epiphany.

"If I eat more of my apple I am bound to come up with a good idea!" He decided.

Lucifer went into his dining room; he said a prayer of thanksgiving, and then lifted the lid over his unfinished apple. He ate the whole fruit in a couple of bites and crunches; even the stem and seeds.

"Well now to wait for some more wisdom..." He angled.

The seraph felt nothing; until his stomach began to burn and make obscure noises. The captain fell to his knees on the floor. He attempted to call on Rofocal or Rahab, but, his throat had gone numb.

"Oooohhh.... My gut sounds like a sick cat!" He panted.

Lucifer coughed up the silver stem, the mirrored ground of his palace reflected his image. He gasped; he was no longer an angel! The son of morning's admission had transformed him into a large white Persian feline with yellow eyes.

"Wow!" He professed as he gazed at himself.

"I think I just gained the ability to shape shift!" He meowed

Lucifer closed his cat eyes and thought himself back to normal. He rose to his feet, as the same resplendent angel he was.

"This is great! Me-el is in school, Rofocal and Rahab are most certainly on level five by now, I know the perfect way to get back at my big mouth brother in Eden!" He revolved.

In the interim, on realm eight Gabriel was pleased with Me-el and how the youth had incorporated Samael into his inner circle. The three smallest angels in her class had brought their desks together in a huddle. Gabriel, after popping a music quiz on the class; had just given them another team project. The students were to decipher what each Hebrew title of God stood for; they were permitted to use their Hebrew text books. Gabriel graded the quizzes as the students went about their labor.

"Wow! Raguel actually got a B! I shall have to give him a Silver Star sticker, it is the highest score he has ever received, and he has earned it." She deliberated.

All the quizzes were graded; Me-el and Samael had tied for highest mark. The rabbi decided to rove around the class room; holding her well known quartz ruler. The more mature angels had completed the Hebrew assignment, and were now reading up on Roman Mythology and paganism. Angels attending Opus Angelorum were all required to be adequately informed on all pseudo gods, Yahweh had personally requested this; Gabriel was not quite sure why, since Abba alone was Alpha and Omega.

"Perhaps," She evaluated.

"Perhaps Yahweh enjoys reading the fanciful tails he himself fashioned, it could also serve to all angels as a reminder; that, no matter how incredible these characters may seem, Yahweh is still the only true God."

The contemplative rabbi reminisced about what Yahweh had said to her upon escorting her through the grandiose building; this was before any students had occupied it.

"Someday Gabriel...now do not even bother asking me what a day is yet, I should say soon, yes, soon you will know what everything in this spectacular structure of archives means! Until then, it would do you well to continue to memorize every plebe of scrolled material within these sacred walls. When you are blessed with angels to teach; I will expect you to incorporate every speck of what you have absorbed into your teaching curriculum! Some things you read will sound silly or even offensive and vile, but do as you are told; for the sake of all future angels. You my dear Gabriel must stay very well read! Besides, I have a feeling you will enjoy doing what I have just requested of you!"

Gabriel smiled as she recollected. God knew her so well. The rabbi casually strolled over to see how her three little musketeers where doing. Raguel's head was on his desk in desperation.

"Why in Heaven's sake does Abba need so many names for?" He whined.

Me-el busily took notes as Samael dictated:

"Okay, last one! Yahweh Rophe; God who heals! That's it you guys, we are done!"

Samael closed his book in triumph as Me-el wrote out the final title in his best calligraphy.

"Hmmmmm...Sounds kinda like Raphael." He observed aloud.

"Very perceptive Me-el!" Gabriel said.

"Rophe means to heal in Hebrew, and the name Raphael is defined as healer or medicine of God; others may also say Rophe means God's remedy, either way you are correct!"

Me-el glanced up at his teacher his cheeks blushed a rose pink.

"Yup! I guess I am really starting to learn more!" He happily claimed.

Raguel sat up straight.

"Sorry I was slouching rabbi, but tell me, why does Abba have so many names? Why not just Yahweh?"

Gabriel was about to give him a response, when the archangel Remiel sounded the noon shofar.

"Ahhh...You can get back to me after lunch!" Raguel determined.

Gabriel grabbed him by the right shoulder, before he bolted out.

"Raguel why don't you discuss what you just asked me with Me-el and Samael over your meal? I am certain one of them might be capable of enlightening you." She broached with a wink.

"Okay! But it's not easy watching Me-el talk with his mouth full; I will probably ask Samael about it."

"I do not talk with my mouth open!" Me-el snapped at his friend over his shoulder.

"It was a joke, come on let's get to the lunch room!" Raguel steered.

Gabriel simpered; the rabbi began shoving the three desks back into their proper places as the students all filed out.

"I suspect Me-el does chew with his mouth open, he seldom has it closed." She chuckled; just then, Yeshua arrived, he was sitting at her desk.

"Hello sweet Gabriel, our Me-el is quite the food maven! But, that is not why I am here, lunch lasts an hour; I want you to accompany me to level one, I have some new planets to show you!"

Gabriel who had been bowing in reverence, now arose, she became aware that Yeshua was playing with the silver marble he had left on her desk after his last visit.

"Of course my lord! I am ready to follow you at any time!" She beamed.

Yeshua took Gabriel by the arm, he situated the marble back on its resting spot; then teleported to the cosmos with her.

Down in Eden, Raphael was picking ripe olives to send up to Jerusalem, his other form was keeping diligent keep over the tree of life. The lieutenant gazed up from his plucking; Lucia was standing right in front of him, looking as lovely as ever. She was holding two empty baskets.

"I am ready to take up your olives lord Raphael." She smiled.

Raphael's eyes lit up, he was going to call on her for his delivery; yet she had arrived without him having even summoned her.

"Perhaps Yahweh sent her." He reasoned.

"Hello Lucia! I still have a few more to pick, but, having you in my presence is always pleasurable! So; if you do not mind waiting on me, I shall be right with you."

Lucia put down her baskets.

"My lord Raphael, have I ever told you how handsome you are?"

Raphael's two middle wings dropped his collection of olives. The seraph's face flushed; Lucia pressed herself against him in an intimate way; her soft lips caressed his. Raphael's two upper wings shot up.

"Ahhh....Lucia, I appreciate your interest, I also find you very attractive; but, I do not think it kosher for us to be getting this close..."

Raphael stammered as Lucia peppered the right side of his jaw with petite kisses.

"I mean Abba has not to my knowledge ever mentioned anything about angels bonding or coupling." He tensely kibitzed.

Lucia backed off; to Raphael's astonishment she did not seem upset.

"My lord, I completely understand, after all, I am nowhere near as fun to look at as Lucifer; I suppose if any angel were to catch your attention, it would most definitely be him."

Lucia knelt down; she began putting the fallen olives into her baskets. Raphael stooped down to assist her.

"Dear Lucia, if Abba did ever permit angels to be joined with one another..."

Raphael paused, he was nose to nose with her, and she smelled of sweet nard.

"Yes?" She asked, her dark lashes ensnaring Raphael.

"Well, I assure you that if that was to ever happen, you would be the first angel I would look for." He divulged as he gave her a small peck on the lips.

Lucia stood up enraged over the lieutenant's actions.

"How dare you kiss me?" She ranted.

Raphael heightened himself, He felt firmisht.

"Forgive me Lucia; I thought you wanted me to kiss you." He anxiously expressed.

"No you fool! Raphael you are a total shmendrick!"

Raphael's emerald eyes widened in shock as Lucia morphed into his older brother Lucifer. Raphael dropped to his knees. He had gone from shock to shear embarrassment.

"My captain?" He gasped as he lowered his head in shame.

"I am so sorry! I did not know you could change your shape! I truly thought you to be Lucia!"

Lucifer cut him off.

"You really think that crude dark feminine type angel is more beautiful than me?" He challenged.

"Get up and answer me Raphael! I want you to face me when I speak to you!"

Raphael rose; he was at a loss for words.

"My captain you know that you are the most beautiful of angels; but, you are my brother; and most importantly you are God's companion! I would not dare anger Yahweh by provoking him to jealousy! Please try to comprehend..." He appealed.

Lucifer now feeling jilted regarded Raphael with even more contempt than before.

"I do not know why I even bothered wasting my time on trying to teach you some kind of lesson! You are correct, I am God's companion! But, I am also your captain! As of today, Lucia is no longer permitted to come to Eden to collect your deliveries! I will instead send one of my own messengers for those jobs! Understood?"

Raphael's head lowered once more.

"Yes my lord, I understand, I respect your authority."

As Raphael stood despondent, Lucifer flew off already devising another tactic to enmesh his brother Raphael with; the captain was determined to get even at all costs for what Raphael had begun over his menial wreath.

Chapter 37

Lucifer now irate turned himself into a serpent.

"With this figure I am bound to edify Raphael with a lesson! I shall fool him into giving me fruit from the tree of life! I will say I am a new creature in Eden who is required to eat from the tree under Yahweh's jurisdiction! After he gives me of the fruit, I will transform back into my angelic form and; he will relent for having acted so incautiously! No angel is permitted to take from the tree of life! If he willingly gives me of the tree while I am yet a snake, he will be breaking the rules without knowing it! It's perfect!" He hissed.

The snake Lucifer had converted into was tall and sleek, coated with gold and silver scales. He could walk upright on two legs. He also had arms and hands. Lucifer had been smitten by the reptile when he had first seen its picture in one of the image books on Opus Angelorum.

Raphael was still shaken by what had transpired between him and his captain in the olive orchard; he stood focused on guarding the tree of life.

"Why did Lucifer do that? Perhaps Yahweh put him up to it; could it be I am spending too much time thinking about Lucia, and not giving enough concentration to my more important duties..." He ruminated.

The archangel attempted to clear his head when a creature he had never caught sight of before entered his scope of vision. The serpent seductively approached Raphael.

"I am going to play him good for preferring Lucia over me, and spilling the beans to Abba about his stupid wreath!" The morning star sulked.

Raphael squint his eyes, he knew all the animals in the garden, and he began to wonder if God had recently created this new one. The serpent was alluring in some aspects, yet more unsettling in others. In Raphael's opinion it resembled a walking vine; it had large slanted black eyes which seemed to rake right to the center of the lieutenant's core.

"Hello," Raphael began.

"Are you new here? Tell me what your name is?"

Cinnamon and Sugar, Raphael's two unicorns were not far from the sentinel's region. The pair of royal beasts trotted over in Raphael's direction when they heard the sound of his voice.

"I am the serpent." Lucifer lied.

"I was told to eat from this tree lest I cease to exist."

Raphael gave the snake a once over. The unicorns remained at his side, one at his right and the other at his left. As Lucifer came closer to where Raphael stood; the two beasts began to snort and stomp their hooves in censure.

"Odd." The lieutenant noted.

"The unicorns act as if they do not trust this new creature..." Raphael deliberated.

He now addressed the serpent.

"Yes, this tree is only to be tasted by animals of Eden; yet, my two friends here say that you do not originate from this place at all. Tell me, is this fact?"

Raphael removed his helmet; he displayed a handsome face twisted in preoccupation. Lucifer resisted his anger and resumed his charade.

"If Abba is correct, you are required to fulfill your duties as a sentinel of Eden and let me partake of this tree!" Lucifer demanded as his long tongue flickered out of his mouth.

The pair of unicorns aimed their glowing horns at the serpent. Lucifer shrieked as his true form came back. Raphael bowed to his captain, and then rose.

"My captain why did you put me to such an ordeal? You know only animals are permitted to eat from this tree. If my two unicorns had failed to unmask you; I could have made a grievous error by allowing the ruler of all angels to taste of its fruit! Unless....did Yahweh ask you to test me as a guardian?"

Lucifer pursed his lips; Raphael had unknowingly supplied him with the perfect alibi; He would not need to tell his brother that he was actually trying to get him in trouble; not that he had really intended to express that at all.

"Yes! Yahweh told me to check and see if you would not fall for a well crafted trap!" Lucifer warranted.

"Abba see's all; you see that is why I also came to you as Lucia. Both God and I wanted to be sure you were not being distracted from your jobs by being frivolous."

Upon completing his sentence the captain felt relief that Yahweh had been looking less into his sea of glass since he had assigned him as his regent. Raphael appeared discouraged with himself; this further pleased the son of morning.

"I do hope you and Abba can forgive me my lord, in the back of my mind, I had feared that might be the case; Lucia does pass through my thoughts frequently, and I do call on her to pick up my deliveries more than any other angel. Abba and you only observed what was obvious...I hope you will both pardon my behavior. I swear to keep my focus on Eden from this day forward, you have my solemn vow."

Lucifer leered at his brother. He desperately desired to rip off his armor and put his own body up against his; yet, the envy remained. He coveted Raphael in a sensual way, but, his fury towards him was even greater.

"He just openly admitted to liking that silly Spanish angel!" Lucifer bemoaned.

"Well I am glad you learned your lesson!" The captain snarled.

"I apologize about the ways I had to trick you, but I had to be certain you were on your toes! Now that you have become aware of your mistakes, I shall be leaving."

Lucifer whizzed away faster than a rouge pixie. Raphael shuddered as he placed his helmet back on his head.

"I nearly lost my employment as protector of this tree!" He repined out loud as he settled back to his post.

Cinnamon and Sugar nuzzled him.

"Thank you both, if you had not been here, Lucifer may have obtained a pomegranate from me, and, accused me with just cause before Yahweh." The anguished angel concluded.

"Damn those meddling one horned horses!" Lucifer raged.

"I was so close to getting a pomegranate! Oh if only I had! Yahweh would have replaced Raphael with another angel! He would have been demoted! Oh well, if I cannot have him to myself, I can rest in knowing Lucia will never have him either!" He devised.

Yahweh was so consumed in preparing Lucifer's solar system that the whole ordeal between Raphael and the morning star fell short of catching his interest. The deity had given no heed to what had just panned out in Eden; aside from that he knew he could trust Lucifer in everything. God was currently in the form of Yeshua, he was hovering next to Gabriel and Uriel in space. Four more planets had just been created. Yeshua smiled his work pleased him. He took the personage of the Ruach and began bouncing among the stars while enclosed in his lucid orb.

"Behold Pater! Clever to name the biggest planet after me your father, using the Roman language Gabriel!"

Gabriel smiled.

"Well, Pater means father, and there is no other father we have except you Abba! Although your books on mythology speak much of a false god by the name of Zeus; he however even if he was real, would never come close to your glory!"

"Thank you," the Ruach hummed.

"Now shall we take a gander at it?"

The angels nodded as they cast their eyes upon Pater with God. Pater was a lush green planet; flocks of griffins flew about, grazing on its flowered mountains.

"They look somewhat like cherubim, except they have heads of eagles and only one set of wings; also, instead of hooves they have talons." Uriel deduced.

"Yes!" Yahweh chimed.

The deity had now returned to his paternal form.

"These mighty creatures will help Lucifer with transporting weaponry and armor with their great strength! Do not worry, all the new animals I have been making can all be fed from Eden's vegetation. None of them will try nibbling on your wings!" Yahweh teased.

Uriel laughed.

"Well Abba, if they attempted to bite mine they would most likely get a nasty burn!"

Gabriel snickered then shifted her eyes to Yahweh.

"My lord it has been a true privilege to see you in all your three forms, you truly are an awesome God!"

Yahweh grinned.

"Thank you my child! I suppose that is why I made up so many books on false ones! I try to duplicate myself in make believe characters; so all angels will know that you can never get any better than the real deal! Forgive me that sounded a tad meshuggina! What I meant to say was I AM and always will be! No others ever existed before me, I alone have been, I am God and there is no other."

Uriel and Gabriel both giggled at their father's dialogue.

"Well, now that you both probably think me *garnisht, shall we take a peek at the remaining three planets?"

"Yes Abba please!" The two angels affirmed.

"Let us gaze upon Mars, named by Gabriel for a fake Roman god of war, good call my child. Especially since I created Mars to be filled with mines of garnets, rubies, red tourmaline, andesine and zircon; specifically to garnish the armor of Lucifer's warring soldiers! If you

* Garnisht: to be beyond help.

look down you can see the inhabitants are mining the jewels as we speak!"

Uriel and Gabriel watched from above as miniature creatures, not much taller than Me-el or Raguel chiseled away busily in tunnels. The cubbles as God called them; favored teddy bears. Each little cub had agile paws with five fingers. They handled things much like a raccoon would; they could easily grasp and clean the precious red gems without any problems.

"The cubbles are adorable!" Gabriel gushed.

"Busy little buggers!" Uriel added.

"These small furry creatures have a diet of honey and milk, I made a point of letting Raphael know that; especially since they are partial to date honey; by the way where is Raphael? I am surprised he is not here with us... anyhow; the gems the cubbles collect will be transported by Lucifer's messengers and lesser archangels to realm four. Of course, no transport will begin until we officially have the formal unveiling. Back to my point, the messengers and other angels will carry the stones to Lucifer's level for adorning not only armor, but, weapons as well!"

Yahweh stopped to catch his breath.

"Now let's move on to Venus!"

The two lieutenants turned their attention over to the next verdant planet upon Yahweh's advice.

"Gabriel's study of Roman myths came up with a suitable name for this exceptional habitation! According to pagan lore Venus was a goddess of love and great beauty! Look and see how this planet lives up to its name!"

Uriel and Gabriel smiled as they surveyed Venus. The terrain was fertile like Eden. Tall trees and opaque beings of light Abba called fairies traversed the hills of this planet. The fairies frolicked through bunches of vibrant magenta, orange and purple arbors. The entities had a feminine likeness, yet, like angels they had no sexual organs; they sang as beautifully as the merbeings on Neptune, whilst they fluttered on wings of glass which resembled those of a butterfly.

"My fairies feed entirely on sun and moonlight." Yahweh mentioned.

"So no food deliveries from angels will be required to this planet. Now, let us head over to our final stop for today; my smallest planet, Mercury."

Uriel and Gabriel followed Yahweh towards the body closest to the sun.

"Now, I personally named this one! The sleek liquid metal which flows in rivers here; inspired me with its name! The metal itself is called Mercury!"

Uriel's eyes bugged out, so did Gabriel's.

"Eeegad Abba! I've never seen metal like that!" Uriel sputtered.

"Nor have I!" Gabriel admitted she was quite impressed.

"Well, with me; all things are possible!" God joked.

"If you two look closely, you will see that I put no living creatures here. I purposely did this, because this planet is so close to the sun. You see my bubelehs' the life I made on the planets; unlike angels can all feel temperature."

Uriel's face took on a blutterbunged look.

"You mean if any life lived on this planet, it would burn?"

"Yes." Yahweh released.

"I created this planet primarily to house the liquid metal, it will be useful to my beloved Lucifer in his fifth realm; he can send messengers, powers, or dominions to gather up as much as he needs; then, they can take it back to him and use it accordingly in the blacksmith shop!"

Gabriel appeared confused.

"But, Abba how will our captain use a liquid metal?"

Uriel turned to God, the same question had also crossed his mind.

"So glad you asked! Allow me to explain, Once Mercury is mixed with other metals, such as silver or gold; it actually makes them stronger! It is what I refer to as an amalgam. You combine another metal with Mercury and heat the two at the correct temperature; thus, forming an amalgam! But we will leave all those details to the blacksmith angels! They are smart enough to figure it out, when I formed them, I saw to it!"

Yahweh snapped his fingers; they were all now back at Uriel's palace seated at the onyx table. Raphael walked in and bowed just as they manifested. The seraph of Eden had brought up a basketful of ambrosial cakes topped with cream and black berries. He set his load on the table. Uriel rose to put on a pot of hot water and fetch some cups and plates.

"Did you bring up some tea leaves from Eden?" Yahweh asked.

Raphael smiled as he pulled out two pouches from beneath his belt; one was filled with mint and rosemary sprigs, the other with hazel nut flavored coffee beans for Gabriel.

"I even remembered Gabriel's coffee!" He winked.

Gabriel gazed at Raphael; he seemed to be faking his cheerful disposition. It was the first time she recollected him ever doing so. Uriel returned and placed four settings around the table. He then went back over to gather the pot of hot water.

"There we go, all set!" He said.

The three archangels bowed their heads to pray, Raphael led them.

"We thank ye Abba, for our lives and for your everlasting love to us."

"Amen." They responded.

Uriel withdrew the lavender silk cloth which covered the cakes, Raphael had brought up. He arose and began serving the company; starting with Yahweh. Raphael waved Uriel off as he approached him; the principal shrugged and sat down. God then spoke:

"I want to thank all of you for all your hard work! I know how much mind blocking you each have had to practice these past few days to keep this project hidden from Lucifer. Tomorrow all the waiting will be over! Lucifer shall receive his surprise!" Elohim crooned.

Yahweh bit into one of the cakes.

"Mmmmm these are very good! Raphael you never disappoint!"

The lieutenant's eyes appeared fogged in sadness; even still, he gave his father a half smile.

"Thank you Abba, I am glad you like them."

Raphael was thinking back to the pair of encounters he had with Lucifer, especially the one at the tree of life.

"If only Yahweh were to find out that I almost gave a pomegranate to an angel....Lucifer must not have told him...if he had, Abba would most certainly know I almost got away with disappointing him for good! Why would Lucifer not tell him?" He quietly revolved.

God continued speaking, he was so caught up in the joy of creating Lucifer's solar system that he entirely missed Raphael's troubled demeanor.

"Tomorrow! Oh I feel ver clempt!" Abba took a sip of tea. He picked up on his schmoozing:

"Yes, tomorrow all of you, the rest of Heaven included, will join me in surprising Lucifer! Now, I know one planet is still left to make, you will all be blown away by it! So; in some respect, there is also a surprise included for the rest of you as well!"

Yahweh's blue eyes gave the three archangels a wink as he blew steam off his cup and sipped. Raphael finally broke the ice and took a drink from his own. He was trying to ignore the queer feeling developing in the pit of his stomach. Uriel at last noticing his brother's decorum nudged a cake onto his plate. Raphael had refused one when the star keeper had first passed them out.

"I say brother why won't you eat with us? You usually do, why only Me-el can out do you in noshing!"

Gabriel nodded as she licked cream and berries off the top of her cake; she dipped it into her coffee to make it mushy.

"I agree brother; by the way it was very sweet of you to remember I prefer coffee over tea! Coffee is way better for a dunker like me!" She bid, hoping to get a real smile out of the gardener.

"Yes!" Abba proclaimed.

"My kind hearted Raphael is so considerate! Please bubeleh join us in noshing! The cakes you brought melt in your mouth like butta!"

Raphael coughed out a tiny chuckle, God's pronunciation of butter made him laugh. He plucked a berry from his cake and popped it in his mouth. It was good. The hesitant angel at last devoured the whole piece.

"Pass me four more Uriel." He said between bites.

Eating seemed to help settle his nerves. Uriel shoved six more his way.

"Tomorrow will be better; perhaps I am just being overly paranoid." Raphael hypothesized as he chewed and swallowed.

Chapter 38

Windsday had arrived; Lucifer was jousting with the power Beleth in level five. Rofocal and Rahab were polishing clean cut prehnite bracers for Azazel.

"Beleth is good." Rofocal commented as Rahab adjusted Azazel's gold arm covers.

"Yes," Rahab agreed. Azazel glanced down at him.

"Yet I must say Azazel can still last longer than him in a duel!"

A satisfied smile came over Azazel's refined face. The angel turned to witness his captain put Beleth into a check mate position, with a malchus sword; once more Lucifer had taken the gambit. The power surrendered and brought in his pair of purple wings.

"You win again lord Lucifer!" Beleth gasped.

Lucifer sheathed his weapon. Azazel now completely varnished, stepped forward to spar the morning star. Lucifer began reviewing the burnished Irish archangel in admiration, as Beleth removed himself from the brawling circle.

"Well Azazel Beleth did not beat your record! He only managed to last three hours!" The captain made clear.

A worn out Beleth went over to Rofocal and Rahab to receive a varnish of his own.

Lucifer prepared to fight Azazel when an unexpected shofar blast resonated throughout the Heavens.

"Sweet shamrocks an ale!" Azazel hollered dropping his mace and shield in a dazed confusion.

Lucifer and the rest of the angels in realm five all had similar reactions; this was no regular shofar, Gabriel was blowing it! The sound of her ram's horn was much louder than Remiel's. Whatever the case, something of utmost importance was about to happen; God was preparing to speak.

"A shofar blast from Gabriel to all nine realms twould be a summons beckon from Abba himself to angels of every rank!" Beleth disclosed as Rofocal and Rahab looked on.

"A summons from our father!" Lucifer bellowed.

"All angels follow me to the throne room!" The light bearer ordered.

Hordes of dominions, powers, and lesser archangels like Azazel scurried after the captain. Lucifer rocketed upwards in a trail of light on his twelve ethereal wings.

Rahab and Rofocal were the only unarmored angels in level five; they shyly filed in towards the back.

"Whatever could be going on?" Rahab wondered.

Rofocal shrugged.

"I cannot say, but, I do know this is the first time Gabriel has sounded her shofar! Of course you did not hear that from me! I once heard Lucifer tell Me-el that Yahweh told him, that Gabriel would only blow the shofar for any type of divine emergency! It does make an angel think!"

Rahab nodded.

"My yes!" He whispered.

Abba had gathered all his angels from every realm, around his transparent sea of glass. Lucifer, Me-el, Raphael, Gabriel and Uriel were all stationed to God's immediate south, east, west and north.

"Listen all my children!" Yahweh commanded.

"I have called you all here on this day for a very special reason! Rofocal, Rahab there is no emergency brewing, so you two may relax." God bantered in good humor.

The pair of messengers blushed as myriads of angelic eyes swiveled over in their direction; then back to their creator.

"You all know," Abba continued.

"That Lucifer is my beloved; I have brought about this summons for a joyous reason, and it concerns him!"

The morning star's face brightened, as Yahweh went on speaking.

"It has been a little over a week now since I manufactured the concept of time; even though in Heaven such a thing can never really exist. If time displayed its true effects on angels; why, you would all have long white beards like me by now!"

Yahweh laughed at his own joke; no angel seemed to understand it.

Me-el hugged Lucifer's right leg; he could barely make out Raguel and Samael in the infinite expanse of gleaming pinioned creatures. The youth glanced down at his protruding tummy; it was making weird noises; it also hurt a little. Me-el had never heard Gabriel blow the shofar before, it had un nerved him a trifle. The rabbi was in her male form and dressed in her coat of arms.

Lucifer affectionately ran his hand through the child's curly dark hair. Me-el's eyes went back to Yahweh.

"Lucifer my love, I have a grand surprise for you! Yes my most dazzling angel, my most beautiful star of morning; bubeleh please come and stand next to me! Me-el I would like you to accompany your older brother too!" Yahweh readily expressed.

Lucifer advanced towards God with Me-el, his princely head and plumage held high. The three lieutenants were quite accustomed to their captain's staggering appearance; it did not affect any of them in the least. The oceans of angels surrounding them however; all began fawning over him in audible voices.

"How stunning he is!" The chorus came.

"My Avi," Lucifer said as he bowed gracefully to Yahweh.

"Oh no! None of that today my most lovely one!" Elohim insisted.

Lucifer arose and lifted a bewildered eye brow at his father; was God stopping him from giving him do reverence? The son of morning was a bit rattled.

"All my angels hearken to me!" Yahweh narrated.

"All of you are commanded to bow to my Lucifer right this moment!"

Lucifer could not believe his ears.

"He really does love me best!" He thought.

Legions upon legions of sparkling entities paid homage in unison, as Me-el, Raphael, Gabriel, and Uriel also fell to their knees. Raphael felt a shiver scatter throughout his wings as he bowed; he still had a peculiar feeling about his captain for some reason.

Lucifer's snow white wings expanded like a marshmallow a child had left in the microwave for over twenty seconds.

"I could get used to this..." He envisaged.

"Good! Now you may all rise!" Yahweh related.

"My children, Lucifer's surprise has been a work in progress, his three lieutenants; Raphael, Gabriel, and Uriel have been helping me with, I have formed eight wonderful new worlds for Lucifer himself to rule over!"

The ninth realm went dead silent; every angel was trying to grasp the idea of other places outside of heaven; that had to be what Yahweh was referring to as new worlds.

"I know you are all wondering what the heck I am going on about! Well, that is why you are all here! Watch my sea of glass and each of you shall view these eight worlds or planets for yourselves! Planets are another term I use for them; they exist outside of Heaven and a few million light years beneath Uriel's realm, so he has the best location to see them, but, they are strictly for my bubeleh Lucifer!"

Yahweh skipped around his five throne angels in giddy excitement. Lucifer tickled pink by Abba's gesture cast his keen eyes onto the still shiny sea; so did Me-el and every other angel.

The planet Playful appeared first. Lucifer and the angels witnessed a large friendly yeti amble through the snow, the world favored Gabriel's level with its spectacular ice formations. God beamed with delight as he saw Lucifer bend down to get a better look. Me-el was on his hands and knees as he sunk his own eyes into the pool. The two siblings faced each other and chuckled in pleasure as a small yeti gazed up at them with large brown eyes.

"Abba they look like Gabriel's pet seal Snow ball!" Me-el alleged.

"Except they can walk on two legs!" He added.

Lucifer wept a solitary tear into the sea; he was deeply touched.

"Abba did you really do all of this just for me?"

Yahweh walked over to the other three resplendent lieutenants'.

"I did! But, your siblings deserve some recognition themselves! They have all been blocking their minds unceasingly so I could bring this surprise to pass! Now that you have eaten from the wisdom tree; it was not by any means the easiest task for them all to do."

Lucifer's eyes glinted at his brethren, he smiled.

"Well that would explain a great deal! I thought all of you were always thinking about the Milky Way, Sea lions and cherubim milking all the day on purpose!"

The three archangels blushed and simpered at Lucifer's statement.

"I love you all! Thank you so much for helping Abba do this for me!" The captain conveyed.

"Well," God resumed.

"Does everyone want to see the next planet?"

The limitless crowd of angels cheered.

"Good! Lucifer my love, behold the planet Neptune!"

Lucifer and Me-el hopped back as images of merbeings appeared; exhibited in a three dimensional holographic form. The creatures were whimsical; their upper part resembled a feminine angel, whilst their lower half displayed a glittery fish tail. The merbeings did flips going twenty feet above the sea of glass; they chanted in hypnotic opera like voices. Little Me-el clapped his hands in rapture, as a blue merbeing clasped tails with an orange and pink swirled companion. The pair of entities waltzed together through a lavender reef of coral, decorated with bright yellow under water shrubbery. The ninth realm marveled at the magical creatures.

"Oh Abba!" Lucifer gushed.

"They are so exquisite! You have out done yourself!"

Yahweh lowered his spectacles and gave Lucifer a friendly once over.

"Bubeleh I out did myself when I created you! All these minute extras are simply to bring you pleasure!"

Lucifer swallowed a huge knot forming in his throat; he was beginning to get emotional. The light bearer found himself becoming more sensitive to everything and everyone since he had finished his apple from the wisdom tree.

He flung his arms around God and gripped him tight. Yahweh was pleasantly taken aback; this was the first time he could recall Lucifer initiating intimate contact with him. God's eyes watered up with love as he observed his favorite seraph lift up Me-el and place him on his shoulders. Lucifer gave each of his three lieutenants' a kiss on the cheek in gratitude.

Raphael had become canny to his captain's new wave of feelings and felt *feh with the smooch. He fought back the urge to wipe the **schmutz off; lest he cause Abba displeasure.

"Now my angels!" Yahweh hollered.

"Prepare to see Urius! I named it after our very own keeper of the stars; Uriel, but, I made the planet especially for Lucifer!"

Lucifer and Me-el rushed back over to the sea of shalom to see what would come up next, so did the entire realm. Yahweh clapped his hands to get every angel's attention.

"My children I think you all might appreciate some nosh about now!"

"It has been a whole hour since I ate..." Me-el thought to himself.

"Before we see Urius, let's get everyone some treats shall we?" God proposed.

Yahweh blew his shofar, three archangels; Remiel, Israfil, and Cassiel emerged above the heavenly throng; they unfurled their enormous wings upon hearing God's

---

* Feh: Disgust.

** Schmutz: Something you wipe off your face.

ram's horn. The myriads of angels found themselves being showered with fresh popped corn from Raphael's farming acres south of Eden.

The immense congregation cooed in satisfaction as they drew together enticing scented puffed kernels of various colors. Raphael had also mixed in walnuts and peanuts to the combination. Excited angels scooped up the party mix in both hands and pinions. Raphael looked up and simply opened his mouth to let some fall in.

"Mmmmm....strawberry, blueberry, and pomegranate, the nuts add a nice saltiness..." He said, sampling his confection.

Me-el bounced off Lucifer's shoulders and filled his green wings; the child had formed a sort of basket with each pair. Raphael could not help but smile; Me-el certainly knew how to use his wings to his advantage.

"Yum! This is wonderful!" The tot declared.

"You should try some Lufi! Look I got some of each flavor in my wings! There are nuts in it too!"

Me-el was now sitting cross legged on his rump, right in front of the still sea. God had provided padded gold stools for his top five archangels, yet Me-el preferred the floor. The fressing tyke looked like a human child holding three extra large popcorn cartons at a fancy movie theatre. He noshed away blissfully.

"No thank you Me-el, I am much too excited to eat! I want to see what Urius looks like!"

"You can do both! Look at me!" Me-el spouted, as he shoved more popcorn into his mouth.

Lucifer pat his younger brother on the head. God began to speak again.

"Well, I hope you are all enjoying the provided refreshments! I know Me-el is! Now let us take our focus back to my sea of glass; shall we? Everyone feast your eyes on the planet Urius!"

The still pool suddenly gleamed with emissions of rainbow light. Two behemoth creatures emerged in three dimensional form; they were both spewing water from holes on top of their heads. The lesser sized creature which was alongside the bigger one, was more slender and agile than its companion. The larger one almost sounded as if it was singing, the smaller one made more of a happy rant of yips and yaps. Both creatures also had crystalline wings which emitted from their sides; in the water they assisted with swimming; however they could also glide above the planet's oceans with their clarion wings.

"Behold the whales and dolphins which inhabit Urius! Not only can they swim, but; as you may all observe, they can also fly!" Yahweh orated.

Me-el leapt to his feet, dropping his popcorn as he did. The creatures had him mystified. The child ran around the sea of glass like a plump puppy chasing its tail. He desperately wanted to pet the dolphin; he even tried throwing some of his discarded popcorn into the mammal's mouth. Me-el seemed to have forgotten that they were just holograms.

Lucifer's eyes had become waterfalls; he wiped away tears of sincere joy from his face. He knelt down and caught Me-el in the midst of his marathon about the heavenly Sea.

"Me-el, you cannot feed them; they can see us though, we cannot actually touch them until we visit the planet; am I correct Avi?" Lucifer asked as he turned towards Yahweh.

God helped Lucifer rise, then placed an arm around him.

"You are correct my beloved one! Do not worry Me-el; soon, you and Lucifer will be at leisure to visit any of the planets whenever you wish! In fact, once you get to Urius, I'll even allow you to feed the dolphins! They just love figs!"

Me-el smiled and began re gathering his spilled popcorn into his pinions. Yahweh waved his left arm over his sea.

"Now, let us move on to the planet Saturn! Or as I like to call it my cosmic carousel!"

Every angel oohed and ahhed as virtues looming one hundred feet above the scintillation body of water; commenced strumming enchanting music on harps; some of them piped on flutes of acacia wood. The angels were playing a familiar merry go round tune. A full size model of Saturn lifted up suspended over the sea. Wondrous white, tan, black, and even pink winged horses frolicked balleticly on the planet's multi colored rings. The horses all had silver and gold hooves.

"Wowza!" Me-el exploded.

"I want the white horsie that keeps changing color each time he runs around!"

Lucifer hugged his small sibling as he began imagining Me-el and he mounted on the dapper beasts together.

"Oh Abba!" He wailed.

"You make my cup runneth over!"

Yahweh beamed at Lucifer.

"Now," He said as Saturn dissipated from their vision,

"Behold the planet Pater!"

Me-el jumped into Lucifer's arms, losing his snacks yet again. A mighty griffin had caught the tyke off guard as it appeared balanced over the still pool on a verdant flower coated mountain.

"What marvelous creatures!" Lucifer cried.

The morning star now attempted what Me-el had with the dolphin; he tried to touch the creature's regal beak. Me-el could not fathom why his older brother was so enamored by the griffin; to him it resembled a giant deformed ugly chicken with a lion's tail.

"Ah Lufi remember what you told me? We cannot touch them until we go there? Of course I think I will let you go visit Pater with some other angel...maybe Uriel, I prefer my chickens smaller and deep fried!"

Lucifer pulled back his hand and glared at Me-el in a puzzled way.

"Me-el when have you ever eaten a chicken?" He asked, as far as the captain knew; Yahweh had not created them yet.

Me-el's face went red.

"Well, I haven't, but I did see them in a picture book in Opus Angelorum! I just got to daydreaming one day about how one might taste like....you know if it was deep fried like Abba's sufganiyot!"

Lucifer winced, his brother sounded a tad barbaric in his thinking.

"Me-el! Chickens have wings like us! Why would you even think of noshing on one?"

"Oh they only exist in library books anyways!" Me-el laughed.

The child was still secretly curious about the flavor of the tantalizing chicken images he had seen; in fact, he had once nibbled on his own wing to test his theory, which had proven quite painful.

The three archangel vendors returned; this time they rained down caramel and cheese flavored popcorn. Me-el now hungrier due to his chicken fantasy, copied

Raphael. He tilted his head up and opened his mouth as wide as possible.

"Deeee_Licious!" He sang.

God glanced towards the pair.

"Well my beloved one how do you like your surprise so far?"

Lucifer fell into Yahweh's arms and wept.

"Abba you are so good to me! I love you so much!"

Gabriel and Uriel dabbed away tears with satin hankies as they witnessed such love. Raphael rolled his eyes and threw some cheese popcorn in his yapper; for some reason Lucifer was still rubbing him the wrong way.

"Maybe I am being a *yutz." Raphael per pended.

The lieutenant decided to shake his silly nerves away.

"I'm just thinking meshuggina!" The healer thought.

Raphael's eyes went over to Me-el, the archangel nearly choked in laughter. He could visibly see the little angel's belly slowly stretching out wider in size as the tot continued to allow popcorn to rain into him.

"Me-el, maybe you should close your mouth for awhile, we still got three more planets left to view!" Raphael advised as he cleared his throat.

---

* Yutz: fool or to be silly.

Me-el looked over at Raphael in alarm.

"Really? If that is the case, I am gonna need some chocolate cherubim milk to wash all my popcorn down!" The youth hinted; hoping Yahweh and the vendors had over heard him.

Chapter 39

Raphael glanced up, Israfil, Remiel and Cassiel were back, it was as if they had read Me-el's mind on wanting frothy beverages. The three captivating archangel vendors were now distributing silver goblets of chocolate cherubim milk; with some assistance from a few virtues and principalities.

"Oh yum! Gimmie Gimmie Gimmie!" Me-el squealed.

Cassiel handed the child a mug complete with a twisty blue straw made of licorice.

"Do not worry," The resplendent angel remarked as he passed Raphael a goblet capped in whipped cream and cocoa shavings.

"Yahweh told us about Me-el's consumption habits; these mugs automatically refill once an angel empties them!"

Raphael raised his goblet toward Cassiel in approval.

"Good to know!" He cheered.

"It is great to know!" Me-el belched as he downed his fourth helping of sweetened milk.

Raphael smiled and lifted his cup again.

"I would like to propose a toast to Abba and our captain, lord Lucifer."

A thunderous clinking of chalices resounded throughout the ninth realm as the boundless angels joined in on Raphael's toast.

Yahweh blew his shofar to regain every angel's awareness. He was ready to continue displaying the remaining planets. Lucifer had Me-el on his lap; the youth was bloated from snacking. The three lieutenants' seemed glad to be getting back to the viewing. God cast his eyes over the assembly.

"Now my children, watch as we look upon the planet Mars!"

A mini replica of the crimson world zoomed out of the sea of glass. Me-el tittered in pleasure as he beheld the tiny mining bear like creatures chisel and bucket red glitzy gems.

"How charming!" Lucifer said.

The captain was amazed at how the furry creatures diligently worked together in synchronized precision.

"I know how much you enjoy red gem stones bubeleh, so I formed Mars to specifically house them!" Yahweh revealed.

"The cubbles reside here to provide you with the best cut rubies, and garnets. All your angels in realm five can now have their armor and weaponry lavished with as many precious stones as they wish!"

Lucifer reclined in his chair, his eyes still fixed on the scarlet planet.

"I love it Abba!" He assured.

"I really like those little bear things!" Me-el tipped.

"I am glad you approve!" God smiled.

"Now let us keep the show going! Everyone get ready to lay your eyes on the lovely planet Venus!" Yahweh announced like a Jewish television game show host.

Me-el hopped off Lucifer's lap as haunting yet, beautiful entities of light with glowing butterfly wings rose above the still pool. The beings were sojourning through trees with blossoming flora. They sang with angelic voices.

"Are those a new breed of angel?" A spell bound Me-el asked.

"They are utterly enchanting!" Lucifer divulged as his corneas digested the fair creatures.

"These are fairies!" Yahweh presented.

"They sound almost as nice as angels, and they do have wings; but, to answer your question Me-el; no, they are not angels. Fairies are a species all their own. I created them just for your big brother Lucifer to admire! It appears I have succeeded! I do hope these brilliant entities do not take all your attention away from me though beloved." Yahweh confessed.

The morning star's eyes went back to Yahweh.

"Abba, you will always be first in my heart!"

Me-el poked Lucifer on the side.

"And...." The child hinted.

"You and Me-el of course!" Lucifer added.

God arose from his chair, causing every angel on the level to bow in worship.

"Alright then! Let us look at the final planet for today! Gaze now upon Mercury!"

Copious amounts of angelic eyes gazed back over to the sea of glass. A small hazy reddish brown sphere levitated on top of the peaceful sea. The planet was teeming with rivers of smooth silver liquid.

"Is that a type of runny metal?" Lucifer puzzled.

Me-el watched as the silky fluid was gathered in bronze buckets by the cubbles. The animals seemed to be remaining cool with special armor made of unmeltable ice. The miniature miners from Mars were passing the loaded buckets to the magnetic fairies from Venus. Yahweh had made the fairies sun and moon light eaters; so the extreme heat of the planet did not faze them. Me-el resumed observing as the luminous fairies transferred the gem studded pails up to Lucifer's black smith shop on level five.

"Wow!" Me-el blurted.

"The cubbles and fairies are working together to bring that special metal up to your military realm Lufi!"

The throng of angels on level nine began applauding as Mercury faded from their vision.

"You see Lucifer, Mercury is not only the name of the planet, but, it is also the title of the liquid metal which it harbors." God explained.

"I also like calling it Quick Silver! You will find that when you're black smiths' combine the Mercury to any other metal on realm five; it will give your soldiers and yourself much stronger suits and weapons! Nergel will not need to buff out as many dents once you apply some Quick Silver to all your artillery defenses!"

"Abba this is all sheer genius!" Lucifer disclosed.

The captain was captivated by the idea of having unbreakable armor and arsenal.

God grew himself five feet and lifted his arms in order to get every angels interest, he was preparing to close the ceremony. The multitude silenced and bowed.

"I would like to thank you all for coming to the summons! *Todah! I do hope you all enjoyed the show! Every angel is now permitted to leave; except for Lucifer and his four primary siblings," God paused. He was searching out Azazel and Nergel in the farrious potpourri of heavenly beings.

"Nergel, Azazel!" Yahweh beckoned upon finding them in the crowd.

---

* Todah: Thanks.

The dominion and black smith regarded God in confoundment.

"I shall entrust you two to assign lesser archangels, powers, and dominions in realm five as supervisors for the new incoming Mercury deposits that have just been taken to your level."

Nergel and Azazel knelt and saluted.

"We shall do so promptly." Nergel asserted.

The leagues of dignified angels swarmed out of God's throne room in an orderly fashion.

"Very good!" Yahweh appraised.

The ninth realm was all but vacant lest for Lucifer and his four siblings. Yahweh had even requested the seraphim choir above his throne to temporarily vacate the premises. God paced over to Raphael, Gabriel, and Uriel.

"I just wanted to offer you three my todah!" Yahweh expressed.

"You three were instrumental in assisting me to prepare this great event!"

Yahweh gave each lieutenant a kiss on the right cheek; he began with Uriel and ended with Raphael. Me-el noticed Abba whisper something into the gardener's ear. Raphael nodded.

Lucifer still to blown away by everything he had just seen, failed to notice the altercation. Me-el also took note of Raphael's perplexed face after God told him whatever it was he wanted. The child quickly decided to mind his own business; maybe they were discussing another surprise for his older brother.

"Alright then!" God cheerfully shouted.

"You three are free to leave; I shall be seeing you all very soon! We still have the finale coming! I myself will sound the shofar for you when the time is right."

The three lieutenants' bowed then descended, leaving Yahweh alone with Me-el and Lucifer. Yahweh motioned for the two to follow him to their corner tea spot.

"Come, I had Cassiel make sure he had our tea and nosh prepared in advance for us!"

Me-el ran ahead of God and Lucifer, eating so much popcorn had made him hungrier. The light bearer and Yahweh walked hand in hand to the domed area together. The two companions sat down together in their velvet rose hued love seat.

God began pouring two cups of tea. Me-el was already eating.

"Abba," Lucifer opened.

"I am dumbfounded! I cannot believe you created all those incredible planets just for me!"

Yahweh passed the morning star his cup, and sipped on his own; Cassiel had left them Chiai tea. God gazed at his favorite seraph with inquisitive eyes.

"All for you my bubeleh! And... I am not done yet!"

Me-el halted his munching, Yahweh's words had caught his interest; he looked rather comical with half a blueberry scone sticking out of his mouth.

Lucifer appeared equally baffled, the captain set down his tea on a table in front of them.

"You mean to tell me you were serious about making me another planet?" He asked.

Me-el sucked up the rest of his scone, he chewed swallowed and burped.

"OY!" The child yelped.

"I second his OY!" Lucifer mumbled the light bearer simply could not fathom anything more lissome than what he had already seen.

"Avi, you have done enough for me!" Lucifer insisted, as tears streamed down his handsome face.

"Ahhh! Your new emotions tell me that you have finished eating your apple from the tree of wisdom! Tell me how do you fancy your new feelings and power?" Yahweh enquired.

Lucifer drew himself closer to God; he felt his heart pound against his chest as he readied to speak.

"Abba, I am feeling things I never felt before," The captain admitted.

Yahweh placed a solitary finger to Lucifer's lips.

"My bubeleh I believe you are beginning to experience the feeling of true love; and, with that comes an array of many other confusing, yet, wonderful emotions! Do not worry; you will become accustomed to all of them in time. You see bubeleh, everything you are feeling I also feel as well!"

Lucifer's eyes widened, he began to wonder if Yahweh ever felt jealous.

"Yes, I do." God winked, overhearing the morning star's clutter of thoughts.

Lucifer's eyebrows jolted up in a mirific fashion.

"My bubeleh that is why I so desperately wanted you to eat from the tree of wisdom! Now our minds are practically one in the same!"

Lucifer ran a hand through his flaxen hair; if what Yahweh said was true, did he too feel desire and attraction? Lucifer thought back about how drawn he felt towards Raphael; and, how envious he had become when he discovered his gardening brother fancied Lucia rather than him.

"Avi, may I ask you a bit of an unsettling question?"

Yahweh nodded, placing his tea cup next to Lucifer's on the table.

"Of course my beloved, you may ask me anything, what is it?"

Lucifer's gaze rapidly shifted to Me-el.

"Oh," God smiled, now understanding that Lucifer did not want the small angel to hear what they were about to discuss.

"Me-el would you please go down to realm five for your older brother and myself? I think you should go make sure the angels there are tending to the incoming deliveries of Mercury. It will also give you a chance to scope out those lovely fairies!"

Me-el stuffed several goodies into his two lower pair of wings.

"Sure just give me a sec!" He pleaded.

The tot found it dreadful for such lavish pastries to go uneaten; Me-el bowed after packing up.

"Okay Abba I'm on it! See ya later Lufi!"

The child took to flight with his pair of free pinions; leaving a trail of scones and cupcakes behind him. After Me-el's less than eloquent departure; Lucifer spoke.

"Well," He managed out.

"Abba this is a bit hard for me to say; I mean I know I was created to be your companion..."

"Please go on beloved." Yahweh urged.

"Well Avi, I'm somewhat ashamed to say this, but, I feel attracted to a certain angel."

"Any particular one?" God casually fished.

Lucifer's face went as red as a ripe cherry in summer.

"I find Raphael very appealing, yet, I do not think he feels the same way about me, I am further dismayed in saying that I have even imagined being intimate with..."

The morning star halted his speech, Yahweh had altered his appearance; he was now an exact replica of Raphael. A startled Lucifer fell off the love seat and onto the marble floor.

"Come to me my love, do all you desire, I am here to serve you my most beautiful son of morning!" Yahweh softly said in his current angelic shape.

God tenderly took Lucifer by his right hand, the light bearer staggered to his feet in disbelief. Lucifer found himself falling love sick into Yahweh's downy wings. The two fused together in one bombastic shock wave of thunder and lightning. The entire realm quaked as they passed through one another; it was similar to an apparition going through a solid surface. Lucifer gasped; he was now seated where God normally was, while God was seated where he had been. Yahweh took Lucifer's hands in his; resuming his paternal figure again.

"That is called two becoming one my love, those feelings you had for Raphael, they are the very same desires I have for you, my fairest of angels!"

Lucifer trembled.

"I want to do it again!" He wailed in ecstasy.

"We shall, but fusing is a very special type of encounter, one that can never be taken lightly. Fusing should not be preformed to simply satisfy one's passing emotions." Yahweh cautioned.

Lucifer's eyes dimmed.

"Forgive me Avi, it just felt so good and I love you so much!" He panted.

"Lucifer I love you too, what you just experienced is referred to as agape love; it is a feeling which is beyond any angel's full understanding; even yours, we will eventually fuse again, but, once will be enough for now!" Yahweh kissed Lucifer on the cheek in a platonic way.

"Well beloved, now that we have fused, I hope Raphael's beauty will not tempt you as often. Lucifer please remember I am a jealous God! I also happen to be the only one!" He vowed.

Lucifer smiled, he took his tea cup and started sipping.

"So he does get jealous!" The seraph evaluated in secret.

"I doubt I will feel anything for him at all now Abba; except perhaps brotherly affection." He jeered.

"Good!" Yahweh replied in witticism.

The deity lifted his own cup of tea to his lips; He put his arm around Lucifer then rested his head on his shoulder.

"Abba, are you really creating yet another planet?" Lucifer asked.

"Of course beloved! I plan to create it on Sunday; the first day of the week! I assure you it will leave you speechless! The ninth planet will be my crème de la crème! Its beauty will nearly match yours! Lucifer the last world will out shine the other eight! Just as you shine among all angels!"

Lucifer's eyes narrowed as he tried to contrive anything more fabulous than what he had already witnessed.

"Abba," He began as he nested his head upon his father's chest.

"The only words I have for you are thank you! I shall be anxious to lay my eyes on the final planet!"

Yahweh ran his hand over Lucifer's golden mane.

"As I have said, I will be creating it on Sunday; however, I will be holding a private rehearsal party this upcoming Sederday. Bubeleh; did you notice how I made each world unique?"

"Yes!" Lucifer joyfully expressed.

"The creatures....then Mercury with its liquid metal! All of them were utterly astounding!" He confirmed.

Yahweh now wrapped both of his arms around his morning star; he turned the angel to face him directly.

"I cannot wait until the run through! Bubeleh; you, Me-el, Gabriel, Uriel, and Raphael will be the very first angels to get a peek at my last planet for you!"

Lucifer surveyed his God with grateful eyes.

"That sounds splendid Abba! Would you like me to inform the others? I mean my lieutenants of course."

Yahweh surfaced to his feet; in a chivalrous gesture he aided Lucifer to stand.

"No need to concern yourself my prince! I have already informed them; all you need do is bring Me-el; perhaps, and, only if you want, I may ask Cassiel and Remiel to join us."

Lucifer nodded.

"Abba I have no qualms with that at all!" He smiled.

"Very well my lovely one, you have my permission to leave. Lucifer I love you! How I wish Shabbat was already here!"

God commented as he planted a kiss on Lucifer's lips.

Chapter 40

Thorsday sessions had just been dismissed. Gabriel sat at her desk; she was unable to grasp how Me-el, Raguel and Samael were all still voluntarily in her classroom. The ruminating rabbi was hoping they would leave soon; she wanted to get back to level two and start pre planning for Sederday; in other words, Gabriel had a busy Shabbat in front of her.

The three little angels had brought their desks together in a circle; they were lying on their backs with their noggins tilted up. Azazel and Beleth had recently inserted new gem stones into the domed obsidian ceiling; after God had exhibited the eight signature planets. Each new stone represented a world in the solar system. Gabriel at last perceiving that the youths were simply star gazing became irate.

"They are getting their theatrics from the school ceiling!" She languished.

A small round quartz depicted Playful. Me-el was pointing out the vivid blue iolite which represented Neptune. Urius sparkled as a green prehnite.

"Hey! That one looks like Raphael's eyes!" Raguel chimed.

"So good at deducing the obvious!" Gabriel thought as she clutched her ruler to calm herself.

Saturn had caught Samael's eye, it was a pleochroic stone with tiny fine cut diamonds of various hues rotating around it as rings. Pater jazzed up the onyx background as a big tiger's eye gem; while Mars was depicted by a large ruby.

"I bet you guys a cubble found that stone!" Me-el spouted.

"Yeah it's cool, but look at Venus!" Raguel bid.

A shimmery round jade portrayed that planet, whilst a tiny circular garnet dusted with silver specs symbolized Mercury.

Gabriel's knuckles were white from her grip on the ruler; she could not take much more.

"I am gonna tell Lufi that I want a ceiling like this one in my egg, and, in my room at his palace!" Me-el touted.

"Hey, do you think me and Samael could get that done for our eggs too?" Raguel implored.

Gabriel who was now gnawing on her quartz ruler, jolted up from her seat; she was no longer able to hold her tongue.

"Enough! I am glad you all are so into your astronomy now, but, you have been staring at the ceiling for almost thirty minutes!" She raged.

The rabbi held up a puny hour glass in her left hand to prove her point. The sands of time were swirling away in it.

"I have been patient, but, you three need to go now! You know if you really want to get a good look at the new solar system; I am certain Raguel could escort you both to Uriel's realm! He knows that place like the back of his hand!"

She seethed through a forced grin.

Raguel flew out without even saying good bye to his friends. Me-el and Samael stood up to face their ranting rabbi.

"Ahhh...that is okay, me and Samael should go catch up with Raguel." Me-el said with a simper.

"Sounds like an excellent idea! Now off you both go! Oh, and have a nice Shabbat!"

Gabriel gently coaxed the pair out the glass twin doors.

Me-el, Raguel and Samael now all found themselves out side Opus Angelorum. The doors of the school now shut and latched behind them. The trio observed daunted as Gabriel whizzed out of the building faster than a long tailed cat in a room full of rocking chairs.

"She is sure hard to figure out!" Raguel sighed.

"Yeah...anyways what do you guys wanna do now?" Samael put out.

Raguel shrugged and looked to Me-el for a response. Me-el had advanced over to the recess portion of the realm; he seemed to be thinking, this worried Raguel. He could not evoke his friend ever appearing so serious.

"I gotta do something with Lufi on Sederday." Me-el said at last.

Raguel and Samael displayed intrigue.

"You and the archangels doing another concert?" Raguel guessed.

Me-el shook his head.

"I am not suppose to talk about it, Abba's orders to Lufi; anyways, I think I better just go back to realm four; for some reason I feel like I should spend some extra time with my older brother."

Raguel and Samael swap troubled glances, Me-el was really sounding deep.

"I cannot really explain why I feel the way I do...It's kinda like I feel like he's gonna be gone for a long time after Sederday...." The child's voice trailed off.

Raguel's brow scrunched, Me-el was making no sense. Samael touched him on the shoulder; it was evident their friend needed some space.

"Come on Raguel, I think Me-el should go do what he needs to, we can still hang out."

Raguel nodded reluctantly, he gave Me-el a big hug; for some reason he was feeling the same way about Me-el as Me-el was about Lucifer.

"Me-el you will always be my very best friend!"

Me-el's heart thumped.

"I know Raguel! I love you and Samael both! I just wanna go be with Lufi right now, I promise I will tell you both all about what happens on Sederday when school starts up again!"

Me-el's eyes twinkled as he took to the sky; the youth was unaware that Yahweh had planned to do the former unveiling of the ninth planet on Sunday; so school would not be back in session until Moonday, of course none of the angels knew except for Yahweh's three assistant's; Gabriel, Uriel and Raphael. Gabriel had been so eager to get out of Opus Angelorum that she had completely forgotten to mention it to all her students.

Raguel and Samael were now alone together.

"So, you wanna go down to Eden? We could check out Raphael's avocado trees." Raguel suggested.

Samael's eyes sparked, he was glad to hear Raguel's offer; it had been Samael's opinion that the sherbet winged angel only was pretending to like him because of Me-el's presence; now he knew different.

"Yeah that sounds super! And if you want we could even go check out that dessert garden you and Me-el always tell me so much about!"

Raguel grinned, he liked Samael's thinking; it helped his sad emotions fade.

"I'm game! Come on Samael let's fly!"

The duo descended to Eden prepared to munch.

Me-el meanwhile was curled up like a purring kitten on Lucifer's lap. He could not sleep; he simply wanted to be close to his older brother. The morning star gently tussle the little angel's hair.

"Tomorrow is Shabbat Me-el; we will be basking upon our beautiful father Abba!"

Me-el released a tiny yawn as a vision of delicacies went through his mind.

"Yeah... I love Shabbat..." Me-el said in a dreamy sigh.

Rofocal and Rahab entered the light bearer's throne room and bowed.

"Yes?" Lucifer bade.

"My lord," Rofocal began.

"Would you like Rahab to carry Me-el to his room or, perhaps to his egg on level three?"

Lucifer rose, Me-el had fallen asleep, he was cradling him in his arms.

"My, he was just awake a moment ago, but no, that will not be necessary, I think I would like to hold him myself until morning." He quietly affirmed.

Rahab and Rofocal knelt, and then exited. Lucifer nuzzled Me-el as a mare would her foal. The captain started singing a lullaby to him. Lucifer's voice chimed throughout the realm as messengers paused whatever they were doing to stop and soak in the tangible sweetness of the morning star's honey drenched vocals.

(Sung to the tune of Hymn: "Holy, Holy, Holy")

"*Seraphim sweet seraphim he who bows before me, my precious Me-el ever will you be...Only God is holy, there is none besides He, Abba our Daddy who loves you and me...*"

Rahab handed Rofocal a silk hanky to dab his eyes.

"Yahweh has made so many wondrous new worlds and creatures," Rahab sniffed.

"Yet, out of them all, none have come close to out doing our glorious captain!"

Rofocal leaned on his friend's shoulder.

"Oh I know! What perfect love! I have never seen such brotherly love!" He gulped between sobs.

Raphael who had been entertaining Raguel and Samael in Eden hiked west of the garden with one child in each arm. Noshing in the dessert lot had proven exhausting to them. They were now both fast asleep. The archangel had Raguel plunked over his left shoulder, and Samael over his right; this made the seraph limp towards the left due to Raguel's heavier body. The lieutenant's wings were reposing, they were a tad sore after he had voluntarily flew the pair around paradise!

"My fault!" He groaned; relived to see the egg patch come into view.

"I was the one who foolishly insisted they sample everything in the dessert garden! I should have known that Raguel would have taken it as a literary challenge! Now my left shoulder and wings are paying for the consequences of my dumb idea! Good thing Samael is as light as a feather; why, if Me-el had joined them, I would most likely be crawling here!" He chuckled to himself.

"Okay you two, time to wake up!"

Raguel and Samael sluggishly opened their eyes at the resonance of Raphael's voice.

"Evening is here! The moment has come for you both to go into your nice comfy eggs!"

The seraph remarked as he cautiously shook the treat stuffed tykes from his aching back and onto the egg patch. The field of elliptical orbs was set aglow with moon light. Raguel and Samael began making their way to their individual sleeping quarters.

"Thank you Raphael." A tired Raguel yawned.

"Yes, thank you very much." Samael repeated.

"Oh it was nothing, truth be told, I enjoyed your company! But now both of you need to get some rest. Tomorrow is Shabbat! You will have a whole day to play and do as you please, so, you better get some shut eye."

The two children settled into their eggs. Raphael trudged over to his own emerald one; he was rather dazed from all the activity he had experienced; this was the first time he had set wing in his egg since he hatched. The healer usually preferred napping at the center of Eden with his two unicorns.

"Sorry Cinnamon and Sugar, but silk cushions and satin sheets sound good to me for this eve." He thought.

Raphael slipped into his egg; he fell into a deep slumber. The archangel found himself in his usual reoccurring dream; the one with Yeshua and the unknown angel, yet, due to his fatigue he gave it little heed.

Chapter 41

Me-el sat on his ottoman shoveling sugar crusted dates and latkes into his mouth. Shabbat had commenced.

"Mmmmm I really like these potato pancakes! They give the dates a nice salty touch!" He expressed about the Jewish delights.

Yahweh and Lucifer sat entranced by one another on the love seat; they were sharing a chocolate milk shake. Me-el upon noticing the new thick enticing beverage halted his noshing.

"What are you two drinking without bothering to invite me to join you for? It looks like chocolate cherubim milk but way yummier!"

The child licked away sugar remnants from his heart shaped lips.

"Ahhh! Our little food maven finally noticed our drink!" Yahweh said with a smile.

"Well," God explained, as he threw a cherry into his own mouth.

"I got to thinking about how much you like chocolate cherubim milk and clotted cream... and that led me to wonder about what would happen if I would combine the two? Long story short, I tried it! Then; I had it chilled on Gabriel's realm."

Yahweh stopped to take in Me-el's hungry eyes and tiny pink tongue; it was sticking out at the right edge of his salivating mouth. Me-el resembled a ravenous fat cat ready to shove his paw into a gold fish bowl.

"Well," Yahweh resumed as Lucifer snickered.

"The outcome of my experiment with the two compounds resulted in what you now see me and your older brother partaking of! Behold! Me-el I now introduce you to iced cream, or; in this form, the milk shake!"

Me-el had slowly inched his way towards the love seat like an inflated caterpillar.

"Hello iced cream!" The tot hummed.

Yahweh lifted up his spectacles and surveyed him.

"Me-el might I offer you one of your own?" He teased.

God handed Lucifer their own shake to safe guard it from its predator. The captain cocked his head as he lapped up whipped cream from the frozen treat.

"Oh I do not think Me-el would enjoy it Abba, he would much rather have regular chocolate cherubim milk." He bantered.

Me-el ran back to his tuffet and stood up on top of it. He put his hands together and began to beg. The small angel started jumping up and down like a crazed ballooned leap frog.

"Oh I do want one! Please Abba! I am so thankful for all your wonderful blessings! Please Gimmie Gimmie Gimmie!!!"

Yahweh tittered, and then snapped his fingers. A tall lavish chocolate milk shake manifested on Me-el's table.

"Nummers!" He shrieked.

The shake was capped with whipped cream, rainbow sprinkles, diced pistachios and three bright red cherries. Me-el stationed himself down onto his seat and grabbed the freezing drink with eager hands; ignoring the twisty pink and white straw, he gulped the immense brew in less than a millisecond. He did not even bother to chew the nuts or cherries. The child fell back on his velvet pedestal and rubbed his engorged belly.

"That was wonderful!" He hiccupped.

Yahweh grinned, while Lucifer laughed.

"I really love our Shabbats together my beloved" The deity expressed.

"I do too!" Lucifer smiled.

God and his regent finished their shake, then; Yahweh placed the empty glass on the round marble table in front of them. He took Lucifer's hands in his own; Yeshua and the Ruach throbbed inside his bosom, they too were content.

"Tomorrow I will be expecting you both here." God said with a sparkle in his eye.

Lucifer nodded, Me-el at last sat up from his milk shake coma.

"Nu?" The youth now drunk off his ice cream had temporarily forgotten that he and Lucifer were both returning to realm nine on the morrow.

"Remember Abba wants us here for the preliminary run through of the ninth planet?" Lucifer lay forward.

Me-el's eyes blinked.

"Oh yeah! Hey, can I have another milk shake Abba?"

"Of course you may my bubeleh!" Yahweh said as Me-el's glass mysteriously refilled.

"Eat and drink all that you want today! Tomorrow I will be concentrating on making your older brother's final planet."

God did not need to tell Me-el twice, he was already slurping on his fifth milkshake; the refilling glass was proving to be quite useful during Yahweh's tea time.

"No problem!" Me-el got out between chugs.

"Just so you know Me-el, I will not permit any sort of noshing tomorrow." Yahweh sternly made clear.

Me-el gaped at God with distraught eyes; he knew Abba was being serious.

"I had better eat more than usual!" The youth deliberated.

"Do not worry Abba, I will behave, I promise; I will just make sure I fill up my tank good today!"

Me-el evaluated as he crammed some macaroons and sufganiyot in his mouth; it was then that a thought commenced going through his head.

"What if Abba just thinks of me as a grob dessert scavenger? I really want him to look at me the same way he looks at Lufi! I can tell how much he loves him."

The child swallowed as the many theories skewered his mind. Me-el glanced over at Yahweh with trembling eyes.

"Abba I will be respectful tomorrow, I love you just as much as Lufi does!"

Elohim opened his arms to the little angel.

"Come here my Me-el, come sit on my lap." God offered

Me-el waddled over to the ornate cedar wood antique love bench. He wiped away crumbs and sprinkles from his face with a blue silk napkin. Yahweh effortlessly hoisted the rather rotund tyke onto his right knee.

"Me-el you are very special to me! Don't you ever doubt that!"

Lucifer bobbed his head up and down in agreement.

"There is no angel in Heaven quite like my Me-el!" The morning star smiled.

"He will make a stately archangel someday!" He added.

Me-el blushed as God and Lucifer embraced with him smack in the middle.

"Oh Lufi," Me-el sighed.

"No angel will ever be better than you! Abba made you as perfect as disc pie and iced cream!"

The child bounced off the love seat and darted back to his ottoman. He resumed snacking on his tray of caramelized fruits and savory cakes.

"I concur with Me-el! No angel will ever out do you my sweet Lucifer!"

Yahweh merged his hands with the light bearer's in a personal manner.

"Thank you Avi." Lucifer whispered.

While Yahweh and his guests were having tea; Raphael and Gabriel were sitting pensively at Uriel's onyx table on realm one in his palace. Uriel casually came in; accompanied by the two archangels Remiel and Cassiel, Lucifer had formally invited them to Sederday's run through upon Yahweh's advice.

"Please sit were ever you wish." Uriel said.

Remiel sat next to Gabriel and Cassiel took a seat by Raphael.

"So," Cassiel communicated;

"Lord Lucifer told us Yahweh wanted us to join you five in realm nine tomorrow; for a rehearsal creation of the last planet of the solar system."

Uriel now himself seated at the table's head nodded in approval.

"Quite so Cassiel, I am not certain why Abba wants you and Remiel there; perhaps because aside from us three,"

Uriel's eyes scanned his fellow siblings before he went on.

"Aside from us three and of course Me-el, you two archangels were not made by Lucifer; yet, rather were hatched from Yahweh's own cherubim; this would thereby make you both archangels of higher rank." He concluded.

Remiel turned to Gabriel.

"So, then it is decided; we shall all regroup tomorrow on level nine? May I ask what time we should be there?"

Gabriel looked to Uriel for the answer.

"Nine in the morning; so please make certain you both watch the sun dials on your realms; unless of course you wear watches." The time keeper smirked.

Uriel ended the short gathering with tea; and, coffee along with some bowls of mixed nuts and figs from Eden. Raphael demonstrated no desire to eat at all; he seemed somewhat despondent. The seraph did not even sip on his tea. Gabriel taken aback by her brother's distant behavior elbowed him on the side.

"Rapha are you okay? You do not look like your normal jovial self; why even Uriel appears more cheerful than you do! Is something ale-ling you?"

Raphael shifted his sad emerald eyes to his concerned sister. Gabriel was currently in her male Anglo form. He addressed her in a hushed voice; not wanting to draw attention to himself.

"I fear I cannot accurately explain it Gabriel; I have bricks in my stomach; yet, I have not eaten a complete meal in two days. There is a knot in my throat, I attempted to unravel the fracas of strife in my befogged mind; yet, it proved fruitless. I do not know the reason I feel as I do, yet; for some reason, I tremble each time I think of Sederday's summons. I know it is preposterous; after all Yahweh's creations have been nothing short of wondrous, I am open for any interpretations, what do you think it could be?"

Cassiel overhearing the lieutenant's monologue without really wanting to placed his palm on the worried angel's shoulder.

"Everything is going to be fine Raphael." He pledged.

Gabriel smiled in agreement as she lifted her mug full of hazel nut java.

"I agree with Cassiel Rapha! You know; ever since we were hatchlings, I have been aware that out of all us lieutenants you are the most sensitive."

Raphael pursed his lips and lowered his gaze. Gabriel put her right hand under his chin.

"My brother it is not a bad thing! Yet perhaps you should try to relax and enjoy these last hours of Shabbat, maybe you simply dread tomorrow because Abba requested we all show up dressed in our armor to honor Lucifer."

A slight frown grazed Raphael's face.

"No...I do not mind wearing my armor, after all it is a direct order from our father, and I always respect him."

Gabriel withdrew her palm; she had not intended to insult him.

"Forgive me Raphael I was joking." She related.

"I know..." The healer acknowledged as he rose from the table.

"Everyone I apologize for my less than cheerful mood, I feel it better to excuse myself. I love all of you dearly; perhaps I need some more sleep."

Uriel arose.

"Raphael if anyone deserves more rest it is you, there is no reason for you to be sorry."

Raphael gave Uriel a meek half smile; it was uncommon for the star keeper to be so amiable.

"Thank you my brother."

Uriel walked over to his sibling as the others looked on.

"Allow me to escort you out."

The fiery seraph politely led Raphael to his palace door.

"You go and rest!" Uriel said as he patted his brother between the wings.

Raphael saluted the remaining archangels as he went through the door and ascended back to Eden.

"I will nap with my unicorns tonight." He thought as he flew.

"After all I still need to acquire that soil for Abba tomorrow, and he wanted it taken from the center of Eden. It will work out well since Cinnamon and Sugar like sleeping by the tree of life; that is where I shall procure it from."

Raphael's labyrinth of thoughts came from a request Yahweh had given to him alone. God wanted Raphael to obtain a six foot bag of Eden's dirt for the

Sederday meeting. The seraph tried to dismiss his nerves as he streaked passed the star lit cosmos.

"Maybe I do just need some extra rest." He conceived.

Chapter 42

Sederday morning had dawned; the ninth hour was quickly approaching, Me-el obediently clung to Lucifer's right hand as they flew up together to realm nine.

"Lufi?"

"Yes?"

Me-el let go of the captain's hand and began zooming around him in fancy circles.

"My armor feels even lighter than before! Look! I can fly just like you now!"

Lucifer grinned as Yahweh's pearly gates came into view.

"That is because I had Nergel dip it; and your sword into the Mercury that was recently sent up to level five; your armor is not only lighter now, but, it is also indestructible! Also once you grow to be as tall as me, the suit will adjust to fit your body at a precise measurement!"

"Wow! Thank you Lufi! You are my favorite brother!"

Me-el seized the captain by the hand as they both landed in unison at the doors.

"Good morning to you my lord!" Uriel saluted.

The chrome lieutenant bowed, then, unlocked the entrance.

"I had to be on the look out over night, Abba wanted me to be certain that nary a stray angel would wonder in."

Me-el whistled innocently, he had thought about sneaking up to realm nine by himself to attempt a sneak peak at his brother's surprise.

Uriel went on:

"Gabriel and Raphael are already inside; so are Cassiel and Remiel."

Lucifer and Me-el followed the poker faced porter in.

Everyone was standing around the sea of glass. Yahweh leapt in joy as he witnessed the morning star march in with his stout companion.

"Our guest of honor and his shadow have arrived!" God proclaimed.

Lucifer smiled and gave Yahweh a kiss. The light bearer's eyes then shot to Raphael.

"Abba why is Raphael dumping dirt from Eden over the sea of glass?"

The son of morning began reviewing the abnormal lump as it levitated above the still pool.

"Oh! That is going to be part of the surprise!" Yahweh confirmed.

"Now, you and Me-el come and stand with all the rest of us around my sea!"

God went over to his tranquil pool; Lucifer stood at his right, while Me-el placed himself at Yahweh's left. God then began to speak.

"I would like to welcome all of you to our rehearsal for the creation of the ninth planet; now, Lucifer you inquired about the soil or dirt as you called it; yet, there is still a more suitable name given to the compound."

Yahweh's eyes fell on Gabriel; he knew she had the proper response.

"My dear silver suited rabbi, would you mind enlightening your siblings and my beloved Lucifer with the more scholastic term for Eden's terrain?"

Gabriel's face went pink, causing her pale male visage to become more handsome.

"I would be delighted to Abba; Eden's soil is referred to as Earth."

"Precisely!" Yahweh bellowed.

"Now, I want each of you to look into my mystic sea, for the moment you may ignore the mound of soil. Keep your gaze on the pool!"

The angels all did as they were instructed.

A sphere of vivid azure blue oceans and seas appeared. Yahweh commenced making hand gestures which seemed to manipulate the bodies of water. The oceans and seas began splitting apart; lush green landscapes manifested between the liquids. The seraphs' watched as mountains, valleys, and animals of every kind; even Me-el's appetizing chickens, began swarming about. Millions of living creatures also filled the huge amounts of water; from the tiniest minnow to the great whale.

"Hey! There are dolphins and whales down there! Except they do not have wings!" Me-el squealed.

The angels resumed sizing up the new world in avid interest. Uriel's realm was visible to all the life on this planet.

"By Jove! Those creatures can catch a glimpse of one of Heaven's levels!" He pondered.

The sea of glass plainly displayed animals of all sorts basking in the sun by day; while others like the raccoon and fox which are primarily nocturnal would roam freely in the night as the moon gleamed.

"Absolutely extraordinary!" Lucifer disclosed.

"The planet I assume is to be formed from Eden's dirt; or rather Earth, I presume..." He hypothesized.

Raphael's face went from sulky to radiant.

"Lucifer you are correct!" He smiled.

The morning star gave him a wink.

"I must confess I was in the dark myself up until now!" Raphael admitted.

"Yet, a planet crawling with so much life; it could only be constructed from a little piece of Heaven itself!"

Raphael's glance went to his beaming father.

"Abba this world is to be created with soil from Eden! That is why you had me bring you a bag full of it! Am I right?"

Raphael's top two wings flapped in excitement; it made him giddy to think that this whole time he had been a sentinel over Yahweh's chosen soil; the soil which would architect Lucifer's chief planet! Now it made sense to him why he had felt so nervous the night before! Yahweh lifted a hand to halt Raphael's dialect.

"My sweet Raphael, Earth will be made out of Eden's soil which will actually connect this planet directly to all nine celestial realms here; but, that is not why I had you bring up the sack."

All the angels' eyes widened in sync as God went on to explain.

"All of you, look closely, as you can see components' of all the other planets I made before can all be found on this one! Me-el was the first to point that out, he noticed the whales and dolphins."

Me-el stood up straight and proud; Lucifer patted him on the head.

"Good job little one!" He whispered.

Yahweh resumed his allocation.

"However, unlike the other eight which were fashioned by my creativity; this one will actually contain part of me in it!"

All the archangels exchanged floored looks.

Me-el, who was still enthralled with Earth, gazed into the sea of glass and laughed.

"Abba this planet is gonna have all the creatures I seen in the picture books at the library in school! Even chickens!" The child said as he licked his lips.

To his credit, the pecking birds were rather succulent.

Lucifer slanted forward, Me-el's chubby hands clapped as various birds of many colors filled the planet's auriferous sky.

"Hey Lufi, the chickens can't fly!" Me-el impishly chuckled.

The youth was still curious about how a chicken might taste; especially if it was deep fried like one of Yahweh's latkes.

"There are all sorts of creatures." Lucifer agreed.

Earth had each chronicled beast which was archived in the texts of Opus Angelorum.

"Why there is the serpent!" Lucifer chimed.

Raphael shivered at his comment; he did not care so much for that creature, ever since Lucifer had tricked him.

"It really is a little piece of Heaven Abba." Lucifer asserted.

"You have truly outdone yourself!"

Raphael and the others clapped, in total agreement.

"Yes! It even contains all the flowers, trees, herbs and vegetation from Eden!" The healer declared.

"Abba if I dare ask... why do I see no unicorns on this planet? Why they have been part of Eden since even before we were created." Raphael examined.

God gave the gardening seraph a smile before he replied.

"My sweet Raphael, Earth is for Lucifer! Not for you,"

Raphael felt his stomach churn; he had not meant to provoke his father.

"Forgive my indiscretion most high..." He begged.

Yahweh winked at him, to let him know there were no hard feelings, and then went on.

"Raphael I can say this, you yourself will also be part of this planet! Once I officially create it tomorrow!"

Raphael now appeared completely commingled; first Abba had said part of him who was God, would be on Earth, now; he too was also being included, how could this all be? The muddled seraph interposed:

"Abba how in Heaven is that possible? If I may be so bold to ask?"

Raphael's observation caused every angel to reconnaissance Yahweh in a fiddled way. Yahweh smiled and continued to articulate.

"All my dear angels I plan to place the entire garden of Eden on this planet!"

Each angel's jaw dropped, aside from Me-el's who was currently drooling over a luscious hen in the pool.

"So Abba you are saying that even though you are making Earth for me, my siblings and you will also be able to reside there?" Lucifer bid.

"Exactly! Angels will or I should say may; co exist with all the creatures on this planet! No unicorns are seen because when I formed them I made them to be a beast of strict heavenly composition, yet; if need be they can be used as guardians I suppose at some time...yet I digress, back to what I was saying before, every angel from highest to lowest rank will be given access to Earth! This will allow you my dear Lucifer to have more help with the major species which will rule over all the different animals! Of course Raphael will obviously reside in Eden."

"Where exactly do you plan to place the garden most high?" Gabriel cautiously hunted.

God directed everyone's focus back to the sea of glass, Me-el jumped up as a three dimensional globe came up depicting Earth.

"I want to put Eden right there!" God said, as he pointed at the model; it was where modern day Israel is located.

"I want to place Eden here because this is where all my chosen people will sprout from!" He revealed in elation.

"People?" Lucifer asked in abashment.

"Avi, I have never heard you speak that term before, which animal is people? I do not recall a creature of that title in any of Gabriel's archives in Opus Angelorum."

Me-el stood up, he was getting equally as curious now. Yahweh smiled.

"Allow me to further explain, don't you all remember at the beginning of my spiel how I said that part of me will always be on this planet?"

Raphael nodded, he had not forgotten. God's eyes now held an extraordinary twinkle; he smiled again and placed his right hand on the morning star's shoulder.

"Before I go on," Yahweh expressed.

"Gabriel, Raphael, and Uriel do you all recall my third form of Yeshua?"

The trio gave God a nod of affirmation.

Lucifer's face went red hot; he did not know his brethren had seen Yahweh in his third form. It made him jealous, yet; he managed to maintain his decorum by telling himself that perhaps that too was a piece of his father's surprise. Yahweh being quick to notice Lucifer's reaction turned to face him.

"My Lucifer I only appeared to them as Yeshua first because I planned on showing you and little Me-el today! You see, Yeshua will be how I am able to walk on this planet! That is how part of me will constantly be there! It was all coming down to this shebang!"

The archangel Remiel now interjected:

"So Cassiel and I will also be permitted to see you as Yeshua today?"

Yahweh nodded.

"Yes! Now before I do reveal myself as Yeshua, permit me to explain why I had Raphael bring up this mound of soil."

Lucifer interrupted.

"Avi have you not already told us; is it not because that is what Earth is primarily made of?"

Yahweh cut him off with a kiss on the temple.

"Yes! But there is yet another reason! Remember how you asked what people were?"

Lucifer nodded.

"Well," Yahweh picked up.

"I am about to show you! Cassiel would you please do me the favor of fetching me my pot of hot water from my tea corner?"

Lucifer searched his brain, he could not comprehend why God was doing things as he was; yet, he was not about to question him.

Cassiel bowed to Yahweh then flew over to get the kettle. He passed it to God.

"Thank you!" The creator smiled.

Cassiel genuflected.

"You are most welcome Abba."

Yahweh commenced pouring the continence of the steaming vessel into the hunk of Earth.

"Remiel," God beckoned.

"Please would you mind touching the soil and telling every angel what it feels like?"

Remiel carefully placed his hand into the moist mixture.

"Well, it feels soft and pliable in texture, almost like clay."

"Brilliant!" Yahweh exhorted.

"That is what I was going for! Now all of you watch as I mold the most beautiful creature any of you will ever see! You see my angels; the singular of people is called a person! With this wet soil I shall make a person called man!"

Lucifer and his siblings along with Remiel and Cassiel now watched in captivation as Elohim began working the loam like a skilled potter would fashion a pot. Every angel was trying to imagine what the man might look like.

"What if it has the traits of one of the creature's on the other eight planets? Perhaps another type of winged horse?" Raphael envisaged.

"Maybe a winged unicorn?" He further hoped.

Uriel started ruminating himself.

"Perhaps it will be a huge towering giant made of rocks! Oh that would be smashing! I could use it to help ward off trouble makers from Opus Angelorum!"

Gabriel inspected the mud.

"I have no clue; everything he has made so far has been wondrous, I really don't know what this man might look like." She analyzed.

Me-el was having his own daydream.

"What if it's a giant cow that squeezes out chocolate milk shakes? Oh I would be its best friend!"

Cassiel, Remiel, and Lucifer were too busy monitoring Yahweh as he meticulously crafted the soil; neither of the three took time to depicture what this enigma might bear a resemblance of. The light bearer started scrutinizing the mushy blend.

"Am I going nuts or does this man display some angelic features...."

Yahweh had just completed the feet and legs. Me-el poked his older brother.

"Lufi, it has feet and legs like Abba!"

Lucifer's eyes became very pensive.

"I know, maybe this man Abba is creating is a type of dirt angel; he did say that these people would govern the animals of Earth, if we have dirt angels to assist us it will give us more time to enjoy the planet."

The morning star whispered to his younger brother.

After what seemed like hours yet, was actually only three minutes; a six foot being stood above the sea of glass. The result was quite unexpected.

Chapter 43

Raphael, Gabriel and Uriel all gaped at the figure in a discombobulated gaze.

"Why the man looks like" Raphael stuttered in disbelief.

"Hush!" Gabriel warned, she also thought the man to be reminiscent of Yeshua; she knew Raphael was about to say just that; however Lucifer and Me-el were still clueless of what the God man resembled, and she did not want Raphael to accidentally give away details.

Raphael got her hint and kept his mouth shut. Uriel maintained his face set like flint; he too did not care to divulge the uncanny likeness between man and Yahweh's form of Yeshua. An epiphany came crashing into the chrome star keeper.

"Of course!" He silently revolved.

"God in three persons! Yeshua is his primary solid form! A person! Yeshua is a man!" He configured.

Cassiel and Remiel were speechless; they had not ever laid eyes on a creature like this. The man did bear a resemblance to Yeshua, except he had no facial hair; nor did he wear a robe. He appeared to be approximately eighteen years of age, with tanned skin and dark hair;

since God had yet to blow life into him, he merely stood as still as a mannequin. Lucifer's face took on a look no angel could recognize, the look of pure warped envy. Me-el on the other hand thought the man to be beautiful.

"Behold!" Yahweh presented.

"My first model of man!" The creator was so keyed up he failed to note Lucifer's scowling stare.

Yahweh reeled on:

"Man is the only creature I made entirely for myself!"

Lucifer began grinding his teeth at that bit of information; God went on to elaborate.

"The Earth and all its animals are for my beloved Lucifer; so, I expect every angel; even you bubeleh," God directed the sentence to the seething morning star.

"All of you are expected to bow before this man; it will be a great gift for all of you serve him!"

Lucifer was now livid, had his father just announced that they were to serve a lower life form?

"Yes, when I officially breathe life into man tomorrow, you angels will all watch over him and be his servants! I myself will serve him!" Yahweh avowed merrily.

The last words made Lucifer want to toss his cookies.

"Me serve dirt? Why that abomination should grovel before me!" He thought. Lucifer was completely enraged; all twelve of his wings were ruffled up like a mad cock.

"Well, what do you all think of my spectacular man? Is he perfect or what?" Yahweh chimed.

Cassiel and Remiel bowed towards the model.

"It is the loveliest creature you have ever fashioned!" They both praised.

"He is fairer than any of us angels!" Cassiel said; adding a coal to Lucifer's kindling inner fire.

Raphael, Gabriel, and Uriel stared enamored at the man; all three of them also bowed in unison. Me-el fell to his knees in reverence. Yahweh turned to Lucifer; he was the only one who seemed less than thrilled.

"What is wrong bubeleh? I assumed you would be pleased by this new being, tell me, what is upsetting you? Remember you are my companion, we are one. Please, tell me what is troubling you." God put forth.

Lucifer began growling in a guttural tone; he tore at his golden tresses, and then audibly snarled directly at Yahweh. His once azure blue eyes had now become slimy bile green. The seraph's raging conduct caused Me-el to run over to Raphael and hide behind him. The archangels all huddled together in a circle, all utterly floored by their captain's uncharacteristic behavior.

"Abba you must be jesting! Do you honestly expect me your most glorious angel to be ecstatic about all of this?" He fumed.

Yahweh stood his ground, yet his eyes were sad. Lucifer encroached his way over to the lifeless man.

"Why should an angel made from the finest ingredients of all nine realms; such as myself, need to bow to a despicable creature composed of dirt? This thing you call man is absolutely repulsive! He is like a hairless ape! Look at him! He has no wings, his complexion is abhorrent! Not to mention, what are those hideous members between his legs? I mean seriously it looks like his abdomen vomited out an unattractive snake! Just look at it! Then look at me? You yourself said that nothing nor no one would ever outshine my beauty! Yet you call this thing perfect?"

Yahweh lifted up both his hands as he tried to calm Lucifer.

"My bubeleh please do not judge the man until I am able to give you a glimpse of me as Yeshua, then; you will know why I worded everything the way I did. Lucifer this man is made in my own image!"

Lucifer's twelve wings shot out in disarray.

"Abba how can you dare lower yourself by saying that! Why it is a direct insult to you! You are light, grace and a pure being like me! No this simply cannot be! I am your regent and right hand! And... I simply will not allow you to degrade either of us in such a vulgar way!"

The self glorifying seraph searched out his younger brother.

"Me-el! Come let us go back to realm four,"

The little angel coward and shook his head; he firmly gripped Raphael's right leg.

"Lufi, I don't like you like this...you do not sound like yourself. I am gonna stay here with Raphael."

Lucifer's nostrils flared. Raphael picked up Me-el in a protective way and held him to his chest. To the gardener's astonishment; Me-el grew a foot taller, he was now at least five feet in length; and, much thinner.

Lucifer who was too flared up did not even notice; he pivoted his glaring eyes back to God.

"Listen! I will not accept this ridiculous concept of yours! I am your son and companion! Not that nasty pile of mush!" He practically hissed.

Yahweh attempted to say more in his own defense, but, before he could get a word out edge wise; Lucifer stomped off without even bowing or saying good bye.

Uriel stepped forward; he gave Yahweh a pat on the back.

"What would you like us to do most high?"

Elohim turned to face the remaining angels. He seemed broken hearted, hurt and dismal.

"Oh if only he would have permitted me to show him Yeshua; then, it may have all made sense to him." He sighed.

Yahweh slump his shoulders; his surprise had not gone as he had planned.

"I will give him some time to cool down; if I know him as I think I do, he will be apologizing profusely by tomorrow."

Raphael felt his stomach sink. He knew at his core that Yahweh was only making a wish by saying what he just said. Lucifer had changed

Chapter 44

Lucifer stormed into his palace, the mirrored abode darted back limitless images of his flawless features. His mind was now poisoned with pride and madness. The teed off seraph began punching through his glass walls. Rofocal and Rahab immediately flew into the throne room upon hearing the tumultuous chaos. The two messengers stood gawking at the farrious shards of glass and quartz scattered abroad. Lucifer was sitting on his chair; his mucus green eyes were aflame with outrage.

"My lord," Rofocal timidly bowed.

Rahab did likewise.

"I gather the summons did not go as you thought it might? Tell us, who has angered our most beautiful one?"

Lucifer's face suddenly became still. A revelation hit him.

"These two would most defiantly agree with me! With their help I know I could start a revolt! Yes that is exactly what I shall do! Then... I will be the one to sit on Yahweh's throne! It should have been mine by now anyway... that old dumb maven has obviously gone raving mad in lunacy if he expects all of Heaven to be okay with bowing to a dirt hill!" He evaluated.

"Rofocal you know me so well, you are correct, the summons was a sheer show of blatant disrespect to me and...every other angel in Heaven! Even to God himself! But he has become a fool, so he cannot fully conceive what he has done!" The falling star bemoaned.

"You know I always thought Abba loved me above all others, why he created all those great planets just for me....but, now....Oh it is bad! This ninth one he wants to form, his supposed icing on the cake, well; it turned out to be a disaster!"

Rofocal and Rahab blinked their eyes in confusion. Lucifer went on:

"It started off wonderfully...until..."

Lucifer paused; to even speak of what his father had done next rallied his anger anew. He thrust his fists into the arms of his crystal throne and cracks commenced running down both sides.

"Until our so called father made a grotesque creature out of Eden's dirt! It has some angelic characteristics, but, it is far too ugly to be one of us! He calls it a man! Not only that, he expects all of Heaven; even me, your captain; the most luminous seraph and his equal to...." Lucifer gritted his teeth.

"He wants us to bow down before it! We angels are to bow to filth!" he thundered.

Rofocal and Rahab put their hands over their open mouths in shock. The messengers now understood why their lord was so worked up. How could Yahweh want

Lucifer the son of morning to stoop before something so primitive?

"That is sacrilegious!" Rofocal yelled.

"Why it is blasphemous!" Rahab added.

"Yes!" Lucifer validated.

"I knew you two would comprehend! He is planning to begin this ghastly project tomorrow! I say that he must be stopped at all costs! Lest all of you lovely angels be put through lethal humiliation! We must start an uprising; Yahweh is no longer suited to rule over Heaven!"

Rahab now came forward.

"My lord is completely justified in his thinking!" He cogitated.

"In fact the day is still young, allow Rofocal and myself to go search the eight realms; I know many other angels will also be just as appalled and join our cause! I gather your siblings are on your side?"

Lucifer tore his gorget from his neck in spite.

"No! Those stupid buffoons! They all bowed! They are *RACA! And, my little Me-el..." Lucifer's eyes went from slimy green to blue again for a moment.

"Raphael! That lousy excuse of a soldier, he has my Me-el! Oh we must get him back, lest they brain wash him against me!"

---

* Raca: Empty ones.

Rahab and Rofocal exchanged stupefied glances.

"Unacceptable!" Rofocal argued.

"How dare your lieutenants betray you in such a way? I will help Rahab; you just leave everything to us my lord! We will muster a sufficient army of warring angels to halt this whole process before it even begins!"

"Indeed we shall!" Rahab put in.

"You give us one hour my lord; we shall bring you a suitable legion of willing angels! Abba has crossed the line by doing this to you!"

Lucifer still dazed by the commotion; grappled to his feet.

"I will go to realm five myself" He posed.

"I know Azazel and Beleth will be on our side for sure! I shall make certain that all our armor is coated in Mercury; we shall be unstoppable! No lieutenants' weapon will come close to fracturing us in the least! Last I knew our blacks smith Nergel; who I am positive will also join our cause; he had just completed a full Mercury coat of arms for me! All angels who join us shall be garbed in Mercury bound suits! Nergel is fast and exact! I shall hurl Yahweh from his realm myself for shaming me as he did! He can then spend his eternal years wallowing through empty space! He will never set a foot on my eight planets! We shall crush every angel who dares to resist us! I will get Me-el back and bring him to his right mind! He and I shall reign together from god's throne! As for those so called siblings of mine, I hope they are prepared to encounter my wrath!"

Raphael was tucking Me-el into his egg for a mid day nap.

"Sleep Me-el, you spurted up a whole foot today! I assume you are tired." Raphael gave the taller child another once over; he could not get over how much more slender Me-el had become.

"Of course it is still early, I could go acquire some food for you, would you like that?"

Me-el's opal blue eyes were clouded with anguish.

"No thank you Raphael, I am not hungry, my stomach feels funny." The stressed youth mumbled.

"No longer a little pudgy ball." Raphael contemplated.

"Why did Lufi yell at Abba? I never saw him act so mean! I thought the man was beautiful!" Me-el whimpered.

Raphael inspected the youth, and then knelt down beside him.

"It is alright Me-el, perhaps Lucifer is simply overwhelmed with all his new abilities; eating from the wisdom tree has given him a good deal more power; who knows...by tomorrow he might be very apologetic to Abba."

Raphael was hiding his true opinions. He knew how much Me-el esteemed his older brother; he did not care to further traumatize him; yet, he felt tomorrow might be worse. He kissed Me-el on the fore head as the lad slid deep into his sapphire egg. Raphael closed the lid; it was then that some odd noises gripped his ears.

"It is not even noon yet, what is with all the commotion?"

Raphael stood up in his armor; the seraph unsheathed his broadsword and began sauntering towards Eden. His two unicorns ran over to him as he passed the wisdom tree. The animals were clearly spooked; and, Uriel was no were to be seen.

"How curious, Uriel would only leave his post if Abba..."

Cinnamon and Sugar started snorting and stomping their hooves, they were attempting to alert the gardener; each of their horns gleamed a fluorescent red.

"A code red? What is it?"

Raphael paid a sharp ear, as the two creatures reported what they had witnessed.

"Impossible! I knew something vile was going to happen. Yet, I could not have ever fathomed anything like this! Nor, did I expect it to happen yet today!"

The lieutenant told his unicorns to guard the egg patch; he then took inventory over what weaponry he had on him.

"Sword in hand, shield, caduceus, oh...I better take my sling and some stones...I handle those much better than this contraption." Raphael said as he sheathed his sword and went to obtain his woven sling. He then took to flight.

Me-el tossed in his egg, he could not sleep; Lucifer's scowling mad face kept lingering in his mind. He pushed the lid off his gem studded egg. Me-el gazed up as he climbed out. He felt his knees go weak as he saw at least one third of Heaven's finest patrolling angels ascend from different realms up to Abba's throne level. The sky darkened like midnight as hordes of wings flapped in frenzy; one set stood out, Lucifer was leading them.

"Oh no! What is going on?" Me-el wailed.

The child knew he needed to get to realm nine, despite the fear that was mounting inside of him. Me-el glanced up again, out of his peripheral sight he viewed Uriel, Gabriel, and Raphael all streak upwards like comets. A boundless battalion followed them; among some of the angels Me-el recognized, were; Cassiel, Remiel, Barachiel, Israfil, Zadkiel, and even Jericho and Razziel. The three lieutenants were all blaring shofars.

Me-el placed his hands over his ears to block out the loud moans of cherubim and thrones. The beasts howled in sorrow; it was as if Heaven was having a hurricane warning with sirens; yet, this would prove to be something much more sinister. Me-el started running to Eden's center; the two unicorns tried to keep pace with him but failed.

"Maybe part of Raphael is still guarding the tree of life!" He hoped.

Little did he know that a call of war had just been issued, every lieutenant was no longer bilocating; but, keeping all their forms gathered in one form in order to do battle. The child arrived at the tree only to be disappointed.

"But Raphael should be here," He fret.

All at once the sky went black again, droves of angels filled every nook, it was as if an immense swarm of sparrows were all migrating up. A big gust of wind spiraled through Eden like a typhoon. Me-el was caught in the midst, he lost control of his six wings and smacked up against the arbor of life.

"Somebody please come and help me!" He moaned.

Cinnamon and Sugar endeavored to, yet, they were pushed backwards by the roaring cyclone winds.

"Help!" Me-el continued yelling.

A tall armored angel appeared.

"Raguel? Is that you?" Me-el asked.

Me-el recognized the sherbet wings and friendly eyes of his comrade. Raguel was at least seven feet tall now, and, very well toned.

"Hello my friend, I heard you calling, I will take you to Yahweh. You once tried to help me by putting me on your shoulders; now, I am here to repay the favor!"

Raguel lifted Me-el onto his back and ascended.

"Thank you friend!" Me-el sobbed.

Chapter 45

Raguel placed Me-el right between Abba's throne alongside his three primary siblings and lieutenants. Yahweh stood surveying the numerous corps of Mercury armed soldiers who were being led by Lucifer. The opposing angels of the morning star were all standing at attention; each held a sword in their hand at a ten hut behind the sea of glass.

"It would appear that one third of my children have convened with Lucifer to contest me. I only hope Lucifer will allow me to show him Yeshua before he tells them to charge; I still value him so much..." God gloomed.

Thrones hovered above along with cherubim; they could only bawl out waterfalls since they lacked hands to grip any kind of weapons. Raphael, Gabriel, and Uriel as well as every other loyal seraph, virtue, power, dominion, archangel, and messenger allied themselves around Yahweh. Me-el's eyes filled with tears, he desperately wanted to run into Lucifer's arms; yet, he could barely identify him anymore. The son of morning's once handsome face was now contorted in fervent rage; even his golden locks seemed dull. The most ghastly change to Me-el however, was that his once brilliant blue eyes, now were a hideous shade of green.

Yahweh stepped forward; the squad of angels encircling him readied themselves by placing their hands on the helms of their swords and various weapons. Lucifer's angels sneered as they did the same.

"All of you just STOP!" Yahweh commanded.

"No angel will touch my bubeleh Lucifer or his army; until I have a chance to speak with him! Is that understood?"

Gabriel who was in her male form signaled the troupe to be to fall back. The angels obeyed yet kept their eyes firmly set on the opposition. God faced Lucifer and began to talk.

"Lucifer my love, please allow me to explain why I wanted you and the others to bow before the man; if after you hear my reasoning and still wish to oppose me, I will sadly respect whatever you and your legions decide to do. After all; I did give each of you free will. Yet; at the very least if you still feel any love for me...which I hope you do..."

Yahweh paused, it looked as if he had hit a nerve, Lucifer's eyes were turning a faint blue, and he was listening.

"I still love you my bubeleh, will you please hear me out?" Yahweh pleaded.

Lucifer's eyes now sparkled in their normal dashing hue, his face also became serene.

"I do still love you too Abba, very well..." The morning star waved a gauntlet at his soldiers.

"You may all stand down; I will listen to what our father has to say."

The ready to pounce army relaxed at their captain's orders.

"Very well Abba, I will listen, tell me one good reason why an angel as exquisite as myself should pay homage to a half angel made of dirt?"

Me-el slowly scooted between Gabriel and Raphael. The youth did not want to risk missing one word uttered between Yahweh and his older brother. He was hoping Lucifer would reciprocate; and everything would return to normal. God orated:

"First, I must say you left so quickly that I did not have the chance to reveal Yeshua to you. Nor to any of the other angels who had come without yet viewing him. Little Me-el included."

Lucifer saw Me-el sandwiched between two of his lieutenants; his eyes went soft.

"You are correct Avi," He frowned, now beginning to regret his bitter actions.

"I suppose I did over react a bit yet...."

Lucifer thought back to how Yahweh had called man his finest creation; envy whirled back into his torn train of thinking; it was as if he was bipolar.

"Yet, even if you show me Yeshua, I doubt it would really change anything!" He heckled as his eyes went green.

Yahweh released a fraught sigh before he went on with his speech.

"Bubeleh, I really think it would! All of you..." God now spoke to the entire assembly.

"My lovely children of light please watch as I show you all my personage of Yeshua. He is in me, and I am in him! Yeshua my dearest ones is actually my most beloved son!"

Yahweh became a blur of light as the transfiguration occurred. Gabriel, Raphael, and Uriel all swiveled their eyes in flabbergasted glances.

"Yahweh has a son?" Raphael whispered to his two equally stunned siblings.

"Blimey! I thought Yeshua was simply another form Abba could take!" Uriel added quietly.

"I as well." Gabriel said in a hushed voice.

"A son! I am your only son!" Lucifer argued.

"How can you have another son? You have always been three in one! That would mean.....I have never really been your only son! No this cannot be!"

The captain's eyes morphed into an unpleasant feline shape, with slits down the center. Me-el took in each angel's startled reaction, he did not know what the huge deal was; Me-el knew from school that Abba could easily create something or someone out of nothing. Also, God had always existed in a triune bond; he could quite simply have a secret son hiding inside of him; it excited Me-el knowing he would now be getting his first official peek at another older brother! God's own son!

"Yes Lucifer," Yahweh said from the light.

"Observe as I split into all three of my forms, as I display Yeshua, keep in mind that I am your father; and, the Ruach," A jolt of lightning struck.

A large white dove flew out of the radiance and perched itself on Lucifer's shoulder.

"The Ruach is my Holy Spirit, he is a guide to all of you angels, he flies were he will; embedding wisdom and grace to each realm, he is also a companion to me; in fact, he was with me long before any of you were."

Lucifer cooled his jets as his father went on.

"You see I have always been three in one, no one helped me create myself! Yeshua has always resided within me as my son, now you will finally be given the chance to see him."

The throng of angels beheld the imperial bird; it began soaring nimbly over the sea of glass. Lucifer was more relaxed now; his eyes went back to blue. He started to recall how Yahweh had told him that he had no beginning or end. This son of his had apparently always been a part of him. Even still; the haughty seraph could not permit his jealousy to leave just yet. He wanted to see this son of God for himself.

"I have seen you as the Ruach Abba! Stop all this stalling! Let us see your beloved Yeshua! Let us all see!" He nagged.

Lucifer's army crowed in agreement.

"Yes! Show us the son! Who cares about a dove! We want to see the son!"

The company around Yahweh now put their hands to their weapons once more. God lifted a hand from his shadow of light.

"All is well, be at ease." He transmitted.

"Lucifer," Yahweh said as he looked the light bearer directly in the eyes from his aura of brilliance.

"Behold Yeshua, my most beloved son; he who was, who is, and shall ever more be part of me; for I am El Rachum, A God of compassion, within me is and ever will reside divine relationship. And; Yeshua is compiled of all the highest love within me! With him I am exceedingly well pleased!"

God's arms stretched upwards from inside the light, the Ruach burst into a resplendent pulsating sphere of rainbow emissions; whilst a crimson flare surfaced from Yahweh's throne. An eerie calm fell upon the whole realm. Yeshua was now seated on God's throne. He was a man; clothed in stark white robes. He was about six foot tall. Yeshua's skin had an olive Semitic trait. He had long wavy brown hair which hung a little past his broad shoulders. He smiled showing bright teeth, obscured by a neatly trimmed beard. His delicate hazel eyes were loaded with love. Every angel on Yahweh's side of the throne room marveled at his incredible unparallel beauty. Yeshua arose from the chair; each angel minus Lucifer and his crew stopped to genuflect in reverence. Yeshua advanced to his Father; he kissed Yahweh on the cheek and then spoke.

"Hello Lucifer, when my Father first created you; I was enchanted by your beauty; it was I who came up with your name. Now; you can see me. I AM Yeshua; and, I AM also your Lord and God..."

As Yeshua introduced himself, Yahweh nodded in approval and the Ruach settled atop the man God's shoulder. Lucifer's internal organs went ablaze with loathing. Yeshua was clothed like a man! The only distinction between him and the model God had configured was that Yeshua appeared a tad more mature than the latter. Yeshua was also in garments, and; although Lucifer detested even wrestling with the idea, deep in his soul; he found Yeshua to be extremely attractive.

"I cannot have him outdoing my beauty!" The envious seraph chafed.

Foam commenced emerging from Lucifer's mouth; his jealousy was getting ready to explode with all the force of an atomic bomb.

"So," Yeshua continued, as he planted himself right in front of the lit rod of dynamite that was Lucifer.

"Now that you know that I AM both your true God and can also be a true man; do you still decline to bow when we; I mean the Father, Ruach and I finish creating your ninth planet with man as its overseer?"

Yeshua's eyes sparkled; he went to touch Lucifer's cheek. Lucifer slapped his hand away in fury. Yahweh now stunned at his favorite angel's rude reaction, held his breath. The angels on God's side of the level went for their weapons again; this time Yahweh did not hinder them. Me-el felt his stomach churn, his chest burned; the child began to hyperventilate as he watched his older brother treat Yeshua in such a crude way. He was feeling very ill. Me-el doubled over in pain and collapsed to his knees; his head was pounding like it had a humongous drum inside it. Every angel was so focused on Lucifer and Yeshua, that the youth went dismissed among the throng.

"Looking at you Yeshua, well...it makes me feel ashamed to know that your breath helped fashion me! You are a wretched beast!" Lucifer hissed.

The ungrateful seraph spat on Yeshua's face. Me-el started to congregate all his inner strength; he knew he needed to get back on his feet.

"My great god? Thou art not so great if you are foolish enough to lower yourself by taking on a sorry suit of dirt!" The captain claimed.

Yeshua wiped his face and did nothing. The Ruach flew into his bosom.

"Lucifer, you know not what you say." Yeshua said in a choked up voice.

Lucifer's brigade clogged out Yeshua's words as they began echoing their new leader's disapproval.

"Aye!" Azazel a power originally created by God himself raged.

"We not be servin god any longer! Not one like him!"

Gabriel flinched as she witnessed a power from her class; Camael, pick up on tormenting Yeshua.

"Yes! We will no longer serve a god who chooses to parade about Heaven as a vessel made of dirt and spittle! We all choose to join Lord Lucifer in his movement to overthrow you!"

"That's right!" Beleth heckled.

"My brethren and I now follow Lucifer a pure seraph made of light! And light alone!"

The rowdy rebels now raised their weapons chanting:

"Cast yahweh down! Give Lucifer his crown! His son yeshua is nothing but a clown!"

Yahweh who now feared for his son Yeshua brought himself back into one solid entity of white fire. He whirled into a massive flaming being; in his righteous anger he jaunted over to Lucifer.

"Do you actually presume yourself to be above me?" God asked in a strident voice.

"Yes! I am better than you!" Lucifer said as he tossed off his diadem and ring; along with the talisman God had bequeathed him with.

"And...I do not require these trivial trinkets anymore!" He growled as he crushed the items beneath his feet like rock candy.

"I have all the power you do and I have mastered it! I AM PERFECTION!" He roared.

His angels cheered him on. Yahweh's eyes went blinding white.

"Well then... you do not need these anymore either!" God yelled as he tore off six of Lucifer's cotton soft wings.

Lucifer moaned in pain; he was more embittered than ever.

"You are no father or companion of mine!" He spat.

"I am more equipped to reign as God of all Heaven! I do not need two extra forms like you! And....I can fly just as well with six wings! You are a dirt loving *nebbish!"

Lucifer plunged towards Yahweh shouting:

"Attack!"

Lucifer's hordes of battle hungry soldiers thrust themselves into God's armed regiment. Me-el fell

---

* Nebbish: Loser.

onto the marble floor and began seizing. The horror of watching the grievous events unfold had made him sick. The Mercury suits were giving Lucifer's agents a big advantage; Raphael, Gabriel, and Uriel who were all experts in fighting; found their weapons shattering as soon as they came into contact with the glossy Quick Silver vestments.

Me-el's eyes frantically searched out Abba. Yahweh was the only one strong enough to keep Lucifer detained. He had the outraged seraph in a headlock. The scene was hideous and brutal. Azazel tore at Raphael's mane; he then split his shield in two using his Mercury coated scimitar. Raphael covered his head with his gold arm bracers, as Azazel went to strike him with a mace.

Beleth wrestled Gabriel to the ground and bit into her wings; although she did not bleed, she was now severely debilitated with only two. Rahab and Rofocal trapped Uriel in a net made of Mercury; rendering him powerless.

"You foul gits!" Uriel howled.

Cassiel and Remiel fell backwards as Nergel and Molech who were both blacksmiths; threatened them with Mercury lances. Feathers flew, swords snapped like china, angels cried in agony. Lucifer grinned as Yahweh kept his pin on him.

"You can hold me back awhile, but, Behold! My warriors are prevailing over your *drek!"

---

* Drek: Worthless dirt.

Chapter 46

Me-el stopped seizing; he shook off the fear that had paralyzed him. The child stood up and yelled.

"No one talks to my DADDY that way! Not even you lucifer!"

The ninth realm went silent. Me-el's voice rung over every clanging weapon.

"Mikha'el?" The youth boomed.

Gabriel limped up on her right leg.

"Who is like my God?" She said repeating what Me-el had just spoken in Hebrew.

A sonic blast blinded all the angels; great orbs of cosmic light began giving off sparks of holy fire. Lucifer's army fell to their knees as their eyes melted in their sockets. Yahweh upon hearing Me-el's voice; shot a thunder bolt directly in the child's direction. Raphael, Gabriel, and Uriel along with Yahweh's entire troupe watched in astonishment as Me-el sprung up four feet in height. He was a wondrous seraph and his appearance was staggering.

"It is him!" Raphael declared.

"Me-el is the archangel I have been seeing in my dreams! Our Father has risen up a new captain for us!"

Lucifer's angels were now rendered powerless, they began pleading for mercy. Raphael, Gabriel, and Uriel along with Yahweh's other loyal subjects rose as they all became rejuvenated in their vigor. Yahweh released his grip on Lucifer. The diminishing morning star had been stripped of his armor. He regarded Me-el.

"My sweet little brother, why look at you! You must help defend me against our shmendrick father! And our less than worthy siblings as well! Together you and I will reign over all realms of Heaven! We can soar through space, and visit our planets! I know what you just said! Mikha'el? Oh my sweet Me-el, I know you were referring to me! Because no angel has loved you as much as I have! Why...I have been both God and Father to you! Oh how absolutely flawless you turned out to be! You are nearly as perfect as me! Come! Let us take down this sorry meshuggina being we once called abba! Him and his foolish squad of angels!"

Me-el's luminous opal blue eyes narrowed in incredible incense. His lengthy flowing auburn hair embellished his fine sculpted porcelain features. The resplendent archangel shined in his sapphire armor which served to bring out his eyes even more. He said nothing.

"Me-el," Lucifer continued on.

"Remember how I told you that I had your armor and sword dipped in Mercury? My brother you can save us!" He whined.

Lucifer walked over to him.

"My sweet perfect Me-el!" He gushed, his eyes streaming tears of pride.

"I know if any angel would remain loyal to me, it would be you!"

Lucifer opened his arms to embrace him. Me-el gazed above Lucifer's head and saw his other siblings. They all seemed to be in a mode of panic.

"What if he was talking about Lucifer?" Uriel whispered to the others.

Yahweh looked at his newest archangel with shimmering eyes; he knew where Me-el stood.

"Lucifer you are not MY FATHER!" He strongly publicized.

"I am no longer your sweet little Me-el either! What I said was a rhetorical question! Absolutely no one can ever be equal to Yahweh! I belong to Abba alone! In school I learned my Hebrew! I know exactly what I was saying! My name is now Mikha'el! Or; Michael and it will haunt you for eternity to recall that on this day, I was most certainly not speaking about a lousy excuse for an angel like you!"

Michael's voice was deep; yet, soft. His emerald wings spread out triumphantly as they reflected an array of several colors.

"How dare you go against our God most high! Our Father! Why, without him you would not even exist!"

Lucifer's eyes welled up with tears as he stumbled to his knees. He quickly hoisted himself up and re veiled his unarmed body; he was now vested in a titanium coat of arms. The fallen star had full knowledge of all his powers now; he manifested a Mercury broad sword for himself.

"You ingrate! I taught you everything you know! You would still be a fat useless lump of feathers if it were not for me! Those three back there!" He pointed back to the lieutenants; Raphael, Gabriel, and Uriel.

"Those three never showed you the same love I did! They never showered you with gifts, or held you when you needed to be held! I did all of that! I loved you even when you did not love yourself! Now you decide to betray me? Tell me when did any of them voluntarily call for your company?"

Lucifer pounded on his breast plate like an angry gorilla. Michael raised his right eye brow at his raving mad foe.

"The answer to that is never! I did it all MICHAEL! I always knew you would grow up to be great! Now you want to disown me? They are the ones that ridiculed you! Me-el come to your senses! I am the one that really loves you! You are like my son! Please do not make the mistake of making me your worst enemy! I am your brother! You're Lufi!"

Lucifer was nearly two feet away from Michael as he finished his plea. He honestly wanted his younger brother to take his side. Michael did not have anything to stew over, he had made his decision. The novel archangel unsheathed his cruciform sword and held it to Lucifer's jugular. Yahweh and his angels watched in suspense.

"Lucifer you are very good at making accusations." Michael disclosed.

"You accuse me of betraying you as a brother, but, you dared to betray Abba! He who made you! That is something I will never do! I know Yahweh loves me! And...I love him! I will not allow you to defame him or his son Yeshua anymore! You are no longer an angel of light! You now embody nothing but vice, gall, and hate! You had the nerve to presume yourself to be better than God, yet you are so far from being anything like him! You refused to bow to Yeshua and then spit in his face! You have no respect for authority! You are no brother of mine! You care only about yourself and your own selfish ambitions!"

"Amen!" Yahweh interjected with an uplifted fist.

"Michael is right! No longer will you be called Lucifer! You do not deserve the name light bearer! From this day forth I disavow you; and, forever disconnect you from that title! All future generations will now know you as Ha-Satan! Or; accuser of the brethren! Part of me will always love you, yet; I now choose to forever disown you! I hereby decree that you are banished to the abyss of space! So too are all who allied themselves with you!" God demanded.

Lucifer growled.

"You cannot do this to me!" He hissed.

Michael's sword nipped at his throat. Raphael stepped forward and spoke.

"Oh Lucifer how thou hast fallen son of the morning! O day star son of dawn, of which you no longer will be known as!"

Michael took his cruciform and shoved it into Lucifer's armor. He had him nailed. Lucifer's eyes went to a most vile hue of green, he hissed at Michael like a snake.

"Go Ha-Satan! As an angel you cannot be killed, but our Father has banished you! I really want you to remember these final words I speak to you; Mikha'el?"

In one swing of his sword Michael knocked Lucifer from the ninth realm with all the potency in his muscular body. Lucifer who was unprepared for such a whopping blow from his younger sibling, hurled past all nine levels of Heaven like a bolt of lightning.

"I am......" Ha-Satan screeched as he plunged down in response to Michael's statement.

"No you are not!" Michael retorted.

The planets which Yahweh had created for the now fallen star caught on fire as Lucifer spiraled down past each one. The prince of morning was no more. Lucifer had fallen.

Chapter 47

Michael stood aloof on the edge of the crater made by Satan's fall. He gazed through the immense hole. Michael observed how Satan had left a similar gaping pot mark on every realm of Heaven. He could easily see right down past Uriel's realm. Raphael, Gabriel, and Uriel now took the liberty of corralling the motley crew which had sided with their former captain. God in his mercy had restored their eyes; yet, voided them of their armor and artillery. He had some choice words for all of them.

"You have all deliberately disobeyed me! Your wretched captain has been forever exiled; you have all been given the same sentence!"

The scuffed up angels gasped as Yahweh waved his hand over all of them. He had transformed their appearances'.

"NO!" The pathetic goons howled.

The entire Pro- Lucifer infantry lost their feathery wings and celestial beauty. They now all demonstrated beastly characteristics. Each Anti –Christ angel examined their once glittery skin, their complexions were now grey, scaly, and oozing protoplasmic fluid. The wings of each fallen angel now resembled the wings of a bat. No longer did any of them have lovely hair; but horns instead. Their wretched eyes all gleamed red or puss yellow.

"We look so ugly!" Rahab wept.

"I have only permitted you all to see again; so, that you might view yourselves as what you truly are!" God hammered.

"You now have horrid bodies to go along with your horrid souls! You are no longer angels of Heaven! But, demons of the abyss! All of you are banished! Leave now; follow your captain Ha-Satan! It would do you all good to leave willingly down the hole he has provided you all with!" Yahweh advised.

God shifted his gaze to Michael who was stationed next to the crater Lucifer had made; his sword still in his hand.

"But, how will we find him?" The demon Dumah queried.

"Well, you all have your eternal lives to wallow around in space and figure that out!" Yahweh answered.

"Also, as usual he shant be hard to find....since part of me will always love the *shanda chaya, Ha-Satan retains his attractive form, minus a few pairs of wings. However, he will never get those back. The six he has left are now black, as opposed to white. And; his blue eyes are now permanently a most gruesome shade of green! I am certain he landed on one of the eight burning planets."

---

* Shanda Chaya: Troublemaking unruly child.

"Which planet can we find him on?" Rofocal begged as Gabriel jabbed him with a spear.

Yahweh who was now losing his patience blared:

"Figure it out! Although the eight planets are engulfed in fire; Ha-Satan to my regret; has all his power. Yes, unfortunately I made that *putz way to smart! The flames will not consume him. As for all of you; well, despite your displeasure of your new looks; I actually acted rather mercifully! That nasty rough skin which so disgusts you, will serve as a natural fire repellent! Now all of you be gone! Or; does our new captain Michael need to lift his sword to each one of you?"

The demons whimpered like miserable dogs; each one holding a tail between their cloven hoofed legs; they all put their claws together in one last plight.

"Forgive us Abba!"

Yahweh turned his back to them.

"I have said all I needed to! My archangels rid me of these riff raffs!"

Raphael placed a smooth stone in his knitted sling, with a perfect aim he managed to bop a quivering Azazel right on his prickly hide. The former power jumped while yelping in agony. Raphael resumed slinging large stones until the revolting creature hesitantly flew down the sink hole; followed by the rest of his sulking platoon.

"The bigger they are..." Raphael surmised.

---

* Putz: Fool.

"The harder they fall!"

Gabriel and Uriel prodded the disgusting regiment with golden lances; making them exit Heaven faster. The last demon to go down the hole was Rofocal. He gazed at Michael with sorrowful eyes before leaving.

"Lucifer, he really loved you! No one up here loved you like our captain! You say your new name will haunt him, but, the fact that you stabbed your older brother in the back will haunt you even more! Michael you are UNFORGIVABLE!"

Michael's mesmerizing eyes widened in annoyance.

"It is Mikha'el!?" He fumed as he finished cramming Rofocal down the opening with the full force of his right boot.

"He always was a blabbermouth and a brown noser!" Michael thought.

Yahweh sauntered over next to Michael. He moved his right hand over the great crevice Lucifer had made; and closed it up. Realm nine, as well as the rest of Heaven seemed to be at peace once more. Yahweh hugged Michael and placed his right arm around him.

"Listen all my angels! Behold your new captain and commander! The mighty Archangel Michael! He who cast out the one who accused you all before me and dared to assume himself above me!"

Michael released a sad smile as he faced his brethren; they were all clapping and cheering. He fought back an impulse to sob like a child. He had always dreamed of this moment; except, Lucifer had always been a part of the crowd; now, the beloved brother he knew was no more. Michael was aware that Ha-Satan had now become his chief nemesis for eternity.

The new captain glanced down, his right foot had touched something; he knelt to see what it was.

"Ha -Satan's armor..." He quietly said.

Michael frowned as he picked up the finding; he easily lifted the coat of arms in his left hand, every precious gem still in its place.

"What of these belongings Abba?" He asked.

Yahweh now appeared a trifle depressed; he reminisced back to the time he had clothed the Devil with the signet suit.

"Ahhh....he really did have it all, oh well...after what just happened I do not believe any other angel should ever again have so much power!" God decided.

"I agree with you completely Father." Michael sighed.

Abba gingerly took the armor in his arms; a tear dropped from his left eye.

"It would be best if I had this put away!" God analyzed.

The deity snapped his fingers; a large quartz courier appeared from out of nowhere. Yahweh opened it and positioned Lucifer's armor inside; the suit of arms hung on a gold hook. God carefully closed the clarion wardrobe then, locked it shut with his finger.

"Gabriel," Yahweh exclaimed.

The lieutenant turned to see the clear cabinet hover over in her direction.

"Yes most High?" She acknowledged.

"I want you to place this showcase in the library of Opus Angelorum; it shall serve as a reminder to all future angels. I will mount a plaque above it bearing the following inscription" Yahweh rubbed his beard as he dictated.

"The inscription shall read: With great power, comes great responsibility, and; PRIDE cometh before the FALL! NOTE: These vestures were once worn by the wisest yet, most foolish seraph of them all! He failed to honor his Father; He was known as LUCIFER, now he will be ever more known as Ha-Satan."

Gabriel nodded as she watched God's words magically engrave themselves on a silver tablet which had manifested right over the courier.

"I will do as my God has instructed." She promised.

Abba faced Michael. He truly was a most ravishing specimen of an angel.

"Look at you! All grown up! No longer a grob chaya!" Yahweh teased in good humor.

"Michael you shall now stand south at my throne!"

Michael genuflected, his six emerald wings changed color each time he took a breath.

"He is literally a dream come true!" Raphael admitted.

"Oh I always knew the little bloke would grow up to be smashing!" Uriel chimed.

Raphael rolled his eyes.

"Sure" He simpered.

"You know it is hard to believe I once pried that svelte archangel out a star shaped window!" The time keeper laughed.

Gabriel giggled as she thought back to who Michael had been before.

"Yes!" She agreed.

"In all fairness, I did turn out to be right about one thing concerning our new captain."

Raphael and Uriel both gave her a smug glance.

"What?" They both asked.

"I was right when I told Me-el, who is now Michael, that he would never grow up to be just like his older brother!" She smiled.

Raguel who had overheard his former rabbi's comment cleared his throat.

"Well...just so you three know, I always knew my best friend was going to be someone really special."

"You came out looking pretty good yourself!"

Raguel turned to see who had just paid him a compliment. It was Samael! He was just as tall and handsome as him.

"Good to see you again!" Samael remarked as he shook Raguel's hand.

Samael and Raguel both bowed as their friend and now captain waved at them with a grin.

"I love you both! Thank you for siding with our Father!" Michael called.

Yahweh blew his shofar to regain everyone's focus.

"All right then," He allocated:

"Tomorrow will still come! Ha-Satan's fall will not hinder me from creating Earth! The planet deserves a chance! I want to make it just for me! All of you will serve as guardians! The other eight planets may someday contain life again....yet, as of now I simply only need use of one. My dear angels all of you who allied yourselves with me, I know I can now trust all of you to assist me once I place all the animals and man there!"

The multitude of angels chanted in approval.

"You may all return to your own levels now," Yahweh quieted as a thought came to him.

"Oh yes...messengers who once served Ha-Satan when he was still Lucifer; would you all please take it upon yourselves to dismantle your former captain's palace and throne. I believe we will use that realm as a museum of sorts. I want all of Ha-Satan's artifacts kept there; minus the cabinet I gave to Gabriel. We should have all future hatchlings very well educated about this day, and everything that transpired, lest history repeat itself."

Jericho stepped up.

"I would be honored to advise and lead that for you most High." He volunteered.

"Great! You got the job! I must say I am rather surprised to see that Rofocal and Rahab were the only two of your kind to rally with Ha-Satan!"

Jericho blushed.

"He was beautiful, but you are the only true God."

Yahweh thankfully patted the angel on the back.

"Oh that reminds me..." God said.

"I want to employ myself with a private book keeper! I need an angel to chronicle everything that has transpired today, and will continue to transpire from this day on...hmmmmm...."

Yahweh's eyes reviewed the angelic throng; his eyes met Razziel; the seraph once mocked by Gabriel for his less than fine pen men ship.

"You!" Yahweh said with a point of his index finger.

Razziel, still fertummect from the battle, looked to his right then left in disbelief.

"ME?" He asked not really convinced Yahweh had singled the correct angel out.

"Yes, I choose you Razziel! From what I recall from the last conference I had with your former Rabbi Gabriel, your writing has really come along nicely! You shall also stand next to my throne; you will chronicle everything I do and say; beginning tomorrow when I create Earth."

A stunned Razziel simply nodded and bowed.

"Rabbi Gabriel actually said something good about me!" He thought.

Yahweh clasped his hands together.

"Alright, now that we have all that taken care of, you may all go about your separate ways; I myself will sound the shofar tomorrow, you may all return here when I do. All of you are welcome to watch me create Earth!"

The numerous creatures soared off, each one saluting Michael as they passed him. Abba walked over to his throne and sat down. Uriel situated himself to the north, whilst Raphael took his place east. Gabriel fluttered to her western spot. Michael for the first time; posted himself at the south.

The new captain tangibly felt some of his older brother's residual energy bouncing off him. Michael was just beginning to come to terms with the aftermath of the melee. He quivered in his armor as he remembered

Ha-Satan's distraught eyes. A big knot swelled up in his throat. He flapped his emerald prism wings seemly; permitting limitless rainbows to obscure the ninth realm.

"I will never see him as my brother again..." He dimly repined.

Raphael who was admiring how aristocratic his younger sibling had become, felt his heart skip a beat as he watched him. A single solid crystal tear drop fell from Michael's right eye.

"My dream has now been completely fulfilled." Raphael mused.

"Michael is the wondrous weeping archangel who I viewed in my dreams!"

The tear that dropped from Michael's eye landed next to Yahweh's throne. A beautiful feminine looking seraph burst up from the ground. Each archangel gaped at her, God stood up.

"Why look at you!" Yahweh smiled at the pretty angel.

The beguiling creature had six wings, two were pink, two were yellow and the last set were a combination of emerald green and azure blue; her hair was long and dark, she had lovely silver hazel eyes.

"Did I do that?" Michael blurted.

The delightful seraph cooed at Yahweh's feet and batted her eyes towards Michael.

"You did! It seems that your tears can give birth to angels!" God disclosed.

Michael's eyes fixated on the becoming beauty; she was as tall as he was; yet, she seemed to have a childlike mentality.

"She acts like a hatchling." Michael observed.

Yahweh pet the angel made by Michael's tear, she stood and bowed before her God; she could not speak; yet sang like a morning dove.

"She seems to be young, but big for her age! I think I will name her Seraphina!" Yahweh expressed.

The pristine feminine seraph commenced flying in circles at the sound of her name. Seraphina cast her glance to Michael.

"Seraphina means the fiery one." The captain added.

"It does." God affirmed.

"She was born after a fiery sword of yours forever rid us of Ha-Satan! Michael I want you to mentor her; perhaps someday she too will be an archangel!"

Michael smiled, Seraphina was adorable. She gracefully soared up above God's throne and started singing like a sweet nightingale.

"Abba, I pledge to do my very best!" He vowed.

"I would expect nothing less from you!" Yahweh said with a wink.

Chapter 48

A defeated Lucifer or Ha-Satan; sat groaning on the former gem filled Mars. The planet was a heap of desert; littered with ash, rocks and Cubble skeletons.

"Ha! I am still looking GOOD!" The fallen star gloated.

Ha-Satan could see his reflection on a lone shard of clear jagged red diamond; dimmed in grime.

"I wonder where my faithful troops are." He sniffed as he rose to his full stature.

The lonely Devil decided to go search for his flock.

Rahab and Rofocal screeched in relief when they saw their handsome leader soaring in their direction. Ha-Satan stopped and squint his eyes at the repulsive rabble of demons.

"Oy vey!" He languished; the Devil realized who the mass of beasts were.

The creatures now embarrassed by their ghastly figures lowered their noggins in shame.

"Rahab? Is that really you?" Satan asked.

"Yes most lovely one!" Rahab wailed.

"I do not suppose you want such terrible looking comrades at your side; after all you have managed to retain your beauty."

The others sniveled behind him, equally upset. Ha-Satan made a slight grimace; then, waved his right arm over the cluster of demons. The grisly host went from wretched to beautiful once more.

"Our captain has restored us to our normal selves again!" Rofocal sang.

Satan chuckled.

"I have; only god and his cohort will be able to see you as undesirable beasts. You shall all keep your beauty, so long as you remain loyal to me!"

The concourse of demons frolicked around Ha-Saṭan in joy; this served to lift the Devil's spirit.

"Listen," Satan asserted as he flapped his jet black feathered wings.

"You must all come take refuge on Mars with me; I still have all my powers! And...I can still see god's thoughts!" He sneered.

"I am very aware of how he still plans to make earth, and, that abomination he calls man! Together we can infiltrate that clump of dirt; with my wit and your cooperation we shall have his stupid man bow down before all of us! Then; when god least's suspects it, man will see me as GOD! That will be our ultimate revenge!"

"What is the plan great Lord?" Dumah humbly inserted.

"Oh it is actually quite simple!" Ha-Satan theorized.

"We will trick the man into disobeying god! Once man goes against his maker; I have no doubt that god will turn his back on him; which will then leave the naked apes to us! Yes...those people will be putty in our hands! Even that ungrateful overgrown disc pie eating brat Michael will not be able to help the dumb dirt wads!"

Ha-Satan's love for Michael had completely vanished.

"I still cannot believe he dared say who is like my god? To me?! That spoiled rotten urchin!" He growled.

Rofocal and Rahab nodded as always.

"You are a far better God my Lord!" The pair bragged.

"I know." Ha-Satan conveyed.

"I am better because I will never lower myself to serve dirt, or take its ridiculous form!"

The clique of tossed out angels cheered him on in agreement.

"Lucifer LIVES! Lucifer LIVES! For us he is our GOD that GIVES!" They chanted.

Ha-Satan grinned, his eye teeth had become fangs.

"Yes, I AM Lucifer! The son of morning will never lose his light! Come my pets let us go to Mars! Mark my words, once god creates man and earth, we will quickly make him regret he ever did! I shall make him wish he would have just allowed the oceans to envelop the whole planet! That is how detestable we shall make this man of his turn out to be!"

Ha-Satan's eyes went into slits of deep thought.

"Yes! I will make god hate man so much that he will someday destroy the earth completely!"

The demons cackled at their captain's clever conspiracy.

"We will make god pay!" The Devil crowed.

Chapter 49

In Heaven Sederday was coming to a close. A full moon glowed over all nine realms. Seraphina had settled herself in Eden; Michael had permitted her to nap in his egg. The captain placed a stuffed pink toy unicorn inside, so she could hug it while she slept. Michael kissed her on the cheek then soared back up to the throne room and kneeled before Yahweh. God motioned for him to come closer.

"You three come here too." He beckoned back to Gabriel, Raphael, and Uriel.

"I want to tell all of you something" Yahweh began.

"Once I create Earth, I have a suspicion that Ha-Satan and his demons will attempt to contaminate it!"

Michael's eyes became alarmed.

"Abba do you think he is going to try to hurt the man and people you plan to put there?" He inquired.

Abba bobbed his head.

"Sadly, I know he will! Yet, I am confident that you my dear Michael and your siblings can match him and his goons tit for tat!"

Michael appeared nervous and unsure.

"Come now Michael, there is no need for you to look so worried" Yahweh assured.

"I know you can do it! You got CHUTZPAH! I also want you to take over realm five; you will need to train more angels as warriors! We will need them now more than ever! Teach them every move that your now fallen older brother taught you! If any angel can beat Ha-Satan in a fight, it is you!"

"I will vouch for that!" Raphael smiled.

Michael bowed.

"I am very proud of you Michael!" God went on.

"You stood up to your own brother to defend my only true son! From this day onward you will be Earth's chief Archangel and prince of my chosen people! You will serve as their guardian!"

Michael's face flushed as his brethren began applauding him.

"Abba I will do it, yet, I do hope my siblings will agree to help me." He shyly stated.

Raphael was the first angel to throw his arms around Michael.

"Thank Abba for you my dear brother! Of course we will help!" Gabriel and Uriel smiled in approval.

"We would be honored too!" Uriel said.

"Indeed! And Michael, I am glad you did not turn out to be anything like your older brother!" Gabriel added with a wink.

Michael returned her smile, he could not agree with her more. Yahweh beamed in *kvell at his angels.

"Good! It is all worked out!" He spouted.

---

* Kvell: To look at someone in pride.

Epilogue

Sunday came and went; Elohim created Earth. Ha-Satan kept true to his words and pounced into attacking man. The Devil's full force assault went into motion when Yahweh formed a woman. Humans have come and gone and Satan continues to see himself as better than God; unfortunately so do most people. God in his immense love permits Ha-Satan to think he is winning; yet, he only allows it because he knows where the Devil will eventually end up. Many years after Yahweh fashioned Earth and flooded it; God's son Yeshua arrived under cover on the planet as a human baby. A sinking hole developed in the Devil's plan; although Ha-Satan managed to lead many people astray; Yeshua won their souls to himself by the shedding of his own blood. Thus, humanity was cleansed of several demonic influences. However, the Devil still prowls about ready to attack!

The Archangel Michael patrols the Earth nonstop, along with Raphael, Gabriel, and Uriel. All of them are ever on the watch for their crazed former brother and his crew of trouble makers. Occasionally Michael may jump into a human to enjoy a slice of pizza; his prodigy, Seraphina follows him about, she still has a bit of growing up to do.

Yeshua now sits at the right hand of Yahweh his Father in Heaven, they peer into the sea of glass together;

the Ruach is on Earth full time now, ever since Pentecost took place. The Holy Spirit has become the most influential being on the planet. Yeshua waits patiently for the day when his Father will call on Michael to lock up Satan in Hell forever; so he might establish his thousand year reign of shalom.

Raphael aside from assisting Michael scout Earth; still attends to Eden. Yahweh placed the garden back on level three of Heaven after Ha-Satan pulled his serpent stunt on Eve and Adam.

As for me, well I wrote this all down because I got selected to! Abba gave me all the details I had missed out on while I was still scribbling in school. You see… I am the archangel Razziel. Oh…Michael knighted me with the position not long after Yahweh promoted me to be his book keeper. I did not see Yahweh create Lucifer; or, any realms of Heaven; as I said earlier God dictated everything to me once I got my job. What I find amusing to this day is how in school, I was known as the angel with the worst handwriting! Oh the irony! Speaking of… remember how Raguel could not blow a shofar when he was a kid? Well, guess who gets to sound it when Yeshua returns to Earth? No! Not Gabriel! Raguel; It is a common misconception though! Raguel was also knighted by Michael as an Archangel, and is now one heck of a shofar blower! Well, now that you all know the rest of the story, keep a few things in mind; if you sit down to eat a pizza and you suddenly get a cold chill; it just might be Michael popping in to snag a bite! If you think about doing something you really should not be doing; well, that just might be his former older brother Ha-Satan!

Hey; every family has issues and loose screws! We really are not much different! Always remember what ever struggles you may be going through, you are never alone! God and his angels are always watching!

To Be Continued in Paradise!

Printed in the United States
By Bookmasters